Praise for the author

JACI BURTON

"Spicy bedroom scenes and a spitfire heroine make this one to pick up and savor." —*Publishers Weekly*

"One hot novel that I could not put down until the last word. Wow!" —*Just Erotic Romance Reviews*

"Burton's book packs a wallop." —*Romantic Times*

JASMINE HAYNES

"More than a fast-paced erotic romance . . . A good read to warm a winter's night." —*Romantic Times*

"Intense, hot, and purely erotic." —*The Road to Romance*

"Try this one—you won't be sorry." —*The Best Reviews*

JOEY W. HILL

"One of the finest, most erotic stories I've ever read." —Shelby Reed, author of *Seraphim*

"A must-read." —*Romance Junkies*

"Sweet yet erotic." —*Sensual Romance Reviews*

DENISE ROSSETTI

"Hot and spicy erotica." —*Romantic Times*

"A sensual pleasure in words." —*Fallen Angel Reviews*

"Not to be missed." —JoyfullyReviewed.com

Unlaced

JACI BURTON

JASMINE HAYNES

JOEY W. HILL

DENISE ROSSETTI

Heat | New York

THE BERKLEY PUBLISHING GROUP
Published by the Penguin Group
Penguin Group (USA) Inc.
375 Hudson Street, New York, New York 10014, USA
Penguin Group (Canada), 90 Eglinton Avenue East, Suite 700, Toronto, Ontario M4P 2Y3, Canada
(a division of Pearson Penguin Canada Inc.)
Penguin Books Ltd., 80 Strand, London WC2R 0RL, England
Penguin Group Ireland, 25 St. Stephen's Green, Dublin 2, Ireland (a division of Penguin Books Ltd.)
Penguin Group (Australia), 250 Camberwell Road, Camberwell, Victoria 3124, Australia
(a division of Pearson Australia Group Pty. Ltd.)
Penguin Books India Pvt. Ltd., 11 Community Centre, Panchsheel Park, New Delhi—110 017, India
Penguin Group (NZ), 67 Apollo Drive, Rosedale, North Shore 0632, New Zealand
(a division of Pearson New Zealand Ltd.)
Penguin Books (South Africa) (Pty.) Ltd., 24 Sturdee Avenue, Rosebank, Johannesburg 2196, South Africa

Penguin Books Ltd., Registered Offices: 80 Strand, London WC2R 0RL, England

This is an original publication of The Berkley Publishing Group.

This is a work of fiction. Names, characters, places, and incidents either are the product of the authors' imaginations or are used fictitiously, and any resemblance to actual persons, living or dead, business establishments, events, or locales is entirely coincidental. The publisher does not have any control over and does not assume any responsibility for author or third-party websites or their content.

Copyright © 2008 by Penguin Group (USA) Inc.
"The Ties that Bind" by Jaci Burton copyright © 2008 by Jaci Burton, Inc.
"Undone" by Jasmine Haynes copyright © 2008 by Jennifer Skullestad.
"Controlled Response" by Joey W. Hill copyright © 2008 by Joey W. Hill.
"Rubies and Black Velvet" by Denise Rossetti copyright © 2008 by Denise Frost.
Cover illustration by Alan Ayers.
Cover design by Rita Frangie.
Text design by Kristin del Rosario.

All rights reserved.
No part of this book may be reproduced, scanned, or distributed in any printed or electronic form without permission. Please do not participate in or encourage piracy of copyrighted materials in violation of the authors' rights. Purchase only authorized editions.
HEAT and the HEAT design are trademarks belonging to Penguin Group (USA) Inc.

First edition: December 2008

Library of Congress Cataloging-in-Publication Data

Unlaced / Jaci Burton . . . [et al.].—1st ed.
    p.   cm.
  ISBN 978-0-425-22381-9 (trade pbk.)
  1. Erotic stories, American.   I. Burton, Jaci.
  PS648.E7.U54 2008
  813'.01083538—dc22

                                                        2008027551

PRINTED IN THE UNITED STATES OF AMERICA

10 9 8 7 6 5 4 3 2 1

CONTENTS

The Ties that Bind

JACI BURTON

One

"You need a vacation, Mom. Actually, you need more than a vacation. You need a life."

Leave it to Lisa Mitchell's eighteen-year-old daughter to state the obvious.

Lisa sat at the old, scarred wooden kitchen table with her daughter, Kayla, Kayla's friend Wen, and Lisa's best friend, Connie, along with Lisa's ex-husband, Rick. A strange group, to be certain, but not at all unusual. Lisa and Rick, though divorced for nearly fifteen years, were still best friends. Rick and Lisa were Kayla's rock and co-anchors. Lisa would have never been able to raise Kayla to be the smart, competent adult she was without Rick's help. Getting divorced was the best thing they could have ever done for Kayla, and for each other. It had saved their relationship.

She stared at the colossal mess that was her family room and kitchen, smiling over the remnants of the successful graduation party for Kayla. She couldn't believe her baby girl had graduated already. Lisa was only thirty-four years old and her daughter was already going to be heading for college in the fall. She felt old. And yet she still felt young. Her life was over, and yet it was just beginning.

"Which is exactly why you need this trip, Mom," Kayla had told her. "You're free of me now. I'm eighteen. I'm going to be gone for the summer anyway, remember?"

How could she forget? Lisa's older sister Amelia—the fabulous, successful sister—was going to take Kayla to Europe for a month. "Yes, I couldn't possibly forget you're going away for the summer since it's all you've talked about for a year." The trip was Amelia's graduation gift to Kayla. Lisa had balked. Amelia had insisted. Kayla had squealed. Rick said it would be good for Kayla, that she was a sharp kid with a sense of adventure.

Lisa had had a sense of adventure once, too. It had landed her pregnant at sixteen.

Of course, her sense of adventure had been a bit wild and out of bounds, totally opposite that of her oh-so-level-headed daughter, thank God. In many ways, Kayla was more like Amelia than Lisa. Which meant her child wouldn't make the same mistakes she had. She'd go to college, become a success, create a good life for herself instead of making bad choices.

"So are you going to do it?"

Lisa looked up at her best friend. "Do what?"

"Mommmm," Kayla said, rolling her eyes. "Pay attention."

"Sorry. I was thinking."

"Are you going to do the vacation with Connie? You know, hit the beach, get naked. Drink fruity drinks. Party your ass off."

"Watch your language, miss," Lisa warned. Kayla rolled her eyes again.

"She's right, you know," Connie said. "You deserve this. No one works harder than you do, both at the hospital and at home. If anyone is screaming for a glorious week of tropical downtime, it's you."

Lisa arched a brow. "I don't recall complaining."

"You never complain, Lisa."

Her gaze drifted to Rick. "I have nothing to whine about. My life is ideal." That was no lie. Kayla had never given her a moment's trouble, Rick had always been there to help out if and when she needed him, and she had a great job as a critical care nurse, working alongside her best friend Connie. All in all, she led a damned charmed life. And she owed a lot of that to Rick. He was the one who should be taking the vacation. The things he'd given up for her and for Kayla . . .

"Your love life sucks, Mom."

Wen snorted.

Snapping a glare at her smart-mouthed daughter, she said, "There's nothing wrong with my love life."

"Except that it's nonexistent."

"I won't find one in the Caribbean."

"It's a good enough place to start."

"True, Mrs. Mitchell. You're still great looking. Even sexy, for a woman . . . uhh . . . your age," Wen said.

"Gee, thanks, Wen. I think," Lisa said, shaking her head.

Connie laughed and laid her hand over Lisa's. "Trust me. Teenagers are ubercritical."

Kayla giggled, then was immediately distracted by the ringtone of her cell phone, temporarily lost in the corner of the kitchen while she and Wen planned the night's activities.

Lisa blew out a frustrated breath. A vacation would be nice. She needed a tan. Some time on the beach, sipping drinks with paper umbrellas, sounded like a slice of heaven. She never took vacations. Okay, she'd had a few, but they'd always been with Kayla and usually involved places like Disney World and Epcot Center and child-oriented functions, or something to do with Kayla's cheerleading or soccer. Never an adult vacation, never alone. The thought of going somewhere with another adult was . . . unfathomable.

"Go, Lisa."

She looked up at Rick. It was difficult thinking of sunning herself on the beach, possibly meeting or dancing with other men.

There'd never been *other* men. There'd only been Rick. Since she was fourteen years old, there'd only been Rick. She'd dated now and then, but nothing serious. She just hadn't been able to be with anyone else. How could she, when the only man who made her panties wet sat across the kitchen table from her? And the last time she'd had sex with him was . . . something like fifteen years ago?

God, she really did need a life.

"You'd really go with me?" She cast a pleading look at Connie.

Connie nodded. "Uh, you bet. Couldn't talk me out of it."

How did she get so lucky to find a best friend and a dynamite co-worker in one? "Do you think the hospital would let us both off at the same time?"

Connie grinned. "Already asked and answered. Beth said she'd rearrange the schedule to accommodate us."

"See? It's a done deal," Kayla said, a satisfied smile lighting up her gorgeous face.

Her daughter was beautiful. Okay, maybe she was just a tiny bit prejudiced, but she and Rick had made one incredible girl. Five feet seven, curvy in all the right places, and thank God the girl liked to eat and wasn't model-stick-worry-your-mother-to-death thin. She was athletic, loved the arts, earned some amazing scholarships, and didn't make stupid choices about boys. She was going to Florida State in the fall to major in elementary education. She'd always wanted to be a teacher, ever since she was a little girl playing school with her friends. The kid had goals. Goals!

"Finished with excuses?" Rick asked. "You don't even need me to watch over Kayla anymore. You're free, Lisa."

Free. What a concept. Free of responsibilities for one entire week. Not having to worry about what Kayla was doing, no guilt over dumping Rick with the burden.

She'd never have that guilt again. The ties that bound her and Rick together were slowly disintegrating.

The twinge in her stomach intensified. She figured it was the cake, not the fact that her link to Rick was evaporating. They were divorced, had been for a very long time. They'd always be connected by Kayla, but it was long past time she let go of him. It was time she let him move on.

Even at thirty-seven, he still took her breath away, probably more now than the day he walked into her life when she was fourteen years old and he was an oh-so-mature seventeen, tall and lanky with his midnight black hair falling over his face. He'd worn it long, shaggy, nearly covering his steely blue eyes. She'd gasped the first time she saw his eyes. No guy should have a face that beautiful, all those sharply angled cheekbones, full bottom lip, and eyes that could make a woman melt.

She'd fallen in love on the spot, and they'd been inseparable after that.

That had been the beginning of the end for her, and had altered the course of her life forever. And Rick's, too. She owed it to him to let him go now. He'd been by her side for all these years, devoted to her and Kayla in ways she'd never expected. He'd been the best father a girl could ask for and Kayla adored him. Lisa admired him for never once failing in his duties. He'd gone above and beyond his responsibilities to Lisa, too. She'd never have the career she had now if not for Rick.

She owed him so much. She owed him a life, love of his own. Even if the thought of it made her stomach ache.

"Speaking of someone who needs to get a life . . ." she said, hardly able to look him in the eyes without bursting into tears. Why was this so hard? She was probably just melancholy at the thought of Kayla growing up, moving off to college. This emotional mess had nothing to do with Rick.

"Working on it," he said, his lips lifting in a sly smile.

Her stomach tightened. "Oh, really? Well, that's . . . great . . . I'm glad."

Kayla grinned. She knew about this, about whatever woman put the gleam in Rick's eye. "And it's about time, Dad."

This was more than she could handle in one night. Lisa pushed back her chair. "Look at this mess. I think I'll start cleaning up."

"Need me to help, Mom?"

"Of course not. You've got your all-night graduation celebration at the high school tonight." She stopped, tilted her head down the hall. "You can take all your gifts to your room, then you'd better get packed."

"I'll drop the girls off," Rick said.

Lisa nodded, busied herself with picking up discarded gift wrap and paper plates. "Thanks. I appreciate it. I'll get her in the morning."

When the girls were ready and Rick hustled them out the door, it was just her and Connie left behind. The three-bedroom house had never been oversized—just enough room for Kayla and her. Right now it felt like a huge, yawning mausoleum.

Connie laid a cup of coffee in front of Lisa. She glanced up and smiled at her best friend. "Thanks."

"You look like you need it. Just like you need this vacation."

Lisa dragged a hand through her hair. "Yeah. I do need it. Both the coffee and the vacation."

"Kayla leaves in three weeks. Beth said the schedule is open. I've already talked to a travel agent."

"This is all so sudden."

"Not everything in life needs a six-month plan, Lisa. Just go with it."

She sighed. "I don't know, Connie. I don't have tropical wear."

"We'll go shopping."

"We don't have flights."

"My cousin is a travel agent. One phone call and I'll get her working on a deal for us."

"Where would we go?"

"I hear Saint Thomas is nice."

She shivered, sank into the thought of turquoise water, sunny beaches, and time to do absolutely nothing. "God, that sounds like the Garden of Eden right now."

"One whole week. That's seven whole days you won't be mooning over Kayla being gone and you alone in this house by yourself."

She glared at Connie. "You, my friend, know me all too well."

Connie winked, her green eyes sparkling with mischief. "That's the truth."

"I'm not going there to find a man. The last thing I need is some disastrous vacation romance."

Connie leaned back in the chair, taking her cup of coffee and cradling it between her hands. "Lisa, you're thirty-four years old, gorgeous, with a body I'd kill for. When was the last time you had sex?"

She gave Connie a blank stare. "I don't remember. I'm sure it was sometime this millennium."

Connie shook her head. "Oh, fuck. Be sure to pack condoms."

"Jesus, Connie."

"Honey, I'm thirty pounds overweight, ten years older than you, and divorced three times, and I get way more sex than you do. There's something wrong with that picture."

"Your kids are both off on their own."

"Bad excuse."

Lisa lifted her chin. "It is not. I couldn't very well bring men back to the house with my kid here."

"There are hotels. And what about when Kayla was staying at Rick's?"

Well, hell. She shrugged. "Good guys are hard to find."

"Not that hard. And maybe you're still carrying a seriously flaming torch for your ex-husband."

"I am not."

Connie rolled her eyes. "Honey, if any one of my exes looked or acted like Rick Mitchell, I'd never have divorced him, and I'd be jumping his seriously sexy bones every chance I could. I don't know why you and Rick don't fuck each other blind whenever you can."

The thought of it heated her. She so didn't need those visuals in her head right now. "Our relationship isn't like that. We're friends."

Connie snorted. "Bullshit. I see the way you look at him."

"What are you talking about?"

"Those big brown eyes of yours just eat him up every time he walks into the room."

Denial hovered on her lips, but Connie knew her too well. She laid her head in her hands. "God. Is it that obvious?"

"Uh, yeah. To me it is anyway."

"Shit. I didn't mean for it to be. I don't want it to be. Oh, Connie, I want to have a life. I want to move on. I don't want to be dependent on Rick. I don't want to feel what I still feel for him. It's not right. Not after all this time."

She hated the tears that welled in her eyes. They made her feel weak and helpless, and she hadn't been weak and helpless in a very long time.

But Connie understood. Thank God for friends. Connie laid her hand over Lisa's. "I wasn't kidding when I said Rick is the type of man most woman would slit another woman's throat to have. He's one in a million."

"I know," she said, her voice choked with emotion. "But he's not mine anymore. Hasn't been for years. And you heard him tonight. He's met someone."

Connie couldn't look at her. "So it seems."

"Which means I have to let him go."

"Then let's have a vacation."

Lisa nodded, determination firing her blood. "You're right. It's time I grabbed my own happiness."

"Now you're talkin'. So are you in?"

Why the hell not? The alternative was growing old alone, feeling sorry for herself, and becoming a pathetic woman holding on to the past. No way was she going to allow that to happen. She swiped away the tears and grinned. "Hell yes, I'm in."

⁂

Wen hopped out of Rick's car with a rapid-fire thanks. Kayla told her to get in line and she'd be there in a sec.

"Dad?" She twisted in the front seat to face him. He knew she'd want to talk after what went down at Lisa's.

"Yeah?"

"Are we doing the right thing? To Mom, I mean."

"Are you having second thoughts? Because we can put a stop to it. All you have to do is say so."

She shook her head. "No. This is the right thing. You and Mom belong together."

Rick leaned back against the seat. "I've always thought so." He turned so that Kayla could see his eyes, could read the honesty in them. "I love your mom, Kay. I never stopped."

Kay's eyes brimmed with tears. At that moment she looked so much like her mother it was uncanny. They both wore their emotions on their faces.

"I know you do, Dad. That's why I think this is the right thing. Sneaky," she said, letting that characteristic Kayla-giggle slip in, "but it's the only way to shock her into facing reality."

"I don't know about that. You and Connie are more devious than me. I prefer the direct approach."

"Oh, come on. You know our idea has merit. You, Mom, stuck together for a week in a tropical paradise. It's your chance to talk to her, to convince her the two of you should try again."

"She'll be pissed." And he wouldn't put it past her to hop right back on the plane and fly home.

Kayla shrugged. "She'll get over it. Who could resist the lure of the Caribbean? Warm sand, tropical breezes, all that hot sex . . ."

"Kayla," he warned, wondering when his baby girl had grown up and become a woman of the world.

"Dad," she said, rolling her eyes. "You're both consenting adults. Even if the thought of you two . . . doing it . . . makes me want to hurl." She let her tongue unfurl and hang out her mouth, making the icky face that made him laugh.

"Gee. Thanks. That's so romantic."

She snorted. "I gotta go. Hopefully Connie is twisting her arm as we speak. I'll talk to you tomorrow, see if Connie managed to convince her."

She leaned across the car and pressed a kiss to his cheek. "Love you, Dad."

"Love you, too, Kay."

And in a flash, she was gone, swallowed up by the hordes of other graduates spending the night at the graduation lockup party in the high school gym. Which meant fun, games, all the food they could consume, and they'd be safe.

As he drove away, he found it hard to comprehend he was the father of a high school graduate. No, a soon-to-be college freshman. Jesus, when had he gotten old?

Fuck that. He wasn't old. Neither was Lisa. Their lives were just beginning. And if everything worked out in the Caribbean, they'd have their second chance.

Hell of a plan. Of course, to Kayla it was all so simple. Lie to Lisa, convince her to go to the Caribbean for a vacation, but have Rick show up there instead. Then spend time together and try to recapture the magic they'd once had when they were younger.

Was that even possible? They were different people now. When they first fell in love, they were both teenagers. They'd lived a life-time since then, had raised a daughter. They had careers, separate lives. Yet they were never really separate, were they?

He knew Connie, knew she'd be able to talk Lisa into going on this trip. Of course, Connie wouldn't be the one accompanying her. Rick would be going. And he owed the entire devious plan to his daughter, who thought her parents should finally consummate the passion that had always flamed between them.

She was right. There had always been fire between Lisa and him. There'd been sparks from the time he met her, even when Lisa was fourteen, when he'd known better than to touch her. But even then it had been damned hard to resist the attraction. They'd waited two years before falling into bed together. And they'd been careful, as careful as they could be when desire consumed them. But condoms weren't the best birth control method, and when Lisa, at sixteen years old, got pregnant, they'd gotten married. They'd been in love. It had been tough. Goddamn, it had been tough. Barely twenty and struggling to work full-time and juggle college part-time, he'd sud-denly also had to deal with a pregnant teenaged wife.

A wife he'd adored.

And when Kayla had been born, he'd hung the moon on his daughter. She'd been perfect, and he and Lisa had given up everything for her, determined that she'd never pay for their mistakes. But they were barely adults, didn't know how to really love each other. Tensions had mounted as high as their bills. They were drowning. Eventually Lisa had to move back home with her parents, taking Kayla with her.

Rick hated failure, but even he had to admit that separating had been the best thing for all of them, had eased the tension between them. By the time Kayla was three, they'd known divorce was inevi-table. They'd realized they weren't ready to face an adult relation-ship, even though they still loved each other. They sacrificed each other to do what was right for Kayla, before they ended up tearing each other apart and Kayla in the process.

Divorcing had been the hardest thing he'd ever done. But he'd vowed never to let either of them go. He was responsible for his child and the woman he'd vowed to love forever. He'd worked his way through college, gotten his degree, and when he'd finally gotten back on his feet, bought a house for Lisa and Kayla. Lisa hadn't wanted it, of course, but Rick said a house was a good place for Kayla to grow up, much better than an apartment. By then Lisa was going to nursing school, and eventually Rick bought a house nearby so he could help watch Kay while Lisa was in school. When Lisa graduated and started making decent money of her own, she took over the payments of her own house. It was important to her to stand on her own two feet and not depend on Rick for everything. It was one of the things he admired most about her.

Over the years they'd developed a perfect relationship, relying on each other, as close to a real family as you could get. Kayla was secure and loved by both her parents, and Rick and Lisa settled into a cozy, comfortable relationship.

A relationship that had no passion.

It suited both of them fine for a long time, while they nurtured Kayla and built their careers. They both dated other people here and there, but it seemed like neither one of them wanted to bring another person into the family relationship they had built among the three of them. Lisa hadn't moved on. Neither had he. It always seemed to Rick as if he and Lisa were both waiting for the time when they could be together again, only neither of them had ever mentioned it. It was like a tenuous, invisible thread between them, and both of them were afraid to do anything to break it. Even if it meant they'd do nothing at all.

No more waiting. That time was now. If they got there and she said no, then that would be it. He'd walk away with no regrets. But he'd regret it forever if he didn't at least try to win back the woman he'd loved almost half his life.

Two

Lisa avoided pressing her nose to the tiny window of the small two-engine plane that swooped and rolled on its way to landing at the tiny island of Saint Thomas. It was difficult, though. Butterflies the size of Tyrannosaurus rex stomped around in her stomach. She was so damned excited she wanted to leap out of the plane so she could get there faster.

The Virgin Islands. The Caribbean. She was almost there. She wished Connie could have traveled with her so she could share in the excitement, but the travel agent had to book them on separate flights. Since they had to schedule at the last minute, seats were at a premium, so Connie would be flying in later today. Lisa was fine with that. She was almost there, and that's what counted.

The previous few weeks had passed in a blur of activity. Shopping for the trip, making travel arrangements, and seeing Kayla off on her own trip, though fortunately those details had already been dealt with months ago, clearing the way for Lisa to concentrate on her own travel plans. Kayla and Connie had insisted on dragging her shopping to buy new clothes. Her suitcase was now filled with sundresses, sandals, swimsuits, and just about anything and everything she could possibly need for this vacation. And would probably never wear again. Scandalous, sexy wear, including stuff for the evenings. And the lingerie? What were her daughter and best friend thinking? It wasn't like she was going to be parading around half-naked for a bevy of men every night.

But at least when she looked in the mirror of her hotel room, she'd make herself blush.

Connie had insisted she go to the salon and get her hair cut and put some highlights in it. More tropical, she'd claimed. Whatever.

Brown was brown. Her hair was brown, her eyes were brown, and she was pretty much average looking. But Connie and Kayla had so much fun doing her makeover that she went along with it. Now she had chin-length hair with subtle highlights that brought out her natural auburn, and even Lisa had to admit it looked pretty darned good. The new makeup was nice, too. Restrained, but sexy. She was ready for . . .

For what? Anything and everything, she supposed. After Kayla's graduation, she'd seen very little of Rick. She supposed she'd have to get used to that since Kayla was now eighteen, out of school, and they didn't have the normal sharing of custody that they used to. Kayla could come and go as she pleased, divide her time between both parents however she wanted to, not according to a court-ordered custody document. Not that that had ever mattered anyway, since Lisa and Rick had pretty much split custody. When one had something to do, the other gladly filled in with taking care of Kayla.

But still . . . Lisa's world seemed emptier without Rick in it.

Too bad. She'd just have to get over that. Rick obviously had a life now. It was high time she got one. After this vacation, she intended to start living again. Going out more. Dating.

Bleh.

The announcement of their impending landing relieved her of that train of thought. In a few minutes, they were on the ground. Lisa grabbed her luggage and went off to find the shuttle to take her to the hotel.

Connie said her cousin had gotten them a great deal at one of the most beautiful resorts on Saint Thomas. A last-minute cancellation or something like that, so they'd gotten it at half price. Lisa didn't care where they stayed. A discount-rate shack would have been fine with her.

But when the shuttle turned through the gates and down the long road leading to the hotel, Lisa caught her first sight of the resort and gasped. It was a villa, a palazzo, a veritable mansion towering above the entire island. Built on top of a hill, rising high and proud and utterly breathtaking, Lisa realized then and there that this wasn't a hotel, it was a damn city in itself. The resort was one of the finest, the ritziest, and Lisa figured Connie was insane and they were both going to be flat broke by the time this vacation was over.

Check-in was like a dream. Her reservation was already taken care of—*bless you, Connie and your cousin!* The room was ready and her things were brought up by the bellman. Wow, this was living. She'd never been treated like this. The bellman took her upstairs via an elevator—everything was trimmed in gold, including the numbered buttons on the elevator. The bellman used another key, sliding it into the slot above the room numbers on the elevator. The light at the top blinked.

"We're on the top floor?"

"Yes, ma'am," he said, looking straight ahead and not at her. "Presidential suite."

"Um, are you sure? Because I'm not important or anything."

His lips curled upward. "Yes, ma'am. Presidential suite. When we get up there, I'll give you all your keys."

The door opened, they took a step out, and there was the door right in front of them. Wow. The hotel room was as big as her entire house. Prettier, too. Open, airy, tropical breezes blowing through the open balconies. Dear God, she could see the turquoise blue waters of the Caribbean right from her room. She knew her mouth hung open, but she couldn't do anything to shut it as she strolled along the pristine cinnamon marble flooring, broken up occasionally by plush, room-sized rugs. The entire suite screamed expensive, from the dark furniture to the king-sized bed. Everything was open, gorgeous, state of the art, and oh, she so couldn't afford this.

"Are you sure?" she asked the bellman again as he set her suitcases on the floor in the bedroom.

"Yes, ma'am." He showed her how to use the elevator keys, gave her a tour of the suite. She gave him a generous tip, then after he left, she turned around and walked outside on the balcony. One of four balconies, one available from every room in the house—because that's what this was. A freakin' house.

Holy crap. This had to be some kind of mistake. She was certain the hotel management would come knocking on her door within the hour, indicating that there had, in fact, been a mistake, and she needed to pack up her things and move to a regular room. One of those "bed and bathroom and that's all you get" kind of rooms. Actually, she wasn't certain she could even afford one of their regular rooms.

This couldn't be her and Connie's room. Even at the discount rate, it just didn't seem possible.

She wandered through the suite and waited a full hour before deciding no one was going to knock at the door announcing an error. Then she decided to unpack.

One king-sized bed in the master bedroom. And another bedroom in another part of the suite. Oh well, she and Connie would figure it out later, and the master bedroom's closet was more than large enough for both their clothes.

She hung everything up, put her things in one of the dressers, then changed into a sundress, trying to figure out what to do until Connie arrived tonight, when the phone beside the bed rang. Her stomach lurched. This was it. The management.

It was Connie.

"Is it gorgeous?" she asked.

"Yes! Oh, my God, this place is a palace."

Connie laughed. "I knew it."

"Are you packed yet?"

There was a slight pause before Connie said, "Uh, yeah. Packed and eager. One problem, though. My flight is delayed."

"Oh, no. What's the problem?"

"Some equipment failure. They're going to bring in another plane, but I won't be able to come in until tomorrow."

"Dammit, Connie. That sucks. You should have had my flight."

"Don't be silly. Anyway, here's the deal. I got you a dinner companion for tonight."

Lisa was sure she hadn't heard that part correctly. "What?"

"My cousin knows this guy who lives there locally. Gorgeous. Great talker. He's available and would love to have dinner with you. You won't have to hide in the hotel room tonight like I know you would have."

She would have. "Connie, I'm not at all interested . . ."

"He'll meet you in the bar at seven-thirty. Dress sexy. I already told him what you look like. Oh, I have another call coming in, I gotta go. Have fun!"

"Connie, wait!"

But she was already gone. Dammit! How could Connie do this to her? A dinner date? Jesus. She so wasn't ready for this.

Okay, she had to calm down before she drove herself crazy. This was just dinner. A nice way to pass the time tonight, and Connie was right. It was better than spending her first night in the room. If the guy was a local, he could fill her in about the island, things to do, and places she and Connie could go. Perfect. She'd have a good time. It would be fine. It wasn't like she was obligated to hop into the sack with the guy.

God, she was rusty at this whole man-woman thing. With Rick it was so easy.

Get over it, Lisa. You don't have Rick anymore. Time to step outside your comfort zone.

Way outside.

She glanced at the clock on the nightstand. It was four. She had three and a half hours until she had to meet her date tonight. Plenty of time to wander around the resort, grab some pool time, and start working on her tan. She could even have one of those tropical drinks, which would help her relax.

She changed clothes again, this time putting on her swimsuit and a cover-up, then slipped on her sandals, filled up her beach bag, and headed downstairs.

After taking so many turns around the hotel she ended up right back where she'd started, she decided she was going to need a map or she'd be forever lost. She stopped at the concierge's desk and picked one up. That would help a lot. Navigating this theme park–sized resort wasn't going to be easy, and she didn't have the best sense of direction anyway.

She made it through the throngs of inside-the-hotel shops, stopped and surveyed the menus at a couple of restaurants, and found the bar before maneuvering her way to one of the pools. She ended her hotel sightseeing right there at the crystal blue waters that seemed to spill over into the turquoise of the Caribbean, as the pool was balanced on the edge of the ocean. It was breathtaking. She found a corner spot, pulled off her cover-up and lathered on sunscreen, then stretched out to enjoy the warmth of the sun.

This really was the life. Her eyes closed, she listened to the water lapping over the rocks, falling into the pool on the first level below. The smell of sunscreen and flowers was heady and tropical. She'd ordered a piña colada from the waiter who'd hurried to her side as soon as she'd laid her towel on the chair, and she took a moment to sip from it before lying down again.

It was possible she might never move from this spot. Though after about fifteen minutes she was hot and sweaty, so she got up and took a plunge in the pool to cool off, swam a few laps, then came out and stretched out on her stomach, tossing her floppy hat over her head to block the sun.

It was delightfully uncrowded, just a handful of people lounging by the pool. She spotted a couple across the pool, lying side by side on their chairs, holding hands, occasionally kissing and whispering. They were about the same age as Rick and her. If she and Rick hadn't divorced, they'd have been married nearly twenty years by now. It might be the two of them on this tropical vacation, soaking up the sun, kissing . . .

She remembered his mouth, the way he used to take it slow, kissing her until her toes curled, until she couldn't stand it anymore and begged him to fuck her. Even now she could still find herself staring at the fullness of his lips whenever they were together, remembering how he tasted, wishing . . .

The pain of longing struck her hard, and the tears began to fall before she could do anything to stop them. Thankfully, the wide brim of her hat camouflaged the ridiculous waterworks.

What the hell was wrong with her anyway? It was way too early in the month for PMS. She was just lonely. If Connie were here, she'd no doubt be drunk and laughing her ass off by now, or fending off some lifeguard fifteen years her junior that Connie had dragged over.

Tomorrow things would be better, when she didn't have all this alone time and nothing but memories to wallow in.

She sniffed, swiped at the tears, angry at her emotions. Rick had a woman in his life now. She had no hold on him anymore. It wasn't like she ever had anyway. Ever since they divorced, he'd been free to date, to find someone else, to get married even.

So had she, though the thought had never crossed her mind. Not while Kayla had needed raising.

Kayla was raised now. No more excuses. So how come she still didn't want to?

The sun had long ago slipped behind the tall columns of the main hotel. She grabbed her watch, realizing it was almost six. Time to get ready. She threw on her cover-up and headed upstairs to take a shower and get ready for tonight. For her date. Where she promised herself she wouldn't once think about Rick.

Who knew where tonight would lead? Maybe this guy would be smokin' hot and she could have some wild, uninhibited, no-strings-attached sex. God, she really needed sex, was tired of her hands and her vibrator and craved the feel of a man's big, hot hands all over her, the feel of a thick cock sliding inside her, pumping her until she screamed, bringing her to orgasm over and over again.

She shuddered and stepped into the shower, staring down at her beaded nipples.

"Hang on," she said, cupping them, sliding her thumbs over them, then reaching for the body wash, refusing to touch herself this time. She was going to wait. Maybe, just maybe, there was hope for her on this trip. Maybe she'd be brave enough to have a fling. Why not? She was certainly old enough, had no one to answer to but herself.

She dried her hair, put on makeup, and selected a nice dress. Black and gold with spaghetti straps and little gold sandals. She wore earrings only. The little threads of gold woven into the tight black bodice were showy enough. As she stared at herself in the full-length mirror and twirled around, letting the skirt settle back around her legs, even she had to nod. She looked damn sexy. Running from one end of the hospital to the other kept her in shape. She had a decent body and Connie had been right—this dress showed it off nicely.

She glanced at the clock. Seven-fifteen. She supposed she should head downstairs and find a spot in the bar, order a cocktail so she could take a few sips, and relax a little bit before her mystery date showed up.

The bar was glorious. Dark and sexy and smooth, with glass walls, tinkling chandeliers that caught the light, and leather furniture you could sink into with ease. There were intimate tables for two or four tucked into dark corners. The entire place was open to the outdoors, bringing a gentle breeze in from the water. There was a nice spot right at the bar where she settled in on one of the high barstools and ordered a drink. A band played, fortunately not too loud so people could hear themselves talk. There was a decent crowd in there. She wondered if this guy would be able to find her from Connie's description.

She was nervous! She felt like a kid going out on her first date. Really, this wasn't even a date. She had to settle down. Maybe he wouldn't even show up.

She felt warm breath on her shoulder and tensed.

"You take my breath away, Lisa."

Oh, God. She knew that voice. She shifted, turning in her seat, but she already knew who it was.

"Rick?"

What the hell was her ex-husband doing here?

Three

"Hey, beautiful," he said.

Rick was dressed in white slacks and a black shirt, both silk and hugging his body in all the right places. The lights in the bar caught on his blue eyes, giving him a dark and dangerous and oh so sexy look. And when he smiled, she couldn't breathe. He was the one who took her breath away. He was so damned gorgeous she was shaking.

It took Lisa a few seconds to find her voice. "What are you doing here?" This couldn't possibly be coincidence, but her mind wasn't working through the possibilities.

He brushed his fingers over her bare shoulders, an intimate gesture, more than he'd touched her in years.

"You can't guess?"

She shook her head. "No." Something formed in the back of her mind, but she shrugged it off. Confusion had taken hold, so again she asked, "What are you doing here?"

He grabbed her drink, laid cash on the bar counter, and found a table for two in the corner. A waitress came over and Rick ordered a drink.

"Are you here with your . . ." She couldn't find the words. "Are you with someone?"

That was all she'd need. Rick here with his new lady love. She would hide in her room. She wasn't ready to handle it. In theory, maybe. In person . . . no way.

His lips quirked. "I am now. I'm here with you."

"I don't understand." Was she being dense? Did she miss something?

He rubbed his index finger over the top of her hand. He never touched her. They were both so careful to maintain a discreet distance, never wanting to give Kayla the wrong idea. And just this tiny caress gave her shivers, despite the sultry heat in the bar.

"Rick, what are you doing?"

And oh, shit, she forgot she was supposed to be meeting someone. "What time is it? I'm . . . I'm supposed to have dinner with someone."

One dark brow arched and he smiled. "I know."

"You do?" How the hell could he know?

"I'm your date."

"What?"

"Connie's not coming."

She frowned. "Okay, I'm confused."

"I know you are, and I'm sorry for that. It was the only way we could come up with to get you here."

"We? We who?" A seed formed in her mind, but she didn't want to say anything. Not until she knew for sure.

"Me. Connie. Kayla."

Her stomach tumbled. She'd been set up, but why? She shook her head. "I'm not really this dense, but I still don't understand. What's this all about?"

He leaned in and oh man did he ever smell good. Not like cologne or anything phony. But like Rick. Like he'd just showered with the best soap ever. Clean and fresh and she really wanted to lick that pulse-pounding spot on his neck. Jesus. She leaned back.

"It's about you and me, Lisa. A chance to reconnect, spend some time together."

"Why?"

He laughed, then, and she felt stupid, like there was some huge joke that everyone got but her. "Why do you think?"

She shrugged. "I have no idea. Obviously everyone I know is in on this but me. Why don't you spell it out in simple terms an idiot like me can understand."

His smile died. "Now you're getting mad. I'm sorry. Let me tell you what's going on."

"That would be helpful."

"I started all this. The idea about the vacation, about setting you up to think it would be you and Connie. Well, actually, it was Kayla's original idea."

Her brows shot up. "Kay's?"

"Yeah." He rimmed his cocktail glass with the tip of his finger. "Seems our daughter thinks there's some unfinished business between the two of us."

"What kind of unfinished business?"

"Maybe the fact that we divorced all those years ago, but neither of us ever remarried, or even really date?"

This conversation was heading into dangerous territory. She and Rick never discussed their personal lives. They only talked about Kayla. "I thought you had . . . someone."

"That someone was you."

Oh, holy hell. Her heart started up with this *thump thump thump* rhythm and she was getting dizzy. She grabbed for her drink, taking a couple long swallows. "Me?"

"Yeah. You. I'm not seeing anyone else. The only one I ever see is you."

"I don't understand."

"Don't you?"

He picked up her hand, held it. When was the last time they'd held hands? She didn't remember.

"You and I have been together twenty years, Lisa. We've been through hell and back. We've married, divorced, and raised a daughter together. And even though we've lived in separate houses most of that time, we're still . . . together. Sort of. You've dated some, I've dated some, but neither one of us have formed any relationships."

"I thought that was because of Kay."

"I don't think so. Lots of divorced people remarry or at least develop relationships with someone else. Kids adapt and accept. Kayla would have, too."

He was right. She had never found someone that sparked her interest enough to keep seeing more than a few times. She never really knew about Rick's love life. Kayla probably knew more about it than she did, but Kay was good about not revealing Rick's personal life to her. Thankfully.

"I never wanted anyone else, Lisa. I measured every woman against you, and they all fell short."

She shifted her gaze to her drink. "I'm nothing special."

He slid his fingers under her chin, forced her gaze back to his. "I disagree. You were barely a teen when you ended up pregnant. You had options to do something about that—your choice to make, but you chose to have Kayla. You finished high school while juggling an infant on your hip. You went to nursing school. You raised a brilliant daughter and you have a successful career. I think you're pretty damn special."

It was hard not to weep under praise like that. She blinked back tears, not wanting her mascara to run. "Thank you. But I didn't do that alone. You've done a damn good job, too. As hard as it was on me, it was doubly hard on you. Working two jobs, going to college, living in an apartment, and then buying a house for Kayla and me. You were always so generous."

"It was my job to provide for my daughter."

"You never missed a child support check. You went above and beyond what the courts required of you."

"I love . . . Kayla."

"I know you do." Rick's love for his daughter was evident in everything he did. That's why every man she dated paled in comparison to Rick. Why there were never sparks hot enough to keep her interested for long.

But was it because he'd been so nice to her and Kayla? Or was it more than that?

"We owe it to ourselves to find out if it's still there, Lisa."

"If what's still there?"

"The magic. The passion. What we once had together."

She inhaled, let it out. "That's what this whole vacation-in-the-tropics thing is about, isn't it?"

"Yes. I wanted to kidnap you from your everyday life, away from our friends, and yeah, even away from Kayla. Back to when it was just you and me."

"We've changed since then, Rick. It's not twenty years ago. We can't go back." She wasn't sure if she was trying to convince him, or herself.

He nodded. "I know. But you can't deny there's still an attraction there."

No, she couldn't. Every time he came over, she longed for him. Every time he accidentally touched her, she felt the spark. But was it because it was Rick, or because it had been so damn long since there'd been a man in her life? She hated being so complacent.

Rick was easy. He was familiar. She'd gotten used to familiar and comfortable. She didn't want to be familiar and comfortable anymore. Kayla was grown. This was her time to go out and get that life she'd denied herself.

Was that new life with Rick?

No. The absolute last thing she wanted was to destroy what she and Rick had built together. Their friendship. The easy way they talked and could be together and care for Kay. How they depended on one another. Would diving back into the sexual waters ruin that? What if it didn't work out? Their perfect relationship would be ruined.

She finished her cocktail, used the napkin to swipe across her lips. "I don't know if this is such a good idea, Rick."

"You're scared."

"Yes."

"I am, too. You have no idea how long I thought about this. Kayla may be eighteen, but she still has a young girl's ideals of romance. She thinks it's easy."

"So did I . . . once."

His lips quirked. "It wasn't so bad."

"It was a disaster. For both of us. I don't want to make it worse by opening up old wounds." They'd gone through hell together. They'd managed to repair the damage for Kayla's sake, but they'd left so much unresolved.

"What are you so afraid of, Lisa?"

"You and I have a ton of history. Not all of it was good." They'd been so young, their notions foolish and filled with fantasy. Reality had been entirely different. Harsh.

"True enough. But we've created a new kind of relationship."

"That's my point. I don't want to screw it up."

He slid his fingers through her hair. Cupped the back of her neck. She shivered at the warmth of his touch. Her nipples tightened and she felt the awakening fires between her legs, the all-too-familiar wetness there.

Rick leaned in and she was mesmerized by the unique turquoise of his eyes. Had they become even bluer over the years? She hadn't been this close to him in so long.

"If nothing else," he said, his breath whispering over her cheek as he drew in closer, "we'll have a great time. God knows we both work so damn hard, Lisa. We need to have some fun."

"Yes." She wrapped her fingers around his forearm, felt muscles that hadn't been there twenty years ago. He'd been no more than a boy when she'd last seen him naked. Her mind was awash in visuals of how it felt then, what it would feel like now. "Fun would be nice."

His lips hovered a fraction of an inch from hers. If she leaned in, they'd touch, tangle, and she could taste him. Oh, how she wanted to take that step. But she hesitated, her mind whirling with the what-if's, the why she shouldn't's.

Rick pulled back. "Not here. Let's go up to the room."

Her eyes widened. "You got the suite."

He smiled. "Yeah. You deserved a real vacation."

"It's utterly extravagant."

He held out his hand and pulled her up. "I have a really good job and I haven't had a decent vacation in years. We both deserve this."

He tucked her hand in the crook of his arm and they left the bar, taking the elevator to the penthouse. His suitcases were inside the door.

"We're going to stay here together?" she asked, then felt stupid. Of course they were. It wasn't like they were strangers, and yet in many ways, they were. It would be like starting over.

"There are two bedrooms." He stared down at her through his lashes. "The decision is up to you."

He meant the decision as to what bedroom he'd sleep in. Well, hell. "This is all happening so fast."

He nodded, laid his hand on the small of her back, and propelled her into the room. "Let's order some dinner and relax. We'll talk."

"Okay." She needed a breather, time to take it all in, think about what this could mean before she made some monumental decision, took a step she couldn't reverse.

They studied the room service menu and ordered food. Rick selected a bottle of wine to go with their dinner. Having the penthouse suite had some advantages, because their food was brought up within minutes, and Rick had them set it up out on the terrace.

Torches were lit below, leading from the palazzo all the way to the beach. Music drifted upward and Lisa could see people strolling on the beach, the walkway alongside it as well as throughout the resort grounds. There was no room next to them, completely isolating them from other people and giving them complete privacy. She felt like a queen overseeing her kingdom. It was peaceful and private and very romantic, having dinner on their small table for two with its starched white linen, a bottle of very expensive wine chilling in a stand next to them.

The seafood was to die for, and Lisa realized she hadn't eaten since earlier that day. She settled into her normal routine with Rick, talking about Kayla. Kay had arrived in Rome with Amelia a week ago. They'd both talked to her on the phone yesterday, but knew she'd be busy a lot so calls would be rare. Plus Kayla said she wasn't going to be in touch while Lisa was on vacation.

"I can't believe the little brat was in on this," Lisa said, pushing her plate to the side and reaching for her wine goblet.

"She can be devious." Rick pulled out the bottle of wine and refilled her glass.

"So it seems. So can Connie. And you as well."

"Only when there's something I really want."

Her face warmed. Wall sconces were their only source of light out here on the terrace, but enough that flickering shadows danced over his face. He looked positively Machiavellian, his lips curling in a wicked smile, his eyes gleaming through the fringe of his lashes.

What was he doing to her? Maybe it was the wine. Maybe it was more than the wine, because when he pushed back his chair and came over to her side of the table to lift her up, she stood, feeling like she was made of water, like her legs weren't going to support her. Which was okay, because Rick pulled her against him and it was oh so good to feel his body pressed up against hers. He didn't crush her to him, just wrapped one arm around her waist and walked her to the balcony railing. Simply having his hand resting on her hip was unnerving. How would she react to having more than that?

For God's sake, Lisa. It's not like you haven't had sex in . . . Actually, she hadn't had sex in . . .

"We don't have to do this if it isn't what you want, Lisa."

"I know." He'd never pressure her. She knew Rick better than anyone else in her life. She could say no and he'd be content to take this vacation with her as friends, him sleeping in one room and her in another.

But is that what she wanted? To keep their relationship the same as it had been for fifteen years? Just friends? Her body knew she wanted more than that. It was pinging and firing all over the place, and all that was going on right now was his hand on her hip.

The only problem was in the what-happened-after? To them, to the solid foundation of friendship they'd built for each other, for Kayla.

He turned to face her, sweeping a windblown tendril away from her face, tucking it behind her ear. Lisa inhaled and held her breath as Rick moved in closer.

"We'll take it slow. One step at a time. Ease into it, rather than rushing headlong without thinking like we did the first time. I'm a little smoother now than I was back then."

God, was he. He slid his palm across her neck—could he feel the wild pounding of her pulse there?

"Slow. Yes. That's a good idea."

At least her mind thought so. Her straining breasts, aching nipples, and wet panties thought something entirely different. She was millimeters away from a hot and sexy man she'd desired her entire adult life, his full lips so close she could feel his breath, inhale the scent of the wine, his soap. Her senses were going haywire and her body screamed anything but slow.

"But right now, I have to do this."

He bridged that gap, inches that seemed like miles, and pressed his lips to hers.

As a shock of electricity curled her toes, she wondered how long slow would last.

Slow was a really stupid idea.

Four

It took every shred of willpower Rick possessed not to drag Lisa into his arms, to crush her against him, to deepen the kiss the way he really wanted to. But she tasted so damn sweet and right now her mouth was soft and yielding under his, and that was going to have to be good enough.

He knew she was hesitant about all this, that he'd hit her with too much too soon. Lisa wasn't one to dive in headfirst without thinking things through. He'd give her time. But damn if it wasn't hard to restrain himself, especially with her leaning into him, her body soft and warm and those sighing sounds she made.

Christ, a man had only so much patience and he'd wanted this for a long time. But he had control. For Lisa, he had mountains of control, even if his dick was hard and throbbing and he wanted to bury it deep inside her.

Control. C-o-n-t-r-o-l. He spelled it long and slow in his head, hoping it would ramp down his libido.

Yeah, right. No such luck. He doubted reciting the periodic table in his head would do much good. Not while he held Lisa in his arms, not when she whimpered and pressed against him, challenging him to kiss deeper, pull her closer, take this kiss one step further.

He tasted wine on her lips. How much had she had? He couldn't remember, he'd been lost in conversation, in watching the cast of light on her hair. She'd gotten it cut and it just brushed her nape and chin now. He wanted to bury his fingers in the softness of her hair, to lose himself in everything Lisa.

Control. With every whispered moan, every slight adjustment of her hips against his, he felt her losing it. Which meant he had to hold on to his, because she'd said she wanted to take this slow. Her breasts pressed against his chest. He swept his hands across her shoulders. How easy it would be to slide those thin straps off, then push down the top of her dress and bare her breasts so he could taste her nipples. Lisa had always had sensitive nipples. Were they still? He wanted to capture them between his lips, nibble them with his teeth, lick and suck them right here on the balcony until she arched her back and cried out.

Control. Not yet. Even though the skirt of her dress was loose and flowy and it would be so easy to draw it up over her thighs, spread his palm over the heated center of her sex and rub her, caress her until she moaned and begged him to pull her panties aside. She'd be wet—he knew she was wet because her scent was already driving him nuts. He'd slide his fingers over her soft, moist pussy lips, teasing her until neither of them could stand it. Then he'd slip a finger between her folds, sliding inside her, feeling her walls clench, grabbing his finger while he pumped gently, finger fucking her while his thumb swirled over her clit.

He used to love to make her come, to watch the way her face tightened, her eyes closed, her hips rose, and she cried out with wild abandon. He wanted to make her come again, right now.

But he promised control. Tonight he was just going to kiss her, even if it tore him apart inside. They had seven days to get to know each other again, to take this one step at a time, a slow, deliberate seduction.

He withdrew his mouth. She opened her eyes slowly, staring into his.

"Slow sucks," she whispered, her voice hoarse.

He laughed, swallowed. "Yes, it does."

She cupped his cheek, ran her palm along his jaw. "I remember kissing you."

"It's been a long time."

"It's better now than it was before."

He arched a brow. "Are you saying I wasn't good at it before?"

She giggled and stepped toward the balcony, placing her fingers on the warm concrete. "Of course not. It's just . . ." She swept her fingers through her hair. "It's just . . ." She turned to him. "Wow, Rick. I don't remember being so . . ."

"Turned on?"

She glanced between his legs, her lips curling upward before shifting her gaze back to his face. "Yes. Turned on. I know we got hot and heavy when we were teens. But we were so new at it. Neither of us really knew what we were doing. Now . . ."

"Now we do know, and we know what we want."

"Not that I'm all that experienced, because I'm not. It's not that I've had tons of lovers since you."

"Neither have I."

She smiled at that. "But I've lived a lot, and thought a lot, and I know what I want now. I know what I need. I've learned a lot of things about my body in the past fifteen years." She turned to him, her face soft, her eyes like liquid chocolate. "You touch me in all the right places."

This conversation wasn't making his hard-on go away. "I've thought about you a lot."

Her gaze shifted, almost as if the conversation were too intimate. But then she looked at him again. "I've thought about you, too. About what it would be like if we—"

"And now we can."

"Yes. We can."

The one thing he'd learned in twenty years of knowing Lisa was the ability to read her. Right now he read desire. As heady as that was, he also read hesitation.

She needed to think. He moved forward, pressed a kiss to her cheek.

"I'll see you in the morning." He left her on the balcony and grabbed his suitcases, took them to the spare bedroom, and closed the door.

Hopefully he'd have to spend only one night there. But even if it was more, he was determined to do this on Lisa's terms. He wasn't going to push her to do anything she wasn't ready for. He'd been thinking about this a long time. For Lisa, it was just a few hours.

Having the night to ponder it might help.

He hoped so, because his dick was rock hard and ready to go off at the slightest touch. And he had no intention of touching it himself. He craved Lisa's touch.

If he was lucky, he might just get it. He prowled the room, stepping out onto the balcony, too pent up even to think about going to sleep this early. He stared at the moonlight glinting off the water, waiting for his erection to subside.

It might take all night, since his thoughts stayed on Lisa, on how she looked, how she smelled, how she felt in his arms, the way her mouth tasted when he kissed her.

It had just been a prelude of things to come.

⋙⋘

Lisa stared at the closed door to the spare bedroom, having half followed Rick after he left her on the balcony.

Left her. Just kissed her on the cheek, told her good night, and walked out.

Then again, he knew her better than anyone, didn't he? He knew she wouldn't want to rush into anything, would need some time to think everything through.

Yes, that was her, wasn't it? Everything carefully planned out. If it was a monumental choice, she'd have to think long and hard about it. She had to ponder every decision ad nauseam. She drove Connie crazy when they went shopping because it took her hours to decide what clothes to buy.

She walked into the master bedroom and closed the door, went into the bathroom, and frowned at her reflection in the mirror.

What was so difficult about this decision? She'd been lusting after her ex-husband for years. What was so wrong about jumping him during this vacation?

Because there would be an after-vacation, that's what the problem was.

So what? They could still go back to the way things were, couldn't they?

Probably not.

Dammit. Sex always screwed things up, got in the way of a perfectly good friendship. She and Rick had spent years mending the tears in their relationship after they divorced. It had been easier back then because they'd had Kayla. Kay had been a toddler, helpless and needing both her parents to care for her. They'd done it for her sake, had put their ridiculously petty irritations with each other aside and taken care of their daughter.

But they'd both been young and immature back then. They were adults now.

Besides, sex had never been a problem between them. That wasn't where their issues had been. And oh God, she needed sex in the worst way, had denied herself over and over again, year after year, mainly because of Kayla, but also because she still carried a major torch for Rick.

Okay, so fine. Rick was here now. In the flesh. She had him all to herself for one glorious week. What the hell was stopping her besides her own stupid head ticking off all the reasons this was a bad idea. Though there were valid reasons. Good reasons. Like why-mess-up-a-good-thing? kind of reasons.

She stalked back into the bedroom and sat on the bed, kicked off her shoes, blowing out a breath filled with frustration.

Could she be more conflicted? Was she doomed to spend this entire vacation being close to Rick, but never taking that step that would lead her into the arms of the man she'd desired for years? What was wrong with her? Why did she always have to be so damn logical?

Any other man would have read the signs and pushed her hesitation, would have stormed over to her and kissed away her uncertainty until she couldn't think straight.

But Rick wasn't any other man. He knew her, knew if he pushed, she'd regret it.

He put the decision in her hands. If this was going to happen, she was going to have to initiate it.

Good God, Lisa, it's just sex. It's not like he's asked you to marry him.

She should go for it, and damn the repercussions. Connie and Kayla wanted her to have fun.

She wanted to have fun. She needed to have fun.

She pushed off the bed and pulled open the bedroom door, shutting down the logical side of her brain, the one hammering at her even now as she walked down the hall toward the closed bedroom door. She knew Rick wasn't asleep yet. Before she chickened out, she knocked.

In seconds, he opened the door. He was still dressed, though he'd unbuttoned his shirt, had pulled it out of the waistband of his slacks. Her mouth went dry at the dark expanse of his chest, the crisp hairs scattered there. Instead, she focused on his face, the way his eyes questioned.

"I want this," she blurted out before she lost her nerve.

Thankfully, he didn't ask her to be sure, instead swept her into his arms, and without saying a word, walked out of the room.

Five

Rick carried her down the hall and to the master bedroom before setting her back on her feet, but he didn't let go of her. Instead, he slid her down his body, letting her feel every hard inch of him. She shuddered as her bare feet touched the soft rug next to the bed. He still hadn't said anything either, but the look of intense desire in his eyes spoke volumes.

Lisa's chest was tight and she found it hard to breathe. She wanted to say something, but didn't dare. She didn't want anything to shatter this moment, not with the way Rick looked at her, the way he slid both hands in her hair—slow and gentle, pulling her face toward him. When he brushed his mouth across hers, it was light, easy, and yet it took her breath away. The tip of his tongue touched hers and sensation exploded. Just that tiny lick of tongues and her clit vibrated, her pussy swelling with need. It felt so good she wanted to reach between her legs to massage the ache, but that was because she was so used to taking care of her own aroused state.

Tonight, she wouldn't have to. What a heady thought that was. Her mind was already awash with visuals of Rick touching her, of the things they could—no—*would* do together.

Wait, she reminded herself. She was getting ahead of the game. She had to stay in the moment, not get lost in fantasy. This was reality, it was happening. She didn't have to imagine sex, didn't have to conjure up Rick as a lover like she usually did when she was alone. He was really here, touching her, sliding his hands down her bare arms, creating goose bumps in his wake despite the warmth in the room.

"You cold?"

Even the sound of his voice turned her on. Deep, low, he definitely had her attention.

"No." She was hot, feverish, every inch of her skin on fire and needing his touch.

"Good." He kissed her neck, his tongue snaking out to lick along her erratically beating pulse before pressing his lips to her jaw, then her mouth, taking her lips in a ravaging kiss that drove her heart rate into danger territory.

And when his fingers slipped under the straps of her dress, her heart rate blipped off the charts, pounding hard and incessant against her chest. Rick could probably hear it slamming against him as he slid her straps down her arms, following them with his mouth, kissing her bare skin. Thankfully, he pulled away from her.

God Almighty, she wasn't a teenager anymore, and this was hardly her first time. She and Rick had had sex before. Lots of sex. But she was—what?—nineteen the last time? She couldn't even remember the last time he'd touched her this intimately, and hell, it had never been like this. The practiced moves of a man, not a boy.

It was wholly different now. She was different. *They* were different. New ball game. But she couldn't deny that she was hyperventilating like a teenager in the throes of first-time passion, couldn't ignore her wet panties, her throbbing nipples, or pulsing clit.

Wow. She hadn't expected it to be this . . . intense. Not with someone she knew so well.

She lifted her gaze to his. "Is it supposed to be like this?"

He smiled, swept his hand down her arm to twine his fingers with hers, seeming in no hurry. "Yeah, babe. It is."

He hadn't realized, but she'd seen it. As he reached for her, his hand shook. He was as affected as she was. He was holding taut to barely leashed control, and he was doing it for her.

Dammit, she'd waited a long time for this. She didn't want control. "Rick," she said, squeezing his fingers. "I'm not made of porcelain. I won't break."

"I'm trying to restrain myself, Lisa."

"Don't try so hard."

Rick sucked in a harsh breath, then released his fingers from hers, grabbed her shoulders, and jerked her against him. She gasped at the sensual violence as he smashed his mouth against hers, reveled in his possession of her mouth, especially when his tongue slid through her teeth and took control, claiming her tongue, licking against it with demanding strokes.

Now there was nothing slow and easy about what he did, walking her toward the bed as he simultaneously freed her arms from the straps of her dress and drew the bodice to her waist. She felt air across her breasts and nipples, her mind trying to process too much. Her nakedness, what would Rick think, where the hell were they going. She felt the back of her legs brush the mattress. Rick pulled his lips from hers, drew back several steps, and stared at her.

"No," he said, blowing out a breath. "We have to slow down. It's been a long time and I want to look at you."

He was right, of course. She expected this big explosion of a consummation, this throwing-her-down-on-the-bed-and-fucking-her-blind situation where she wouldn't have to process, to think about anything. But their first time together after all this time was monumental, and they shouldn't rush through it.

Now he was looking at her. Really looking at her. And for the first time, she felt shy. He hadn't seen her naked in a long time. She didn't have the youthful, waif-thin body of a twenty-year-old any longer. She resisted the urge to cover her breasts. This was her body now.

"I've always loved your body, Lisa," he said as he shrugged out of his shirt, his gaze never leaving her chest.

She couldn't help but smile. "You liked my boobs."

He grinned and met her gaze again. "Well, yeah. I'm a man. We're obsessed."

She laughed, grateful he wasn't taking this so seriously. She needed a little levity so she could breathe.

And he was damn beautiful, too. His shoulders had broadened, his chest had filled out, and he definitely spent a lot of his free time working out. He might be over thirty-five, but Rick was all chiseled muscle and very little body fat. She knew he ran every morning, went to the gym after work, and he ate well. It showed. She wanted to feel that body next to hers. She reached behind her for the zipper on her dress.

"No. Let me." Rick stepped forward, their noses practically touching as he located her zipper through the tangled mess of her dress. He drew it down, all the while staring into her eyes. So intense, intimate.

So utterly adult.

So new.

"We're not kids anymore, Rick," she said as he moved in, grasped her dress, and pushed it down over her hips. It draped in a puddle at her feet.

"I'm well aware of that." He held her hand while she stepped out of the dress. She kicked it away. His grin was so damn sexy. "What's your point?"

Her lips curled. "I have no idea." She reached for his pants, flipping open the button and brushing his erection with the backs of her fingers as she drew the zipper down. She shuddered a breath, dizzy from nervousness, from excitement. This was all happening so fast. She wanted to slow it down and speed it up at the same time.

"Are you nervous? Should I slow down?"

He was teasing her. She cocked a brow. "I'm hardly a virgin."

His brows waggled. "Don't I know it, since I'm the one who took your cherry."

She snorted. "As I recall, you were rather adept at convincing me you were the one for me."

Once he was naked, he pushed her onto the bed and climbed on after her. "As I recall, you didn't put up too much of a fight."

She worked her way up onto the pillows. "So you're saying I was easy?"

They lay side by side now. Rick palmed her stomach. It rippled under the warmth of his hand. "Nothing about you has ever been easy, Lisa."

That might be the biggest compliment he'd ever paid her. Or was it a compliment? Did he mean she was difficult? She opened her mouth to ask the question, but Rick placed his finger against her lips.

"Shut up."

She thought about objecting, but he was right. She always thought too much, and now wasn't the time to think. Instead, she threaded her fingers through his hair. Dark as a moonless night, and so thick her fingers got lost in its depths. It felt good to touch him again, to lie side by side together in bed like this, not to feel the rush of having to fuck like they did when they were kids. There was so much more to lovemaking than just getting naked and penetration. There was touching, looking, kissing, and just being with someone you cared about.

Rick seemed to understand that, even if his erection lay prominent between them, a constant reminder of what was going to happen.

He leaned over her, brushed his lips over hers. Soft, oh so soft, it was like a feather across her mouth. And yet it was electrifying, making her nipples pucker. And when he touched her, his fingers lazily mapping her skin from her shoulders to her collarbone to the valley between her breasts, her heart rate kicked up again.

Rick deepened the kiss, pressed over her more firmly, grasped her hip to draw her closer against him. Her breasts flattened against him, her nipples rasping against the crisp hairs of his chest. He lifted her leg and draped it over his hip, putting her pussy in direct contact with the hard ridge of his cock.

She gasped as he began to surge against her, rocking his erection against her pussy. A wildfire of sensation rolled along her nerve endings, every single one connected to her pulsing clit. She dug her nails into his shoulder, tilted her head back to look at him, needing to see his face.

Lines of concentration formed along the outer corners of his eyes and across his forehead. She traced them with her fingertip, memorizing every single one. Rick grasped her hand and kissed her fingertips, then licked them, placing them one by one in his mouth and sucking them gently until she whimpered. She'd been way too long without a man to hold out much longer. Just the sliding motion of his cock against her pussy made her crazy.

"Rick, please."

"I'm nowhere near ready to fuck you yet, Lisa. I haven't even tasted you."

Oh, God. He pushed her onto her back, took her mouth in a long, deep kiss that made her feel drugged, then dragged his lips over her jaw, her neck, and down to her breasts, moving his body over hers and spreading her legs apart with his knees so he could settle between them. He palmed her breasts—oh, to have them touched by someone other than herself was heaven. He caressed her nipples with his thumbs and the sensation shot straight between her legs, making her throb and squirm underneath him. He held her still with his body, continuing to torment her by rolling his fingers around her nipples, then bending down to take one into his mouth.

His lips closed over one peak and she wanted to die from the pleasure. She stilled, watching as he flicked her nipple with his tongue. An arcing shot of pure liquid heat pooled between her legs, throbbing incessantly. She rolled her hips, grinding her pussy against him.

Rick looked up at her and smiled, then licked the other nipple, grasping her breasts between both hands and torturing both with laps of his tongue until she writhed in uncontrollable delight. This was exactly what she needed, what she'd craved when she said yes to Rick. His touch, his mouth on her body, making her feel like a desirable woman for the first time in . . . she couldn't recall how long.

She needed more. So much more than this. The waiting was unbearable. She wanted his cock inside her, stroking her until she screamed in orgasm.

But when he slid down her body, pressing a kiss to her ribs, the dip in her stomach, her belly button, she wanted something else entirely, now anticipating the hot, sweet pleasure of his mouth taking her right where she needed to go.

He shouldered her legs apart and she felt his breath against her thigh. It was so unbearably intimate, so familiar and yet so new. And when he kissed that spot on her inner thigh that made her laugh, she remembered how many times he'd done that in the past, how well he really did know her body—like no other man ever could. They'd shared the intimacy of first-time lovers, because they'd been each other's first. They'd learned about sex with each other, had explored the basics, the how-to's, had fumbled around and figured out this whole sex thing together.

But now, as Rick laid his hand over her lower belly and let it slide lower, using the practiced moves of an adult, it wasn't at all fumbling. It was smooth, caressing, moves meant to relax her and ratchet up the sexual tension at the same time. He knew exactly what he was doing to her. And when he pressed his mouth over her sex, laying his tongue flat over her clit so she could simply feel the hot wetness pressed against her throbbing sex, she knew it was nothing like the old days. Nothing at all.

She lifted up, her body swelling with heat and need, arching toward that pleasure. He gave it to her, licking the length of her pussy, driving his tongue into her and using his hand to stroke her clit. Embarrassingly, she was already there, rocketing into orgasm like drought-stricken tinder, engulfed in a fire of the sweetest pleasure. Rick was right there with her, licking her, his hand pressing down on her as she rode out her surprising climax until she shuddered into some semblance of reality.

But he gave her no time to relax, instead climbed up her body and planted his mouth over hers. She tasted the tart sweetness of her own completion on his lips and it drove her into fresh arousal. His erection slid along her wet pussy lips, making her aware of how close they were to consummating, and how much she wanted to feel him inside her.

Tension coiled low in her belly, a desperate need that had her raking her nails along his back, to lift her hips in silent invitation. Rick rolled over and grabbed a condom from his pants pocket, tore open the wrapper, and applied it in a hurry before turning back to her and capturing her again in his arms.

"Don't want to make the same mistake twice," he said with the hint of a smile.

She traced his mouth with her fingertips, then palmed the back of his neck and drew him forward, needing his lips on hers. He kissed her, his mouth pressed hard against hers, his tongue sliding inside at the same time his cock pressed between her pussy lips and penetrated her.

Feeling him inside her, joined with her, made tears spring to her eyes. It was so incredibly monumental that for a moment she felt silly at getting so choked up like this. It was just sex, after all. She shouldn't make such a big deal out of it. Yet it seemed like so much more—felt like so much more.

She really was a basket case, wasn't she? Pushing the emotionalism aside, she concentrated on simply feeling Rick, on the way he moved inside her. Slow at first, pulling out, then sliding back in, dragging his cock over her sensitized nerve endings. Lisa dug her heels into the mattress, losing herself in the sensations, on the way her pussy tightened around his cock each time he withdrew. It was as if her own body objected to him pulling out, wanting to grip him harder to prevent him from leaving her.

Symbolism much? She really had to learn to shut her brain down. Sex was supposed to be mindless, about just feeling and not thinking. But how could she not mix the two together? Her brain was as involved in this as her body. She had to think about everything she felt—what it meant as much as the sensations zipping through every nerve ending.

She opened her eyes to find Rick staring down at her, his face hard and tight. She inhaled, the heady, exciting aroma of sex surrounding them. Their bodies were slick with sweat as they slid together, Rick's pelvis grinding against hers in a way that stroked her clit into indescribable sensations, ever flaming the fire inside her.

Rick grasped her hands, moved them out to her sides and entwined his fingers with hers, then began to move in earnest, his chest scraping her nipples as he drove inside her, his shaft rubbing her clit as he rocked against her with hard, deliberate thrusts.

"Rick," she whispered.

"Yeah," he said back, seeming to know she was close to coming again. He was relentless, not even giving her a second to catch her breath as she caught the wave and rode it over the crest, crying out with the force of her climax. He stilled, letting them both feel the way her pussy convulsed around him as she came in violent bursts that left her whimpering. And then he started up again, moving slowly this time, refusing to let her even come down from the high before he brought her right back up again, rolling his hips over the sensitive spots until she was cresting again and again, mastering her body in a way that only he could until she was begging for mercy.

But he wouldn't give it to her, not until she was limp as a rag doll and couldn't possibly come again. And when he tensed, claiming her mouth in a heated kiss that left her wet and helpless and climbing again, that was when he went with her, groaning into her mouth as he shuddered with his own orgasm. She held tight to his sweat-slickened back and wondered that it had never, ever been like this before.

This was magic. It was amazing and frightening because she wasn't certain she could ever give it up.

Six

Rick stared down at the sleeping beauty next to him. Her hair had fallen over her face, shielding her eyes, though he knew they were still closed, because she was snoring.

He'd forgotten that she snored. Cute, girly-type snores, but she did snore, especially when she was exhausted. He supposed the flight, the shock of finding him there, plus the sex last night would have been exhausting.

He rolled out of bed and into the sizable bathroom to turn on the shower, unable to keep the grin off his face. So far everything had been perfect. More than perfect, actually. But he knew Lisa well. She wasn't the type to accept at face value. She might have enjoyed the sex, but she was going to be a hard sell.

He was good at sales.

After his shower, he dried off and slipped out of the bedroom to head into the other room to grab his clothes. He'd be moving into the master bedroom today. The thought of what they'd shared last night made him harden easily. Lisa was so responsive, like melting butter in his arms. He wanted that every night, not just on this vacation. The key would be to convince Lisa that it could work between them.

By the time he got dressed, Lisa was awake and in the shower. He made a couple of phone calls, planning their day, then went into the bathroom just as she turned the water off. He was waiting, towel in hand, as she stepped out. Her eyes widened before she smiled.

"Not used to finding a man in my bathroom," she said with a tentative smile as she accepted the towel from him.

He leaned against the counter and admired the pink tinge to her skin as she dried off and combed her hair. She turned away from the mirror to throw him a look. "Are you intending to stare at me?"

"Maybe."

"Stop it. It's unnerving."

He laughed. "Hurry up. I'm starving."

She shook her head. "Men. You only think with your stomachs and your cocks."

"That shouldn't surprise you," he said, then left her alone and walked out on the balcony to wait.

Perfect day. Sun was up and he could already feel the heat. He couldn't wait to get outside. This was as much a vacation for him as it was for Lisa. They both needed to unwind after the intensity of Kayla's graduation and all the prep that had gone into that. Of course, Lisa had done all the planning for the party. And she stressed about every little detail, as always. The key to this week was for both of them to relax. To put everything out of their minds, including their daughter, and focus on just the two of them. That would be a first. They hadn't done that in . . . too many years to remember.

"Hey."

He turned at the sound of Lisa's voice.

She stood in the living room, wrapped only in the white fluffy hotel towel.

"What should I wear today?" she asked.

It took him a minute to engage his brain, since all the blood had rushed to his dick at the first sight of her. "Uh, shorts, tank top. Whatever's comfortable. And pack a swimsuit."

"Okay." She turned and padded barefoot back into the bedroom.

Rick swallowed and faced the ocean, trying to calm his raging cock. You'd think a woman in a towel would be nothing to write home about. Not sexual at all. Yeah, right. One look at Lisa in the towel and his imagination went haywire. He wanted to drag her onto the balcony and do a hundred different things to her with his hands and mouth, all while she was wearing that towel. He filed those thoughts away for later. His goal was to show her that being together wasn't going to be all about sex. That would be hard to do if everything he thought and did *was* all about sex. But dammit, he'd spent a lot of years without her. So sue him if he had a one-track mind. It had been a long drought.

She came out in khaki shorts and a body-hugging tank top, carrying a straw bag overflowing with beach things—swimsuit, towels, sunscreen—everything they'd need for the day, or so she told him. It was typically Lisa to be prepared.

He'd arrived the day before so he'd have a chance to scout out the area, figure out what he wanted to do. He grabbed her hand and took her out the back door and toward the beach.

"Aren't you hungry? I'd love some coffee and breakfast," she said as their sandaled feet hit the sand.

"You'll get both shortly." He didn't give her any other clues, just led her down the beach to the dock. There was a floating restaurant at the end of a long pier. It was still early enough that they managed to snag a decent table near the windows overlooking the water.

The bay was smooth as glass this morning. Boats docked alongside the pier, undulating against their moorings, as Rick and Lisa settled into their seats and placed their food orders.

"This is wonderful." Lisa sipped coffee and stared out the wide windows at the activity on the dock below the restaurant. Shops were beginning to open and people bustled with activity, both tourists and the locals getting ready to start their day. Lisa looked over at him and smiled. "Thanks for finding this place."

He knew she'd like it better than an air-conditioned restaurant in the hotel. "You're welcome."

"So what's on tap for today?"

"We're going out on a boat. Do a little snorkeling."

Her eyes lit up with an unmistakable sparkle. "I love the water."

"I know." He hadn't taken any vacations with her—ever. They'd been too young, broke, and then Kay had come along so there'd been no time, no money. But over the years, Lisa and Kayla had taken a few vacations, and Kay had filled him in on Lisa's love of the water. How sad was it that his own daughter knew more about Lisa than he did? Oh sure, they'd gone to the lake a few times, and he knew Lisa loved going out on their friends' boat. But apparently she had a huge love for boating, for water, and for beaches. Kayla also told him that Lisa had really enjoyed the snorkeling they'd done off the Keys one summer.

He was going to indulge her love of all those things they had never done together but should have. He felt like they'd missed out on so much.

They ate a huge breakfast, then Rick led her out the sliding glass door at the back of the restaurant and down the dock where the rows of touring boats were moored. Seagulls soared around them, diving down near the water, hoping for a chance at their own breakfast.

Rick inhaled, loving the smells here at the dock. He used to go fishing with his dad every weekend when he was a kid. Until his dad got too sick to go.

Lisa slid her hand in his as they walked down the dock. "You're quiet."

He glanced over at her and lifted his lips. "I was thinking about my dad. The smell of the water and fish reminds me of going to the lake and fishing with him."

She squeezed his hand, leaned closer to him. "He died way too young."

"Cancer has a way of ripping those we love away from us."

"I know. I see it all too often at the hospital."

"Makes you want to hold on to the people you care about and never let go. We only get one chance to do this, you know."

She stared up at him, the sunlight making the subtle red highlights in her brown hair look like they were on fire. "Yes. I know."

He found the pier he was looking for and dug into his pocket for the tickets.

"This is it?" Lisa asked.

"Yeah. You like it?"

Her jaw dropped. "It's incredible."

He'd booked a catamaran with a large flat deck off the back, so there was plenty of open space for just lying around in the sun. And the best part was yet to come. He handed their ticket to the captain, a quiet older man with a worn cap pulled low around his face, who grinned and hurried to let the ropes loose, saying they'd get right under way. As soon as Lisa situated herself on the deck, her legs slung over the side, she shifted, looking for other people.

"Aren't we waiting for the others?"

He grabbed a spot on the deck next to her, watching the dock disappear as the captain pulled slowly away. "There isn't anyone else. I chartered the boat for a private day-long cruise."

Her brows shot up. "Are you serious?"

"Hey, I've spent years sharing you. I want you all to myself for as long as I can."

She shook her head. "You amaze me. Thank you."

The ride was like sailing on smooth glass as the captain took them out across the turquoise water. There was a shade awning available to get out of the sun, but once they'd gotten going, Lisa went below to change into her swimsuit. She came out in a strapless bikini, green and pink with palm tree patterns splashed across the fabric. It hugged her curves perfectly.

He went below and changed into his swim trunks. When he came back, Lisa was lathering on sunscreen.

"Let me do you," she said.

He waggled his brows. "I thought you'd never ask."

Laughing, she pushed at his back. "I meant sunscreen."

"So not what I had in mind." He turned his back to her and she lathered lotion on him. He did the same to her, but took his time smoothing his hands over every inch of her skin, enjoying the feel of her shoulders, her muscles, the way she seemed to relax when he pressed into her.

"This is nice," she said, leaning against him. She tossed on her floppy hat and stretched her legs out on the deck.

It was very nice. Lisa always had the best legs. With all the running around she did at the hospital, they stayed in great shape, with well-toned calves and slim ankles. Her toenails were painted a bright pink. She looked at him over her shoulders, saw the direction of his gaze.

"Kayla's idea. She said the pink was tropical."

He let out a laugh. "Very." He slid his hands under her thighs and drew her legs up to her chest so he could play with her feet.

"You know my feet are ticklish," she said, sliding them away from his reach.

"I do seem to vaguely remember that."

"Ha. Vaguely my butt. You used to torture me by holding me down and tickling me until I had hiccups."

"I did not."

"Did, too."

"I seem to recall it making your nipples hard."

"Can I help it if it my feet are both ticklish and an erogenous zone?"

"I like things that make your pussy wet."

The rumble of her purr rolled through her back and against his chest. His dick stood up and took notice, too. He wrapped his arm around her waist, letting his fingers dip to the top of her bikini.

"Rick."

They were cruising along slow and easy. The captain was in the main cabin, his focus on steering the catamaran. No other boats were in sight, and even if they were, who could see anything but the blur of a boat cruising by? Rick slid his fingers under her waistband.

Now all he heard was the rush of water along the side of the boat and Lisa's breathing, which grew heavier, her chest rising and falling with deliberate, deep swells. There was a lot of swelling going on between his legs, too, his cock throbbing as it hardened and pressed against Lisa's butt.

"Rick," she said again, though he wasn't sure if it was in warning or invitation. He dipped his hand into her bikini bottom, resting it just above her mound. It was like dipping his fingers into molten lava—hot, steamy, and utter temptation. He couldn't resist sliding farther, cupping her sex, all that heat surrounding his hand. He felt Lisa shudder against him. He had to admit to doing a bit of shuddering himself. Holding a hot, wet pussy in his hand, and doing it in public, wasn't something he did every day. Or even every year. It was one hell of a turn-on.

Another factor to consider was that this was Lisa, his ex-wife, someone he cared about. He had to protect her, and he was torn between wanting to do just that and not giving a damn, because he really wanted to rip off that little excuse of a bikini bottom, spread her legs, and bury his mouth against her soft, wet flesh. Especially since she was wriggling against him, lifting against his hand and throwing off every signal in the book that told him she enjoyed what he was doing. And he really liked doing it to her, enjoyed the feel of her soft skin, how wet she got when he slid his finger along the plump folds of her pussy.

"You like that?" he asked, leaning his cheek against hers, whispering in her ear.

"I think you know I do. You can feel what you do to me."

"Yeah, I can. Wet, quivering. You want me to put my finger inside you, don't you?"

"God, Rick, this is . . ."

"What? What is it, Lisa? Don't tell me it's wrong, because it isn't. No one can see us. The captain is driving the boat. Let me drive you." He skimmed her flesh again, a light touch. She quivered in response, lifting her butt off the deck, pressing her sex against the heel of his palm.

He slid his fingertip inside her and she rewarded him with a pulse of hot cream. Encouraged by her silence, he dipped farther, knuckle deep, keeping his movements slow and rhythmic. In and out, in and out, caressing her clit with the pad of his thumb, his intent to drive her slow and easy and right over the edge.

The lull of the water, everything around them, was quiet except for Lisa's rasping breath, her fingers digging into his forearm as he moved rhythmically against her, inside her, until she tensed, let out a soft whimper, and jerked against him as she came, driving her head back against his collarbone while she rode out her orgasm with sharp, shuddering motions.

God, he was hard now, and really damned uncomfortable. Making her come like this had been easy. Fucking her in such a public place would be impossible. He withdrew his hand and licked her sweet, salty cream from his fingers, which only made the torture worse. He was going to have to wait.

Lisa settled against him, tilting her head back to stare up at him. "This hardly seems fair."

He smiled down at her. "I'll get my chance."

She righted herself and wriggled back against him, rubbing her butt against his erection.

"You're enjoying that, aren't you?"

The vibration of her laugh echoed against his chest. "Maybe a little," she said. "But I promise to make it worth the wait."

He could already imagine it.

In a short while the captain pulled into a private, white sand beach carved into a U-shaped cove. Cool blue water lapped against the shore as they disembarked and the captain helped Rick unload their supplies. Rick made arrangements for him to pick them up before dusk, and the catamaran took off.

"He's leaving us here?" Lisa asked.

"Yeah," Rick said, turning to her. "I wanted us to be alone for the day. There's a reef out there for snorkeling, we have a picnic lunch and some drinks in the cooler over there, we have fins and snorkel gear, beach chairs and towels, and I have a cell phone to contact him in case of an emergency."

She stood ankle deep at the lapping water's edge, hands on hips. "You think of everything, don't you?"

"Not everything. Just some things. So what do you want to do first? Swim or eat?"

"Definitely swim. I caught a glimpse of the reef on the way in and it looks gorgeous."

"Let's go."

They spent the afternoon snorkeling, diving under and taking pictures. The reef was a splash of colors, from orange to blue to purple to green, coral and waving tall grass hugging the bottom tight while rainbow-colored fish swam in and around it. Lisa seemed to really enjoy herself. Rick did, too, though he mainly enjoyed watching Lisa. She took to the water, the coral, and all the sea life with a childlike exuberance. He grabbed the camera and took pictures of her interacting with everything around her. Those were going to make some great photographs.

When they tired of swimming and snorkeling, they climbed out of the water, dried off, and ate lunch. Rick had ordered a picnic basket from the hotel, and it was full. They had sandwiches, fruit, wedges of cheese, and a bottle of wine along with water. Plenty to eat and drink while they relaxed in the beach chairs. It was a perfect, private paradise.

"This is heaven," Lisa said, sipping her wine out of their acrylic glasses. "I could get used to this."

"It would be easy to live the decadent lifestyle, wouldn't it? If only we were rich and useless."

She snorted. "Yeah. It's that whole needing a job and money thing. The lack of independent wealth."

"Dammit. There are always roadblocks."

"I could start buying lottery tickets."

He drained his wineglass and grabbed the bottle out of the cooler to refill both their glasses. "Yeah, there's a good use of your money."

"Hey, I'm working on my dream retirement here. Don't shatter my illusions."

"You'd never be happy as part of the idle rich."

She lifted the glass, swirled the liquid around before taking a sip. "You're probably right. I'm way too twitchy. I always need to be doing something. This is nice, because it's temporary, a break from my normal frenetic pace. But to do this every day, lie around and have nothing to do?"

"You'd be bored."

Her lips lifted. "Yeah, I'd be bored. I'm already wondering what I'm going to do to fill the time after Kayla goes off to college."

"No more cheerleading events," Rick reminded her.

"No more soccer games. Sleepovers. Shopping trips."

Despite her trying to hide it behind teasing amusement, Rick could see the misery reflected in Lisa's eyes. He wanted to turn that around. "You're worried your life is over because your baby girl is going away to college. That she won't need you anymore."

Her cheeks pinkened. "I know it's silly. But we've always been so close. I know we're not best friends, because I'm first and foremost her mother, not her buddy. The house will just be so empty after she's gone."

He hoped it wouldn't be, but he wasn't going to get into that just yet. "You have a full life, Lisa. A career. You've worked hard. Your life isn't all about Kayla."

She shrugged. "I know that. Logically anyway."

He also knew that part of her was afraid to take the next step. He knew her so well. "Yeah, but you're a woman. Emotional."

She tipped her sunglasses down the bridge of her nose and gave him a look. "Oh, don't give me that. You're going to miss her, too."

"Of course I am. But she's grown up. She's ready to move on to her next adventure. To get out there on her own and test the waters."

Lisa slid the glasses back up to cover her eyes, then clasped her hands together in her lap. "And we have to let her go."

"Yeah, we do. But instead of thinking about the emptiness, why don't you think of fun ways to fill all that spare time you think you're going to have?"

She glanced over at him. "For example?"

"Well, I'll be available."

Seven

Lisa gave him a thoughtful look. He'd hooked her, which was good. Sometimes he liked her thinking, especially if it was about him.

"You'll be available for . . . ?"

"I don't know. Bowling."

She snorted. "You hate bowling."

"Good point. We could go to movies."

"We used to love that."

"I hear they're reopening the old drive-in."

"Really?"

"Do you remember when we used to go?"

She laughed. "Yeah. You, me, and about ten of our friends, all piling into a couple pickup trucks packed up with lawn chairs and coolers. It was fun."

He reached for her hand. "I liked it better when it was just the two of us there."

"Of course you did. Because we did more making out, less watching of the movie."

He had vivid memories of the times they spent cuddled together in the car. "Duh. Why do you think I liked it?"

"You would."

"Though I think I got you pregnant at the drive-in."

"I think you might be right. Maybe it's not such a good idea for us to rekindle our love of drive-in movies, then."

He tilted his head back and laughed, then stood and dragged her out of the chair, pulling her against him. "Okay, no bowling. No drive-in movies. I can think of other ways to pass the time."

Lisa locked her arms around his back, her hips brushing his legs. She tilted her head back. "You can, huh?"

"Yeah." He pulled her sunglasses off, needing to see her eyes. So clear, bright, filled with the passion he felt, too, whenever he got close to her. She made him feel like a kid who couldn't control his own libido. Hell, he got hard whenever he was around her. That didn't happen with other women. He definitely had a thing for Lisa.

"What are you thinking about?" she asked.

He refocused his attention on her face. "What? Nothing."

"Not true. You get this glazed look in your eyes whenever you're thinking about something. Kind of unfocused, like you're deep in thought and miles away."

"Sorry. I was actually thinking about you."

She quirked a brow. "You were?"

"Yeah. And how I get a hard-on whenever I'm around you. It's kind of embarrassing. I'm too old to pop an erection whenever I'm near a woman."

She grinned and rocked her hips against his. "Oh, I don't know about that. I like it. It's a compliment."

He slid his hand down her spine, palming the small of her back and pushing her closer to him so he could press his erection against the softness of her body. "You say that now. What if we were in the grocery store?"

"Hey, it's your hard-on, buddy. People will be staring at you, not me."

"I'll be pointing the finger at you and telling everyone it's your fault because you're so damn sexy."

"You wouldn't dare."

"Try me."

"I just might do that."

She laughed, and he loved seeing her so free and relaxed. It reminded him of when they first met.

"God, you're beautiful, Lisa. I can't believe how much time we've wasted." He tangled his fingers in her hair and brought his mouth down to hers, tasting the sharp sweetness of wine on her lips. He pulled back, licked along her bottom lip, then pressed his mouth to hers again, sliding his tongue inside, letting the flavor of her mouth burst along his taste buds. He wanted to devour her, but he kept his desire in check, keeping the kiss light and easy. She inched closer and let out a soft moan as he held her, kissed her, let sensation take over for both of them.

A warm breeze blew over them, the sound of the water crashing against the shore equaling his passion for Lisa. He savored every minute he spent holding her in his arms, feeling the buttery softness of her skin, the fullness of her curves, the way she was so pliant against him. He moved his hand along her neck to her shoulder, learning her body all over again just as he did last night, still in awe that she let him touch her like this. It could have gone the other way and he knew that. She could have easily said no, but she hadn't. That she wanted this, wanted him, kind of amazed him.

He pulled back, searched her face, the way her eyes darkened when they were filled with passion and need. Her lips parted and she swallowed, breathing hard, her breasts rising with every deep breath. He took her hand and moved to the bag, dragged out the beach towels and spread them on the grassy bank above the chairs.

She didn't say anything, just reached behind her, unhooked her top, and tossed it over the chair. Rick blew out a breath, admiring the way the sun bronzed her skin, cascaded off her hair. Everything about her was perfection, right down to a few little stretch marks across her lower belly, the marks that said she had once carried his child. He loved those, loved her because she never cared about them or tried to hide them. She'd always seemed proud of them. He moved toward her and dropped to his knees in the grass to plant his mouth across them, kissing and licking each one. With a low moan, Lisa buried her hands in his hair while he reached for the ties on the sides of her bikini, undoing them so he could pull the material away and bare her sex.

He looked up at her. She watched as he slid two fingers between her legs.

"Spread for me," he said.

She parted her legs and he entered her with his fingers. She was already wet, her damp heat gripping him as he finger fucked her with slow, easy movements. She laid her hand on his head, her lips parted as she breathed in heavy, panting bursts while he pleasured her with deliberate strokes. When he planted his mouth over her clit and licked her, she cried out, thrusting her sex against his mouth. He felt her grip him from the inside, contractions tightening inside her as he sucked, and she came against his mouth, over his fingers in a shuddering rush. He loved doing this to her, knew what she needed and how. He loved that she trusted him enough to let him do this for her. For them both.

Rick stood and untied his board shorts, let them drop to the ground, and stepped out of them. He grabbed a condom and put it on, then lay on the towel, bringing Lisa down with him. She straddled him, giving him one hell of a sexy view of her pussy as she slid down on his hips. She leaned forward, her hands on his chest as she kissed him, rubbing her pussy against his cock, his balls, all that sweet moisture coating him before she pulled back, grabbed his shaft, and lifted herself up to glide over him, enveloping his cock with excruciatingly slow movements. It was so sweet to watch her face as she gripped him, moved against him, rocking back and forth, each time gliding over his balls and making him clench his teeth as he held back.

He reached for her hips, needing to hold her, to feel her flesh and grab on to her as she rode him. The sun shined down on them both, making them sweat, slick, easy for Lisa to slide over him. She laughed at their stickiness, seeming to thoroughly enjoy the ride. He enjoyed watching her, seeing the light in her eyes, the way her breasts swayed with every movement, the way her fingers curled against his skin whenever her clit dragged against him. She sucked her bottom lip into her mouth, concentrating on her pleasure—exactly what he wanted her to do, because if it was good for her, it was damn great for him.

He rose up, driving harder into her, and she gasped, dug down deep, and ground against him, giving him back what he gave to her. She leaned forward, curling her back up like a cat's as she slid over his chest to grab on to his shoulders, then rode him, driving her pussy down over his cock until he was at her mercy.

"Christ, Lisa." He dug his fingers into the flesh of her hips now as he held on tight, letting her guide their movements, giving her free rein to do as she pleased. She was a wildcat, immersed in her own pleasure, lifting up and slamming down against him. He knew she was close, felt her tightening, convulsing around him. She surged forward, took his mouth in a wild kiss, biting him, sucking on his tongue, groaning into his mouth. When she came, he knew it because she cried out into his mouth, and he let go then, too, holding her tight against him as he surged upward, flooding come as wave after wave jettisoned from deep inside him in incontrollable bursts.

Spent and panting, they lay together in sweaty silence for a few moments. God, he couldn't move, every part of his body drained.

"Ugh. I'm a mess," she finally said, lifting her head from his chest to smile at him. "How about a swim?"

"Great idea."

They cooled off in the sea, guzzled down bottled water, then collapsed on the beach chairs.

"That was nice," Lisa said.

"Uh-huh."

"Sex is . . . a lot different now than it used to be."

He slanted his gaze in her direction. "In what way?"

She shrugged. "I don't know. Before we were just kids. Experimenting and kind of new at the whole thing, so we really didn't know what we were doing. Now there's more . . . finesse. And it's a lot more intense."

He knew why. At least from his perspective. But he wanted her to figure it out on her own.

"Yeah, it's intense all right. But I always thought sex between us was good."

"You're a guy. You think any sex is good sex."

He laughed. "Spoken like a true woman."

She shifted in the chair and half turned toward him. "Isn't that true, though? At least with men?"

"No."

"Men can have bad sex?"

"Honey, there's great sex, there's average sex, and there's lousy sex. A guy can tell. Trust me, we prefer great sex."

"What's lousy sex?"

"Barbie pussy."

She spit out a deep laugh. "Barbie pussy?"

"When a woman just lies there stiff and doesn't move. You know, like a Barbie doll. As if she expects the guy to do all the work. Then he's supposed to be grateful that she's allowed him to get some, so that should be good enough."

"Oh." She snorted. "I could see how that wouldn't be very enjoyable."

"Yeah. Like I said, sometimes no sex is better than sex with someone who isn't really involved."

"Have you . . . had sex with someone like that?"

How much was he supposed to reveal? They'd never discussed their sex lives during the years they'd been divorced. But if he had any hopes of reconciling with Lisa, he owed it to her to be honest. "Yeah, I have."

He expected her to be pissed. Instead, she wrinkled her nose. "Yuk."

"Exactly."

"Have you had the other kind?"

"What other kind?"

"You know . . . the great kind."

"Yeah. A couple times."

She turned again, this time staring out over the water instead of looking at him. "Kayla never told me about anyone you were dating. She was always very discreet."

"Kayla never met anyone I was dating."

She snapped her gaze to his. "Why not?"

"Because I never went out with anyone seriously enough or long enough to introduce them to our daughter."

"Oh."

"Lisa, having sex with someone doesn't make a relationship."

"But if you had great sex, wasn't that worth . . . exploring a relationship?"

"Not necessarily."

"Why not?"

"They weren't you. They've never been you, Lisa."

Eight

Lisa stepped out of the shower and dried her hair, her mind preoccupied with everything that had happened. It had been one hell of an eventful few days, both physically and emotionally.

After that day at the private beach with Rick, something had changed between them. Maybe it was what he'd said about the other women he'd been with, that he'd never formed attachments with any of them because they hadn't been her. She'd changed the subject immediately, because the topic had been careening toward a road she didn't want to head down—overwhelming and heavy. She wasn't ready yet.

Not just yet anyway. It was all too much to take in, and she and Rick were having fun together. That was all she could handle at the moment.

Just being with him—alone with him—was a whirlwind enough. She had been besieged with sensation. Being with him one on one without interruption, not having Kayla as the main topic between them, forcing them to be just a twosome again. That hadn't been the case since they were very young. This was entirely new territory for her—for both of them. It was like starting all over again, but with someone she was very familiar with.

Yet being with Rick was brand new, too. Everything about him was different now. She supposed she was completely different, too. So many years had passed, they had both learned so much, changed completely, had more life experience to bring to the table. They really were two different people now than when they'd been together as kids.

A brand-new relationship with the same old couple. A couple who had been together, yet apart, for over twenty years. Now if that wasn't confusing as hell, what was?

They'd spent the past few days simply playing together. They'd snorkeled, swum, taken boat rides, shopped, and toured Saint Thomas. She'd probably taken two hundred pictures of all the architecture. Rick had been a wonderful companion, patient and indulging in everything she'd wanted to do. She couldn't think of anyone else she'd rather be with. And he really seemed to enjoy every activity, seemed to love exploring the buildings and the towns, taking all the tours and soaking up the local atmosphere. They were in sync—well, except for the shopping, but what man enjoyed that anyway? She knew she wasn't merely dragging him along, that he was having as much fun as she was. And every moment spent with him made her realize how much she'd missed . . . being with him.

That was the problem, had always been the problem. She never wanted to be with anyone else. But was that because of Rick, or because Rick was safe, a known factor in her life?

"Ugh," she said, staring into the mirror. "Stop thinking so much." She had to get ready for their date tonight and she was running out of time. Rick was in the other bathroom, and here she was musing on . . . what the hell was she musing on anyway? Everything and nothing, as usual. Overthinking everything, of course, just like she always did. She made herself crazy.

She dried her hair, put makeup on, then pulled the sides of her hair back and affixed a jeweled clip at the crown of her head. Fancy, but not overdone. She liked it. Now she had to get dressed. Rick had told her they were going to dinner, then to a club to go dancing and to do some gambling. She decided to dress up, and she had just the outfit in mind, something Connie had insisted she buy. It was a bit over the top for her tastes, but Connie had sworn Lisa looked knock-'em-dead sexy in it, so she figured that would be the outfit to wear.

She went to the closet and pulled out the dress. A royal blue satin, it was one piece of skin-tight, lace-up, made-for-sin heaven. The bodice was strapless, shirred under the bust in front and boned in corset fashion that ended just at her hips, with crisscross laces in the back. Fun. The rest of the dress flowed down into a pencil skirt that hugged every one of her curves, with slits on both sides of her thighs, the material ending just at the knee. She had silver strappy stiletto heels to complete the look. When she'd tried it on at the store, she couldn't believe how the corset molded to her curves, drew her less-than-ample breasts upward, making her look like she had serious cleavage, and the rest of the dress was dynamite. Plus the color was perfect for her. She had to admit, Connie was right. It was as if the dress had been made just for her. She loved it.

She didn't want Rick to see her in it until she was fully dressed, but she needed help with the laces, so she dialed housekeeping and one of the ladies was up there in a flash to help her. Fortunately, Rick was busy in the other room and didn't even notice when she let the woman in. The woman smiled and was more than happy to lace up the back of the corset. Lisa tipped her when she was done, then sucked in a breath as she surveyed the finished product in the mirror.

Not bad. Not bad at all. With the corset laced tight, it molded close to her body, accentuating every curve. She slipped on her shoes, added silver earrings and a bracelet, and she was ready. She opened the door and found Rick standing in the living room, dressed in a black suit with a white no-collar shirt. He was leaning against the arched doorway to the balcony, a vision of dark-haired perfection as he sipped a brandy. He was so handsome he could have been on the cover of a men's fashion magazine. He took her breath away. Maybe they could just stay in tonight and make love. Her nipples tightened as she stepped into the living room.

He must have heard her heels clicking on the marble flooring, because his head turned in her direction, his eyes widened.

"Holy shit, Lisa."

She warmed under his perusal as he pushed off the wall and came toward her, walked around her, and whistled.

"Goddamn, did someone sew you into that dress?"

She giggled. "Nearly."

He came around to face her, took her hand, and kissed her fingers. Their eyes locked. "You look beautiful."

She could feel the thumping of her own heart. "Thank you. You look pretty smokin' hot, too."

With a wide grin, he took her hand and slid it in the crook of his arm. "Then let's go show off."

They took a taxi across the island to another resort, this one containing a club situated on an enormous rock hill overlooking the bay and alight with purple spotlights swaying back and forth. The atmosphere in front of the club was charged and exciting, people lining up to get inside. Beautifully dressed people, too. Rick told her this was a pretty exclusive nightclub and there was a dress code, so it wasn't like you could walk up from the beach in your cover-up and flip-flops and get inside. And you had to have your name on the list, which wasn't an easy thing to do.

Their name was on the list, thanks to a hefty tip to their hotel's concierge, so they went over to the "reservations" side of the line and walked right in.

Lisa realized two things immediately. There was a quiet part of the club, and an earsplitting part. Even though there was a closed door cutting off the bar and dance club, you could still feel the pounding rhythm coming from beyond the doors, could see the lights bouncing around, and hear the music. As they moved in the opposite direction toward the restaurant and through the doors into soothing music, Lisa marveled at the amount of money the resort must have spent on soundproofing the walls, because it was some feat to isolate that driving rhythm from the rest of the patrons.

The restaurant was all dark paneling, cherry woods, and candlelight. How romantic. They were seated at a table in the corner. Very private and intimate. A waiter came by with menus and a wine list. She deferred to Rick, who ordered a bottle of sauvignon blanc. The waiter brought the bottle, poured their glasses, took their food orders, and left them alone.

"Did you enjoy your nap today?" he asked.

"I passed out for two hours. I was exhausted after you dragged me around town half the day."

"You like shopping."

She sipped the wine, pleased with the crisp, dry flavor. "I do. You hate it."

He shrugged and took a swallow of wine, rolling the liquid around in the glass. "I like being with you. I suffered through it just fine. The shops were interesting. I wasn't bored."

He hadn't seemed to be, but she wondered. "We can do things you like, too, Rick."

"We *are* doing things I like. We've snorkeled, parasailed, Jet Skied, taken a deep-sea fishing excursion, and gone to the marine mammal exhibition. We've also shopped, taken a wine tour, and hung out on the beach. We've eaten nonstop and drunk our way through this island. I've hardly been bored, Lisa."

"Okay. You have a point. I haven't been bored either." Sometimes she forgot that, maybe with the exception of shopping, they enjoyed many of the same things. That's probably why neither of them had ever moved from Florida. The beach, water, and marine life were all things they both loved. And Kayla, of course. There was always that tie that bound them together and always would. But that wasn't enough to sustain a relationship. A child was never enough to hold a couple. It hadn't been enough when they were younger and it wouldn't be now. There had to be more, something besides Kayla, besides the years between them.

"Shadows."

She met his gaze. "What?"

"The candlelight casts shadows across your face. But there are already shadows in your eyes."

"Wow," she said, reaching for a wry grin as well as her glass of wine. "That's pretty deep. You dabbling in psychology on the side now, Rick?"

He laughed. "Sorry. I just know when you're doing that whole deep thinking thing."

Her gaze drifted down, then back up again. "Yeah, you do, don't you? Sorry. I'll stop."

He reached across the table and laid his hand over hers. "You don't have to stop thinking. I just wonder if your thinking doesn't tend to run toward the all-the-reasons-you-shouldn't-do-something area."

"You do know me well. Yes, it does tend to do that."

He slid his hand from hers, leaned back in his chair, and grabbed his glass. "Why can't you just accept what is and go with it?"

She shrugged. "I'm a chronic overthinker. You said you know me. You must know my affliction."

He shook his head. "Yeah, I do. I guess I'll have to come up with ways to banish thoughts from your head."

"Trying to keep me witless, huh?"

She caught his smile as he tipped the glass for a drink.

Rick was right, though. Why overthink everything and plan for the future when she was having a wonderful time right now? What was wrong with right now? They had made no plans for what happened after this vacation was over. Maybe nothing would happen, and they would go back to their lives the way they had been.

Just have fun. Enjoy. Forget about everything else.

She would. She'd try.

Dinner was a sumptuous feast of lobster, dripping cholesterol-laden butter, and a plate full of delicious steamed vegetables. Lisa ate way more than she should have considering her already too tight dress, but she couldn't resist. It was simply too decadent a meal. By the time dinner was finished, they'd polished off their bottle of wine. She was stuffed and utterly relaxed.

"Time to dance off those calories," Rick said, pulling her chair out.

Overly full, she felt like she was waddling from the restaurant to the dance club, which she could have found blindfolded. One only had to follow the sound of the thumping bass that led to red velvet ropes attached to brass stands, directing them to wide, rich wood double doors and two scary-looking bouncers. Rick gave one of the guys his name, and they were allowed entrance.

Wow, some security setup. What was inside that was so special? The doors were held open and they walked in. Lisa was immediately assailed by flashing bright lights, brain-melting music, and wall-to-wall bodies. Thankfully, Rick had hold of her hand, because they hadn't walked in ten feet before the crowd closed in on them from all sides. Good thing she wasn't claustrophobic. The ceiling was lit with a rainbow of colors cascading down from track lighting that seemed to follow her like a spotlight wherever they walked. She'd feel like she was on display if the lighting didn't appear to follow everyone else, too, in a muted, dark purple sort of way. It was funky, and kind of fun, almost like a laser tracking system. Maybe it focused on body heat or something, because everyone was lit up like that. How cool.

There was a long bar against every wall, scattered high tables and tall chairs set in front of each bar, and the rest of the club was nothing but dance floor, the biggest floor she'd ever seen. Good thing, too, because that seemed to be what everyone was doing—gyrating to the music. There had to be at least two hundred people out there on the football field–sized wood floor. The really awesome thing about it was the dance area was so huge, there was plenty of room for people to move around instead of feeling as if you were packed like sardines in a can.

"Drink first or dance?" Rick asked, leaning close to her ear so he wouldn't have to shout.

"Definitely dance. I need to work off dinner."

He pulled her onto the dance floor and they wound their way out into the crowd. The energy there was infectious and Lisa soon found herself immersed in the music, a sexy R&B song that had her swaying her hips back and forth and raising her arms over her head, turning around and laughing so much her sides ached. How long had it been since she'd been out dancing? Too long, just like every other fun thing associated with dating. Because she hardly ever dated.

Rick was a phenomenal dancer, had a killer rhythm, and knew how to move his body in a way she found incredibly sexy, especially when the music slowed to something hot and sensual and he pulled her into his arms. Their bodies touched in all the intimate places and Lisa lost herself in the music, in Rick, in the way she felt in his embrace. She focused her attention on his hips rocking back and forth with hers, her nipples sliding against his chest, the way his hand pressed against the small of her back, bringing her even closer. She felt his cock against her hip, felt it harden as his eyes turned darker. The room grew suddenly smaller, her breaths shorter, and everyone else fell away but the two of them locked in this dance with no words. And yet the dance expressed everything she wanted to say.

She suddenly wished they were alone—like right now—because there was a magical spell being woven over her. Rick moved against her, still in control of the dance, but one hand moved up to press against the side of her neck, his fingers tickling the nape as he drew her forward to kiss her. The kiss was light, a soft brushing of his lips against hers. He teased her with the tip of his tongue, no overly dramatic public display of affection, but enough to curl her toes and make her wet. Make her want. She breathed against his lips, letting out a soft sigh.

She knew he had this entire exciting night planned of dancing at the club, then gambling at the casino, but it wasn't what she wanted anymore. She just wanted to be alone with him.

"I want you, Lisa," he whispered, releasing her mouth and giving her such an intense look it left her shaken.

Maybe he had changed his mind about what he wanted to do tonight, too.

She nodded, rested her chin on his shoulder so he could hear her. "This is fun, but would you be terribly disappointed if we left?"

He leaned back, smiled, and shook his head. "No. Let's go."

He took her hand and led her out the door. Instead of hailing a taxi to take them back to their hotel, he looked down at her feet. "Take off your shoes."

She didn't even ask why, just slipped her heels off and put them in his outstretched hand. He led her down the stone stairs and onto the walkway leading to the beach.

The night was balmy with just the slightest breeze. It was difficult to see anything at all since there was barely a sliver of moon visible in the sky, but that made her other senses come alive. She smelled the salt spray from the ocean, heard the birds trilling calls as they flew overhead. All the night creatures were out, the human ones content to party at the resort above them. She and Rick were completely alone out there on the beach.

They walked hand in hand just along the water's edge, neither of them saying a word. Once they were out of sight of the bright lights of the resort, he pulled her away from the water, trudging over the sand and underneath a rocky overhang, flipping her around so her back brushed the craggy stone.

His mouth came down over hers in a demanding, passionate kiss that told her without a doubt what he wanted from her. There might have been a part of her that would have objected to sex out here in public, but she was too far gone, too much in need of this man she still wanted so desperately. He lifted one of her legs and draped it over his hip, sliding his fingers under the silky fabric to caress the bare skin of her leg. His touch, the clarity in her mind that he wanted her this much, sent hot shivers across her skin, making her nipples tingle, her clit quiver, because she wanted him with an equal desperation.

He moved his free hand under her thigh and toward her sex, cupping her, caressing her until she writhed under his touch. He tore the fabric aside and buried his fingers inside her, pumping her with soft, measured strokes. She moaned against his mouth and he kissed her harder, relentless in his pursuit and coaxing an orgasm from her that she had no hope to hold back. She bucked against his hand, reaching down to grasp his wrist and hold him there while she shuddered through the waves of pleasure that swamped her. He kept his mouth planted on hers, his tongue like velvet fire, inducing moans and whimpers and reducing her to a wet, needy mess.

She finally tore her mouth from his and reached for his face, cupping his cheeks and forcing him to look at her so she could choke out one breathless word in between panting breaths. "More."

She barely held on while he reached into his pocket for a condom, unzipped his pants, and positioned himself between her legs. He swept one arm around her back and lifted her. With a loud groan she settled over him, her toes sliding into the sand as she impaled her pussy onto his cock. Ripples of sensation crashed over her, and she let herself drown in them.

Delicious. Decadent. Hot. Rick pushed her against the rocks as he began to pump between her legs, his movements grinding his shaft against her already raggedly sensitive clit. She had no idea if there were other people walking by. They were enshrouded in pitch darkness, yet she knew she wasn't being quiet. Not when Rick continued to pound her with relentless, steady thrusts, and her pussy gripped him with tight convulsions. Not when he bent his head low and swept her mouth again with a kiss meant to devastate, to turn her mind to mush.

Then she didn't care if they had an audience of hundreds, because she only wanted these amazing sensations to continue, wanted to climb this ladder of torturous pleasure rung by rung with the only man who could do this to her, who could make her feel on fire from her toes to her hair. Only Rick could take her from one climax to the next without even catching her breath, could make her want to die and in the next moment cling to him in ragged desperation and beg him to do it to her again until finally, he groaned, grinding against her with a wild orgasm of his own. She held tight, dragging her nails over his sweat-soaked back as he shuddered against her, pulling his mouth from hers to kiss her jaw, her neck.

Finally, reality intruded and she realized where they were.

"I hope there weren't witnesses," she said.

"With cameras," he added. "I'd hate to end up on some sex site on the Internet."

She laughed.

They fixed their clothes and Lisa swiped her hand over her hair. "My body is still throbbing."

"Good," he said, taking her hand. "Because I'm not finished with you yet. Let's go back to the room."

Nine

They'd barely shut the door to their suite before Rick turned her around and kissed her again.

She loved kissing. There were some serious nerve endings in her lips, and every time he pressed his mouth to hers, it sent shock waves directly to her pussy. She wondered if kissing had the same effect on his cock. As he leaned against her, pressing her up against the door while he thoroughly explored her mouth, his cock rocked against her belly, hard and insistent, and she decided that his mouth must be wired the same way—right to his cock.

Then he shocked the hell out of her by sweeping her up into his arms and carrying her down the hall—so romantic, so sexy—and depositing her on her feet next to the bed.

"I could have walked," she said.

"You make it really difficult to be Prince Charming, you know." He shrugged out of his jacket and yanked off the tie, then started unbuttoning his shirt.

What he was doing now was definitely charming. "Sorry. I did enjoy you carrying me. I could get used to it."

His lips curled as he reached the last buttons on his shirt and dragged the hem out of his pants. "I like holding you. You feel good."

She sat on the bed and held on to the bed post while he pulled the shirt from his shoulders and cast it aside, then undid his belt and drew down the zipper of his pants. He kicked his shoes off, dropped his pants and then his boxers until he was naked. She was at a decided clothing disadvantage here, since she wouldn't be able to undress without Rick's help. Plus, she was kind of mesmerized watching Rick take his clothes off. She'd never realized how sexy it was to see a man strip. She was definitely going to have to pay attention more often when he shucked his clothes.

"I need help," she said.

He came over to her, his cock already semierect, and knelt in front of her. He slid one shoe off. "With your shoes?" he asked, sliding the other one off and holding her foot in his hand, flexing her toes and massaging her foot.

"Uh, no, but that feels really good."

He lifted her foot and kissed the tip of each toe, continuing his oh-so-heavenly massage. He gently laid her foot down, lifted the other, and gave it the same care. He was so tender, making sure to avoid those spots that tickled, that all she was aware of were the spots that made her body tingle to life, that made her pussy swell and warm.

When he'd finished, he stood and moved between her parted legs. "So what do you need help with?"

His cock, now fully hard, presented itself at the level of her eyes. Any help with undressing was lost as she reached for him, holding his thick shaft with both hands as she tilted her head back, stroked him, watched his eyes drift half closed. He groaned as she rubbed her fingers over the soft head, swirling her thumb around the pearly liquid gathering there. She lifted her thumb to her mouth to lick off his salty flavor, then bent down and captured the head of his cock between her lips.

Soft, unlike the rest of him, which was hard and throbbed in her hand. She stroked and sucked him, all the while watching his face, watching his reaction, loving the way his eyes closed, then opened, as if he wanted to savor the pleasure, but wanted to watch, too. And she wanted to give him something to watch. She released her hold on his cock and used her lips to take it into her mouth, inch by inch.

"Jesus, Lisa," he said with a soft croak, reaching for her hair, stroking it with his fingers while she licked around his shaft, admiring the way her saliva made it glisten in the half-lit room, then grasped his cock between her lips again, using her mouth and throat to squeeze it all the way back until she had him deep. And oh, she loved capturing him like this, holding him enthralled. It gave her such a sense of power and delight.

Rick groaned, fisted her hair in his hand, and began to guide her movements, slow and easy at first, then harder. She found it amazing that she could get so turned on by sucking his cock, but she did. Her pussy throbbed and her nipples felt tight and achy as she pulled his cock out of her mouth and licked the underside of his shaft. She was amazingly excited by all this.

Rick grasped her wrists and leaned back. "Enough or I'll come in your mouth."

She smiled up at him. "That would be nice."

His eyes were slits of dark desire. "You're killing me, Lisa."

She liked the harsh, gravelly tone to his voice, that barely leashed control he seemed to possess as he pulled her up to stand, then turned her around so her back was to him.

"I love this dress," he said, pressing against her to kiss the nape of her neck. "It's very sexy."

She shivered, her skin popping up goose bumps all over. "I thought you might."

He moved closer, his body molded to hers as he cupped her breasts over the silken fabric of her dress. "Your breasts are beautiful in this dress. I like this part," he said, caressing the upper swells of her breasts where they rose above the fabric of the corset. The reaction of her body was instantaneous, like lightning sizzling through her veins.

"I want to fuck you while you're wearing this dress." He laid his hand on her back and gave her a gentle nudge forward. The front of her thighs hit the mattress and she bent from the waist, planting her hands on the bed. Her ass shifted against his crotch, his hard cock rubbing the soft material of her dress.

She felt Rick's hands on her legs, lifting her skirt, his fingers smoothing along her skin to reach under her panties. She quivered at his touch, forcing her legs to stop trembling as he drew her panties down her legs, then off. He used his knee to nudge her legs farther apart, then lifted her dress, draping the skirt over her hips.

"You have the prettiest ass, Lisa." He took the globes in his hands, gave them a gentle squeeze, parted them, then slid one hand between her legs to cup her sex.

She was glad she was holding on to the bed because her knees went weak. The pleasure was incredible, his hand sliding back and forth over her wet, ready sex.

"Please," she whispered, biting her lower lip to keep from further begging for his cock.

"Okay, babe."

She heard him get the condom out and then he was back between her legs, his cock spreading her lips apart and sliding in. Her body welcomed him inside with a tight gripping that made her whimper in pleasure.

Rick grabbed hold of the corset laces on her dress and began to rock against her, slowly at first, then picking up intensity. In this position he could fuck her with deep, penetrating thrusts, filling her, swelling against her, making her insane with pleasure that tore against her normal reserves and made her feel savage, primal, desperate to reach orgasm. She fisted the blanket and bucked back against him, needing more of his cock.

"Harder," she said, pushing back again as he thrust forward. He responded by pulling on the laces of her corset, lifting her up against him, arching her back so he could fuck upward into her pussy. With the other hand he turned her jaw, met her halfway so he could take her mouth in a hard, passionate kiss. He moved his hand down the front of her dress, savagely pushing the front of the bodice down to bare her breasts so he could get to her nipples. He circled them with his palm, the roughness a harsh contrast to the softness of her flesh, inflaming her passions to a feverish level.

"You get wetter when I touch your nipples," he whispered over her shoulder.

She could feel it, the sensations both inside and out making her feel crazed and out of control. He pushed her forward again and rode her, driving up hard against her, his balls slapping against her sex as he thrust. She reached between her legs, wanting even more than this, needing to massage the throbbing ache centered at her clit.

"Fuck. Yes. Make yourself come for me," Rick said.

The harsh tone of his command only fueled the flames of her fire even hotter. She rubbed her clit, feeling her pussy tighten like a vise around his cock. The dual action of her own hand and his tunneling cock brought her close to the edge.

"Rick, I'm going to come."

She'd no more gotten the words out than she spiraled out of control, unable to stop the vortex of sensations that hit her as she climaxed. She braced herself on the bed as Rick pushed her hard, then planted his hips against hers, gripping her buttocks as he shuddered against her, and came right after she did with a loud groan and a curse.

Wiped out, she fell forward onto the mattress and Rick went with her, kissing the back of her sweat-dampened neck before rolling both of them to the side. Still inside her, he continued to stroke her with his cock while he smoothed his hand over her body and kissed her shoulder.

It had never been like this before. Never. Not such wild, uncontrollable passion, this hard edge that had taken her beyond the point of reason. She was drained, emotionally and physically.

"Come on," Rick said, sliding off the bed.

She went with him, her body on autopilot now. He turned her around and untied the laces of the corset, pulled her dress off and draped it over the chair, then took her by the hand into the bathroom. He turned on the low-level lights so the bathroom was dimly lit, then ran water in the whirlpool tub while she leaned against the counter and yawned, enjoying the steam rising from the tub.

Rick stepped in first, then held out his hand, holding hers while she climbed in and settled down in the water. He pulled her against him, her back to his chest, his legs spread so she could sit between them. He hit the jets and warm, frothy water swirled around them.

Soon, every limb was a lead weight and she dropped her head helplessly against him.

"I'm going to pass out on you," she murmured. "I hope you weren't planning to assault me again."

The deep vibration of his laugh rumbled against her back. "I'm sure I could manage . . . somehow . . . to get it up again for you, babe, but only if you force me."

She snorted. "Yeah, right. You're probably already thinking of ways you can fuck me in the bathtub."

"Hey, you're the one who brought up sex in the tub. I'm just try-ing to relax you."

"I am relaxed. Too relaxed. How will I ever adjust to real life again?"

He reached around her, wrapping his arms under her breasts to pull her closer. "Reality isn't much different, is it?"

She tilted her head back to stare up at him. "Are you kidding? This life is too easy. We've been living a total fantasy all week."

He cocked a brow. "Have we?"

"Yes. A great vacation filled with hot, sunny days and warm, breezy nights. Lazing about with nothing to do but swim, see the sights, loll about in the water, eat and sleep whenever we want."

"Don't forget all that sex."

"Yes. All the sex, too."

He continued to stare down at her.

"What?" she asked.

"I'm waiting for your point."

"Don't you see?" She shifted around so she faced him, pulling her legs in and crossing them over his. "It's not reality. None of this has been."

"And that's a bad thing?"

"No. Yes. I don't know." She pulled her hands through her hair. "I'm confused, I guess."

"What do you want, Lisa?"

That was the million-dollar question. "I guess what I'm trying to say is, this vacation will end."

"Yes."

He stared at her expectantly. God, how was she going to say this? She supposed the best way was simply to put it out there. "And I don't know how to . . . end things with us."

His lips curled. He laid his hands on her thighs, leaned forward, and pressed his lips to hers. "Do we have to?"

"I don't know, Rick. I don't know where we are. Like I said, this has been a fantasy. It's been wonderful. I've enjoyed the time with you so much. But it's not reality. It's not our lives, not who we are, who we've been for the past fifteen years."

He leaned back. "You mean divorced. Separate."

"Yes."

"Is that what you want?"

Did she? She didn't know anymore. "I can't say."

"I arranged this week as a way for us to reconnect, Lisa. To rediscover each other, to see if we still had the magic."

There was definitely magic between them. More so now than there ever had been before. But was it enough to sustain a relationship, to build a future on? She reached for his face, sliding her palm along his jaw. "It's been amazing. More than I could ever hope for."

"But?"

She sensed his tension, knew anger simmered just under the surface. But she owed it to him, and to herself, to be honest. "I just don't think it's enough. I think we're trying to recapture something that's long gone, Rick.

"I think our time is past. I think it's time we both move on with our lives."

His jaw clenched, the parts of his body touching her tightening, too. All the joy, the relaxation she'd felt tonight, evaporated in the steam rising from the water.

She'd hurt him. And that tore her up inside, made her stomach clench with pain.

"Is that how you really feel?" he asked, not making a move to rise from the tub, but draping his arms over the sides. He seemed casual and relaxed, but Lisa knew he was anything but. "Do you really feel like we're over, or is that the line you're using because you're afraid?"

Defenses up, she lifted her chin. "I'm not afraid, Rick. I just don't think you and me together is a wise idea."

"Because?"

"Because it's too much history."

"All bad?"

"No. Of course not. We have Kayla."

"We have more than just Kayla between us."

She rubbed her head, knowing where this was going. "Do we? There's always been Kay between us. She was the reason for our marriage, the reason we fought it out for three years before finally giving in and divorcing."

"We divorced because we were too young, not ready, not able to handle a relationship and a child. We needed that separation until we both grew up."

She nodded. "Yes. But still, would we have stayed together if Kayla hadn't come along?"

He shrugged. "I don't know, Lisa. I think we would have. We're still together now."

She let herself smile. "Not really. We're divorced, we share custody of our daughter. We raised her together. But everything has always been about Kayla. Now that she's heading off to college, I'm afraid there'll be nothing left for us to build on together."

"There's a lot we can build on, Lisa. We have amazing chemistry, we love being together."

"Great sex doesn't make a relationship. I'm afraid we're both holding on tight to the past because we're afraid to move into a future that doesn't include our little nuclear family. Maybe it's time we consider it."

He took in a breath, blew it out. "You've dated other men since we've been divorced, haven't you?"

"Yes."

"Slept with a few?"

"Yes."

"Find that magic with anyone?"

She looked down at the water, then back up at him. "No."

"I dated a few women, slept with a few. No one . . . no one gives me what you do, Lisa."

How could she feel so giddy and so awful at the same time? "I'm the mother of your child, Rick. I can't help but think your feelings for me are tied into Kayla."

He pushed off the sides and stood, water dripping down his body as he stepped out of the tub and grabbed a towel, not bothering to dry off. He dragged both hands through his wet hair and turned to her, his eyes gone storm dark with anger.

"Our entire life isn't about Kayla. At least mine isn't. You and I aren't together, didn't come together and stay together, simply because of our daughter. And if you'd step back from the past twenty years for just a few minutes, step away from your fear of being alone, your fear of losing your daughter, of losing who you are, you might just see that I've *always* been there. And I wasn't just there for Kayla. I was there for *you*, for every step you took, every time you fell, every time you needed me.

"Not just for our daughter, but for you. That divorce decree was just a piece of paper, Lisa. I never left you. But you know what? I think you're right. I think it's time I did."

He opened the door and closed it behind him, leaving Lisa still sitting in the tub, his words ringing in her ears and tears sliding down her cheeks.

What had she just done?

Ten

Stupid. God, she'd been so damn stupid.

Tears racked Lisa's body until she had nothing left to give. It hadn't gone the way she'd envisioned at all.

But what had she expected? That Rick would just say that things would go on the way they had always been? That she could live in her safe little cocoon and nothing would ever change? She knew that couldn't happen. Not anymore.

By the time Lisa had gathered her composure enough to get out of the tub, dry off, and throw on some clothes, Rick was packed and gone.

Cold dread filled her at the realization that he'd left her, and she had no idea where he could be, no way to track him down, no way to reach him. She could try his cell phone, but would it work down here?

What would she even say to him if she called him? She'd told him it wasn't going to work, her intent to thank him for a wonderful time, but to make it clear she didn't want to continue a relationship with him beyond their vacation. So he'd left. She'd gotten her wish, hadn't she?

So why was she so freakin' miserable? Why did she feel she'd just made the worst mistake of her life? Why did it take such a cold slap in the face for her to realize how much she cared for him?

He was right. Dead-on accurate with everything he'd said to her. She had been hanging on to Kayla, on to her role as Kayla's mother, afraid to take a step into adulthood and try life on her own. As a woman. She'd kept Rick at a distance all these years, still feeling that pang of longing for him but too damn afraid to say or do anything that could shatter the perfect world they'd created for Kayla. So they'd done this careful dance around each other, remaining friends—close friends—when they could have been so much more. All this time they could have been more.

And now, this week, Rick had given her that opportunity again, and she had thrown it back at him and told him it wasn't at all what she wanted, because again, she'd been afraid. Afraid that it wouldn't be perfect, that it wouldn't meet her expectations, that she would fail, just like she'd failed him the first time, like she'd failed Kayla the first time.

Better to take no chance at all than fail at the chance you take, right?

But what if she and Rick tried, and it didn't work out? That would kill Kayla.

Wouldn't it?

She lay on the bed and dug the heels of her palms into her tear-swollen eyes. Oh, God, she couldn't think anymore. She had to talk to someone. She needed advice. Someone had to tell her what to do.

She stared at the phone. Connie. Kayla maybe? She'd really love to discuss this with her daughter, get Kayla to weigh in on this.

Then it hit her. No. Absolutely not. This was her life. Her choice. Her decision to make. No one else's. It was time to grow up, to stand on her own for once. She didn't have Rick to rely on anymore, and she sure as hell wasn't going to cry on her daughter's shoulder.

Only she could decide what path to take next. And from the way her heart twisted, it was clearly obvious how she felt about what she'd done. Her feelings for Rick went way beyond guilt at hurting him.

Great time to figure that one out, Lisa.

She'd screwed this up so badly. A week of romance, sex, spending time with a man she—

Loved. Yes, she was in love with Rick. She always had been, had never stopped loving him. She'd depended on him to be there for her, and as he'd said to her before he walked out, he had been. Every time she needed him, he'd been there. Not just for Kayla, but for her. And she'd used him, had never given anything back to him, but had only taken. Even this week, she'd taken, and instead of shouting out how she'd felt, she'd crawled back into her shell of fear and complacency and announced that she didn't want what he offered.

What a bitch she was. How could he love her? How could he care for her? She wasn't worth it.

Fresh tears sprung in her eyes, but she swiped them away, refusing to feel sorry for herself. Dwelling in misery wasn't going to accomplish anything. She'd spent the past fifteen years letting Rick take care of everything, take care of her. That was going to change. It was time she grew up and took charge of her life. It was time to make some decisions about her future. About their future.

She knew what she wanted now, even though she'd been an utter dumbass and the truth had hit her about an hour too late. But maybe it wasn't too late. She had an idea. A wonderful, impossible, romantic, scary-as-hell idea.

Their flight back to the United States wasn't for two days. Unless Rick was so pissed he decided to grab an earlier flight . . .

She picked up the phone and called the front desk, confirming her suspicions. He'd checked into another room, but he was still in the hotel. It figured Rick wouldn't just leave her there alone. Even as angry as he was, he would stay there to look out for her, would still be there at checkout time to fly back with her.

She so didn't deserve him. It would serve her right if he laughed in her face and walked out on her when she presented her plan to him.

She lay down on the bed, knowing she'd get nothing done the remainder of the night. She fell into a fitful sleep, waking nearly every hour, hoping Rick would walk through the door so she could apologize and tell him how wrong she'd been. When the sun rose and filtered through the bedroom balcony, she got up and called room service for a pot of coffee, eager to start on her plan. There wasn't much time and a lot to do. She was going to look ridiculous if Rick said no. She didn't care. After what she'd put him through, what she'd said to him, she deserved it if he turned around and walked out on her.

After breakfast and a shower, she dressed and went downstairs, making arrangements, hoping like hell she wouldn't run into Rick. Not yet anyway. She coaxed the front desk clerk into keeping tabs on him and letting her know if for some reason he checked out. She didn't think he would, but just in case he did, she'd have to know. Her plans would be ruined. Everything was going to take place tonight. The coordinators were wonderful considering she was throwing this all together at a moment's notice, but since it wasn't a weekend, everyone had openings. She found a dress that fit perfectly at the designer shop in the hotel, and it was all scheduled. She was giddy with excitement, nervous with anticipation, and also dreading facing Rick again. But she had to if this was going to work. She had a hair and makeup appointment in an hour. All she had to do now was write the invitation, have it sent to Rick's room, and hope he showed up. If not, she'd go to his room and beg him in person.

She had a lot of apologizing to do. And a lot to accomplish before eight o'clock tonight.

～❈❈❈～

Rick stared out the balcony of his room, tired of pacing, tired of his own thoughts. He'd spent some time on the beach today—too long, walking a couple miles in one direction before taking a long swim, climbing out, and walking back. It had helped clear the cobwebs somewhat, but he had no more answers now than he did when he left the room earlier.

He still didn't know what to do about Lisa, how to convince her they did belong together.

He couldn't make her love him.

That was the worst part. He'd gotten this all wrong. Maybe his feelings were one sided, but he didn't think so. It was fear holding her back, not her feelings for him. But there wasn't a damn thing he could do about it. He'd done all he could. The rest was up to her.

At least he'd tried. This vacation was his attempt to get them alone so they could talk, get away from everyday life, and become a couple again. It had worked, too, for a while. But he knew it was just a matter of time before Lisa would start overthinking everything again. Why did he think he could change her? That's who she was, who she'd always be. He was either going to have to accept it, or walk away.

Which was what he'd done last night. Not a very smooth move on his part. Instead of staying with her and talking through her fears, he'd gotten pissed off and stormed out. *Way to be mature, Rick.*

Maybe they hadn't grown up enough yet. Either of them. Maybe they both needed to take a step back and really think things through.

Maybe Lisa was right.

He was pushing her. Too much too soon. His expectations had been too high. He was rushing her. After they got back home, they'd talk, take things slow. Lisa wasn't the type to rush into anything—he knew that about her. With time . . .

He turned at the knock at the door, frowning. No one knew he was here and he hadn't ordered room service. When he opened the door, a bellman stood there with a sealed envelope. Rick took it, tipped the man, and closed the door, staring at the handwriting on the envelope.

Lisa's. She'd found him. He arched a brow and slid his finger under the seal to open it, scanning her elegantly printed words:

Rick

Words can't express how wrong I was. How sorry I am.

Sometimes I have to lose something to realize how much it means to me. Maybe it's taken me fifteen years to understand, to realize what was right in front of me the entire time, and I was too blind to see it. You've been everything to me. Friend, lover, and husband. You were right. Paper means nothing. We have always been meant for each other, I just didn't see it. I do now and I don't ever want to lose you again.

Meet me on the terra cotta terrace, beachside, under the white
canopy at eight p.m. tonight.
Wear your suit.
Marry me. I love you. I've always loved you.

Lisa

He read the message several times, unable to believe what it said.

She loved him.

Marry her? Here? Now? Tonight? Was that even doable? Was she insane? It was so impulsive, so not Lisa at all.

Jesus.

He dragged his hand through his hair, glanced down at his watch. It was six o'clock. He headed to the shower, cleaned up and dried off, then went to the closet for a suit, shirt, and tie.

He couldn't believe Lisa was doing this. So impulsive. His lips curled.

Maybe she could change, after all.

He grabbed his clothes and started getting dressed. There were a few things he wanted to do before eight o'clock.

<hr>

Lisa stood under the white canopy, gardenias spread all around, their sweet scent helping to relax the giant butterflies in her stomach.

What if Rick didn't show up? She'd be mortified, crushed.

And it would be no more than she deserved after the way she'd treated him last night.

The way she'd treated him for years, actually.

Her hands shook as the hotel's wedding coordinator handed her the bouquet of creamy roses.

"You look gorgeous," Amanda said, her bright pixie face lit up with a smile. For someone so young, Amanda was incredibly organized. She'd pulled this wedding together in one day, from minister to marriage license—and oh, the strings she'd had to pull to get that together—to the tent to music to probably more details than Lisa even knew about. Lisa owed her a debt of thanks. As well as the astronomical bill she was going to have to pay for everything, but she didn't care.

She turned, the cream silk shift she wore swirling around her knees. God, she loved this dress. It was actually her first official wedding dress. She and Rick had gotten married at the court house the first time. Lisa had been ill with morning sickness, had worn an old dress, and the entire event was a cloudy blur of nerves and nausea.

This one—if it actually happened—would be different.

Her hair was piled up on top of her head, loose ringlets cascading alongside her face and along her neck. She wore a pair of matching stiletto sandals that made her legs look long and sexy. The outfit was amazing.

Now all she needed was a groom.

When she spotted Rick coming around the corner of the building, her heart rammed against her chest. Tears welled in her eyes and she almost sank to the floor. Her legs were shaking as he stepped under the tent and took her hand in his, kissing her knuckles.

"I'd love to marry you, Lisa. I love you, too."

Just like that, she was forgiven.

"I don't deserve you," she whispered, fighting to keep the tears back.

He pressed his lips to hers. "We deserve each other. We deserve this."

She sniffed, smiled up at him, unable to believe how happy she was.

"Are you sure?" he asked. "Kayla's not here. Your friends, our families."

She placed her fingers at his lips. "This is just about us, Rick. No one else needs to be here."

One side of his mouth curved upward. He nodded.

"Shall we begin?" the minister asked.

The ceremony was short, but achingly sweet. The minister was perfect, spoke to them about love and commitment, and how important it was to remember to value each other. Lisa cried and she was certain her makeup was a mess, but she didn't care. Rick surprised her with rings for both of them. He would think of that—she had forgotten. Matching platinum bands that were simple, but absolutely stunning. When the minister pronounced them husband and wife, Rick pulled her into his arms and pressed his lips to hers, kissing her with a brief, dazzling kiss that left her breathless. The flash of a camera popped around her, they toasted with champagne, and then they were finished.

Married. Again.

This time, forever.

They spent a few moments talking with Amanda and the minister, the photographer took a few pictures, then they were off.

"I have dinner being delivered to our suite," Lisa said.

Rick held her hand as they walked through the lobby toward the elevator. "You do?"

She nodded. "And champagne."

"Great."

"And I bought something special to change into."

He arched a brow as they entered the elevator. "You already look pretty special. Beautiful, in fact."

Her cheeks warmed. "Thank you."

"You're welcome. Wife."

Wife. They'd really gotten married. "We're married."

"Yeah. Kayla's going to be pissed."

The moved into their suite. "She'll get over it," Lisa said. "She'd want us to be happy."

"Yeah, she would." Rick pulled her into his arms. "Are you?"

She twined her fingers around his neck. "Am I what?"

"Happy. Are you sure this is what you wanted?"

"Yes. God, yes. I'm so sorry, Rick. About last night . . ."

He shook his head. "Don't. I overwhelmed you and I know it. I pressured you. I just hope I didn't push you into this."

She smiled. "You didn't. I've always wanted you. I guess I was just afraid that maybe Kayla was why we were together in the first place."

"I loved you way before Kayla ever entered the picture. And even more after. We both just needed to grow up."

"We both have."

He let out a sigh. "I should have asked you to marry me again long before now. I don't know what stopped me."

"Probably the same thing that stopped me. Fear of shattering the perfect arrangement."

"You're right. We made the divorce too comfortable."

"Our friendship was too easy."

"We put romance, sex—us—on the back burner."

She leaned into him, loving the feel of his body against hers. God, how she'd missed it, and how excited she was to realize she wasn't going to have to let him go. "Never again. We come first now. Always."

He untangled her arms from around his neck and led her out onto the balcony. As usual, the night was perfect. People walking below, music coming from somewhere, a soft breeze sailing upward, warm and filled with the fragrance of the island.

"I'm going to miss this place," she said.

"We can stay longer."

She turned to him. "I have to get back to work Monday."

"Call in. Tell them you're on your honeymoon. I'll bet they give you a few extra days."

Tempting. The old Lisa would come up with a hundred reasons why that was such a bad idea. The new Lisa already had a hundred reasons why she wanted to stay here. "I'll call tomorrow."

"So will I."

"After that we'll call Kayla together."

"We'll probably hear her squeal all the way from Europe without benefit of the telephone line."

She laughed. "You're right. She's going to be so excited. So will Connie."

"I have a lot to thank both of them for. They were instrumental in helping me with my plan to get you here."

"Then I'm the one who's thankful. To them, of course, but especially to you. If you hadn't made this happen, we might never—"

"But we did. And that's all that matters." He swept her into his arms, kissing her in a way that left no doubt as to how much he loved her.

Passion ignited and Lisa felt the immediacy, the need to consummate their marriage. She'd made plans for that. A silken, floor-length nightgown, rose petals strewn across their bed, champagne chilling next to the bed. A whole romantic, seductive scene that she no longer cared about, because all she wanted was Rick inside her, right now, right here. She had this silly need to "cement the deal." Immediately.

She tore at his suit jacket, pulling it off his shoulders. It fell to the floor. She kicked off her shoes while Rick toed his off. Their lips stayed glued together, their tongues doing a wild mating dance that left Lisa hot, feverish, and desperate with need. When he lifted her dress and slid his fingers between her legs, she cried out, not caring if anyone could hear them.

"Yes," she said, biting down on his shoulder as he drove two fingers into her pussy. "More."

"You're wet," he said, his voice tight. "You want me to fuck you out here?"

She loved when he went all harsh and all male on her. Her nipples tightened, her breasts swelling higher over the bodice of her dress. She leaned back and searched his face. "Yes. Fuck me here. Do it now."

He dragged her to the balcony edge, planting her hands on the cement. "Bend over," he commanded.

She did, and he lifted her dress, pulling her panties down to her ankles. She stepped out of them and spread her legs, waiting for his cock. Needing his cock. Instead, she felt his tongue probing between her ass cheeks, flicking out to lick at her pussy lips. She tossed her head back and moaned as he licked her, lapping at the wetness there, driving her crazy by teasing her with his tongue and fingers, taking her so close to the edge she mumbled incoherently, unable to form the words to tell him what she needed.

But he knew. He slid his fingertips up to her clit and moved them in circles while fucking her pussy with his tongue. She shattered right there, digging her palms into the rough cement, lifting her ass against his mouth and hand while her nerve endings exploded against him.

She was still shuddering when Rick rose and unzipped his pants, put on a condom, and plunged his cock inside her. Hard, demanding, he fucked her with long, measured strokes, wrapping one arm around her waist and planting his lips along the nape of her neck. He licked her, even bit her, and her body caught fire. She raised the front of her dress and massaged her clit, wanting to come again with him.

"Do you think someone's watching us?" he asked. "Do you think maybe some guy is jacking off watching us fuck?"

"I don't . . . I don't know," she said, trying to catch her breath, visualizing someone hidden in the darkness on one of the balconies, his cock in his hand, stroking it fast and hard while he watched Rick fuck her.

"Your pussy is so wet, babe. Does that excite you, the thought of people watching us?"

"Yes," she said, whimpering as he surged into her, filling her, expanding inside her, and it was all she could take. "Rick. Rick, please."

"Tell me what you want."

She didn't know. She just wanted more. Her throat was raw from panting, her breath gone, so she backed up against him, pushing her pussy onto his cock.

"Oh yeah. I know what you need." He held her tighter, plunged deeper, and she strummed her clit with a fury, taking her right to the edge. Her pussy tightened, and with Rick's final hard thrust she went over, taking him with her. They both shouted their pleasure into the night. It was wild, sensual, a little bit crazy, and absolutely the hottest thing she'd ever done. Rick pulled out and turned her around, kissing her until she was dizzy with pleasure all over again. She palmed his chest and pushed back. "I can't breathe," she said, laughing.

"Wife dies from pleasure on wedding night. Story at eleven," he said, in mock news anchor horror.

She giggled. "I just might."

He fell into one of the cushioned chaises, taking Lisa with him. She snuggled up against his chest and watched the stars above them.

"Yes, we definitely have to stay a few more days," she murmured. "I think you're adjusting to this decadent lifestyle."

"I could get used to it. We'll need to redo the backyard." She lifted her head. "Will you move into my house? Or do you want me to move into yours?"

"We can figure all that out later. Don't worry about the details."

"Okay. No matter what, we definitely need a private back porch."

He laughed. "I've created a monster. One who likes outdoor sex."

"Hey, we live in Florida. Might as well take advantage of year-round nice temperatures."

He tilted her chin back and kissed her. "I love you, Lisa."

"I love you, too. Thank you for not giving up on me."

"I never have. I never will."

She was so lucky. A wonderful husband, an incredible daughter, and an amazing future. They were bound together now, tied with invisible bonds that had always been there. She'd just been too blind to see them.

Now she saw clearly.

"Dinner should be arriving soon," she said.

"Good. You're working me to death on this vacation. I'm starving."

She grinned. "It's a good thing the food is great here, then. I need you to keep up your strength."

He stood and pulled her out of the chair. "There's also a matter of that special outfit you said you bought for later?"

"Oh, yeah. The one I'm going to wear when we consummate our marriage."

He snorted. "It's going to be a long night."

There was a knock at the door. Their dinner, no doubt. Lisa smiled and batted her lashes at Rick. "Better go eat your spinach. You're going to need it."

Jaci Burton is thrilled to be living her dream of writing passionate romance.

She lives in Oklahoma with her husband.

Visit her at www.jaciburton.com.

Don't miss her exciting new novel, *Riding on Instinct*, coming in April 2009 from Heat. Turn to the back of the book for a sneak preview.

Undone

JASMINE HAYNES

To my husband, Ole
For always coming up with the great ideas when I think there are none left!

As always, thanks to Jenn Cummings, Terri Schaefer, Lucienne Diver, and
Wendy McCurdy. And to Shannon Hollis, for letting me try
on a real corset and giving me a few particulars.

One

"You've been off your stride since Richard left." Lorie cut right to the heart of the matter. "It's been a year. You need to move on, at least go out on a date."

"I'm over Richard. But you know the last year has been a nightmare professionally." Margo Faraday sipped after-dinner coffee, curling into the corner of Lorie's leather sofa. As a mortgage broker, Margo's business had taken a nosedive with last year's subprime mortgage debacle. The San Francisco Bay Area was especially hard hit because of the high cost of houses. She was still in major recovery mode.

Lorie narrowed her eyes. "I know you, girlfriend, and it isn't just business. You've been pensive since your birthday."

Pensive? Yeah. Maybe. Her birthday had been a couple of weeks ago, before Thanksgiving. "Well, turning forty-five is not exactly making me feel tiptop," Margo admitted.

Lorie was a couple of years younger. "You look gorgeous. Blond hair, green eyes, a hot bod men drool over."

Wasn't that exactly what best friends were for, to help you rebuild your self-esteem? "You're so sweet." Margo did try hard to keep herself in decent shape. "But I'd rather have red hair like yours." And quite frankly, Lorie's bra size, too, not that Margo would actually say that.

Lorie swiped at her short red curls. "The color doesn't stay in long enough. I spend a fortune at my salon."

Margo had heard the complaint often enough. Luckily her own blond was natural. But it wasn't just the age thing getting to her. It *was* Richard . . . and it wasn't. After eight years of living together, Richard had walked out. One humongous fight, and he was gone, just like that. Since her birthday, she'd felt that lonely year finally catching up to her.

"Come on," Lorie pleaded with a pout. "Tell me what's really both-ering you."

She and Lorie had known each other ten years, meeting at work right after Margo's divorce. "I guess it's getting older, not dating since Richard left, the business problems"—she shrugged—"everything." And the fact that her two major relationships had failed spectacu-larly, first her ten-year marriage, then Richard. She'd been with him almost ten years, too. Why couldn't she get past that ten-year mark? Margo's mother still bemoaned the fact that her daughter couldn't keep a man. In her mother's eyes, she'd never quite measured up.

Lorie heard only the one thing. "It's not like you've even been open to dating anyone. Carl's got this great VP of Sales—"

Margo held up her hand. "Please don't set me up with one of Carl's friends." Lorie had been dating Carl for two years and living with him for six months. He was great, but his standard for an ideal date was a man's rung on the corporate ladder.

Right on cue, as if mentioning him conjured a call, Lorie's cell phone rang with Carl's special tone. Grabbing it off the magazines and papers on the coffee table, Lorie answered with that gooey smile she still managed to wear for him. "Hi, sweetie"—pause, a quick head shake—"let me check." And she popped up from the sofa to head down the hall to the bedroom.

Lorie had a point about dating. The year since Richard left had seemed to rush by her so fast Margo couldn't stop it. Topped off with turning forty-five, she badly needed a boost to her self-confidence, something to make her feel alive, attractive, and desirable. Maybe she couldn't make a success of a relationship, but she did need a man, or at least some sort of a connection. Even if it was only for a night. Or a week. Or a month. Vibrators only went so far.

Margo shuffled through the magazines on the coffee table, look-ing for something to entertain herself rather than thinking about her love life, or lack thereof.

Instead of a magazine, she came across . . . what on earth was that, a personal ad? A plain sheet of paper, it had been printed off one of those personals Web sites. Good Lord, were Lorie and Carl looking on the Internet for extracurricular activities? The thought stole her breath, made her think of Richard . . . and what had really ended their relationship. The thing she'd never had the courage to reveal to Lorie. Instead she'd let her best friend think the break up had been about Richard's new girlfriend, Katrina.

Margo almost put down the ad. It wasn't her business. It was snooping. It was . . . she couldn't help it, she *had* to read.

Amateur Photographer Looking for the Perfect Model. Ever thought about posing for erotic pictures? We can start out with you clothed, then various stages of undress until total nudity. Pose as erotically as you're comfortable with, perhaps even touch yourself, use a toy or two. Let your inhibitions go, I want you completely undone for the camera. The disposition of the pictures is up to you; if you don't want me to keep any, I won't. I'm not looking for a professional model; I want a real woman. I know you're out there.

The last line seemed to call to her. She felt a hitch in her breath, a sweep of heat through her body as she read. And imagined. She was a real woman, she was out there. And she needed *something*.

But what was *Lorie* doing with the ad? Maybe Carl wanted naughty pictures of Lorie. That was harmless enough. Lorie couldn't intend doing it on her own or she wouldn't have left it on the coffee table for Carl to find.

But why hadn't she told Margo about it?

For the same reason Margo hadn't told Lorie the real reason Richard left. There were just some things secret to any significant relationship.

She barely managed to get the paper back on the table before Lorie returned, breezing into the living room with that gooey smile on her face. For a moment, Margo felt a pang of envy.

"You'd never know the man has an MBA. He can't even remember if he returned the rented tux from that benefit we went to last week." Whether he was forgetful or not, Lorie was crazy about him, and Margo suspected she loved the quick little calls for this, that, or the other that made her feel needed.

"What's this?" Margo hadn't intended saying a word about the ad, but it was as if her mouth opened and the words fell out all on their own.

Lorie grabbed the paper, flopped back down on the sofa, and put her slippered feet on the edge of the chrome-and-glass coffee table. Then she laughed. "Oh God, that's my brother's friend. They went to college together."

"Your brother's *friend* wants to take erotic pictures of you?" With her brother being ten years younger than Lorie, it meant this guy was in his early thirties.

Lorie huffed out another laugh. "No, silly. He just put the ad out for a model. And Zach"—Lorie's brother—"thought I might know someone." She made a horrible face. "Yeah, like one of *my* friends would do it."

Yet Margo's whole body hummed with the thought of having a young man take nude photos of her. *Erotic* photos. She'd never admit she had a bit of an exhibitionist streak lurking within, but the idea heated her on the inside. Yes, one of Lorie's friends would *think* about doing it. Not that she'd act on it.

Margo had to know more. "An 'erotic' model? What is he, some sort of pervert?"

"Actually, Dirk's the sweetest guy. But he's gotten into the photography thing, and there's some contest coming up in the new year that he wants to practice for."

"Practice?"

"You know, posing the model, getting the lighting right, stuff like that, technical photography things."

Right. "Is this some sort of porn contest?"

Again Lorie laughed. "No. It's artistic. Showing the female form in all its glory"—she waved her hands, the paper flapping—"not that he only does nudes." Lorie tipped her head. "In fact, I'm not sure he's done nudes before. Which is probably why he needs practice." She punctuated with a sly smile.

"Then why doesn't he just hire a model to practice on?"

Holding up the ad, Lorie pointed. "Because he wants a real woman. Not some model-thin, unblemished young thing. According to him, it's all about showing off a real woman's beauty." She shrugged, as if only a man could come up with that line. "He's sweet, but I don't think he's going to get a 'real' woman to pose. If anything, he'll get a reply from some skank."

Margo smiled at the face Lorie made. "Right. No ordinary woman would go for that. I mean, what if he put the pictures on the Internet or something?"

Lorie shook her head. "Oh, he'd never do that. Dirk's your boy-next-door type. I'm just waiting for the right woman to come along and sweep him off his feet." She snapped her fingers. "Not to mention finding someone for my brother. Now talk about a perv." Lorie rolled her eyes, but Margo knew darn well she adored her younger brother. Tossing the ad on the coffee table, Lorie narrowed her eyes. "And don't think you're fooling me. You're trying to sidetrack me so I'll forget our discussion about Richard and why you're not moving on."

Lorie had it wrong. Margo wasn't avoiding at all. In fact, she was terribly intrigued. With Dirk, and his ad. He might be the perfect solution to her "pensiveness," as Lorie called it. She could have a hot interlude, give her self-esteem a boost, then walk away with no one the wiser, not even her best friend.

Margo memorized the e-mail address at the bottom of the ad.

❦❦❦

The A-frame house nestled among the pine, oak, and redwoods was ablaze with icicle Christmas lights.

Of course, once she'd gotten home that night after dinner with Lorie, Margo had vacillated. In the end, though, it was the echo of Richard's accusations that had her finally answering Dirk's ad. Richard claimed she was unwilling to take a chance and worried excessively about what everyone else thought, especially her mother and her mother's friends. That drove him crazy. It was ultimately why he left. It wasn't Katrina, as she'd let Lorie believe, it was Margo herself.

Just once, she wanted to do something wild and crazy, kinky and hot. She wanted to prove to herself that Richard was wrong. She could get down and dirty, and have fun while she was doing it.

Parking her sedan by the stand-alone garage, Margo shut off the engine, and the silence of the forest settled in around her. The house was isolated. She'd passed several driveways coming up the long, winding road, but the homes were set too far back to see more than a porch lamp beaming through the trees.

The boy next door, Lorie called him. The Christmas lights twinkling along the roofline attested to it. And Lorie had vouched for him, not to reiterate the fact that Lorie's brother had known him since college. Dirk Araman. The name appealed to Margo in a warrior kind of way. If someone accosted a woman in the street, a guy named Dirk would run the mugger down.

Over the week, they'd exchanged several e-mails. He was articulate, funny, and well, sweet. She felt like she knew him. Mentioning how she came to see the ad, she'd asked him to keep it quiet. Explaining herself to Lorie was out of the question. All right, the secrecy was shades of excessive worrying, but honestly, even Richard would agree she didn't have to broadcast her intent. Dirk agreed to keep it to himself. She also made it abundantly clear that the pictures would be for her use only. Not for this contest of his, not even for him to keep.

She'd told him her age, and though he was twelve years younger, it hadn't fazed him. All he wanted was to take her picture while she . . . The photos were hers after they'd looked through them together and he'd made all his notes. He explained about the competition, that if he won, he stood to get national attention for his work. His goal for their session was to work on posing, lighting, and a host of technical jargon that had passed right over her head. He'd also asked her measurements for some special lingerie he wanted to photograph her in. The competition was for nude portraits only, but he was honest enough to admit he'd added the erotic part for the titillation factor. Well, hell, she was in it for the titillation, too.

That made them equal perverts.

Could she get naked for a stranger? She took care of herself. Her breasts were small, but they didn't sag. She didn't consider herself a bad-looking woman. But it was one thing to say you'd do it, another to actually *do* it. And touching herself for him? A hot shiver raced through her. Yes, she was nervous, but she wanted it. The idea was kinky, decadent. She'd just wasted one precious year ignoring her needs, and she wasn't about to lose another.

Margo threw open the car door and stepped out. The chilly December night bit through her coat. Opening the rear door, she stuffed her small purse, phone, and keys in her gym bag, which was packed with makeup (camera lights could be harsh), lingerie (despite his having something special for her to wear), a bottle of wine (she liked the sweet stuff), and her vibrator. She didn't know if she could use it for him, yet the fantasy had haunted her. Her toy had seen extra duty every night this week.

The three-story A-frame loomed above her. A balcony ran the length of the second floor, and the third was obviously a loft. The scent of wood smoke tinged the air. Stepping up on the porch, she detected the soft sound of a woman's musical voice drifting through the panes of opaque glass in the door.

This was it, her last chance to rethink. She might have except for the distant echo of Richard's voice alleging that, just like her mother, she'd grow old in her pristine, picture-perfect life, and find out she hadn't done a damn thing with it. No risks, true, but no rewards either.

Margo pressed the bell.

A giant answered her ring. Oh. My. God. Though she was five-six, with four extra high-heeled inches, the man at the door towered over her like the Incredible Hulk. He had to be at least six-five. His thighs in black jeans were the size of tree trunks, his chest beneath a red-and-black flannel shirt rippled with muscles, and his hands would span her waist, with room left over. With a face made up of blunt angles, square jaw, sharp cheekbones, and a slightly crooked nose that had been broken at least once, he looked like the warrior his name implied.

Margo clutched her bag to her chest, and her heart pumped fast and hard. What had she gotten herself into?

"I'm glad you didn't change your mind, Margo."

His voice was liquid smoke easing over her nerve endings. The stuff of wet dreams, it trickled down her spine, settling between her legs. She'd always been around average men, and Dirk was anything but average. Truth to tell, there was something bone-melting about his sheer body mass, all muscle and no fat.

He watched her watching him, his eyes an extraordinary shade of blue totally unexpected beneath that short cap of thick, dark sable hair. "Maybe I should have sent you a picture before you agreed to meet me," he said.

Then he smiled, and Margo's libido went into overdrive as a single boyish dimple appeared at the left corner of his mouth. It transformed his face from Boris Karloff's Frankenstein to . . . well, Margo didn't know exactly. Except that the combination of his smile and size made her panties damp.

"You can back out right now, if you want." He held the door wide, standing slightly to the side so she could enter. If she wanted. Yet he didn't touch her with anything but that smile.

Right. That's exactly what Richard would expect her to do. Turn tail and run. *You're so afraid someone might actually find out you've got a dirty mind. Newsflash, Margo, most people have dirty minds. You're nothing special.*

She realized she'd been staring rudely. "I'm sorry. You're just so . . ."

"Big," he supplied. "You'd never believe my mother is only five-one and a hundred and five pounds."

Margo gaped. "No way."

He nodded, a hank of brown hair falling across his forehead.

"What about your dad?"

"Five-eight and the proverbial ninety-pound weakling. He always claimed I belonged to the milkman." The dimple appeared again, his blue eyes twinkling like Christmas tree lights, and Margo imagined everyone laughing over the family legend.

The night air was creeping beneath her long wool skirt, and all his central heat was whooshing through the wide open door. She couldn't take forever to make up her mind. She'd wanted the titillation of doing something out there and kinky. She wanted the erotic photos. She needed to feel *alive* again, needed a connection. But whereas before she'd fantasized of stripping down for a total stranger, now she realized she wanted to do it for *this* man.

Dirk Araman held out his hand. And Margo took it.

⁂

"Would you like to take off your coat?"

He said it almost gently. In the kitchen, he'd poured her a glass of wine out of the bottle she'd brought with her, adding a couple of ice cubes to cool it. Then he'd retrieved a beer from the fridge for himself. Yet in all that time, she still hadn't let go of her gym bag or removed her coat.

"I won't bite." He quirked one dark eyebrow over a scintillatingly blue eye. The dimple bloomed once more, and she knew what he'd left unsaid. *I won't bite unless you want me to.*

Her breath caught in her throat. She wanted him to. She hadn't planned on letting him touch her, but the idea was a bud waiting to bloom in her mind. He smelled so good, all woodsy, as if he'd been out splitting logs for the fire that burned in the living room. The Christmas tree stood tall in the corner, wrapped in tinsel and red and blue ornaments, a star winking on the top. Braided rugs covered the hardwood floors. Margo set her wineglass on the burnished oak coffee table, tossed her gym bag on the brown leather sofa, and undid her coat.

Dirk's fingers brushed hers as he took it, and a tiny shock raced through her body. Her thank-you sounded a bit strangled. He tongue-tied her. What did you say to a man you were about to undress for?

After hanging her coat in a closet, he held up a hand—God, he had huge hands, with long, supple fingers—and pointed past the entry hall to the stairs. "I'll show you the studio."

Slinging her gym bag over her arm, Margo picked up her wineglass, and the sudden cold on her fingertips made her nipples peak against her soft, cowl-neck sweater. He tipped his head, his lids lowered, and she knew he saw, but he was gentleman enough not to mention it. Polite boy next door, just as Lorie had said.

The second level had three bedrooms, a bathroom, and a montage of pictures adorning the long hallway wall.

"Are these all *your* photos?" Her wine sloshed slightly in her glass as she pointed. "They're beautifully done."

Good God, the man blushed. It was adorable. "My sisters are a bunch of hams, always wanting their pictures taken."

She counted four women about his age, all gorgeous and petite, and surrounded by varying numbers of children, husbands, and animals. There were also three shots of a stunning lady dressed in a flowing caftan cavorting amid long meadow grasses. Margo leaned in to study the trio of photos.

"That's my mom."

Margo felt her jaw drop. "You're kidding."

He rolled his eyes. "I know the pictures are . . . unusual, but she wanted me to take something special for her new lover—"

"The milkman?" She didn't mean to be funny; she was astounded, and by more than the milkman legend.

But Dirk laughed, a hearty sound she felt in her chest. "Naw. My dad made her dump the milkman after I was born."

Certainly none of his sisters were of his same behemoth proportions.

"My dad died of a bad heart about three years ago, but my mom met this great guy, and she wanted to give him some special . . ." His face reddened. "I didn't know how to tell her no." Then he flipped up a hand. "Not that they're *that* sexy." Yet he seemed embarrassed, like a little boy.

Margo studied them once more. They *were* sexy, but not because of the clothing or the poses, nor from anything the photographer had done. Rather, the sensuousness came from the woman herself, as if she'd been thinking of her lover.

"How old is she?"

He shrugged, as if he couldn't figure out why she'd even ask. "Sixty-two. No, wait, she's almost sixty-three."

"She's not sixty-three *until* she's sixty-three." Which is how Margo's mother would think. Her mom certainly wouldn't be thinking about "lovers." According to her, women over fifty didn't even *like* sex. Her mother probably hadn't liked sex before she was fifty, either, when Margo's dad was alive.

"I stand corrected," Dirk said. "Mom would kill me."

"Not that she even looks sixty-two." The photos were gorgeous. Every single one of them, not just his mom, but his sisters and the family, even the family dogs and cats.

Margo wanted him to do that for her. To make her feel beautiful and dazzling in front of the camera, young and alive.

And she planned on giving him a show like no other he'd ever had.

Two

"Well, I'd certainly say you have talent," Margo said at last, indicating the wall of family pictures with a wave.

Dirk didn't quite meet her eye. "Thanks." Then he held out his hand. "Enough of my family."

Her perusal of his photos made him self-conscious, as if he were uncomfortable with receiving approval. Artists could be touchy, she knew, and his photography was definitely an art. His loving touch had made a magnificent array of family photos.

Her hand in his, she let him guide her up the spiral staircase to his loft. Large hands, warmth. She'd never been a woman who needed pampering, but it was somehow sensual being taken care of by such a big man. Her high heels clicked on the metal stairs, and he ducked his head to avoid a rafter as he pulled her up into the surprisingly spacious room.

Margo dropped her bag by the railing. Good Lord, what a setup. Lights, camera, action.

In the loft's far corner, next to a cast-iron potbelly stove, he'd arranged a vanity with mirror and lights, presumably for his models to make themselves up, and a screen behind which they could change. Outfitted with two backdrops, one blue, one black, he'd created separate settings for the actual photographs. Surrounding both were several light stands, each fitted with umbrellas to direct the lighting from the sides and overhead. Shiny silver and gold inserts inside the umbrellas would cast the model with different shades of coloring. A complicated digital camera topped a tripod, and an impressive array of lenses and other technical-looking equipment were laid out on a table. The black backdrop was graced with a classy burgundy chaise lounge, and before the blue, he'd set a single wooden barstool.

For a moment, she could only stare at that chaise. She was going to get naked for this man. Right now, right here. He'd see every flaw. What had been a naughty fantasy would soon be reality.

She wanted to do this. She just needed to . . . calm down, talk about something else because she refused to let him know she was nervous. What better way than pouring on admiration for his impressive setup? "No fooling. You *are* a photographer."

"No fooling." He moved farther into the room so he didn't have to stoop beneath the sloped, raftered ceiling.

"How long have you been doing this?"

"About five years. I've got some of my stuff on stock photo sites." He flashed her that dimple, looking boyishly proud. "I received my first royalty check a couple of months ago."

"So you're making a living at it. That's cool. Making your dreams come true in life is the most important thing."

He glanced up, in the process of lighting two candles on a small carved oak table by the divan. A peach scent perfumed the air. She couldn't read his expression—assessing maybe, gauging the veracity of her compliments.

Taking her wineglass, he set it within easy reach of the chaise. "Far from making enough to pay the mortgage." Yet the blue of his eyes intensified. "Someday, though."

"So what do you do for a living now?" she asked, then immediately regretted the question. It was too personal.

But he gave her a smile. "Nothing of much consequence." And thus forgave her intrusion.

Really, she didn't want to know anything more about him. This was a hot interlude between strangers. Something she could trot out of her memory banks years from now and say, "I took a risk. And God, was it worth it." That was all she wanted.

"We can begin with you on the stool and work to the lounge."

At least he was starting her out easy. "That's fine."

"Let's do some test shots to make sure the lighting's okay."

He positioned her, seating her on the barstool, his hands in her hair, fluffing it, tilting her chin, fitting the cowl neck of her sweater just so. His body heat seeped through the wool of her skirt, and rather than frighten her, his light touches set her blood on simmer. When he stroked away strands of hair that had wisped across her cheek, she wanted to lean into his palm.

"Tilt your head." His voice whispered across her hair as he tapped her temple. Then he squatted beside her, flaring her skirt around the stool, fingers brushing gently.

He rose to survey his work. "Perfect."

His words made her *feel* perfect, even if he was only referring to his own arrangement of her body.

Removing the camera from the tripod, he held it to his eye rather than looking at her on the viewfinder. He clicked off pictures, murmuring instructions as he did so, then finally held the camera away and looked at what he'd taken.

"Hmm." He grimaced. "The silver's too harsh. Better if we use one gold and no silver." He tore a couple of the colored Velcroed panels from inside the umbrella lights. "Okay, now lean over the stool like a World War Two pinup girl."

She smiled as she posed like Betty Grable. Bracing her elbows on the seat, she gazed over her shoulder at him.

He smiled his approval. "You're a natural."

Her heart beat overtime. She loved his compliments. But could she bare all? Margo closed her eyes, the whir of the camera lulling her as she imagined removing her clothes. Lying down on the chaise lounge. Touching herself. For him.

And her panties were drenched. God, yes. He was big, he was hot, and his throwback features fascinated her in a way she'd never have thought possible. Even his age was a turn-on. She'd always been attracted to suave, sophisticated, older, charming. But this man was blatantly male, all caveman style.

For once, she wanted to step out of her comfort zone. She never had to do it again, but this time, she wouldn't let her fears get in the way. After all, no one but she and Dirk would ever know.

"The lighting's just right. Do you want a look?"

She came out of her reverie to find him holding the camera out to
her. "No," she said. "I trust you."

She did. He wouldn't touch her unless she asked. He wouldn't
steal her pictures and disseminate them on the Internet. The assur-
ance didn't come just from Lorie's good opinion. It was the way he
blushed when she admired his photos. His laughter when he talked
about his sisters and mom. The slight mist in his eyes when he said
his dad had passed on.

"I'm ready for a close-up, Mr. Director." She batted her lashes.

He chuckled. "I'm no DeMille. And you're a helluva lot prettier
than Gloria Swanson even in her heyday."

She loved that he knew the line was reminiscent of *Sunset Boule-
vard*. She liked it even better that he'd thrown her a compliment so
easily, as if he really meant it.

"Now get on the divan and show me that beautiful leg." A small,
wholly male smile creased his lips, and a hot light blazed in his
shockingly blue eyes. "And keep the shoes on."

Back-seamed thigh-highs and lacy thong panties, that was all she
wore under the calf-length skirt. In her fantasies, she'd revealed the
sexy lingerie one bit at a time, not a striptease so much as leisurely
dropping her barriers.

Margo put the sole of one pump on the burgundy chaise, slowly
raised the skirt to her knee, then bent over to slide her hand down
her calf, smoothing the seam of her stocking straight. The camera
clicked beneath Dirk's finger.

"Are you sure you've never done this before?" he asked.

"Only in my fantasies," she answered, her voice husky.

Christ, she was hot. He hadn't expected that. He hadn't cared.
He'd needed the technical exercise to ready himself for the competition, but he'd also wanted the pleasure of a lady's company, the
eroticism of taking her picture as she lay naked for him. He hadn't
wanted a model, he'd wanted a real woman whose beauty wasn't
manufactured as if she were a commodity to be sold. He worked in
the entertainment industry, where sometimes the only real thing

about a woman was her breast enhancements. Though that was a
pretty shitty thing to think. In his career, he was just as shallow and
self-absorbed as the women he met. It was the bane of the business.
You were an object, not a person. You could never be yourself. Which
was why he wanted someone real for this session. A real woman was
a beautiful creature in all her incarnations, no matter her hair length,
eye color, facial structure, size, or age, as long as she *felt* beautiful.
True beauty was strictly attitude.

This lady had it all, with a tantalizing hint of vulnerability in her
gaze.

"Take a sip of wine," he murmured, "and wet your lips."

She leaned over, giving him a sweet view of her ass. When she
turned back, her red lipstick shone lush and rich with the shimmer of
wine.

"Now look at me while you pull the skirt high enough to give
me a taste of thigh."

She raised the fabric to the tops of her stockings, baring lace but
no skin. Holy hell, a woman of surprises, all elegant business on the
outside, but underneath, luscious lingerie. Blond hair past her shoulders, small breasts, toned muscles, and a pert ass, she was ageless to
him. With a slight tilt to her nose, green eyes, and sculpted cheekbones, she was one fine lady.

"Perfect."

She smiled, then stroked a hand beneath the skirt to her butt, the
wool covering the act, but affording the camera a provocative hint.

He hadn't specified in the ad, but he'd been looking for someone
older. The taut skin and natural beauty of younger women came
across well through the lens, but somehow they lacked confidence.
As if they weren't sure of their inner beauty as much as the outer
trappings. Older women's sense of style shone through. They'd accepted who they were, had gotten past their inhibitions, and came
across the camera with grace.

"Smile for me again."

He wanted a picture of that smile. It lit her face, showed the hint
of laugh lines at her eyes, her mouth. She laughed a lot, perhaps

frowned a little, a woman who'd lived her life. Another reason he wanted to photograph a real woman versus a paid model. No Botox, no surgery.

"Lie down," he whispered, and she obeyed.

His heart beat faster as she spread herself out on the divan, one high-heeled shoe on the floor, her skirt primly covering her knees as she flung her hands above her head. She fluttered her eyelashes coquettishly. "How's this?" she asked.

"Perfect." Her small breasts—ones he'd figured for the real thing—thrust high against her sweater, her nipples hard beneath the soft wool. If she was wearing a bra, it was thin, maybe lacy. He snapped a shot.

"More?" she queried with a sexy rise to her brow. She didn't wait for him to answer, tugging on the skirt, bunching the material in her fingers, raising it slowly, teasing the camera.

The black stockings were sheer, her legs toned. She'd cared for herself without going overboard. The lace of her thigh-high appeared, then creamy skin, and finally a black satin thong.

"Are you going to take a picture?"

He met her pretty green eyes. She was laughing at him. He had to laugh at himself. She had him mesmerized.

"Maybe I should start worrying that you're a pervert."

"Of course I'm a pervert. I advertised for a woman to do nasty things for my camera." The most beautiful thing in the world was a woman in ecstasy. He'd wanted to capture the sight. But he was still a pervert. "I swear I'm harmless, though."

He could only imagine what Lorie had said about him. She was a kicker, always teasing him, about his height, his size, his career choice. He was thankful she hadn't scared Margo away.

Again Margo raised the sexy brow and let her eye travel the length of him. It was almost a touch the way that look made his cock jump. He'd known he'd get hot watching, just not *this* hot, where he'd forget to grab the shot.

"I'm going to show the other leg, so don't miss this time."

He sensed that his fascination put her at ease. Or maybe it was the fact that she enjoyed knowing how attractive he found her. He still couldn't believe she'd understood that photography wasn't a hobby to him, but a dream. He'd longed for a woman who would believe in his dream and his ability to achieve it. Most of the people he knew thought he was crazy to consider giving up his lucrative career for taking pictures. Then again, "taking pictures" was a close reminder of the paparazzi, who, while they were disdained, could also make or break a career.

He raised the camera and for once didn't like the distance it put between him and his subject. She gave him a tantalizing satin-thong view, reveling in the power of a desirable woman, which was exactly what he wanted to encapsulate on camera.

Without prompting, she turned over and tucked the skirt to her waist. One foot firmly on the floor and a knee on the chaise, she leaned forward on her hand, revealing her gorgeous ass in the barely there thong. The woman had excellent taste in lingerie. Then she rose, her blond hair tumbling around her shoulders, skirt falling to cover her, and stretched like a cat, one arm in the air, fingers kneading as if they were claws.

"I want to get naked," she purred.

This was the woman he'd hoped to release once she stepped in front of the camera. Hot. Ready. As if she were anticipating a man between her legs. It hadn't taken her long to feel the lure of being naughty for an inanimate object.

He was so damn hard he needed a slug of beer to cool off. He positioned his camera back on the tripod.

"I have something I want you to wear."

She startled, as if she'd forgotten there was a man behind the lens. Turning, she held her arms across her abdomen, looked down, realized the defensive posture, and dropped it. She wasn't quite as assured as she'd like him to think.

Opening a drawer of the vanity, he pulled out his prize.

"What"—she pointed, coming closer—"is that?"

"A corset."

She laughed. He was beginning to get that she laughed when she was a tad nervous. "You mean like a *real* corset?" She put out a hand to touch the fabric, then one of the stiff bones.

"I want you to wear it."

She tipped her head and eyed him, a taste of a smile at the corners of her mouth. "Is this some sort of fetish thing?"

"There's something sexy about a garment that a woman needs a man to help her get in"—he raised a brow—"and out of."

She snorted out a little puff of air. "She doesn't need a *man,* just a maid." She said it with the slightest edge and had him wondering about her *real* life.

"Consider me your servant for the time being." He unfolded it as far as the bottom laces would allow. "Game?"

"Isn't it hard to breathe with one of these things on?"

"I won't lace it that tight."

She clucked her tongue softly. "It's kinky."

He chuckled. "Hell, asking you over here is kinky." He itched to lace her up. He could do it without touching skin, but she'd be close, so close. Just achieving something different on camera had been his original intention, but now, the idea of her sweet body in the corset had become a need, the ultimate in sexy.

The camera would adore her figure, her waist tiny, her breasts small but plumped by the corset's stays.

Easing her in front of the vanity mirror, he stood behind her, her body heat a hair's breadth between them. Then he leaned in to whisper, "Take off your clothes."

She swallowed, her throat tensing in the reflection. Then she reached down, grabbed the hem of her sweater, pulled it over her head, and tossed it aside. Her hair settled back around her shoulders in a sexy muss. Her scent, sweet shampoo and fruity body lotion, rose up. He almost closed his eyes to breathe her in, then he looked in the mirror.

Holy hell. Her breasts beneath the black lace bra were everything he could have hoped for.

"Perfect," he whispered.

Her nipples beaded. He knew it was what she needed to hear

when her fingers went to the back of her skirt. He held her gaze in the mirror as the light rasp of her zipper filled the air, then she dropped the skirt and kicked it aside.

Her stomach was slightly rounded, there was a dimple or two in her skin that she probably hated. She had a nipped-in waist and a flare to her hips that might not have been the height of fashion in a world that demanded no woman should bear a single extra ounce. She was his ideal.

"The corset's going to love your curves," he whispered. Her breath whooshed out as if she'd been waiting for his approval.

Her eyes on his in the mirror, she undid the front clasp of her bra, shrugged, and the lacy confection fell to the carpet. Clad only in her satin thong, thigh-highs, and heels, she stole his breath.

He held the corset in front of her. The flower print on a cream background enhanced her skin. She glowed with vitality.

"Just step into it." He'd left the bottom laces in the eyeholes so that he wouldn't have to fiddle once she held the garment to her. Taking the two edges from him, she put one foot through the laces, the round curve of her ass coming perilously close to his cock.

"Hold it at your waist so I can thread the rest of the loops and tighten it."

She looked at him in the mirror. "Have you ever done this?"

"No. But the salesgirl said to lace it like a tennis shoe."

"Hah. So now I'm an old shoe." Her laugh was genuine, but again he recognized that touch of vulnerability.

"Not old and not a shoe." He stopped to give her body a long, savoring look. "A sexy woman."

"Darn tooting," she whispered, then held the corset around her at the waist as he began threading the holes.

He felt almost clumsy as his fingers brushed the skin at the base of her spine, just above her ass. Her body heat almost singed. The scent of her lotion wafted up, and something else, a faint aroma of woman, a touch of arousal.

She shivered.

"Are you cold?" He'd stoked the wood-burning stove earlier, and he was toasty. She, however, was damn near naked.

"No, it's fine." Her cheeks deepened their rosy tint.

The shiver had nothing to do with room temperature, and everything to do with bare skin. Looking down to the gape of the undone corset, he found her nipples hard, pearled. "I can put on another log," he said as he pulled the laces together.

She sucked in a breath, then let it out slowly. "No, really." Then she laughed softly. "I'm hot enough."

He allowed himself a smile at her obvious pun.

He laced another couple of loops, and her skin's warmth began to seep through the material. "The fit will get tight now."

"I've heard that a tight fit is a good thing."

Oh yeah, she was getting into it with him. He'd imagined touching her like this, soft, accidental caresses. He'd imagined himself with a hard-on as she fell into the heat of arousal. But he'd never considered how badly he'd need to be a part of it, not just an observer, but a participant. Her skin was smooth, soft to the touch. Her scent made his mouth water. He brushed aside her hair, baring her shoulders, though the length wasn't at all in the way of the laces. He simply craved a touch.

Four eyelets left, he tightened. She gasped.

"Too tight? Can you breathe?"

"I'm okay. It's just"—she tipped her head to one side—"it feels good in an odd way, makes you stand straighter."

Another eyehole, and the corset plumped her breasts. Though barely covering her nipples, it effectively hid them from view. Too bad. "A couple more laces, can you handle it?"

"I'll let you know when you've done it all the way up."

He threaded and pulled, but with none of the strength Mammy had used on Scarlett in *Gone With the Wind*.

Tying the laces off with a neat bow, he stepped back. In the mirror, the effect was perfect. Her enticing breasts plumped above the lace edging of the corset. Cinching in her waist, the bones gave a luscious flare to her hips. Over her flattened abdomen, the point in the front arrowed down to her black satin thong. The globes of her delectable ass begged for his touch, and the back-seamed thigh-highs were a sexual hedonist's fantasy. Her blond hair had fallen to frame the upper swell of her breasts. He raised his gaze to her green eyes. The artist in him needed to photograph her like that, while the man in him wanted to bend her over the vanity and bury his cock in her.

"So how's the fit?"

She drew in a shallow breath, her breasts rising. "Just don't make me run or try to touch my toes." She smoothed a hand down her stomach. "But I like it. Though you can certainly see why the women didn't eat much at their big galas." Grinning at the mirror, she added, "But it makes me feel sexy."

But could she make herself come for him? More than anything, Dirk wanted to capture her face aglow with ecstasy.

Turning this way, then that, she cupped her breasts, plumping them higher. Reaching around her, Dirk gave a slight tug on the bottom, and the tops of her nipples peeped out. It was the ideal combination of gentle lady and sexy woman.

How had he gotten so lucky? Margo was more than any woman he could have fantasized.

Three

"Did you bring makeup?"

Margo pointed at her bag she'd dropped by the stairs. Grabbing it, Dirk set it on the vanity stool. She bent straight-backed, which was all the tightly laced corset would allow, and pulled out a small cosmetics kit.

"We need some of that blush stuff," he said.

She thought her cheeks were fine, but Margo retrieved the powder and brush. Dirk looked first at the compact, then at the brush, glanced at her, and smiled that wickedly handsome smile.

"What are you planning?" Whatever it was, she had a feeling she'd like it.

"Look in the mirror and watch."

Behind her, his body barely touched hers, yet his heat turned her wet on the inside. The fleeting caress of his fingers as he'd laced her up had driven her mad. His arms bracketing her, he opened the blusher compact with one hand, then powdered up the brush with the other.

So big, so warm. In the mirror, standing behind her, his arms around her, he was massive. Despite her high heels, he was still a head taller. He could crush her completely with one big bear hug, yet every stroke, every caress had been slow, gentle, like a lion playing with a mouse.

If he were a mere five years younger than her, she might have . . . Margo stopped herself. No "might haves." This was a lark, a naughty interlude. Her best friend would freak if Margo even thought about dating—or anything else—Lorie's much, *much* younger brother's buddy.

Then the brush caressed the visible aureole above the corset, and she forgot about Dirk's age. She bit her lip to trap the moan in her throat.

"The camera loves deep color," he murmured, bending to his task.

He smelled like soap and yeasty beer. All bubble and fizz around her. She wanted to melt against him. In the light of the vanity lamps, his features were growing on her. He was, in fact, eminently doable. Not that Margo intended to go *that* far. Why, she hadn't even brought condoms. Making herself come while he watched was the ultimate in safe sex, next only to celibacy.

Yet what he did to her nipples was so completely erotic, the soft stroke of the brush back and forth. Then he lowered his head to blow the excess powder away. Oh Lord. There was such a thing as spontaneous combustion. She could shudder to climax with nothing more than the shush of his breath across her nipple.

Then, brush and compact in midair, his gaze caught on the sight of her nipples in the mirror, and his lips formed the word *perfect*.

One simple word burned away Richard's accusations. She *could* take risks, let herself go, revel in her sexuality. The feeling was like a drug. It wouldn't last, but for that moment, Margo didn't give a damn. For now, her doubts evaporated like steam out of a hot springs.

"Shall we get started?"

God, yes. This hot, gorgeous man would get the pleasure of watching her make herself come. "The chair or the stool first?"

With a finger at her elbow, he guided her to the stool. "Let's do the pinup girl pose again."

In the mirror, except for the tops of her nipples above the corset, she'd appeared almost decently dressed. But now, hands balanced on the stool, her thighs were bare above the stockings and her ass cheeks were naked but for the tiny thong.

He tapped the back of her knee to adjust one leg, setting her high heels a few inches apart. "Lean on your elbows."

Margo laughed, the corset restricting even that to a mere giggle. "I cannot bend over any further in this thing." As it was, the point rested snugly against her tummy. Any more, and it would dig. The edging chafed her nipples when she shifted, and a shiver of pleasure coursed through her. Even a slight movement was like a caress. She was hot and wet, and it didn't help that he kept touching her, changing her position with a stroke of his hand, the tip of a finger.

"Do you want me to loosen the corset?"

"No." Then she realized how quickly the answer shot out of her mouth. "I mean, I'm fine." More than fine. "It's actually very erotic, the way it moves on my breasts, how sensitive it makes them." Then she blushed for having revealed so much. Yet the binding made her aware of every breath, every bit of skin, even the shift of air currents over her body when he moved.

He snapped photos, tilted her head, placed her hair just so across her shoulder blade, clicked a few more times, and on and on. He was here, there, everywhere. In constant motion, he directed her, talked to her, praised her, photographed her, and turned her into a bowl of jelly. His scent intoxicated her, the room got hotter, and Margo got wetter.

"Perfect." His favorite word. He probably said it to all his models.

"Shall we move to the chaise now?" He indicated with the lens of his camera. "And have a sip of wine. You must be thirsty." Like an eager little boy, he held out the glass.

The ice had melted in the sweet white wine, yet hadn't diluted the flavor. She felt the sip all the way down, just as she felt the lick of his gaze along her throat. The corset forced her to bend at the hips to set the glass back on the table, and when she sat, she had to dip at the knees to avoid being impaled by the bones.

"Why don't you recline?" he suggested.

She lay back and was suddenly eye to eye, so to speak, with his jeans. Good Lord. She was parched again. The man was hard. Like the rest of his body, his erection was sized accordingly.

He was as turned on as she was.

She put one arm above her head, the corset shifting over her throbbing nipples. Leaning in to place her hair along her collarbones, he whispered, "Don't worry. I'm not going to take advantage. I just can't help it when I look at you."

It didn't matter if he was feeding her bullshit lines. All that mattered was the illusion. He found her attractive. She got him hard. She didn't care about anything else. It was all she'd really come here for tonight.

"I'm fine. Take your pictures. Pose me the way you want."

He breathed her in, as if her scent would somehow help him put together the ultimate photograph. She couldn't remember if Richard had ever been that sensual. Perhaps it was the fact that Dirk was a photographer. He saw things other men didn't.

He backed off, took his pictures, a flurry of them, and was back again, on his haunches at her side. "Sit up."

With the corset binding her, forcing her spine straight, she couldn't roll up and had to hold his hand as he pulled her. Then she still had to lean back on her palms because it pushed into her belly. She knew there was a proper way to sit, but she certainly hadn't mastered it in less than half an hour. "How did women live with these things?" she mused aloud.

"I would assume they never got down in a prone position."

"They sure couldn't get back up again. So much for all those romance novels where the heroine gets done with all her clothes on." She couldn't believe she'd said that, yet with him, the idea of getting done in the corset was extremely appealing.

Her pulse rate shot to the top of the charts as he gave her that special devil smile. "I wouldn't have figured you for a romance woman."

"I love romance." Historicals were her favorite at the moment. And what did it mean that she wasn't a "romance woman"?

"I can see that." He had her set one high-heeled foot on the carpet. "But I would say you make your own romance rather than read about it." He tapped her knee to get her to cross her legs, and his touch lingered a second longer than necessary.

His little caresses enticed her to beg for more. It took her a moment to formulate an answer. "Thanks for the compliment, but that's like saying you know everything so you don't need to read to learn anything new."

"Not a know-it-all. Just a woman with a fertile imagination and a huge sense of adventure." He smoothed the seam along the back of her calf.

She almost lost her train of thought. Again. "Another compliment. Thank you." During their last fight, Richard asserted she had *no* sense of adventure. He was always coming up with kinky ideas, and she was always finding a reason why they wouldn't work.

"Hey, where'd you go?"

She realized Dirk had been snapping off pictures while she ruminated over Richard. She wondered what he'd see when he looked through the photos again.

"Sorry. Daydreaming." Pondering regrets. Perhaps answering Dirk's ad hadn't been so much about showing Richard that what he said wasn't true, but about showing herself that she could change. She was capable of taking a few chances.

"Tell me what you were daydreaming," Dirk cajoled, the camera to his eye, making it less personal than sitting in a café telling your best friend why your relationship failed.

Suddenly Margo wanted, needed to unburden herself of the secret she'd carried all these months. Dirk was a stranger. He wouldn't judge. Or if he did, all she had to do was walk away. It was like telling a psychiatrist, but without the expense. "My boyfriend answered an online personal ad."

The clicking silenced. "You've got a boyfriend?"

"We broke up a year ago."

Her answer seemed a tension release, and he shifted on the carpet in front of her, catching her from new angles. "Go on."

"This ad was for the two of us." She paused a beat, her cheeks heating. "To find another couple for some mild kinky stuff." She'd been freaked at first, but they had fantasized different scenarios during sex play before. It gave her some of her best orgasms. So she'd agreed. "Except the couple turned out to be our neighbors."

"How very coincidental," he murmured.

"I swear it, in the entire Bay Area, the couple advertising for

exhibitionist sex lived around the corner." Could you get more bizarre? It was one thing to get kinky with strangers, another to
broadcast your proclivities to the neighborhood.

"Busted. How awful," Dirk said with a British accent.

"We only e-mailed with them, and I don't think they figured it
out. They gave a few more personal details than we did." Her natural
hesitancy, which had irritated Richard, too.

"Well, well, Miss Margo, I'm shocked you'd consider doing such
a naughty thing." The camera didn't hide his dimple. Laughter
threaded through his voice. "And get caught at it."

She snorted lightly. "You're not shocked."

"You're a very dirty girl."

Margo bit her lip, trying to stifle her own answering smile. Good
Lord. His teasing felt good. Liberating.

"What about your boyfriend?"

She shrugged, remembering Richard's disgust with her nervousness. "He said we couldn't be sure it was them"—she'd been 99 percent
positive—"but he didn't think it was such a big deal even if it was. He
wanted to go ahead with it." She shifted, the corset suddenly too binding, digging into her stomach. "He was upset when I backed out."

Richard blamed it on her anxieties, called it an excuse to give in
to her fears. Yet the idea of having sex in front of strangers, of watching them, had all been so titillating. She'd wanted to try. She just
didn't want anyone to *know* she'd ever do anything like that. Margo
also suspected that Richard found the wife attractive—prettier
than Margo, more fit, with larger breasts, and younger—and was
disappointed he wouldn't get the opportunity to see the couple
make love.

"And that was the beginning of the end," Dirk finished.

"It *was* the end." Richard had had enough of her so-called anxieties. He left, and soon after, he'd found Katrina, who surely did every
kinky thing he wanted.

"Lucky for me, then, or you wouldn't be here." Dirk didn't let her
stew about it. "So get kinky for me now, sweet Margo. Show off a
little of that sexy body." He winked. "Show off a lot of it." Going

down on one knee, he slipped the shoe off her heel and let it dangle from her toes.

He couldn't know how good his words were. Months of angst melted away. She hadn't sought his approval. It was simply that the man took her revelation in stride, as if it were nothing out of the ordinary. As if both her kinky side and her anxieties were equally acceptable. As much as she loved Lorie, Margo feared she wouldn't have gotten the same easy reaction.

He went on without a clue of what he'd just done for her. "I like the look." His gaze trailed up her leg. "Give me a sultry little moue."

Margo laughed. It felt so damn good. "What *is* a sultry little moue?"

Standing back, he puckered his lips and sucked in his cheeks.

She would have gone into hysterics if the corset wasn't cinched around her. "You look like a blowfish."

"Then you do it better."

She did, but she felt so silly, she started laughing all over again. All the while, he shot her, one after another.

"You have the most glorious laugh."

"Thank you." She tried to stifle it for the sake of her ribs in the corset. "You don't have to keep complimenting me."

"It's merely an observation."

His observations warmed her beyond measure. "Okay. I'm ready to try my moue again, Mr. DeMille."

"Give me a show, baby."

She tipped her foot and set the shoe in motion, dangling from her toe. Leaning back once more, she moued, and was sure it came off as part laugh, part smile, part blowfish. Yet with him, it didn't matter if she looked ridiculous. He made it fun.

"Now fling the shoe."

She did and squealed when it hit his knee.

"Let me see you remove a stocking."

Slipping the other shoe off, she slowly rolled down the thigh-high, until the corset wouldn't let her bend any further. The camera clicked, and Dirk issued orders, suggestions, murmured encouragement. She lay back and thrust her leg in the air, the only way she could reach to slide the stocking all the way off.

"Beautiful."

It probably gave him a great view of her satin thong, but Margo was amazed at her own dexterity. She didn't think she had it in her. The second stocking went the way of the first, and she lay back to catch her breath.

He was at her side, his hip next to hers. "That deserves a drink." He held the wine to her lips.

"You forgot the cheese and grapes to ply me with."

"I'm such a shitty host."

He was, in a word, perfect.

He held up the glass. "Mind if I taste?"

"Of course not."

He took a long swallow. "It's good," he said. "Sweet. Just the way I think you'd taste."

Her skin flushed. She imagined him tasting her lips, her nipples, between her legs. Lord. "It's one of my favorites."

He smiled. "I want to see you in just the corset."

Without her thong? She felt the heat in his gaze from her fingertips to her toes.

Oh yes, without her thong.

Four

She'd gone to the mirror to check her lipstick and fluff her hair before they started another round of photos. Dirk realized she'd needed a few moments to ready herself. Now she sauntered to his side by the chaise, the sexiest sway to her hips, a seductive smile, and a fire in her green eyes. He loved a woman who could let her sexuality loose when it suited her.

He also loved a woman with a kinky streak, even if she had a few anxieties over it. It made him hot that she'd confided her presumably terrible secret, especially since he'd gotten the sense she'd never told anyone. It tripped an odd protective instinct that he didn't know he had, the desire simply to validate who she was. *Hey, no big deal, baby, you're normal, you're fine.* It took her from being a sexy model to a woman with emotions and a need he could fulfill.

"You should take a picture while I dispense with my thong." She saluted him with her glass, sipped, then set it down.

"I intend to, sweetheart." The endearment slipped off his tongue as he backed off, the camera to his eye. "You have a delectable ass." He wanted to stroke his cock down the crease.

"Thank you." She gave him a brief little moue. And it in no way resembled a blowfish. A woman's sense of humor was another thing that attracted him.

"Now take it off, sweetheart."

Her back to him, a hint of bare flesh peeped through the corset lacings. She slipped her fingers into the thong riding high on her hips. Pushing the satin down, she cupped her bottom, spreading her cheeks the barest amount. Then the thong slid free and fell to the carpet. With the camera in continuous mode, he captured every moment rather than single shot. Sometimes you wanted time to set up every photo precisely; others, you didn't want to miss a thing. The difference between the slow rolling down of her stockings versus the fall of her panties.

Then she climbed on the chaise on all fours and, one hand on her ass, glanced at him over her shoulder. Yeah, single shot required for this.

"Stay like that." He closed in on her, positioning her chin until the lights hit at the right angle. Then he laid her hair across her shoulder, the fine strands like silk in his fingers. He wanted to touch, hold. Instead he backed off.

The pink lips of her pussy peeked out at him. "Too fucking hot," he whispered, and even through the viewfinder, he saw her eyes widen. "Sorry."

"I like it." There was the tiniest trace of shock in her gaze, as if she hadn't recognized the full value of dirty talk before. And was shocked that it made her hot. He immortalized every nuance.

She rolled down to her side, one knee up to cover the bare essentials, elbow supporting her, cheek resting on her fist. The peak of her nipples glowed above the corset's trimming, her breasts plumped and full. Yet there was a hint of the boning causing her to hold herself more stiffly than was natural.

"Do you want me to get you out of the corset now?"

Her gaze shifted down to her chest. "No." Then back to him. "My nipples tingle whenever I move." She drew a lock of hair back and forth across the visible upper half of an aureole. "It's a very erotic garment." Her mouth lifted in the barest of smiles. "Which is why you chose it." She fluttered her lashes. "Are you sure you've never dressed a woman in a corset before?"

His mouth went dry watching her, and his finger clicked the shutter release as if he'd had an involuntary muscle spasm. "This is a first," he said, "both erotic photos and the corset."

She laughed. "Ooh, I'd never thought I'd be a man's first."

It would also be a first if he came just through the act of photographing her. Yet he was damn near that hard. "I've never had the pleasure of being a woman's first either."

"This is my first," she whispered, and he lowered the camera to drink in the sight of her with his naked eye.

He wondered if any woman would give him the same reaction, but an innate sense told him no. There was something about *her.*

She slid her hand from her knee to her thigh, then dipped down between her legs where he couldn't see. "Have you ever photographed a woman down here?"

Her sweet, delectable pussy, of which he'd gotten a rear view. "No." The word came out a bit strangled. He'd never before been so enthralled by a woman. Instead of fighting, he simply went with the feeling. "Show me."

She slowly drew up her leg, revealing a dusting of curls darker than her hair. This was no longer about winning a contest or gaining national attention for his work. It was about her. For the first time in his artistic life, he actually wanted to set down his camera, yet the photos simply flowed through him as if he were channeling them.

One step, two, then he was down on one knee for her close-up. Moisture glistened on the pink folds, beckoning him to taste. Yet he kept physical distance even if he couldn't sustain full emotional distance. He was no longer a photographer.

And she was the sexiest of God's creations.

"You're wet." He memorized every drop from afar. "Does the camera turn you on?" Or was it him?

"The pictures make it hotter." She licked her lips, her gloss shimmering. He captured that, too.

Then, his eye to the viewfinder, his lens on her, he reached down and cupped his cock. "It turns me on." And he let her see the rigid outline in his jeans, encapsulating another moment in her journey, his journey.

"All men are very visual, not just photographers." She drew her knee higher, parting her legs wider, giving him not only the sight, but the musky scent of her arousal.

"*You* turn me on, not just the photos."

"You say that to all the girls." She played with the hem of the corset, teasing him with her fingers' proximity to her pussy.

Dirk slowly raised his gaze, traveling over her abdomen, her nipples, and finally to her eyes. "It's not the photos, the camera, or the situation." He tipped his head back, eyes closed, and arched, his jeans binding his cock. "It's you."

And Margo wanted to do anything for him. Everything. There would never be another night like tonight. He was twelve years younger, a flawless male specimen, yet he wanted her. His eyes fairly glowed with blue heat as he dropped his head down once more. She lay back against the chaise and preened, her legs slightly spread, giving him a look but not a full shot.

He snapped a photo of what he could.

Her ego needed this. This adventure was more than getting over her anxieties. Her self-worth had been trashed, and she'd lost her belief in her own desirability.

With a look, Dirk had given it all back, and she didn't give a damn that it was an illusion. Life was an illusion; you just determined whether you wanted to see through it or not.

Then he said the unthinkable, the thing she needed. "Touch yourself for me."

The reverent hush in his voice seduced her. She'd always been a foreplay girl. Doing this for Dirk, a big, wholly masculine stranger with a massive hard-on for her, made it all the more potent. She smoothed a hand over her chest, and pinched a nipple. She moaned into it, hips rising. Then her hand traveled downward, and through the slits of her eyes, she watched him as she burrowed her fingers into her pussy.

He never stopped photographing, never stopped watching, and she grew wetter under the camera's keen eye. Parting her folds, she touched her clitoris. A hard, aching nub, she rubbed it. God, what else should she do? What would look the hottest?

What would make him go wild? Because, to quote his ad, she wanted *him* completely undone.

"Close your eyes, pretend you're alone." His voice enthralled her. "Show me what you'd do. Let it all go."

She did, but she never lost awareness of him in her mind, watching her, desiring her, getting hard for her. The biggest part of what she wanted and needed was *him*.

The overhead light beat down on her, heating her skin. She fell into sound and sensation, the soft click of the camera, his subtle moves about the chaise, the scent of man, soap, the peach candle, the lingering taste of wine on her lips, and the rhythm of her fingers on her own flesh.

"That's beautiful, gorgeous," he murmured encouragement.

She was slippery with her own juices, and she arched into her hand. The corset hugged her, restrained her, yet its tight binding added to the intensity. She moaned, dipped a finger inside, back out, around her clit, then straight on.

She was so wet, hot, and behind her closed lids, she imagined his touch joining hers, rough male fingers caressing her. She was barely conscious of the sounds she made, soft moans, sighs, her voice catching in her throat, a light pant—the only thing the corset allowed—as she drew herself higher.

God, she wanted a cock inside her. Big, hard, warm, hitting deep, forcing her to the pinnacle. His mammoth cock.

"Make yourself come for me."

His voice was so hot, husky, needy, she was almost sure she'd imagined it. Just as she imagined his cock driving into her, tasted the salt of his skin, smelled the musk of his come. Her hips rose, undulated as if he were between her thighs.

The explosion hit her without warning, sliding inside her, then shooting out to every nerve ending, and she gave full voice to the ecstasy, crying out, panting, working her fingers to make it last as long as possible. Until suddenly it was too much, overwhelming, a sharp pleasure-pain.

"Damn, that was hot." Setting the camera on the floor, he sat on the chaise by her waist, nothing more than his body heat touching her. "I love the flush on your skin when you come."

She couldn't utter a word. So beyond herself, she didn't even close her splayed legs, letting him look his fill, loving that he did so without hesitation.

"Your face was the most beautiful thing I've ever seen."

He went on feeding her ego, and she lapped it up as she slowly drifted back to normalcy. Or as least as normal as one could be lying naked and prone with a virtual stranger less than an overheated inch from her.

"Need a drink?" He lifted her wine and set it to her lips. She sipped, the light fruity taste quenching.

Then he held the glass, his gaze traveling the length of her body, catching on the sight of her pussy, her spread legs. Slowly, as if he were thinking over each infinitesimal movement, debating, imagining, he stretched out his hand, the glass over her mound. And he tipped it.

Cool wine drizzled over her heated flesh, between her folds, over her clitoris, the sensation so rich, such a contrast of hot and cold, that she almost came again.

Closing her eyes—"Oh God"—the words slipped out as she shivered with the delicious sensation. She barely contained the rest. *Touch me. Lick me. Please. Oh God.*

When she could open her lids, she found herself trapped by his hypnotic gaze. She hadn't planned on physical contact. She'd gotten creamy thinking about how naughty she could be for the camera, but she'd never thought about more. All right, she had, but it was only fantasy.

Yet now . . . his hands . . . those big, delicious hands.

Really, why not? *Come on, Margo, let go, take a risk.*

"I want a special photo," she murmured.

"Tell me." His eyes were like the hottest part of the flame.

"Your hand." Her imagination running rampant, she drew in air as deeply as the corset would allow. "I want it on me."

After setting the wineglass down, he put one big hand on her waist, his heat seeping through the corset. "Where?"

"Between my legs." Her breath caught in her throat, and it had nothing to do with the tight lacing.

He trailed down to the corset's rounded front piece, which pointed directly to the hot spot that ached for his touch.

"Kneel beside me," she went on, "and take a picture of just your hand on me." A shallow bite of air slipped down her throat. "Just my body and your hand."

"From which direction?"

God. The man was definitely an artist at heart. Anyone else would have put his hand between her legs right now. She was glad, though, that he wanted to create the perfect experience.

She pointed above her. "From over my shoulder."

He glanced at her tight nipples fully exposed above the corset. She knew he understood exactly how she wanted it. Her rouged nipples, stomach flat beneath the boning, the tight curls of her mound, and his hand.

As if she were looking through her own eyes. She needed the moment saved, a sight she could have forever.

"Don't move," he said, then his warmth was gone. Turning her head, she relished the ripple of muscles in his arms, back, ass, and thighs as he secured the camera to his tripod, fiddled about with its knobs, then carried it behind the divan. Whipping out his light meter, he tested.

The delay was maddening, yet also enhanced the blood rush to her clitoris. She literally ached, one pulse, two.

Then he was back. "Are you sure?"

Of course not. Then again, in the big scheme of things, what difference did it make whether he touched her? If he licked her? Even if he did her? It wouldn't be the end of the world. What awful, terrible consequence could there be? God wasn't going to strike her dead. Gee, even her mother wouldn't know.

She wanted to try this, with him, taste the experience, feel it. The chance would never come again. "I'm sure."

Dirk went down on one knee beside her, palming the camera's small remote shutter release in his hand. "What exactly does touching mean? I need to know your limits."

Margo blinked, twice, then swallowed.

He realized she wasn't entirely sure, as to her desires or her limits. Still, he had to see her come again. He caught the full glory of her orgasm on digital, yet he'd been farther from it, distanced by the lens. Her own hand giving such pleasure to herself had been overwhelming, taking him almost to the point of implosion himself. Except he hadn't been a part of it, and despite the rules they'd established in the beginning, he wanted to feel the shudders ripple through her body, needed to own her orgasm right along with her. And he wanted to carry the image of his darker hand against her fair skin.

She wet her lips. "Ask. If I don't want it, I'll say no."

It spoke volumes about trust, though she probably didn't recognize it. She believed he'd take no for an answer. She would accept his hand between her legs and trust that he'd stop at just that. Unless she chose more. Oh yeah, the simple words said a helluva lot. Equally important was how much her trust meant to him.

He laid his hand on her abdomen, testing the textures of both corset and bare, deliciously scented flesh. Her arms over her head, she shuddered, spreading her palms across the top of the chaise as if she needed something to hang on to.

"You have very big hands."

"Like the rest of me."

She smiled. "I figured that out."

Splaying his fingers, he headed down to her pubic curls. He used the remote to capture it all on camera. His eyes on hers, he slipped down to palm her mound. He could almost feel her clit pulse. She closed her eyes for a brief moment, then snapped them open and focused on his tanned hand between her thighs.

"Spread your legs a little."

Keeping her knee flush to the chaise, she opened herself to him. He slid farther, cupping her without delving deeper, and her juices dampened his hand. He caught every movement.

"Does it look the way you wanted it to?"

Breath puffed between her lips. "Yes. No." Then she sighed. "It's better. You make me feel so petite."

She *was* petite. Her flesh burned for him. He burned for her. She was beautiful, sexy, imaginative. Given time, he was sure she could take him places he'd never been. But Dirk didn't have time. He had only tonight.

He rubbed her in gentle circles, almost like a trainer settling an excited filly. Her clit was still safely tucked away, untouched but for the light massage of her own pussy lips. She stretched imperceptibly, perhaps straining for more.

"What else do you want?" He was damn near ready to beg.

Her eyelashes fluttered, as she savored the slow roll of his hand, then she raised her gaze to his. "Tease me."

How long could he play without letting her come? How high could he take her? The longer she was on edge, the more spectacular the come.

He'd likely drive himself insane, but what a way to go.

He handed her the remote, realizing that her face wouldn't be on camera, just her body, his hand. Part of him shouted out to change the position, but this was the way she wanted it.

"Watch and push that little button"—leaning over, he put her finger on it—"when you like what you see."

She clicked immediately, immortalizing his expression. "I loved what I saw." Her green eyes fixed on him.

He wasn't concerned about his looks. He knew he was a big ugly lug that women found fascinating simply for his size. He wouldn't win any beauty contests, but he'd never given a damn about that. He figured he was a decent guy on the inside, and that was enough for any woman who was worth it. He'd just never found that special woman in the glittering, objectified world he worked in. Yet Margo's gaze made him feel he was more than he'd ever considered himself to be. As if she'd snapped a picture and found the very core of him.

"Now touch me," she whispered, and he would have done anything for her.

Touching was the simplest act of all. He parted her sweet lips and dipped low to find her creamy and warm. She hummed her pleasure, closed her eyes, arched into his hand, and clicked.

"How many pictures can I take?" She squirmed at his touch.

"As many as you want." This flash card was all hers, and he'd chosen one with a high capacity.

"Good." She smiled, her eyes still closed. "Now get busy."

"Yes, ma'am." It made him hot that she could tease even now. "Like this?" He caressed her clit with a fingertip.

This time she looked at him. "Nice. But not enough."

"I'm just warming up." He shifted close enough to draw in her scent without getting in the way of the camera. Her sweet feminine musk made his mouth water. Her juices covered his fingers. "I need something."

"What?"

She sounded so testy, he smiled. "To lick you off my hand."

At that, her eyes flew open. Her lips parted. She blinked a couple of times as if she couldn't believe he'd consider it. Then, "Yes"—a pause—"I mean, please, be my guest."

Holding her gaze, he rubbed his fingers across his lips, wetting them with her essence. Then he waved them beneath his nose as if he were sampling the bouquet of an expensive wine. Finally, he licked her from his lips. Sweet. Expensive. Intoxicating. She made him drunk with need.

He didn't realize he'd closed his eyes and leaned in until she clicked, the lightest sound of the shutter release most people might not even have heard.

"Ambrosia," he whispered.

Her eyes turned a primal green. "No one's ever done that."

He actually reveled in being the first. "I'm neglecting you." He let the need to make her come take over completely.

He dipped deep inside her, fast, two fingers. She moaned at the unexpected assault and grabbed his arm just as the camera went off again.

He pumped, the heel of his hand working her clit at the same time. He'd planned a lingering rise, but now he wanted her on the edge immediately. A tear leaked from the corner of her eye. He backed off to gently stroke her pussy lips, all around, everywhere but her clit.

"Bastard tease," she muttered, eyes closed. He didn't think she was even aware of the epithet.

"Don't want you to come too soon. You need plenty of time for photographs." He needed plenty of time to raise her to a level where she was ready to come spontaneously, where he could back off and her body would simply orgasm on its own.

He teased her clit, slowly this time, not pushing her too far. Her hips moved against the chaise, and her fingernails sank into his shirtsleeve. She bit her lip, moaned, and he felt a new, lush streak of moisture. Yet he kept the pace slow.

"Did you bring your toy?"

She hummed her answer, accompanied by a nod.

"Is it in your bag?"

"Yes," rushed out with a hiss, as if she were once again impatient with all his questions.

"I want to use it on you."

Her body stilled despite his slow clit massage.

"May I?" Waiting for her answer, he forgot to breathe.

Five

"Yes." Her answer was a soft purr strumming along his cock.

Oh yeah. "I'll get it for us." Then Dirk took her hand and pulled it down between her legs. "Keep stroking yourself. Keep wet. Keep hot. Don't stop"—he pointed—"but don't come yet."

"Yes, Master," she murmured, a teasing light in her gaze.

He licked his finger one last time as she watched, and the light in her eyes turned to smoky green.

Her bag was personal. As the youngest with four older sisters, he'd learned one thing pretty damn quickly, that you *never* touched a woman's bag, be it purse, gym bag, briefcase. But she'd given him tacit permission to rummage.

He riffled through the lingerie she'd brought, satin, silk, lace, a profusion of colors from flower pink to dark purple. He smelled her sweet natural perfume on them, and the textures slid off his fingers like warm silky water. He wanted to rub them all over his face like a lion marking himself with his mate's scent.

He glanced back to find her watching him. Her fingers moved lazily. Then she waved her other hand imperiously. "I'm going to have to speed this up if you don't hurry."

Despite the annoyed tone she affected, he sensed her sudden nervousness. He was leaving her alone too long. Then he found her cold, plastic vibrator. He was so much hotter. Rising, he warmed it in his hands. "Hold it while I move the camera."

She took the toy, but stopped touching herself altogether. "Where are you moving it?" Again, an undercurrent of nerves laced her voice.

He shifted the tripod down the chaise, close to her knees.

"But that'll be just my—" She stopped.

He bent over her, arms bracketing her body. "It'll be you, me, and the vibrator."

He was close enough to kiss her, but he hadn't asked permission for that, and somehow kissing would be going too far. He wasn't sure he could hold himself back from taking more.

He backed off so he could breathe.

She pursed her lips. "I want classy, you know, not porn."

He huffed, pretending offense. "I would never do porn."

She looked along her body, her pert nipples, the corset, her curls, her bent knee, then glanced at the camera and finally at him. A cloud tarnished her forehead for a moment.

"It'll be perfect, I promise." Dirk stroked a single finger down her cheek.

Margo closed her eyes and breathed, once, twice, then focused on him once more. "Yes. I know."

It would have been easier if the vibrator had been sitting on the table next to the wineglass. Then she wouldn't have had time to think. Instead, she would have simply begged. Why the thought of Dirk taking pictures from that angle suddenly bothered her, Margo couldn't say. Except that she'd seen her share of porn movies, and well, she didn't think a close-up of a woman's splayed anatomy was particularly attractive.

Yet Dirk made everything perfect, just as he said. His touch had driven her high on the precipice, so close so quickly. It was in the way he looked at her, the way he saw her.

The remote was in her hand. She was still completely in control. She didn't have to take a picture at all.

Rounding the back of the chaise, he grabbed her wineglass. "I think you need another drink."

She propped herself up to sip, the corset teasing her nipples, and drank deeply. The alcohol hit her toes in a rush, tingling up her legs, then settling in her belly, the exact opposite of what it should have been. And Margo knew it was a release of the tension knotting her insides. Sitting beside her once more, Dirk took the glass, finished the bit left at the bottom, then rolled his lips together to dry them off.

He took hold of her chin. "Look at me."

As she did, he slid the vibrator down her center, wetting it, rubbing her with it, teasing her without the batteries on.

"Is it cold?"

She shook her head. Her body was already warming it.

"I think it's cold." He slid it in his mouth, sucking off her taste. "There, I think it's warm enough now."

God, he was a kinky one. She loved it. She settled back against the chaise, and when he touched her with it, the vibrator was warm, wet from his mouth. He turned the control, setting it to buzz on low. He strummed her clit, and she jerked, her pussy ultrasensitive.

"Was that good or bad?" he asked.

She opened her mouth, breathed, then managed a word. "Good." Intense.

"Perfect." He gave her a glimpse of that adorable dimple, then he went down on the carpet beside her. "You have a gorgeous pussy."

He let the vibrator worship it, sliding the length along her opening, then beneath her clitoris, around, right on. She didn't have a voice to even laugh at his comment. The buzz was light enough to be maddening yet not enough to come. And he never stayed long on her clit. She was sure that was by design.

"You're not taking pictures," he chided. "Do I need to handle the remote as well?"

Her finger acted on its own, almost spasming against the button, as he gave her a higher blast of vibrator. Only a second before turning the speed back down.

"Good girl. I'm sure I can't handle the hard work of fucking you with this and photographing as well."

His dirty talk, his teasing, made her hotter. "Please."

"Please what?"

"More." It was all she could manage.

"More what?"

"Just quit fooling around and fuck me with it, dammit." It didn't even sound like her voice and didn't feel like her words.

"My pleasure." He grinned. She had the presence of mind to capture it.

Then the vibrator was filling her, humming against her walls, in, out. He angled it, hitting that special spot inside and making her rise right off the chaise. She bucked, forcing the vibrator deeper, and she attacked her clitoris, rubbing it in time to his thrusts. She could barely think to hit the camera's button, two tasks at once almost beyond her. His voice flowed over her, a litany of words, encouraging her, urging her to the edge. And she was so close, so very close. Yet . . .

She threw one hand over her head, grabbing the back of the chaise, and fought to catch her breath. "I need you."

"What do you want me to do?" His voice, a question, she could barely hear over the rush of her blood.

"Lick me. Please lick me." She needed the wet of his tongue, the warmth of his mouth. A man's touch. This man.

The vibrator thrummed inside, and oh-yes-thank-you-so-damn-much, he bent his head to her. She looked down, and the sight of this huge man between her legs overwhelmed her.

"More. Please."

He suckled her with his lips, then circled his tongue all around. She twisted her fingers in his hair. The corset bound her tightly, restricting her movements, somehow intensifying each single shift of her body, rubbing the underside of her exposed nipples. The sensations threw her high, then the click, click, click of the camera drove her over the edge until she screamed. She simply came undone for him, her orgasm so hard for so damn long, tears trickled from beneath her tightly closed lids.

Dirk had heard the telltale flicker of the shutter release. He'd wanted to watch her come, but when she'd begged him to lick her, he'd needed the taste of her so much more.

The way she went off, her cries, her moisture flooding his mouth, the tremors coursing her body, he'd felt like a real man. Of course he'd made love to women. He'd enjoyed it, they'd enjoyed it, but with her, it was . . . beyond. He'd given without needing anything but the pleasure of making her feel that good.

Turning the vibrator off and setting it on the carpet, he soothed her legs with his hands, nipped her thigh, kissed her gorgeous little mound.

Her chest rose and fell, her nipples begged for his mouth, and her scent was like a caress along his cock. He ached. Yet the pieces of herself that she'd shared astounded him. Making a woman come with his mouth had never been so powerful.

She flung a hand across her eyes and groaned. "Please say that wasn't me wailing like a banshee."

"It wasn't you wailing like a banshee."

She uncovered one eye. "If it wasn't me, then who was it?"

He grinned, then licked his lips, her sweet taste stunning him again. "You didn't wail. You gave these hot little cries that made me want to take my cock out and stroke it."

She sucked in a breath.

He'd forgotten she was too much a lady for that kind of language except in the heat of the moment. "I didn't mean——"

She held up her finger to cut him off. "If it didn't have that effect, it wouldn't have been so much fun."

Fun wasn't the word he would have used. More like earth-shattering. But she wriggled beneath him as if the fact that he was still lying between her legs made her self-conscious. It was time to take her downstairs, see to her comfort, but he wasn't anywhere near ready to let her leave.

Sitting up, he pulled her with him, then stood, still holding her hand. "Let's look at some of the pictures."

Her face flushed. "Together?"

"Yeah." He laughed, wanting to take the sting out of it. "I told you the flash card was yours, so if we don't look now, I'll never get to see them." The words struck a chord in him, vibrating right down into his belly. This was a one-shot deal. When she walked out of his house, he wouldn't see her again.

But hell, it more than met his expectations, and Dirk was never one to look a gift horse in the mouth. "I want to make sure you're happy with them before you go."

She hitched the corset higher, setting it once again above her nipples, the way it was supposed to be worn. Then she crossed her legs almost as if she were trying to hide her pretty little bush. *Too late, sweetheart.* He'd seen it, caressed it, tasted it, and her scent would haunt his dreams.

"Do you have something I could put on?" She tipped her head. "Unless you get me out of this corset so I can dress."

Hell no. The sooner she got dressed, the sooner she'd be out the door. He wanted her beside him as they viewed the photos, her pussy bare, sensitive, the corset rubbing her nipples the way she'd said she liked. "I've got a robe you can use."

The Chinese screen in the corner of the loft hid a dressing area. On a wooden coat rack, he'd hung a silk wrapper.

"Thank you." She rose gracefully from the lounge, the corset giving her body a regal bearing.

Pink cherry blossoms on red silk, the robe suited her hair and creamy skin perfectly. He captured a couple of unguarded moments as she slipped it over the corset. Flipping her hair out, she let it settle around her shoulders again, the lights shimmering in its golden streaks.

"Can I use your restroom?"

"Sure. Down the stairs to the left, third door. I'll just turn off the equipment, then I'll meet you in the living room. I can run the pictures through the TV."

For some odd reason, he was loath to let her out of his sight, as if she were a figment of his imagination that would disappear. But for the taste of her on his lips, he might have dreamed the whole thing.

Now he just had to convince her that once wasn't enough.

❦

Margo put her hands to her face and talked to the woman in the mirror. "Oh my God. I can't believe you did that."

Yet she'd loved every moment. She wouldn't trade a single one. She simply wished that a woman could ride the orgasmic high longer, because coming down meant you had to face that you'd gone overboard and done more than you wanted to.

"Except it was so damn good," she whispered.

She pinched her cheeks for color, since she'd left her blusher upstairs, then took a steadying breath. They were going to view the photos on the TV. She'd be up there in flat-panel living color. Thank God the man didn't have a sixty-inch screen.

He was already downstairs, the wine on the coffee table, glasses filled, one for each of them this time—he'd hardly touched the beer earlier—and a plate of white cheese with crackers and grapes. Just as she'd ordered. A log crackled in the fireplace.

Down on his knees by the TV, he was plugging in cables.

"I was kidding about the grapes and cheese."

"Your wish is my command," he quipped over his shoulder.

Her wish was to stop feeling so tense. She wondered how on earth you could be nervous with a man after he'd gone down on you. It was the most intimate of acts, and yet . . . it had been easier to do that in the intimacy of the moment than to make small talk now that it was all over.

Especially when she actually had to look at herself doing all those things. A chill shimmied through her, followed quickly by a burst of heat. They'd be watching together.

She allowed herself a deep swallow of wine to calm herself before settling back into the couch. The corset keeping her back straight, she tucked her legs beneath her, the front point resting on her abdomen. She sipped again and twirled the stem of her glass in her hand.

Finally he rose, and the blue screen made way for a shot of her in the pinup girl pose.

Margo laughed, and the thought slipped out. "I don't look half bad."

Dirk gave her a look. "You're fucking gorgeous."

She loved the word on his lips. Just as she'd loved it when he'd said he wanted to stroke his cock. Crude was effective in setting her on fire. Yet a thank-you was all she could manage.

He sat on the couch beside her, concentrating on the photos. "Dammit, I should have moved that light a couple of inches. I don't like the shadow it puts on your face." Leaning forward, he grabbed a composition book off the table and jotted down a line. Then he glanced at her. "I want to make some notes so I can fix the things I didn't like and duplicate the things I did right."

Margo couldn't help herself. "I definitely think there are some things you did very right."

His lids dropped to half-mast, his gaze heated, and he gave her a long second's look. "Should I duplicate them?"

Her breath caught in her chest. "You should certainly record the technique in your little book there."

He wrote another line, never taking his eyes off her. "Duly noted."

The pictures went on. Some he skimmed because they were multiples of similar poses. "You can choose your favorite."

She liked most of them. "You're very good."

His coloring deepened. Just as it had when she'd complimented the pictures of his family.

"I mean it. You really made me look good."

Tipping his head, he turned, giving her a frown and a pair of narrowed eyes. "I photographed what was already there."

"But the lighting——"

"Good lighting only enhances."

Thank God for Photoshop, too. But he was missing her point. "A good photographer knows the right moment to capture."

He'd stopped on the photo of her rolling off a stocking, the satin of her panties flirting with the camera, a sultry smile gracing her lips as she smoothed her hands along her legs. She didn't remember that smile, hadn't known she was capable of it.

"I do look beautiful," she whispered, then turned to him, "but your talent brought it out."

His lips parted, and something hovered in his mind. But instead of voicing the thought, he pointed to the plate of goodies. "Eat a grape with a piece of the cheese. It's tart and best with something sweet."

Wasn't that true about most things? Life was best with contrasts. Such as his big hulking body matched with that adorable dimple.

But she wasn't going to let him get away with ignoring her. Taking his face in her palms, she forced him to meet her gaze. "*You* made me beautiful."

"You *are* beautiful." He wasn't giving in.

"I'm talking about your photographs, Dirk, how you find a person's soul. They're magnificent. They are art." Then she let him go to clasp her hands in her lap.

His gaze roamed her face, settling on her lips, as if he didn't want her to see whatever might be written plainly in his eyes. Then he wrapped a grape in a slice of cheese and pushed it between her lips.

Argument over. He'd won. For now.

Six

Watching herself remove her panties on camera excited Margo all over again. Yet other than murmuring "perfect" and "gorgeous," Dirk was engrossed in his composition book.

Even so, his words filled a need yawning inside her.

The corset fit her snugly, enhancing all her existing attributes. As he said the camera did. She was already beautiful, the camera and the corset just made her . . . more. Yet would she have seen that with any other man?

Then she was naked but for the old-fashioned yet extremely sexy garment. In a close-up, she'd pinched her nipples, the aureoles red. And her face . . .

"So fucking perfect."

She held her breath. He was right. On screen, she was totally enamored of her own body, her own sensations. Even her pussy looked lush, wanton, and yes, beautiful. Her touch on her own body wasn't sleazy or porn-star tawdry. It was passion personified. She remembered how it felt, his voice pushing her on, telling her to touch herself for him, to make herself come.

She squirmed on the couch, and he glanced at her, his eyes the deep, dark blue of the depths of the ocean.

"I've never just watched a woman come like that." He looked from her to the TV screen and back again. She could hear him breathe. "Women don't really need men at all, do they?"

Her cheeks blazed, and she laughed or she would have melted into an embarrassed yet highly aroused puddle. "It's better when there's a man involved."

Yet she hadn't had a man in a year, and she'd been . . . all right. It wasn't the sex itself that she'd come searching for. It was the connection. It was to liberate something in herself. Then she'd found him.

"I want to see the ones with you," she said.

He clicked through to his hand, so big, so dark against her skin. She heated between her legs all over again. The bright red of her nipples, the dusky curls between her legs, and his fingers. She could almost feel it, hear the sounds she'd made.

What he did on film wasn't porn. He'd given her a memory she'd tuck close, like a diary she'd take from beneath the bed when she was eighty and say, "I did that. And I loved it."

Suddenly she had to have it all.

Sliding forward, the corset giving her grace, she wrapped a single grape in cheese and held it out to him. As she had done, he ate from her fingers, licking the tip as she drew away. Then she went to her knees on the braided rug like a geisha.

"I want another picture." She put one hand on his knee.

"Of what?"

She detected a slight crack in his voice. "Of you letting me pleasure you with my mouth." She could have put it crudely. But she liked dirty words better when he said them.

He rubbed a hand on his jeans. "You don't have to do that."

"I know." She rolled her lips together, tasted wine, cheese, the fruit, her lipstick. "I want to taste you."

He didn't say a word, didn't make a move.

"I will die if I leave here tonight without that." She'd never wanted it more, never needed a man as much.

He rose slowly, until he was high, high above her. Then he held out both hands and helped her to her feet. "By the fire," he said, "where it's warm."

She wasn't cold, far from it, but she went to her knees once more by the blaze, the corset keeping her straight, the silk robe caressing her arms, her legs, her butt. Delicious contrasts.

He whipped the TV connector cable from the camera and towered over her. God, he was hard, huge, filling out every ounce of his jeans.

"Take off your shirt," she ordered.

"Yes, ma'am." He handed her the camera and unbuttoned.

His chest was one big wall of muscle, tanned, hairless, massive pectorals. She'd never seen real washboard abs, but the man had them in abundance.

"Hmm," she mused, "pants on or off?" She glanced up. "Which would be sexier in the photograph?" She couldn't decide whether to choose the purity of his naked body or the decadence of his clothes hanging open. She put a finger to her lips before he could answer. "Decadent," she said as if he could read her mind. "Just the belt and fly open." Then, handing the camera back, she gazed up at him. "Don't miss a moment, okay?"

His laugh choked off in the middle. "I surely won't." He smoothed the hair back from her face in an oddly reverent gesture. "Take off the robe and show me your nipples."

The silk pooled in her lap, and she plumped her nipples above the corset. The blush had worn off long ago, but each was a bright, sensitive, rosy red.

"Perfect." He put the camera to his eye.

She would never again use that word without thinking of him.

His belt buckle was stiff, and it took a moment to loosen it and the buttons on his jeans. Beneath, he was naked. His curls were a dusky brown lighter than his hair, and he'd trimmed. Fresh soap and the musk of his precome mingled with the wood smoke of the fire. She parted the placket of his jeans and gasped. He was even more than she'd expected. Stretching back, she couldn't read his expression past the camera.

"What they say about big hands is definitely true."

The camera clicked as he said, "Actually they say the size of a man's hand is inversely proportional to the size of his—"

It was his turn to gasp as she wrapped her fingers around him. "This is definitely not inversely proportional."

Even as she watched, a bead pearled on the tip. Her mouth watered. She'd had wine, grapes, now this. He shuddered as she licked him clean, savoring his salty-sweet taste.

"Delicious," she whispered, and he pulsed in her hand. "Gorgeous," she added, and felt a pressure against her grip as he grew. "Beautiful, wonderful, and eminently suckable."

He laughed. "You're gonna make me come before you start."

"I never knew mere words could mean so much."

He shifted the camera enough to gaze at her. "Under certain circumstances, words are everything."

"I thought a picture was worth a thousand words."

"Not when you're telling me I have a gorgeous cock." Then he reached down to stroke her hair and give her the slightest push toward his crown. "But it's even better if we have both."

"You mean you want me to talk to it while you photograph?"

For just a moment, there was such a look in his eye. "You're fun," he said, and Margo had the feeling it was the highest of compliments, more important than any of the others.

She rewarded him by sliding her parted lips down his underside, trailing her tongue. She would never be able to fit all of him, but gliding back up, she opened, took him. Circling his crown, she tasted once again the ambrosia of his come, then slid down to meet her fingers fisted around him.

He groaned, and she looked up in the lens of the camera. He could see her while she couldn't see him, and it gave her an odd little kick. When she retreated all the way to his tip, she paused, gazed, blinked, then sucked on the end like a lollipop.

"Wench," he muttered, but she felt his heat, his pulse, and relished a fresh burst of flavor.

His hips shifted in rhythm, begging her to take him deeper again. Twice, three times, then a hard suck on the crown that sent a shudder through his body. She grabbed his big meaty man thighs, slid his cock inside until her eyes watered. He filled her, not just his girth or length, but the essence of the man.

He sifted the fingers of one hand through her hair, guided her, flexed and rolled against her until he was pumping between her lips. With a deep groan rising from his gut, he bent to set the camera on the rug. Then he held her face in both big hands, taking her mouth with his cock as if he were deep inside her body. The pleasure radiated through her limbs, possessing her.

Then he flew apart, shouted her name, and came undone completely in her mouth. Just as she was his, he belonged to her in a way no other man ever had before.

<hr>

He couldn't remember how he ended up on the floor, his head in her lap. His knees must have given out when orgasm roared through. He'd gone mindless, the silk of her hair, her scent clouding his head, and her mouth dragging him straight to heaven.

She stroked his eyebrow. Her lipstick wasn't even smudged, lighter maybe, but not a single misplaced mark. She looked the regal lady, even the robe draping her shoulders once again.

He'd never had a woman make him lose time and space. He recognized it was the circumstance, days of anticipation, the kinkiness, yet it was also Margo. Her elegance and grace, her smile, her trust. And her belief in his talent.

His body still reeled. He splayed his hand across her abdomen beneath the silky robe, her body heat seeping through the corset. "Do you want to finish the photos?"

Soothing his other eyebrow with her finger, she had the prettiest smile. "I think maybe you should get me out of this corset instead."

His heart plummeted. He didn't want her out of it. Everything would be over too fast. As long as she wore it for him, she couldn't leave. He sat up anyway, slowly, missing the warmth of her as he did so, then on his hands and knees, he moved behind her. "Undo the robe."

She let it fall. He couldn't help dropping a kiss to her shoulder. "You didn't have to do that, but it was the best."

Turning her head, just enough for him to see her smile, she whispered, "You taste good. I'll always remember that the most."

He hated the finality in her words, yet this had been designed as a once-only interlude. He loosened the laces, starting at the top to unthread them through the holes.

She let out a satisfied sigh, then laughed. Just as she would remember the taste of his come, he would always hear her laugh as much as anything else they'd done.

"Was it that tight?" He kept his voice light.

"It wasn't bad, but you realize how much it pulled you together when you take it off."

She lifted her hair up off her neck as if that would help to unlace her. All it did was make him want to sink his teeth down on her nape like a lion and have at her. Despite the powerful come, he wanted her that way, from behind, his cock sunk deep.

His fingers were suddenly clumsy with the laces, then she was free as he tossed the corset aside. The stays left red marks on her skin that faded even as he watched. He rose to his full height over her. She was naked except for the robe covering her lap, yet the blue screen of the TV hid her reflection.

"Mm, it feels delicious to be free." She shook her hair, then slowly drew the robe over her shoulders. Rolling to her feet, she turned to him, tucking the lapels close to her throat.

In bare feet, she was so small versus his hulking body. Her gaze roamed his features, and for the first time, he feared what a woman thought of his face. Even before he'd gotten his nose broken, he hadn't been a beauty.

Then she smiled. "Thank you for tonight." She stroked his chest. "You can't imagine how good that was for me."

"Ditto." It was all he could say. She was getting ready to go. He wanted to beg her to stay. Words failed him.

"I'll get dressed and be right back." Then, up on her toes, her hand along the back of his neck, she kissed him lightly.

It was the first time his lips had touched hers, so damn sweet. And sort of lonely as she headed back up to the loft.

Their night was over long before he was ready for it to end.

⋙⋘

It was such a perfect way to end the evening. God, now he had her using that word.

She'd left off every stitch of underclothing yet her cowl neck sweater trapped all her body heat inside. Minus the corset, she found her spine remained straight, shoulders back. Sashaying down his stairs, she felt sexy, hot beneath his simmering gaze as she entered the living room. She only hoped she could maintain the feelings once she left his house.

"Shall we finish off the photos?" An eager little-boy expression animated his features.

And he was a boy. Compared to her. It was exhilarating to touch his gorgeous physique, to take him in her mouth, to be desired by him. She would always be a tiny bit in love with the memory because of what he'd given her. He would forever be her younger man fantasy. But he was just a fantasy.

"Why don't you just send me the cream of the crop?"

He blinked over those startling blue eyes. "But that means I have to keep the flash card."

"Yes." That's exactly what it meant. The pictures would be his, as was the choice to abuse the gift. He wouldn't. Dirk was a different kind of man, though she hoped he would look at them over and over, remembering. "Pick out the ones you think are best and e-mail them to me." She smiled to herself. "Don't forget the last ones. They're the most important." She wanted to savor them just as she'd savored the taste of him. If she ever had a lonely night when she lost faith in herself again, she'd pull up the picture of Dirk Araman filling her mouth and be reminded of this release from her anxieties.

"Well, I gotta go." She hugged her gym bag, palmed her keys. "Thank you for tonight."

He retrieved her coat from the hall closet and helped her into it. Then he held out a hand, his lips parted, as if he were weighing his words. "It was my pleasure. I'll send you the best. You won't be disappointed."

She backed up one step to the door. "Nothing you do could ever disappoint me."

He'd given her back so many pieces of herself she'd tossed away when Richard left.

⊗⊗⊗⊗

She was gone. He wasn't ready. He'd wanted to beg her to kiss him. A real honest-to-God kiss, one that would stain his soul permanently.

Instead, she left him with the photos. If he chose, he could submit them for the competition or post them on porn sites.

Did she know how much trust she'd laid in his hands?

He punched a couple of buttons on the hand remote and the TV blazed to life. She stared up at him in living color, her lips wrapped around him as she took him to heaven.

He'd never seen a more beautiful sight in his life. He wanted to see it again and again. For real, not just a photo.

⊗⊗⊗⊗

Saturday morning she woke to the sun on her face. She stretched sinuously. Sensuously. Like a woman who'd had the absolute best sex of her life last night. And she'd have the pictures to prove it, beautiful, erotic photos of . . . her sucking a man's cock. Her face.

Margo sat bolt up in bed. She'd left him with the pictures. Suddenly the voices of reason were warring in her head.

What if everyone finds out? What if he puts those pictures on the Internet?

Dirk wouldn't do that.

But how did she *know*? She'd trusted him when her mind was clouded with his scent, his taste. A woman had no sense at a time like that. Good Lord, what had she been thinking?

Without dressing first or even starting the coffee, she turned on her computer. The machine took forever with that damn virus software upgrade. Her fingers trembled when she finally got into the Internet and entered her user name and password for e-mail. She'd created an account specifically for answering the ad, an unidentified e-mail address he couldn't trace her to.

Thank God she hadn't given him her full name, not even her cell phone number. Yet she'd still been stupid and let her emotions carry her away because he made her feel good.

Good Lord, what if he asked Lorie about her? All it would take was her first name, and Lorie would know . . .

Her heart beat faster and her blood drummed in her ears when she saw the e-mail from him. With an attachment.

His message was brief. "Thank you for what you did. I stayed up all last night going through the photos. You brought out the best in me. I have never experienced anything more wonderful nor created a more perfect image."

God. Why did he have to sound so sweet?

Holding her breath, she opened the attached photo. The air whooshed out of her, and her heart stopped for several beats.

Taken from above, he was large, thick, filling her mouth, light tufts of brown pubic hair brushing her pinkie as she wrapped her fingers around him, her nail polish bright, red hot. Her face filled the photo. Not a hair out of place, not a wrinkle that didn't give her grace and character. Her eyes wide, she gazed up at him as if he were the most important being in the world. This was his view of her. There was nothing tawdry or dirty. God, she was truly beautiful.

His skill took her breath away all over again. Margo could only stare for long moments. She wanted to be that woman. She needed to believe she was, but less than twelve hours after her revelations of last night, she'd started doubting again.

Her fingers hovered over the keyboard. She could search him out on the Internet. She'd simply taken Lorie's word that he was a nice guy. She'd never checked for herself.

Yet that was ripping away the gift of trust she'd given him.

He'd never know she'd done it, that sane voice whispered. He'd expect her to do it. He'd wonder why she hadn't.

Except that after meeting him, seeing his family photos, begging him to make her come, taking him in her mouth, it seemed an underhanded way to treat him.

She'd trusted her instincts about him last night. She'd trusted herself and her own judgment of character. If anyone saw that picture, hell, they'd be jealous. She was a catastrophizer. The only possible outcome was always the worst one. Her career would tank, she'd lose her house, and be out on the streets. Worse, she'd had to move in with her mother.

Take a chance. Stop worrying.

Instead of searching, she hit Reply and began typing. "Thank you. I want to always see myself this way. But I did get a little frightened that I'd left the pictures with you."

He replied so quickly, he must have been sitting at his computer. "I will never hurt you. You are safe. Would you like to talk to my mother and have her tell you what a nice man I am?"

Shades of what Lorie said about him. She laughed out loud despite her anxiety. She was riddled with anxieties; she always would be. Unless she took a chance and let them all go. "I'll give you my vote of confidence without your mother's endorsement. I love the picture. You have such talent. Send me more."

When his e-mail came in, she was such a slut, she clicked on the attachment first. In it, she sat on her haunches, the red silk robe pooled in her lap, the corset plumping her breasts. His gorgeous cock would soon be in her mouth. Anticipation colored her face, lids half closed, that sultry little moue he'd asked for adorning her lips. This wasn't a pose. This was her, the woman in her craving the man.

Her skin heated, her body moistened, and her mouth watered for another taste of him. How could he do that to her with a mere picture? Yet he did, because he had some innate ability to draw out a woman's essence.

If these photographs ever made it to the Internet, she'd be proud to acknowledge them. She'd adore sending one to Richard.

She went back to the e-mail to tell Dirk how much she loved it. His answer made her heart stutter through several beats. "You are the sexiest woman alive. I want to see you again."

See her again? As in another photo session? Or something more? She closed her eyes and imagined his hands on her, his mouth, his cock deep inside her. And God, yes, she wanted that.

But he was twelve years younger, and when he got tired of her, she wouldn't be able to handle the loss. She knew she'd invest way too much in how he made her feel. You didn't have to fall in love with someone to get hurt. You could simply have your needs met, then find it all ripped away when you least expected. Sex was never *just* sex. Walking away from his offer wasn't the same as not taking a chance; it was nipping a problem in the bud before it started. She'd gotten everything she needed last night. More than she'd ever dreamed of or hoped for. It was silly to ruin it now by letting things get away from her.

Besides, Lorie would totally freak if she ever knew what Margo had done.

Yet her temple began to throb as she typed. "That's not a good idea, Dirk. I'm older, at a different stage of life, and all that. But thank you. And thanks for a wonderful evening. I will always treasure the memory."

She sent it off. She was fine. This was the best thing to do. Time to get dressed. Time to return to the real world. Dirk Araman was a beautiful fantasy.

It was best to leave him that way.

⁂

Shit. Okay, it was only a minor setback. He'd e-mail and give her time to get used to hearing from him. Until she expected his e-mails, wanted them. Hell, he had enough photos of her to keep this going for months.

Her last lover had walked away because she wasn't willing to take a chance. Dirk wouldn't let Margo make the same mistake. He would get into her life, some way, someday. He didn't give a damn how old she was, she was perfect. She believed in him.

He would show her how good they could be together.

Seven

He drove her wild. So many seductive pictures. She was like Narcissus, always staring at herself. Except that it wasn't just her, it was Dirk. Touching her with a big hand. His brow furrowed in concentration as he used the vibrator to make her mindless. His blue eyes ablaze as he tasted her the first time.

With every picture he sent, one by one by one, he asked her for coffee, or dinner, a walk in the park, a bike ride.

The seventh day, she couldn't stand it anymore. She wanted sex with him. One night of passionate sex with a big, strong, hot young man.

Just once, she told herself on Friday evening as she dressed in a black Lycra top that laced down the back. It reminded her of the corset. She wanted to remind him, too. She paired the top with a leather skirt that zipped straight up the front and straight up the back. Richard had called it her easy-access skirt. After a painstaking makeup job, she gave herself the thumbs-up. She'd hold her own with a woman even Dirk's age.

She didn't call ahead to tell him she was coming, and by the time she hit his driveway, she was hot and wet with anticipation and nerves. She parked behind a car by the garage. Lights blazed inside the house, as did the Christmas icicles along the roofline. He was definitely home, but what if he had a woman with him? She hadn't thought of that. Butterflies in her belly added to her excitement.

Her high-heeled shoes clicked loudly on the front porch, and if she wasn't mistaken, she could hear the TV. The condoms were in her purse, she was here, sexy and needy. It was now or never. She didn't want to be eighty and regretting that she never took advantage of this gorgeous specimen of a man.

A shadow passed over the door's opaque glass. Somehow, it seemed too small for Dirk's bulk. Margo held her breath.

An older woman answered. A very short lady, especially since Margo was in heels. Lord, Dirk *was* a changeling. This was his mother, though she'd left behind the flowing caftan in favor of a chic red jogging suit that wasn't meant for a workout.

His mom gasped. "Oh my goodness, you're Dirk's friend Margo." She grabbed Margo's hand. "Come in, come in."

Lord. How did the woman know about her? What had he said?

"Is Dirk here?" It was the only thing Margo could think to ask that didn't accidentally reveal how she and Dirk had met.

"No, silly." The woman's two white eyebrows tugged together. "He's down in L.A., of course."

"Oh." Maybe he had business there. But why hadn't he told her? Because in her e-mails, she'd been adamant about not seeing him.

The woman gave her an assessing look. "I'm Dirk's mom, Betsy, by the way." Then she beamed, and Dirk's adorable dimple appeared at the side of her mouth.

"He gets his blue eyes from you." The same startling blue.

"His daddy had blue eyes, too." She'd dropped Margo's hand, but now picked it up again. "I was watering Dirk's plants, and his TV is better than mine, so I decided to watch the show here." She surveyed Margo, her eyes twinkling. "You don't have to go right away just because Dirk's not here, do you?"

Margo had forgotten her sexy easy-access skirt and tight Lycra top with a strip of her skin showing down the back. Lord. What would Betsy think? Certainly not that Margo was here for a cup of sugar. Giving an excuse, though, would only make the situation worse. "I'd love to watch the show." Whatever it was.

The living room was toasty warm, a fire crackling, the TV on mute as commercials played. A wine bottle, crackers, cream cheese, and a bowl of salsa littered the coffee table.

Betsy followed her gaze. "I know, bad for the old arteries, but it's a special night, and I always treat myself." She picked up the wine. "Dirk said you brought this. I love it. I've never had Gewürztraminer before." She leaned in to whisper conspiratorially, "Dirk told me how to pronounce it."

Odd how good it made her feel that Dirk gave it to his mom.

"Don't stand there," Betsy said. "Kick off your shoes and put your feet up on the couch. I'll get another glass."

Margo didn't have a chance to tell the woman she didn't want anything. She had to keep her head about her. What if she let something slip? For instance: *I met your son through a personal ad, and I did a zillion naughty things for him a week ago, and the fact that you answered the door instead of him is killing me.*

The commercials ended, and the show began. Some wrestling thing. Obviously not Betsy's program yet. A log sparked and cracked in the fireplace. Margo's gaze rose to the mantel and the row of pictures. She hadn't noticed them on Friday. Nerves, and the fact that she was thinking about taking Dirk in her mouth.

Her tummy flipped over. Good God. *She* was on the mantel. That's how Betsy knew who she was. She stood before the fire and gazed at her photo. He hadn't sent her this one. A pinup pose, before she'd taken her clothes off for him. She wore a secret smile, hinting at a woman with depths yet unfathomed. It was a picture to make a man want to fathom those depths.

He was so good. His pictures saw beyond the outer shell and seemed to reveal the inner thoughts and soul. The man was magnificent in so many ways.

"I'm proud of him, you know." Betsy waved the glass in the air before she poured, then set it on the coffee table as Margo sat down. "He's talented in so many ways."

"I love the pictures he took of you." The ones upstairs.

"Yes"—Betsy preened a moment—"the things he can do even for an old bag like me."

"You're not an old bag. You're gorgeous." Margo didn't add the common "for your age" because, in truth, Betsy was beautiful for any age. She'd weathered her years terribly well.

She took the compliment. "Thank you, my dear. Now let's not miss the show."

Margo kicked off her shoes. She was here, Dirk's mother was nice, and what the heck, she'd drink wine and enjoy the show.

Betsy punched the remote, and the sound blared to life. "It's time." She giggled.

Margo marveled. The little lady was a smackdown fan. There was the posturing, the jostling, the two contestants growling at each other like dogs at a fight, the referee trying to shove them apart, them shoving the referee back. All the while the crowd screamed, jeered, cheered, hurled insults, and generally went wild. It was a madhouse. Betsy sat with her legs tucked beneath her, a pillow clutched to her stomach as she nibbled on a cracker. The TV screen earned her rapt attention.

Ironman was fighting Maximum Bob. The names made her laugh, but not too hard so she didn't offend Betsy.

"Oh my God, look out," Betsy cried at the screen. "He's going to do a clothesline!"

Maximum Bob threw himself against the ropes, bouncing out again, ready to smash Ironman to the mat. Obviously Ironman figured out the strategy because he spun, grabbed, and slammed Bob into the mat instead. They rolled and growled, and sweat dripped off their brows. Ironman was huge, two heads taller than the referee who'd just hauled him off Maximum Bob for some infraction. Not that the relatively tiny ref would have budged Ironman if the big guy hadn't allowed it.

Wasn't all this fake? Margo didn't ask, once again for fear of offending Betsy, who was shouting instructions, name-calling, and all the rest of it, just like the audience.

"Get him with a high flyer, Ironman." Then Betsy shouted a few mild epithets as Ironman ran, jumped up in the corner of the ropes, flipped, and threw himself down on the hapless Maximum Bob.

So, was Dirk down in L.A. on business? Or a photo excursion? Margo didn't know a thing about him. She still didn't want to know anything. She just wanted life-transforming sex with him.

Yet she was dying to know what his mother thought their relationship was.

"He won, he won." Betsy bounced on the couch, giggled, cheered, spilled wine on the braided rug, which she promptly rubbed away with her foot so the stain wouldn't set in. God, Margo's mom would have had the spot remover out immediately. Though she'd never have bounced with glee in the first place. Betsy's antics would have given her conniptions.

Thinking her own thoughts, Margo had missed the win, but she clapped anyway. "Well, that was just marvelous."

"He's going to be champion this year, I know it."

"Ironman?"

Betsy huffed out a disgusted breath. "Well of course Ironman. Who else?"

On the TV, there was all the back-slapping, cheering, booing from the other side, the referee trying to hold Ironman's beefy arm in the air. The big man's skin glistened with sweat, his tight trunks outlined every muscle, and even his . . . though she knew he was wearing a protector, his package still had to be one impressive member. And he wasn't bad looking—

Oh my God.

Her heart beat so furiously she was sure she was having an attack of angina. Get out the nitroglycerine. Did they even use that anymore? Who cared? Oh my God. Dirk "Ironman" Araman took center stage in all his glory.

"Isn't he magnificent?"

"Definitely." Questions bounced around her brain, knocking against her skull as if her head were hollow.

"You didn't know, did you?"

She hadn't realized Ironman's mother was staring at her. "I haven't known him for very long. I guess he didn't get around to telling me yet." Just as she hadn't told him anything, he hadn't revealed himself to her. But why hadn't Lorie mentioned it? Hello, because she didn't have a clue Margo would ever answer that ad.

"I'm going to have a talk with that boy," his mother said, a diabolical scowl disfiguring her features.

"Please don't." God forbid. Dirk would already be having a fit at the fact that Margo had shown up at his house without an invitation and found his mom instead.

"I've taught him better than this. If he's interested in a woman, he's got to share himself."

"It isn't like that. We're just friends. I'm a lot older than him, you know." And God, she wished she hadn't said *that*. But really, what would people say? It was even worse now that she knew he was a celebrity.

Betsy flapped a hand. "Pah. Age doesn't mean a thing. Why, my lover Orson is ten years younger than me." She winked. "I haven't seen Dirk this animated about a woman . . ." She trailed off, tipping her head. "Well, never. He dates, and he's brought women home to meet me, but"—she curled her finger around her chin—"but he's just *more* about you."

Oh God. Margo did not want to have this discussion with Ironman's mom. "Well, that's really nice. I better be off now." She rose. "It's been so nice meeting you."

"You don't have to go yet. They'll be doing an interview with Dirk in a minute."

"No, really, I have to go. Thanks for the wine."

She left, speeding out to her car in case Betsy decided to follow her with more tales of the enthusiastic things her son had said about a woman twelve years older than he was.

Betsy didn't get it. The distance between fifty-two and sixty-two was a drop in the bucket. The contrast between thirty-three and forty-five was like the difference between a 7.0 earthquake and an 8.0. The damage was astronomically higher.

＊＊＊＊

She'd come to his house tonight. If her outfit—as described in detail by his mother—meant anything, she hadn't come merely to say thank you for the photos.

Hope made him slightly light-headed.

Mom had called him after tonight's match-up with the tale, going on about what a lovely woman Margo was. It had been a long night, a party afterward, and it was midnight before he got back to the hotel and the computer. His gut rolled when there was no message from Margo. He'd expected something. Even if it was an accusation over why he hadn't told her about Ironman.

Not that it freaking mattered. It was a good living, but it wasn't a passion, just something he'd fallen into after being on the wrestling team in both high school and college.

He cracked his knuckles like Ironman would and settled his fingers on the keyboard. What to say . . . "My mom thinks you're lovely. I think you're lovely. I'm sorry I missed you tonight. I'll be down here a couple more days, till the day before Christmas Eve." He heaved a sigh, then typed. "I'd like to get together when I'm home."

He stared at the message for a while, deciding what he didn't like about it. Too much or too little? He wasn't the type to angst about what to say, what to do, or worry whether he'd said the wrong thing. All his angst went to his art. He'd never been like this over a woman.

"Just send the damn e-mail," he muttered. In the end, he deleted the parts about his mom and where he'd said Margo was lovely. It was too . . . ingratiating.

He was about to shut down when his e-mail beeped. She was up. Dare he hope she'd been waiting for his e-mail?

He could only smile when he read her message. "You looked very cute in those tight leggings."

Cute. He laughed harder. The woman was fun. He wanted to be a part of her fun. Yet she was so damn hard to pin down.

"You didn't say anything about going out with me when I get back." He hit Send, questioning whether he was being too pushy.

His e-mail beeped again. He wanted to beat his head against the wall as he read her words. "Let's talk about it when you're home."

Godammit.

She was a challenge. He would not give up. Not until the day she gave him an unequivocal no and stopped answering his e-mails.

Eight

After almost five days and so many of Dirk's increasingly explicit e-mails and naughty photo attachments, she was mad for him. There was no question that she'd see him again the very day he arrived home. A date, Margo wasn't so sure about, but she would seduce him. Just once. She even planned on wearing the same outfit, skimpy Lycra top and easy-access skirt.

If his mom answered, Margo would expire on the spot.

Afraid she'd lose her courage, once again she didn't call ahead to make sure he was there and alone. This time no extra car occupied the driveway, the garage door was closed, the Christmas lights twinkled, and smoke puffed from the chimney. Lamps gleamed through the loft's windows, but the ground floor lay in darkness. He'd said his flight got in midafternoon the day before Christmas Eve. With smoke, there had to be fire, in more ways than one.

She rang the bell but resisted putting her face to the glass to make out any movement inside. If he was in the loft, he had two flights of stairs to descend.

Why was she so jittery? It was worse than the night she'd shown up on a stranger's front porch. Because she had intention this time? Or because the last time, she'd plucked up her courage for one thing only to be faced with something far scarier. His mom, for God's sake.

When he opened the door, she realized it was none of those things at all. It was how much she craved his touch, a need that had grown exponentially since she'd last seen him.

"Hey." He didn't even turn on the hall light, just grabbed her hand, hauled her inside, slammed the front door, and shoved her up against it. "I've never kissed you, not a real kiss."

He took her, with lips, tongue, mouth, his body pressing her to the door, his hands through her hair, holding her for his possession. Her purse fell from her fingers as she clung to him.

Deep, passionate kisses were for later. This was a heady sampling, but oh so good. She opened for him, licked his lips, stroked his tongue.

He punctuated each taste with words. "God, I needed this." He traced the seam of her lips. "I've thought of nothing else for weeks." He nipped, sucked, took his tongue deep, retreated. "You've unhinged me." He grabbed her butt and dragged her up close and personal with the bulge in his pants. "You should have called. I'd have made it special."

Pulling his head down, she shut him up with her kiss. He tasted of beer and man, smelled of pine and wood smoke. "This is special," she whispered, then stroked her tongue inside his mouth, backed off to his lips, then his jaw. "I missed you." She held his face in her palms, such a gorgeous rugged face.

"Fuck." He put his head back a moment, revealing the long column of his neck.

On tiptoe, she licked straight up his Adam's apple.

He swore again, then dropped his head to meet her gaze. "I don't want to be an animal. But I'm fucking crazed wanting you."

"Be an animal." She lifted his big hands to her breasts. She'd never had a man crazed for her, wild to get inside her. She wanted to feel it, taste it, revel in his need.

"I'm afraid I might eat you right up." Tugging her shirt down, he stuck his hands inside her bra. Her nipples peaked at the first graze of rough fingers across them. When he pinched, she closed her eyes, moaned, strained up against the door to give as much access as possible.

He bent to lick her nipple, blew on her, and the shock of air was as mind-altering as the pinch. Her knees felt weak. Leaving her breasts bared, he trailed down her sides to the skirt, yanking it up with his fingers.

"There's a zipper." She gasped as he rolled his hips against her. "Starts at the bottom."

He squatted in front of her, big, solid, all male, grabbed the bottom of the skirt, and zipped all the way up to the elastic of her thong. Looking up, his eyes glittered in the darkened hall. "You're a naughty woman wearing this to entice a man."

"You're a very naughty man for unzipping it."

He covered her mound with his mouth and blew warm air. Margo groaned. He'd teased her with pictures and innuendoes for days. One more second, and she'd spontaneously combust.

"And these are very naughty panties." He pulled the thong down with his index finger until it dropped to the floor, then delved with the tip of his tongue, barely stroking her clit.

She shuddered at the feel and the sight of this big, hot male down on his haunches before her. All hers to command.

"You like that," he whispered. He did it again, licking a little longer this time. "You're very, very wet. I can smell you, like honey." He probed once more. "Taste like honey, too."

Her legs began to tremble. He dipped his finger inside her, then stroked the digit across his lips, and stood.

"Taste it," he said, wrapping his hand around her nape, bending close, his lips such a temptation.

She tasted herself, sweet as he said, mixed with his heat.

"Do me," she whispered against his lips. No man had been inside her in over a year. "There's a condom in my purse."

"Came prepared, didn't you."

She leaned her head back against the door. "I haven't thought about anything else."

He grinned. "I've thought about all the different ways to have you." Bending slowly, keeping his gaze on her as he went down, he grabbed her purse on the first try and rose all the way back up until the rapid pulse at his throat was at eye level.

"I hope you brought more than one." He held the purse out.

Margo wiggled her fingers in the front pocket and came out with four. "Even you couldn't use more than that in one night."

He laughed. "You shouldn't challenge a man like that."

Oh yes, she should, because if he could use all four condoms in eight hours, she'd take him up on it. "It's a bet then."

"I'm pretty sure if one of us loses, then we both lose."

She took the purse from his hands, tossed it to the side, and gave him all four condoms, three of which he shoved in his jeans pocket.

"Let's make sure we both win," she said. She palmed Dirk in her hand. "You are so big."

He put an equally big hand over hers and rubbed himself, his head falling back as a low growl rose up from his throat.

"I unzipped you, you undo me," he said, bringing his gaze back to hers. The Christmas tree lights winking in the living room were reflected in his eyes, catching them on fire.

She popped his button fly slowly, revealing miles of naked flesh, commando again. Leaning fully against the door, she slid her fingers inside, down to his balls, and held them in her hot hand. Squeezing gently, she then trailed the tip of her fingernail back up to his crown. Come beaded on the head.

"Fuck," he whispered.

"You fuck," she murmured, then smeared the little pearl back and forth through the tiny slit of his cock.

He gave a full-body shudder.

She worked just the tip with her fingers, using his own moisture to coat him. The head was smooth, tight, beautiful. She'd never had a man so large, but she was hot enough, creamy enough, woman enough to take every inch.

She sucked her finger clean, then looked up at him. His irises weren't even visible anymore, just deep pools of need.

"Put it on." She flicked the unopened packet he held.

He startled as if he hadn't even remembered it in his hand. "Yes, ma'am." Ripping it open with his teeth, he plucked out the condom, and threw the wrapper to the floor.

"Do they come in extra large?" she asked, with the most innocent of tones. "I don't remember a size on them."

He laughed, choked it off. "You're a tease."

Then he rolled the condom on and pushed his jeans low on his hips, past the globes of his butt. Dipping down, she slid her fingers through her own moisture, gathered it, then cupped his clad cock, smearing herself all over him for lubrication.

"Fuck, that's hot." He gulped air. "Do it again."

She went deeper, then slid out to circle her clit. So wet, so hot, she slathered him with her essence.

He simply turned primal. With a low growl from his belly, he shoved his hands in the open zip of her skirt, grabbed her butt, and hauled her high against him. Throwing her arms around his shoulders, she spread her legs over his hips. His cock nudged her pussy, and Dirk held her still a moment.

"I'll be slow," he whispered, but his body trembled.

"Just do it." She bent her head to nip his neck, hard.

Bracing her with his hands on her butt cheeks, he surged forward. She breathed hard to accommodate him. God. It was . . . there were no words. A little pain, her pussy quivered, heated, shifted.

She locked her ankles at the base of his spine and squeezed. Lightly, then harder, forcing him deeper. "Fuck me, Ironman, just fuck me."

He slammed her against the door. Deep, high. Oh God. He touched something inside her no man ever had, and with every thrust, he shot her closer to the edge until she begged him to throw her over. And still he went at her, his breath in her ear, his scent all over her, every inch of her body taken hard.

She came from the inside out, a burst of colors, fragments of herself flying out, falling, screaming, crying, until she couldn't hear anything, see anything, and all that existed was this man's body filling every crack and fissure inside her.

God help her, once wouldn't be enough. Even the whole night wouldn't be. She'd have to come back a second time.

❦

Slumped on the floor, he cradled her in his arms, his cock still buried inside her. He didn't apologize for taking her against the door. It was too hot for words. He'd give her tender lovemaking later. That's exactly how they'd needed it, fast, hard, cataclysmic. There was time for the rest later.

She hugged him tightly, her lips against his neck. Her bite would leave a mark. He'd wanted her to mark him. He was hers.

"You a very bad man," she whispered.

Her warm breath along his skin heated him on the inside. His cock flexed.

She pulled back. "Don't tell me you're ready again."

He grinned, his heart feeling oversized, bursting. "Who said I won't win that bet to use all four condoms?" He stroked the tangled hair back from her face. "You are so beautiful when you come."

She blushed, the heat rising beneath his fingers.

"You say too many nice things. They'll go to my head."

"I'm going to keep saying them." For a woman so gorgeous, she didn't have enough belief in herself. He could give that to her. "Over and over. Tomorrow. Next year. The year after."

"The year after, I'll be on the wrong side of forty-five."

She was so damn sensitive about her age. "Women only get better. Like fine wine."

She snorted, then rubbed noses with him. "Lucky you won't have to test that theory." She stretched. "Ooh, those muscles."

He wouldn't let her change the subject. "I don't care how old you are. I want the woman inside." He tapped her chest. "It won't matter when you turn fifty. My mother's boyfriend—"

She cut him off. "I know, he's ten years younger than she is. But I'm not your girlfriend . . ." She held her mouth open as if she had something left to say, then tipped her head.

He knew what she was thinking, what lay on the tip of her tongue. "It's not just sex."

"No, it was great sex."

"And more." His heart was in it. So was hers. "A woman doesn't come like that for a man unless she has feelings."

She tried to wriggle away. He held her fast, stayed inside her, so she would feel him all the way up to her heart.

"I have feelings. You're a very sweet young man."

"Don't patronize me. You just fucked me, and I don't even know your last name." He hadn't realized it bothered the shit out of him that she'd never given her name. He could have asked Lorie, but that would be violating Margo's trust. Besides, he wanted to hear it from Margo herself.

"It's Faraday. Margo Faraday."

He swallowed, hard. It bugged him that she gave her name now, her tone cold, as if it didn't mean a thing. Hell, it bothered him even more that she'd called him Ironman while she was fucking him, as if he were a prize to be won for the night, instead of the man he wanted her to see him as.

He took more seconds than necessary to answer. "I want more than tonight. Even if tonight is four times, I want more. Corny, but I want a relationship. A boyfriend-girlfriend thing."

Margo sucked in her cheek, chewed on it lightly. "I don't think we should ask for more than is reasonable."

"Fuck reasonable." His jaw worked, and he turned his head, neck cracking. "I mean that I think we could be good together."

She was sure they could be. For a little while. Until the world intruded. He was young, she didn't want to hurt his feelings. "You're twelve years younger, so I'm sure you don't see it the same way. But at your age, that many years is too much." She hitched herself a little closer on his hips. "What we did was wonderful, beautiful, and we can do it again if we keep it secret. But it's not something we can count on."

"Your age doesn't matter. I don't care."

Yeah, well, he was the hot young stud. She was the old lady. "I don't want to be gossiped about."

"Nobody will say a thing."

All right. He was only thirty-three and a man. But honestly, didn't he have any idea what people would say? "You're a celebrity. Everyone will talk. Not to mention my clients."

"You're afraid, that's it."

She tried to push away, but he wasn't called Ironman for nothing. "I'm not afraid. I just know how to face facts. The world can be cruel."

"And you're not willing to stand up for something you want."

God, he was so warm between her legs, so real, hard again. Her body tensed to take him, her chest fluttered. She wanted. Yet she'd never considered wanting him for more than this, what they'd done tonight. Anything else was always impossible. Only that seemed far too harsh a thing to say. "I've seen how people can be. They have the ability to destroy fragile relationships."

His cheek muscles flexed, ending with a flare to his nostrils. "You're afraid to take a risk. Like you were with your boyfriend."

That sliced right through her. "You don't need to be mean."

He grabbed her under the arms then, and rose as if she weighed nothing. His cock pulled free, and cool air rushed in where all his warmth had been. He set her on her feet.

"Don't you move," he said, eyes glacial. "Don't you leave."

Something in the way he pointed his finger touched her ire. "Don't point."

He didn't apologize, simply pinned her with a glare as he retreated through a door behind him. The light flipped on, a bathroom. He rustled, ran water, while Margo put her bra to rights, stepped into her panties, tugged her shirt in place, zipped her skirt, and grabbed her purse from the floor.

He stepped out, jeans all buttoned up, the condom obviously tossed. "I'm sorry."

"Gosh, a man who knows how to apologize." She didn't like her own bitchy tone.

He ignored it. "I want to give this thing a shot."

For a moment, she imagined. She owed him that. The thought made her warm, breathless, desired, special. But when she opened her eyes, she saw the stark reality on his unlined face.

"Relationships like that can't work, Dirk. Older men can get away with it, but not older women."

His features resembled Ironman in the ring, hard, tense. Yet his voice was the antithesis, low, barely a whisper. "Take a chance."

A voice screamed inside. *Say yes. Do it.* But she knew it would never work. "No."

She didn't apologize. She merely found the doorknob with frozen fingers. He didn't stop her as she shut it behind her.

She didn't start to ache until she climbed into the front seat of her car, started the engine, and headed down the hill.

No. Just like that. He stared at the door even as the sound of her car faded away.

He wasn't worth taking a chance on, at least not for her.

He slid down the wall and laid his head in his hands. Fuck. You couldn't fight someone else's insecurities, you could only fix your own. Her fears outweighed her belief in herself.

No really did mean no. And he just had to live with it.

Nine

With only half an hour to go until the New Year's ball dropped in New York, the house party was jumping with thirty couples and a few singles, lots of laughter, and a truly spectacular guy on the white baby grand piano. He knew all the old standards.

"All right, spill. You've been moping all night." Lorie wasn't the kind of hostess who felt she had to hover over the caterers, wait staff, or her guests. She provided good food, top-notch wines and mixed drinks, pleasant company, and let the rest take its natural course. For now, she enjoyed a respite from the fun, collapsing in a corner grouping of chairs by the fire.

Margo set her champagne cocktail on a side table. "I don't mope." Yet something was wrong. Less than a month ago, she'd been fine. Now she was . . . broken. Like a pinhead crack in the windshield that grew into a huge fracture right down the middle.

Lorie retrieved the flute and put it back in Margo's hand. "Your mother drove you crazy over Christmas, right?"

It was almost a week later, and Margo had to admit she was just recovering. She'd gone to her mom's in Napa on Christmas Eve and returned the day after. Being an only child and her father having passed away, it was she and her mom for a day and two nights. Ugh. "No worse than usual."

Her mother's litany of do's and don'ts rattled around in her brain. If nothing else, it showed her what she was in for if she dated a younger man. Yet she couldn't stop aching for Dirk's touch, his big hands, massive body, and adorable dimple.

His words echoed. *You're just afraid to take a risk.*

Lorie kicked off her high heels and tucked her legs beneath her. "No, really, tell me what Mommy Dearest did this time."

"She's not Mommy Dearest." Nor was she the person Margo needed to talk about. In the days since she'd walked out of Dirk's house, she'd realized the disservice she'd done to her friend by not trusting her with the truth. Lorie would never judge, and Margo needed to talk badly.

"I never told you why Richard left," she said. Starting with Richard was a step closer to telling Lorie everything.

"I thought he met that bimbo Katrina."

Margo had allowed Lorie to believe Katrina came before the breakup. It was easier than the truth. "The problem was that he wanted us to do a few kinky things with another couple." She'd said it. And the earth hadn't shattered or the sky fallen.

Lorie merely tipped her head, her nostrils flaring slightly even as her eyes widened. "What kind of kinky things? Do tell."

Margo glanced around. Their corner had gone unnoticed for the moment. "He wanted us to have sex in front of another couple. You know, they watch us, we watch them."

Lorie's glance strayed to Carl for a moment. "What a naughty boy. Of course you told him no."

Margo fortified herself with a sip of bubbly. "I said yes."

"Get out," Lorie whispered, leaning in avidly. "Did you?"

"No. The couple turned out to be neighbors of ours."

"Oh my God." Lorie let out a breath. "Have I met them?"

"No. And I put the kibosh on the whole thing."

Lorie gave her a sly smile. "But you would have done it if it wasn't the neighbors?"

Honestly? "It seemed pretty exciting at first."

"Aren't *you* full of surprises." Lorie tapped her chin with her champagne flute. "And Richard dumped you just for that?"

He dumped her for the same reason Dirk had let her walk out the door. Because she wasn't willing to take a risk. *Any* risk. "He said the neighbors were an excuse. That I'd never want to try anything that added a little pizzazz."

"Honey, I say good riddance to him. If he didn't accept you the way you are, then he wasn't worth it." She patted Margo's hand. "But why didn't you tell me all this?"

Margo didn't have the right words.

"Oh my God, you'd thought I'd disapprove of you. Me, your best friend." Hurt glittered in Lorie's eyes.

"I didn't approve of myself even thinking about doing it."

"You need to lighten up." Lorie lowered her voice. "Once, Carl made me come in a restaurant." She widened her eyes. "He put his hand up my skirt under cover of the tablecloth."

"You're kidding." Margo knew Lorie wasn't straitlaced, but she'd never have imagined something like that.

Biting her lip, Lorie looked at Carl once more, a gleam in her eye. "It was the hottest thing I've ever done in my life."

Dirk was the hottest thing Margo had ever done. He was the reason she'd started the confession. "You remember that ad you had from your brother's friend?"

"Zach's friend?" Lorie looked at her a moment as if the question didn't even compute.

"Dirk? He wanted a model?" Margo prompted.

Lorie tucked her chin and frowned. "Yeah. Okay."

"Well, I answered his ad." She could hear her heart beating in her ears waiting for Lorie to say something, anything.

Lorie just stared before finally answering. "I don't get it."

It was so beyond comprehension that Lorie couldn't even fathom it. Lord. Margo had to spell it out. "I modeled for him"—pause, heart beating faster, flush creeping up her skin—"erotic photos."

Gradually, a smile kicked up the corners of Lorie's mouth. "You naughty little girl." She laughed. "Good for you."

"Good?" Margo gaped. "He's the same age as your brother."

"So? It's not like he's jail bait." Lorie tipped her head. "Did you have sex with him?"

And when Margo nodded slowly, Lorie giggled, then glanced at Carl. "Don't give me away, but I've always thought Dirk was hot. All those muscles." She shivered dramatically.

"His hands," Margo whispered. God. Lorie didn't freak. She actually *approved*. "Why didn't you mention he was some wrestling star?"

"Because I didn't have a clue you were interested." Lorie sighed.

"But you could have told me what you intended. I'm not your mother, you know."

"I should have let you know what I was thinking. I'm sorry." Then Margo told her best friend the whole story. It took the entire glass of champagne. "Now he wants to *date* me."

Lorie signaled a waiter for refills. When he left, she clinked glasses. "A younger man, it's better if you just have sex with him." Then she jutted her chin out. "Isn't it?"

Margo had been going round on that issue. "He pretty much said it was all or nothing." Either she was his girlfriend. Or she wasn't.

Lorie shook her head. "Doesn't he see it can't last?"

Margo knew why she'd told Lorie the truth. She wanted someone to validate what she wanted. Her heart plummeted when she didn't get the answer she craved. "He seems to think it can."

"You know how important your image is to your business. He can't expect you to just throw all that away."

Yes, he could. Which didn't seem quite fair. He wasn't the one they'd hold up to ridicule.

"I mean, he *is* a celebrity." Lorie wrinkled her brow. "Even if it is that wrestling stuff."

Margo itched to defend him. Wrestling wasn't *stuff.* Just as his photography wasn't a mere hobby. But Lorie was right about everything else. He'd have groupies and paparazzi following him. Margo would be a laughingstock.

"You're saying all the things I've been telling myself." Yet she wanted him so badly that she had trouble sleeping, eating, getting up in the morning, working . . .

Lorie patted her knee. "You'll get over it, hon. The right guy is out there, someone you have more in common with. Dirk's a big old sweetie, but . . ." She held her palms out in a you've-gotta-know-what-I-mean gesture.

"You're right." Yet it left her with that broken feeling inside. "One or both of us would get hurt in the end."

"Yeah. Better to nip all that pain in the bud."

But what if it didn't hurt? What if things worked out? Like

Betsy and her lover Orson. At that age, people merely said, "More power to you, baby."

"Besides, your mother would have a stroke *and* a heart attack at the same time," Lorie added, like icing on the cake.

Her mother would never in a million years approve of Dirk or his mother, Betsy. But Margo's mother was also alone. She'd likely die that way, too, with her high standards, her highbrow friends, her orderly house, and never a whisper of gossip.

No one had ever said anything bad about her mother. Because she'd never taken a chance. She'd never risked.

And she was alone.

Margo didn't want to be alone. The question was whether another man would turn up in her life who made her feel the way Dirk did.

Did she want to risk never finding that feeling again? Or take a chance on Dirk?

⌘

Maybe he'd made a mistake. He should have told her sex would be fine and let time work its magic.

Pinned by Dirk's hammerlock, Pain Freak grunted, groaned, and strained. The referee counted to three, grabbed Dirk's arm, and declared him the winner. The crowd went ape.

The New Year's Day exhibition fight in Sacramento was packed. Cheering, jeering, shouting, you could count on a match crowd to be enthusiastic. Turning in a circle as Pain Freak crawled off the mat, Dirk ran in place to bleed off the adrenaline. Fight fans shoved up against the ropes shouting out a chorus of "Ironman, Ironman, Ironman." Two teenage girls screamed for his sweaty towel, then fought to the damn near death when he tossed it. A woman pulled her shirt up for a glimpse of her breasts before Security dragged her off.

Women had offered him any sexual favor he could think of, some he didn't believe were possible. He'd even had a few guys hit on him. There were always the groupies hanging out when he left, or at the after-parties.

Dirk just wanted to make the three-hour drive back home in one piece. His manager threw him his robe, and Dirk caught it in one fist, crushing the red and yellow satin before he yanked it on. He spat out his mouth guard in the bucket and grabbed a clean towel to wipe the sweat off his head and face. The stadium lights were intense. He got a few spots before his eyes.

Which would explain the hallucination. Margo. Down there in the crowd, six or seven people back in the stack. He wanted her so bad he'd conjured her up. God, she was beautiful, all streaked blond hair, gorgeous green eyes, body that wouldn't quit, and a perfect smile. He'd gone crazy for her smile, of all things. She seemed to be saying something, but his ears were ringing in the din. He climbed through the ropes, held on a moment because she didn't disappear like an apparition should.

Security stepped up, ready to escort him to the locker room.

He shouldn't have been able to make out a damn thing in the cacophony of music and sound, but he heard his real name, not Ironman, but Dirk. And the haunting figure waved her arm at him.

Holy Hell, that was no figment. Margo was here.

Below him, he grabbed Jamie's arm, head of Security.

"That woman," he shouted, pointing. "Bring her here. I need to talk to her."

The crowd pushed and shoved, flowing, and seemed to carry her away, but two security guys reached her, wrapped her in protective custody, and elbowed their way back, handing her up into the ring with him.

Dirk couldn't hear a damn thing over the roaring in his ears. So he gathered her in his arms and kissed her, hard, lips, tongue, her taste sweet and hot. Then he remembered he was sweaty from the fight, and they were in the middle of a crowd of thousands. Yet Margo kissed him back and clung to him.

He lifted her right off the mat. The crowd went freaking manic, camera flashes filled the stadium, and Margo smiled.

"What are you doing here?" he bellowed in her ear.

She pulled back. "I missed you."

He had to read her lips, and his heart beat harder than when he'd body-slammed Pain Freak.

He was getting another chance, and he wasn't going to screw it up this time. He had to get her out of here before the reporters started asking who she was. Handing her through the ropes into Jamie's arms, he then climbed down himself. Her hand tucked securely in his and surrounded by the cocoon of Security, they headed into the stadium underground for the locker rooms.

There'd be reporters in there, too, cameras. Dirk grabbed Jamie's arm. "I need somewhere private. So she and I can talk."

Jamie grinned. A short, stocky guy with state-of-the-art communications equipment coming out his ears, Jamie knew the rabbit den down here like the back of his hand. With a series of hand gestures like an NFL referee, he sent his guys away, ushered Dirk down a corridor, unlocked a door, and flipped on a light.

"I'll be back in fifteen minutes to let you out." Then he winked. "Enough time?"

Christ, the man thought he was going to fuck Margo, and in this dinky little cleaning supply closet.

"It's enough time." He closed the door on Jamie's shit-eating grin and grabbed Margo's arms. "What are you doing here?" His heart pounded so loudly, he still had to read her lips.

"I came to tell you I was wrong."

"You weren't wrong. I asked for too much when you barely knew me. I should have backed off. We can do the private thing until"—he shrugged—"you're more comfortable. If you never—"

"Would you please shut up?" Her smile took the bite out.

"Yes, ma'am." He'd wanted everything on the table.

"First, I love the way you fight."

An odd kick started low in his gut.

She pulled his head down to Eskimo-nose him. "It was hot."

"Only because I didn't get beaten this time."

She put his hand on her breast beneath the dark wool coat she wore. Her nipples were hard under her sweater, filling his palm. Her heat rose, sweet, musky arousal. "I've got a hotel room, and I want you to take me there and do me all night long."

Okay, sex, he could handle that. After months of good sex, she'd be his forever. Right? He'd convince her. For sure. He'd never given up on anything in his life, and he wasn't giving up on Margo Faraday. "I can do that."

"But I also want you to know that I'm not like my mother."

Dirk nodded. "Uh-huh."

Margo didn't expect him to get it. He was moist, sweaty, yet he smelled all hot, heavy, hungry male, and she reveled in the scent of him. But really, she had to tell him what she'd figured out last night with Lorie. She'd called him, and when she couldn't get hold of him, she'd Googled him, found his Ironman website, and like a smitten groupie, driven at breakneck speed to attend his fight. To tell him.

"My mother has the ideal image. Everyone thinks she's the most wonderful woman, the head of all her charity committees, she dines with the mayor." Margo made a face. "She's simply smashing in all her friends' eyes, a paragon of virtue."

"And you're not?"

She enjoyed the incredulity in his voice. "No." She'd never been enough in her mother's eyes. Wriggling closer to him, she slipped her hands beneath his satin Ironman robe. "I'm not virtuous. I like doing nasty things to younger men." She waggled her eyebrows lecherously.

"I'm into nasty," he agreed.

She rubbed her belly against his erection. "Good. Because I want us to think up naughtier things to do. Give it all a chance, take a few risks. I don't want to regret that we didn't try something because we were afraid someone might not approve or that it wouldn't turn out the way we wanted it to." Like her mother. Who never took a chance on anything so that her image could never be tarnished. "I will not be virtuous yet unhappy."

He slid his hands down to her butt. "I'm going to make you happy." He captured her mouth, kissed her sweetly, deeply, then pulled back. "No one has to know about us."

She knew how much that cost him. "You don't want that."

"I don't give a shit as long as you're with me."

She smoothed a hand across that adorable brow of his. Then she went up on her toes to kiss his once-broken nose. "Ask for what you want, Dirk. Don't let anyone stop you. Not even me."

He tilted his head back, staring at the bare bulb hanging from the ceiling. Then he came back to her. "You're right. I want you to come to my fights and go to the parties when I win, and fuck me all better when I lose."

"You won't lose."

"I want you to look at my photos and tell me what you like or what I should have done differently. I want you to pinch my arm when we're out and say, 'Holy shit, honey, there's a great shot, please get it for me.' I want you to believe in me."

Her heart turned over. He wanted so much. "I want to be sixty-two and still calling you my lover," she whispered. "I want everyone to know I'm yours no matter how much younger you are or how old I am."

He took two quick breaths, emotion rolling over his face. "We don't have to tell anyone yet. We can wait until you're ready."

She cupped his cheek. "I'm ready." She closed her eyes for a moment as her mother's voice echoed in her head. "I'll cringe when my mom asks me where on earth my head is these days, but I will never hide you. I'm sorry I wanted to keep you a secret."

"Baby, don't apologize, okay? I'm the one who gets exactly what he wants, and you're the one making the sacrifice."

She went on her toes and nipped his lip. "I don't want to be my mother's age and regretting that I never took advantage of the most adorable younger man I've ever had the hots for."

"Shucks," he said, but the loud thump of his heart so close to her ear told his story.

Then she held her watch up to the light. "It's only been five minutes. You've got ten more before your friend gets back." She smiled. "Wanna do me against the door? I'll scream so everyone knows exactly what we're doing."

He laughed. And that gorgeous dimple appeared at the side of his mouth. "You're such a romantic."

"Oh yeah," she murmured, her lips close to his, "I don't want to leave this supply room without everyone in the entire stadium knowing you just did me in here."

He pushed her coat apart, lifted her, pulling her legs to his waist, and braced her against the door. "Make sure you scream my name really loud, baby."

He ran his hands up her skirt, and she saw the moment he figured out she wasn't wearing panties. His blue eyes blazed.

"And," she said as he rubbed his fingers across her, "I think you should use one of my photos for the competition." Her mother would absolutely die, but Dirk made Margo feel beautiful. And she was damn proud of those pictures.

His eyes glowed hot, then he kissed her, and finally whispered in her ear, "In that case, I'll win everything I've ever wanted."

How could she lose? Betting on Ironman was a sure thing.

Jasmine Haynes has been penning stories for as long as she's been able to write. Storytelling has always been her passion. With a bachelor's degree in accounting from Cal Poly San Luis Obispo, she has worked in the high-tech Silicon Valley for the last twenty years and hasn't met a boring accountant yet! Well, maybe a few. She and her husband live with their cat, Eddie (short for Eddie Munster, get the picture?), and Star, the mighty moose-hunting dog (if she weren't afraid of her own shadow.) Jasmine's pastimes, when not writing her heart out, are hiking in the redwoods and taking long walks on the beach.

Jasmine also writes as Jennifer Skully and JB Skully. She loves to hear from readers. Please e-mail her at skully@skullybuzz.com or visit her website at www.skullybuzz.com. Her newsletter subscription is skullybuzz-subscribe@yahoogroups.com.

Don't miss her exciting new novel, *Fair Game*, coming in June 2009 from Heat. Turn to the back of the book for a sneak preview.

Controlled Response

JOEY W. HILL

One

Forty-five miles. God, the only thing better than this was sex. Sex done exceptionally well. As Lucas crested the hill, pushing the burn in his legs, he snagged his water bottle to take a measured draught. Releasing the bike handlebars to coast hands-free, he shifted his hips to negotiate the inevitable curve. No such thing as a straight line or a flat expanse this deep in the Berkshires. Every downward slope followed by a challenging upward one. Like the curves of a woman's body. Or her mind.

Ben had given him shit about hopping a charter here for the weekend when they were still figuring out how to make the numbers work for the Mancuso plant operation. But it was all bullshit, because Ben knew Lucas did his best problem solving while cycling, just as the legal advisor did it by finding the prettiest ass available and immersing himself in it. When they came back to the office Monday, Ben would fix the legal snarls, and Lucas would crunch the numbers into manageable pieces. Hell, Matt should save the money on their corner offices. Though Lucas had to admit he liked his Baton Rouge city view, with the backdrop of the Mississippi River.

It was time for a lunch break and a stretch, if he could find the spot his buddy Marcus had told him was right off the road around here. He was pretty deep in the Berkshire farm area, but tourists did have a way of finding the hot spots. Still, Marcus had stressed "hidden," even giving him GPS coordinates for the exact location, give or take ten feet.

There it was. As he rolled across the shoulder, he saw the narrow deer trail. A couple broken twigs and some spoor suggested the brown-eyed creatures had passed through recently.

It was a short hike, so it worked as a good cool-down. The light racing bike was easy to carry, even with his gear. Marcus had said the glade would have a stream, soft grass for a nap, and a frame of trees for the sky that would make Lucas think he'd fallen into a nest made by Heaven itself. Marcus was a gallery owner, brushing shoulders with New York art types, so such metaphors were to be expected. Or maybe the description had come from Thomas, his spouse, or life partner, whatever they called it. It sounded like a good place and Lucas wouldn't dwell on what they might have done there. To each his own, but his preference definitely ran to heart-shaped asses of a different gender. Skin like cream, and tender pink lips hidden like treasure between not-too-firm, not-too-soft thighs. Just like Goldilocks, he knew when they were just right.

Lately, it had been just okay. Some lovely ladies, intelligent, beautiful, and willing. Business associates on the same time schedules, which discouraged anything deeper on either side but ensured dinner dates and sexual release were no farther than a cell phone call. He was CFO for Kensington & Associates, after all, so he didn't have trouble with that.

But maybe it was watching Matt, the head of K&A, with his new wife, Savannah, during the past year. The way they'd taken the leap of faith together, and their love just seemed to grow and grow. Not like a molasses flood, drowning everyone in reach in gooeyness. More like the quiet reassurance of the ocean's murmur. Timeless, clean, overwhelming. Proof that there was a greater purpose here. Maybe Lucas was ready for something deeper himself. Maybe that was why he was cycling and Ben was hip deep in pussy by now.

As he stepped into the clearing, anticipating the tranquility, he came to a dead stop, his thoughts scattering like a game of 52-card pickup.

Marcus hadn't mentioned the spot came with a half-naked girl on a motorcycle.

Either that, or Lucas had been run over by a minivan and didn't realize he was dead, stumbling into everything Heaven should be. If so, he was profoundly thankful to the minivan driver.

He blinked. Yes, it was definitely a woman, stretched out on the curved seat of a Night Rod series Harley. At one time, she'd apparently been wearing black jeans with riding chaps over them, for they were in a crumpled pile next to the bike, leaving her lower body clad only in a pair of silky ivory panties. Her feet were braced on the handlebars, legs spread, ass snugged down in the driver's seat while her upper body was arched over the hump to the passenger seat. The toned legs and generous ass were taut, for her fingers were tucked into the panties. Thanks to the blessing of filmy material, he could see their individual movements.

She was wearing a corset. Ivory colored as well, with one strap falling off her shoulder and elevating her breasts so they were accentuated by the slightest breath. Just a touch of lace at the low décolletage that tempted full exposure from the crescent stretch of her torso. The corset hooked in front, so would lie flat under the heavy white T-shirt she'd been wearing, also lying in the grass.

Tiny earphones for a music player were tucked into ears as delicate as porcelain, half-hidden by her hair, skeins of white gold long enough to fall over the top of the rear tire. A few strands were scattered across her face by the breeze, teasing wet, parted lips. Her bare feet flexed against the chrome bars as she apparently hit a good spot, biting her lip. Since her eyes were closed, golden lashes fanning her cheeks, he imagined she was deep in some fantasy, picturing her fingers as someone else's.

Or perhaps she was thinking about someone watching her, getting hungrier for a taste of the pussy she'd teased into a wetness that had soaked the crotch panel. Someone who wanted to slide his hands under her, grip that delectable ass, and tongue her first through the saturated silk. Bite her clit through her panties. Women loved that, the buffer to stimulation that provided friction, helped warm them up, so that when he finally pulled the cloth out of the way and tasted creamed flesh, they would be writhing, begging.

God, he loved eating pussy. Second best thing to fucking it.

A gentleman—not to mention a smart man—would have backed away. But he couldn't make his feet move. This was undeniably a gift from God, and he was a devout Methodist. Okay, at least when he went home to Iowa during Christmas and attended church with his parents. Regardless, there was a higher power, a higher order. Hadn't he just been thinking that? Maybe this was an answer.

Yes, Lucas. In your search for a deeper relationship, God has sent you to a private photo shoot from Penthouse.

Hey, crazier things had happened. Like his spontaneous decision now to become part of her fantasy. As he moved forward, he hoped she wasn't armed.

⋙⋘

Oh, she'd so needed this. Cassandra didn't like being away from home, but she'd had to come to Hartford to close this deal. Two days of managing the negotiation had been bad enough, but she'd had to deal long-distance with crisis after crisis at home, from the minor issues that came up with her younger siblings to a frantic call from the nanny saying her black-sheep brother had gotten as close as the security gate. Fortunately, the guard had sent him on his way. Everything was okay there, and she'd been waiting to fly home to Baton Rouge in time to listen to her baby brother Nate sing her a new song he'd learned. That had been before the general manager had put in a frantic call telling her the deal she'd just finalized had unraveled. Knitting it back together had involved a trip back to the Hartford office and some corporate diplomacy, along with a little tactical bullying of the key players for having almost dumped a sixty-million-dollar contract over some childish perceived insult.

That detour had kept her in the area an extra day, so when she'd passed the motorcycle dealership and saw that they did day rentals for enjoying the Berkshire scenery, she'd thought, why the hell not? She'd chosen the Night Rod and headed out with a map.

Finding this glade had been an extraordinary accident. Pulled over to take a break, she'd seen a pair of deer slipping into the forest. She'd brought a camera, wanting to take some pictures for the kids, so when she'd followed their path, heard the inviting rush of water, she found a stream with a small waterfall, a spot too far off the beaten path for anyone to find. Perfect. Even though she was far from home, the idea of being far from anyone, out of the eye of the world completely, was exactly what she needed.

It seemed sometimes that all she dealt with were children. She much preferred her siblings to those well into supposed adulthood. Was every man in the world looking for Mommy? Did any of them know how to use their brains *and* take charge, hold the reins comfortably? She'd met precious few like that.

As she'd sat in the grass, leaning against the comforting bulk of the bike, she'd closed her eyes, imagined that hard bulk as such a man. Lying back between his legs, the two of them enjoying the quiet beauty of the setting. His hands would slide up to cup her breasts, tease the nipples with relentless skill as he pushed her hair aside to kiss her throat, holding her fast as her legs moved restlessly in the grass, needing his touch between them, something he held just out of reach to drive her need higher.

In a house of five kids, with her responsibilities as their guardian, there was little privacy, even to do this. Often she felt like a bottle of soda, shaken to the point of near explosion. Jesus, she'd even resorted to adolescent metaphors for her sexual frustration.

She wanted to stretch her body out on the seat of the muscle bike, strip down to nothing but panties and corset, and make herself come, imagining herself as the pinup of some virile god's fantasy, watched by him through the trees. She'd know he was there, so her movements would be provocative, blatantly carnal, until he couldn't resist any longer and came to her. He'd turn her over the back of the bike, bind her wrists to the pedals, spread her legs wide over the rear tire, the sun's heat on the chrome burning her flesh, and oh, God, she'd be dripping for his cock. But instead he'd kneel first, go to work on her with his mouth, until she was screaming, begging . . .

She'd put on her ear phones so she wouldn't worry about every rustle of woodland creature, the snapping of twigs. No one was out here, and she didn't want to care anyway. Truth to tell, it wasn't a bad fantasy, imagining someone stumbling upon her. Someone whose name she didn't need to know, who wouldn't let her negotiate or get away with anything. Who would see through every ploy and sweep her choices away.

"Please, let me . . ." She knew she'd spoken it aloud, a whisper, though she couldn't hear it over the hard bass line. When her eyes opened on a brief flicker to let in sunlight, they stayed open. Widened.

Apparently, some perverse nature god had answered her silent plea.

He was outlined by the midafternoon sun, but the shadowing only enhanced everything she wanted to see. Tall, which she liked, because she was five-eight. Golden blond hair pushed back, highlighted with darkened streaks from sweat. He was shirtless, the muscles glistening as if oiled. She'd seen bodies with swollen and bunched muscle, but he was as compact as a spring. Flat pectorals, one or two faint veins following the curves of his biceps. The small silver medallion he wore, perhaps a religious symbol, fell in the ridged vee that divided the pecs and coaxed the press of her thumbs. There was nothing wasted on him. While the arms were muscular, she could see the architecture of his collarbone and rib cage, the frame it provided for the tight stomach that wasn't a six-pack, just a slab of smooth muscle, with an indentation of navel that looked as firm. Tanned, he wore nothing but a pair of tight bike shorts and biking cleats, showing off a pair of calves and thighs also roped with taut muscle.

He was a young god by anyone's standards, but the shorts and shoes said he was definitely of her species. A man who'd interrupted something embarrassingly personal.

She wasn't the type to jump up shrieking over it. Kind of beside the point now, anyway. She *was* the type to tell someone to fuck off and let her get on with it, and watch him run in terror. But unlike some of the infantile examples of manhood she'd been dealing with the past couple days, he didn't strike her as the bolting kind. It interested her, made her blood ratchet up a few degrees, her body obviously enjoying the view as she weighed what to do next. Or maybe she'd just see what *he* did next.

While she waited, her gaze lifted to his mouth. The lean, athletic face which matched the body confirmed he didn't play—he competed. He had the long, sloping jawline she imagined an Egyptian prince might have. Lips with a touch of sensual fullness to them, and a short hairstyle, just the points of the strands scattered over his high forehead. A tapering to short sideburns. He had a hairstylist who knew his or her business, which said money, but the body was a hundred percent from the sweat of his brow. She liked the way the silver medallion lay on his bare skin. She wanted to taste the metal chain and the sweat of it beneath, the salt of him.

As he noted her regard, he casually dropped to a squat, his forearms propped on his spread thighs, fingers grazing the earth. Maybe because he could see her earplugs, he didn't speak, but it intensified the moment, encouraging her to continue.

She had a Beretta in the backpack and knew how to use it. She'd also had self-defense courses, enough to know isolating herself was stupid, since the first line of self-defense for a smart woman was not to put herself in dangerous situations. But she doubted many psycho serial rapists went out on their bicycles in the rural Berkshires, seeking chance encounters with lone women.

His attention was on her lips now, her throat, sweeping down over the corset, a question in his eyes, for of course it wasn't most women's choice of practical underwear. But then he moved his gaze back to her hand. Though she'd frozen at his appearance, she still held two fingers inside the panties, lying on her quivering clit, the other two fingers on the outside, her thumb in the crease of her thigh.

Keep going. He mouthed it, she was sure. From the look in his steady gray eyes, it wasn't a request.

She stared at him. *Breathe slow. Even. Hold it steady.* The corset required that. Even an orgasm could get too out of hand, and she had a feeling it was about to, for as his lips formed the words, her clit shuddered under the bare friction of her still fingers.

He was waiting to see if she was the type of person who would continue. She had no idea what that would make her in his eyes, but why should she care? He wanted her to continue, and hell yes, she wanted to continue. She was far from home here.

When she began to move her fingers, his gaze immediately returned there. Holy God, who knew that actually *being* watched was ten times more stimulating than fantasizing about it? And it had been a pretty good fantasy at that. Still, she closed her eyes. Reaching over her head, she found the crisscross of black bungee cords holding her pack. When she slid her free hand under them, the cords cut against her skin, goading her imaginings about her god binding her as he spread her this way, while his mouth . . .

⋙⋘

She sought restraint for her pleasure. That alone spiked Lucas's response. With his casual bed partners being primarily businesswomen who felt they had to hold the upper hand, it wasn't easy to find one who naturally desired the more dominant forms of sex he preferred. He wondered if that was the reason she wore a corset under her clothes.

God in Heaven, what was a woman like this doing in a secluded glade, having to pleasure herself? The way she'd looked at him, that half challenge, daring him to run or stay, laced with a sensual desperation that said *Don't ruin this*, had added to the intrigue.

Now he rose, moved to her. As he laid a hand on her raised calf, her gaze sprang open. He stayed that way, not retreating, giving her time. As he smelled her arousal, his nostrils flared, for her gaze registered it, her breath quickening. When she made a visible effort to modulate it, he noted she seemed to be using the corset to control the level of her own arousal. *Interesting.*

He leaned forward, just enough to have her blue eyes widen a fraction. Pausing, he listened to the faint sound of what was coming through her player. "Hot Blooded," by Foreigner. It told him what pace she'd been setting for herself. But if he was the stimulus, rather than Foreigner's bass line, he thought something else might work better.

Since the player was tucked into the open flap of a saddlebag, he drew it out by the cord so she wouldn't think he was rummaging through her things, then scrolled through the menu.

She had eclectic music taste. Ballads, rock, jazz of the smooth variety. But she also had some things that were off the beaten path. Edgy music that could take the mind to a new place, where the unimaginable might become acceptable. He hit the song he wanted.

⚜

"Destiny," by Zero 7. Had he played the song because of the title? No, this guy wasn't that cheesy. He'd known the song, knew it had a dark urgency to it. The haunting opening strains talked about a woman alone in her hotel room, watching pay channel porn and dreaming of her lover. There was a loneliness to it. It was about desire, not thought. The need for someone to understand her, down to the dark, below-the-soul levels.

So he knew the song. But how did he know it would be the right song for this moment, for her?

He was still leaning over her, his gray eyes studying her with an intensity that suggested . . . not invasion, but as if he was figuring her out. When his gaze finally dropped to her mouth, she had to swallow. As his attention continued to descend, he might as well have put his hands on her, because she *felt* the weight of his touch in his gaze. He smelled of sweat. Basic earth, male strength.

Men fell short in many ways, but they could sometimes be relied upon for this. He'd just happened on the rare moment when his abilities and her needs were in perfect accord. Lucky him. Lucky her. In this clearing, where he didn't know her name, she'd take it, because he'd done all the right things, made all the right moves, the stages of the dance all male animals had to know to win the willingness of a female. Circling, nonthreatening approach, respectful, but knowing when to switch gears and make the request a demand, bring the force of passion to the mix. It was amazing that humans, supposedly the most intelligent of all species, often fumbled the steps even a field mouse could handle.

As his gaze rose, pinned her again, she gave a bare movement of her head. A nod. *Yes. God, yes.* But she wouldn't help him. She was tired of orchestrating the whole damn world so it would work the way it should. She wanted to see if someone else could do it.

Usually, she felt compelled to direct. *Touch me here, squeeze that. Kiss me more.* But when sex was like choreographing a major Broadway production, it was too exhausting to be worth the bother, really.

Putting his hands on her waist, he spanned it, his hands over the tight lacing. Then he moved upward, slow, not as if he was doing it to please her, but as if he was learning her for himself, which pleased her more.

Slow, slow, he held her firmly as his strong fingers moved up over her rib cage. This was a man who not only knew how to touch women, but that each one needed to be handled uniquely, an important component of the foreplay.

As he reached her breasts, he stopped, his forefinger and thumb fitting beneath each.

She wanted to draw a deeper breath, but couldn't. She had to keep herself calm. Even. She could do that. If she could do it right now, she could do it anytime. She wouldn't touch him. That would help. But Jesus, the body this man had. She wanted to trail her fingers down his sides, feel the prominent ribs that racked into the muscular abdomen, play at the snug band of the cycling shorts which showed the sleek curve of a sizable erection. Hadn't she heard somewhere they didn't wear any underwear under those? When she made herself look up, she couldn't prevent a groan as he cupped her breasts, squeezing just enough so they swelled farther out the top of the corset. Not gentle. He didn't hurt her, but he conveyed his desire. The dangerous spark in his gaze at her groan told her he could get a lot rougher, if that was the direction the tone went. He didn't mind getting down and dirty as needed to make it blow-your-mind sex.

If she could get all that from one look, she was still fantasizing. But that was okay. For once, she wasn't going to scale back her ex-pectations just because they appeared unrealistic. If he did everything perfectly, she'd know she was dreaming, no harm done. Even if he did a couple things wrong, she still wouldn't be tossing him out anytime soon.

Then his hand went to the first hook of the corset.

Freeze fantasy.

Automatically, Cass caught his wrist with her free hand, an unspoken direction. *That needs to stay on.*

The god toyed with it, his fingers shifting beneath her grip. She suspected he could make short, deft work of the undergarment. It was an effort to hold on to her resolve, because she wanted those long fingers, wanted to explore the shape of his knuckles, the lines between them, the broad shape of the palm. One more moment, and she knew she'd give in.

Then he gave her an inclination of his head, a twist of the sensuous lips. Not capitulation. He was just letting her have her way. For now. It stoked the need in her, and pulling her hand away from his flesh didn't ease it.

Now one large hand slid back down to her waist. The other closed around her wrist and withdrew the hand she had in her panties. The motion dragged her fingers over her clit, and that, combined with his intent, was like electrical current. Bringing her damp fingers to his mouth, he took them between his lips, sucked them in deep.

A man who took the reins from a woman in a sexual situation so effectively that it left no doubt who was in charge. That was what she'd wanted, right?

"Ah . . ." Her body undulated on the seat, a sinuous emulation of what it wanted, before she could stop it. Those full lips were firm and soft at once, his mouth hot, teeth nipping, laving at fingers covered with her scent. As he drew them out, he lowered her wet hand, as if he was going to place it on his chest.

Too much temptation, the idea of trailing damp fingers over his muscled flesh, marking him. She closed her fingers into a ball, drew it back to herself.

Again he allowed it, watching her closely all the while. The music had changed once again. Back to Foreigner's "Hot Blooded." It sparked a fire in her, such that she raised a leg, intending to place the sole on his tempting chest and shove him back, force him just to watch her. Instead, in a smooth motion, he closed his hand on her ankle, pushed it up to his shoulder, and then dropped to one knee.

As he hooked her leg in a firm grip she couldn't shake, panic came and went, gone fast, because he put his mouth on her, over the silky fabric of the panties.

"Oh . . ." The music boiled through her, warring with any protests, egging him on. The bass line was her heartbeat, pounding hard against her chest, the guitar riffs her gasping breath, too much, overwhelming.

If he'd stumbled around like most guys did down there, she might have freaked out and shaken him, but she was too aroused, and his mouth knew what to do even better than her way-too-familiar fingers. A scrape of the clit with his teeth, long, dragging licks of his tongue up the filmy fabric, the friction of it galvanizing her hips to his mouth, wanting to feel the press of his nose, the rasp of his cheeks on her thighs. Tomorrow, she wanted to see the marks, wanted it to chafe when she walked. Evidence that she'd had this over-the-top moment with a stranger.

She twisted, he held her still. She bucked, he moved with her. His mouth was relentless, taking her over from the second it was on her. Foreigner was as merciless as he was, moving from "Hot Blooded" to "Urgent." No fucking kidding. She wanted that climax so badly, but she wanted more, too, an uneasy, yearning feeling she couldn't stifle. Her vision was graying. Oh, damn it all, she couldn't breathe.

He knew that, too. Already rising, moving up her body, hands reaching for the corset.

"No. Don't take it off," she gasped. "Don't."

He muttered an oath she could hear even over the music, with his mouth so close to her ear, but he slid his hands under her arms and lifted her so she was leaning into his body, her cheek on the slick chest muscle. His fingers went to the adjustable laces at the back. Yeah, right. Most guys took five minutes fooling with a bra strap. She was an idiot. She'd probably asphyxiate before . . .

The garment loosened, more than she wanted to admit was needed, but she could breathe. Of course, she was inhaling him at the same time as the oxygen. Sun-warmed flesh, dense muscle. Feeling the touch of his hands on her and oh holy hell, what was he doing now?

Sweeping aside her hair, he laid his lips on the bump of vertebrae, just at her nape, still holding her close against his upper body.

The climax swept over her so fast, there was no anticipating it. It ricocheted up from where the ribbed seat pressed against her pussy—still spasming from the memory of his mouth—to her neck, where his lips rested now. He kept a tight grip on her hair, holding her head still beneath that erotic kiss. As she rocked herself against the seat helplessly, he grasped one of her buttocks, squeezing hard to add male demand to her jerking rhythm, working her against the friction of the seat until she was making frenzied cries, pushing against the solid wall of him. God, she wanted him between her legs, instead of a beast of metal. Hammering into her, holding her down . . .

The thought brought her down quickly, quicker than she wanted. She was shaken. Shaking, still catching her breath. As he'd pulled her up, it had yanked her ear phones free, so now the music was her own rasping breaths, the birds, the rush of water, the wind. The drumming of his heart, his own ragged sounds.

"Little idiot," he murmured, his jaw along her temple. She heard a faint Midwest trace under the blatant edge of desire. "You could have passed out."

"Well, who knew you'd be good at this?"

She said it without thinking and cursed herself. Guys got off on that kind of flattery, took it as invitation for more. She didn't want to stroke his ego, not when he'd ripped her open like that. Forced her to loosen her self-imposed restraints and turn control over to him.

Wrapping his hand in her hair, he canted her head back. Before she could think of something more quelling to say, he shocked her again by slamming his mouth down on hers, taking it over, and everything attached to it. Drinking deep, he made it everything a kiss should be. Fire, mind-altering, wet, demanding, scraping things raw that would scream in the open elements when he took his mouth away, so that she'd beg for it to return.

Raising his head when she was nowhere near sated, he held his grip so she couldn't try to follow his mouth. "I was just getting started, sweetheart."

Since he was still giving her that penetrating look, it suggested he was used to assessing things closely, determining what made them tick. But he disrupted her anxiety over that when he released her hair to run his hand beneath it, caress her nape in a way that said every time he touched her there, he'd remember what had shattered her. "Now, let me give you a real climax." As his gaze heated, she began to moisten again, anticipating. "If you thought what I did before was good, there've been too many losers in your life who didn't appreciate how they could make you sing."

A backhanded compliment for sure, she told herself, trying to keep the sensual intent of the words from muddling her mind more than he already had. Implying she was sexually deprived if she let something like a couple minutes of lip play get her off. Bastard.

"What's your name?"

She shook her head and he tipped up her chin, a trace of impatience in his eyes. "I want to know."

"A name comes with expectations."

"Identity," he agreed. "Repeat dates."

She couldn't afford a man like this in her life, for certain. He'd almost made her smile. "I'm taken."

He blinked once. "No, you're not."

Someone more inexperienced would have retorted, "How do you know?" But when words were used as weapons, she could hold the upper hand. She merely met him eye to eye and stayed silent, trying not to think about the fact she was wearing only soaked panties and a way-too-loose corset. While he was wearing a pair of shorts that should be illegal.

"If you were taken," he said, a sexy, rough edge to his voice, his

hand tightening on her sensitive neck, "I'd see him
There'd be a hint of his aftershave on your breasts, whe
the day by suckling your nipples, or razor burn where hi
your tender flesh. Your lips would be swollen from his k..... vv iicii
she tried to turn her head, he dragged his jaw along the side of her
neck, then placed his mouth there, spoke against her tingling skin.
"Or I'd have smelled him on your cunt. Because if he doesn't mark
you as his every morning before you walk out the door, he's insane."

Hadn't she compared this man's initial approach to that of an
animal? After a statement like that, he was pure animal for sure,
stating possession in terms understood by beasts of the forest. As
well as alpha males with a primal code like this, an undercurrent
that she knew women sensed but most could never truly understand.
Even as they were hopelessly drawn to it.

Still, women had their own code to survive such a devastating
assault. Drawing her head back, she managed a cool smile reflected
by no other part of her quivering body, but it was a starting point. "I
said I'm taken. I didn't mean by a man. I'm taken by the demands of
my life, and you're not part of it. Nor am I inviting you. Only into
this moment."

"So that's what this is about." He dipped his finger into the crevice between her breasts, tugged at the corset.

"What?"

"You wear it beneath your clothes. It's not fashion. Control is very
important to you."

"It's important to everyone."

"A woman in a corset has to be constantly aware of the state of
her body," he observed. "Never getting too flustered, stressed. It's an
armor of sorts, but a paradoxical one. Because while the parts so
tightly laced inside it lose some sensitivity to a man's touch, the parts
above and below become far more sensitive because of the constriction. The trail of a finger along the buttock, just below the corset
hem. Or the lightest kiss on the pillow of a breast. Or even the
nape . . ." His hand passed there again. When he put his lips back
on her shoulder, she had to ball her hands into fists to keep from

sliding her hands down the curve of his bare back, feeling the ridges of spine, how low those shorts came on his hips. Whether she could slip her hands beneath the band to explore the design of his lower back, the rise of his tight ass.

"Let me go down on you again, sweetheart. Let go of your precious control. Give me the bliss of eating your sweet pussy and hearing you scream for me."

She closed her eyes. *I really, really want to, which is why I can't.* "I need some water first. Do you have any?"

A pause. Raising his head, he studied her. "I do. I left my bike just over there. But playing the coward doesn't seem to be your style. If you're going to leave, you're the type who'd just knock a man flat on his ass and walk right over him, not look for a running head start."

"And you're the type who wouldn't get out of the way."

"Not if the fight is worth winning."

I can't say no to you. She'd had her twenty minutes, and that was all she could afford. "I'm out of time. I've got to go." Moving away from his intoxicating proximity, she grabbed up her jeans, pulled them on while he leaned on her bike seat, watched her silently. She tied on the chaps, fingers trying not to fumble beneath his gaze as she performed the intimate task. When she found her T-shirt, she looked down, realizing she needed to tighten the corset laces. Her breasts were in danger of coming out entirely. It was possible she'd even given him a glimpse of her nipples once or twice in her haste. Well, she'd call it just compensation for taking off on him.

"Allow me." He'd shifted when she'd been pointedly ignoring him, hoping he'd just vanish, and so now he was right behind her. "Stand still."

As she stiffened, uncertain whether to move away or not, his hand snaked around her waist and up, lifting the corset so the underwire was more fitted beneath her breasts. While he almost impersonally ran his hand over the cups, her nipples hardened from the passing heat of his touch. The liquid pooling between her thighs increased. He adjusted the laces, tightening, tightening again, until a breath escaped from her, a hint of a moan to it.

"You like that, don't you? You like it when a man binds you." His voice had lowered, animal urgency to it, his hands starting to slide downward, taking her resolve there as well.

She jerked away, knowing if he pulled her back so she could feel the hard line of his cock, she'd be lost. She'd let him plow her like a field. Yanking on the T-shirt, she turned, found her boots, and yanked them on as well. A quick grab at the handlebars and she had the twist for her hair she'd left there, whipping it up into a tight bun on her neck.

"Transformation. All armor in place now."

She ignored him, pleased when she managed a flippant tone. "The room's yours. If you want to continue." Though she really didn't want the provocative image of him stripping off his shorts to lie naked in the grass as God made him, his hand pumping what appeared to be an impressively proportioned cock. All muscles straining as he thought of her, as come spewed from him, wetting his thighs, his smooth ball sac, that hard belly where she could lick it off . . . *Sweet Mother Mary.*

"Don't cheapen it." He stepped forward, but surprised her when he didn't reach out to touch her. Even so, she felt the need to pick up the helmet, hold it as a casual barrier between them, trying to give him a diffident look.

Finally, when she thought she couldn't stand his silent scrutiny another moment, he leaned in. His body pushed against the helmet, brought the pressure of it against the churning in her belly. Despite herself, her lips parted, her eyes seeking his. "My mistake was in giving you a choice," he said. "Next time I get you alone, I won't do that. I'll restrain you the way you wanted to be, and then I'll make you come so hard you'll think you've died. You won't run away from me again. And I'll have the truth about why you feel you need to run now."

Unclogging vocal cords glued together by aching lust was not easy, but she managed it. "To the next time then," she said. A taunt, because of course they'd never see one another again. Moving around him, she strode to the bike.

She wished she could let him know how much she wanted to stay. She was sorry that she'd turned it into this. But he'd managed to kick in the door to her darkest needs in less than twenty minutes, and she couldn't afford to get lost there. It was for the best.

No, the best thing was to let him sate them both, spend another volatile hour together, and then go their separate ways as two strangers who'd enjoyed the novelty of an unexpected sexual encounter. Leaving a challenge in the air like this wasn't good. But he was right. She was being a coward, because if she stayed, she might just want to take him home. And she wouldn't embarrass herself, wouldn't reveal she was so desperate for this type of intimacy she would cling to a stranger. That was almost as pathetic as losing her perspective, making this about more than sex, and ruining it for both of them.

Because she wanted to apologize to him for that, she thought instead about clipping him, enough to make him stumble backward. She didn't, but he did something worse to her. As she passed him at a slow idle, her booted feet balancing her, his hand closed on her arm, so she released the handlebar. He didn't do anything to bring her to a halt, just followed the line of her arm down to her elbow, the tender skin of her forearm, and closed briefly on her fingertips before he let her hand pull free.

She could escape him, but not the irony of it. In his grasp, under the tantalizing hint of his control, she'd felt freer than she had in a very long time.

No, she definitely couldn't afford a man like him in her life.

Two

"Turns out they're sending over someone else to help us work out the final contract points this morning," Jon commented, setting his organizer on the conference room table. "Allan contracted the flu. Johnson called over to Pickard Consulting to send one of their people instead."

Lucas swore, slapping his legal pad down. "This is the type of pissing contest Johnson's been doing throughout this whole thing. I'll bet he talked to Pickard a week ago."

"They're sending Cassandra Moira," Jon added.

Ben whistled. "Big guns, that one."

When Peter lifted a brow, he chuckled. "And those aren't bad either, you complete tit addict."

Peter shot him a grin as Ben continued for Lucas's benefit. "She's one of Pickard's best, groomed right out of school. She's known for getting the job done and walking away from the table with more than you wanted to give away, but making you feel damn good about it. Be particularly careful about her, Lucas. She's hell on wheels on details. I think Pickard had her brain replaced with a CPU."

"We should cancel. We don't have to take this shit. Hell, let's make him think we're pulling out. Maybe he'll have a fatal heart attack and we won't have to deal with this crap anymore."

Jon lifted his brows, exchanged a look with Peter, but it was Ben who stated the obvious. "Are you getting laid enough? You've had that stick up your ass since you got back from the Berkshires last month, right before the Mancuso thing."

"Some of us don't need sex every night of the week," Lucas retorted, but he waved a dismissive hand and turned toward the window, cutting off further comments.

Yeah, he knew he was out of sorts. And he was sick of being out of sorts, and not knowing what to do about it.

He'd thought about lying down in the grass where her clothes had lain, where the crushed grass suggested *she* might have lain, and jacking off to relieve the seething frustration in his balls. Instead, he'd pedaled another thirty miles at a cardiac arrest RPM and cursed himself for not memorizing her plate. But it was just fun and games, right? He'd played sex games enough to know the edge during was as serious and purposeful as it should be, to give the fantasy a sense of reality. But afterward, it was supposed to become a fond memory. Not a damn possession of his mind.

He could have called ten different women when he got back, but he hadn't. He was still thinking about her, the honeysuckle scent of her hair and skin, the enormous blue eyes that had shifted away from desire at the end, when he'd put his foot in his mouth, intruding on their fantasy with a too-close-to-home observation about her reality.

Damn it all, he had more finesse than that. If it was fun and games, you didn't poke at the underlayer. But she'd been so armored, not only in the corset but everything he sensed it represented to her. He believed in pushing a woman far beyond what she believed her capacity for pleasure was, because that was what brought them both the most pleasure. To do that for his blue-eyed mystery, he'd known he needed to strip those layers away. Maybe that was what was bugging him. He didn't like leaving a woman unsatisfied, even if the retreat had been her choice.

My mistake was giving you a choice . . .

She was protective of something in her life, something that couldn't afford romantic entanglements. "I'm taken." That meant kids, though he'd seen no evidence of it on her body. Even on a fit woman, signs of childbearing lingered. Still, he was sure that was it. She was also doing it alone. A woman who would take a Harley deep into the Berkshires, who could assess him and let herself go just that small amount, was a hell of a confident woman. On the other hand, that quick, guilty climax had nearly been strangled out of existence by her own will.

Kick-ass confident, but way too tightly laced. Literally.

All five of the K&A management team grouped in this room knew how to read people, but the other four acknowledged he was the best at it. His assessment, based on their short interlude, was that she was tough, determined, and wary of any perception of vulnerability, but she didn't have the weakness in her that many damaged women did. She'd fought for respect in her world and won it, if he didn't miss his mark. She wasn't going to allow anything to derail the forward motion of that train.

"She might just be your soul mate," Peter observed.

Lucas struggled out of his thoughts. "What?"

"Cassandra Moira," Jon supplied helpfully, studying Lucas with midnight blue eyes that saw too much. Kensington's Archangel was what they called Jon. He had a side passion of studying ancient religious and philosophical texts, and a pacific personality that could calm any temper. His emotional radar was as finely tuned as a *Star Trek* empath's. He also held a dual finance and engineering degree that was merely a footnote to his genius-level mechanical skills. "Lady has a reputation a lot like yours. She could play championship poker. You'd have crossed her path by now if Matt hadn't had you scrambling all over the Central American start-ups these past couple years. When I met her at Pickard's last year, she reminded me of that Ginger Rogers' quote, modified. She goes balls to the wall with any of the guys, but she does it in a corset."

Lucas's head snapped around so hard he winced at the crack in his neck. "What?"

"Geez, man, don't give yourself whiplash. You *are* hurting, if the mention of Victorian underwear will get you worked up. I know a girl . . ."

"Shut up, Ben. What do you mean, Jon?"

Ben O'Callahan, the green-eyed, dark-haired legal advisor for K&A who had a passion for fast, expensive cars and extreme bedsport, grinned, but closed his mouth.

Jon moved one hand in a thoughtful stroke along the satin surface of the table, as if recalling something entirely different and far more sensual. "I put a hand on the small of her back when I opened the door for her. She's tall, but somehow delicate, too. I did it on instinct. Expected her to take a bite out of me, but she just thanked me. You know we notice women. The details. She was wearing a corset beneath her clothing."

"Devil is in the details." Ben flashed a look across the table that matched the comment.

"What does she look like?" Lucas asked in what he hoped was a casual voice, even as he battled back a baffled desire to take Jon's hand off for thinking it was okay to touch her.

"You're about to find out." Matthew Lord Kensington, K&A's CEO, entered the conference room. The expression on his aristocratic yet rugged features—the combination of an Italian mother of noble lineage and oil-rich Texan father—was that of an alpha wolf initiating a hunting party. "Alice said she just arrived in the lobby."

"Warning, guys," Jon said. "Now that I've got you all worked up thinking about her underwear, it's only fair to tell you she's all business. Don't mix it up with her. She's extremely good at this, and could pull the rug right from beneath us."

Matt slanted a calculated glance at Lucas. "Sounds like we need your A-game."

Great. Fucking great. He saw the concern in Matt's eyes that matched Jon's. Matt was his best friend as well as his boss. No one had pressed Lucas about his attitude, but they'd all noticed. It was time to shrug it off. Worry it like a terrier on his own time. Because there was no way it was the same girl. He wasn't entirely skeptical of kismet, but the idea of a stranger he'd met entirely by chance, halfway across the country—in the middle of a fucking forest, for Chrissakes—waltzing into this business meeting, was more than fate. It smacked of burning-bush, freaking miracles.

He heard Alice, Matt's admin, greeting their visitor. When the woman responded, his reaction bounced through his chest and slammed right down into the base of his testicles as if she'd kicked him in the balls. It was her. He knew it, even though she'd only said about six sentences to him that day.

He arranged his legal pad, pen, and PDA at his chair, though he usually put everything away, anything that he might toy with and give away his thoughts. He didn't take notes because he'd remember, if it was important. Yeah. He could see himself reporting on the smell of her perfume, the way the blond cascade of her hair glimmered when the sunshine hit it.

"Man, seriously." Jon laid a hand on his shoulder, bringing his unusual wave of serenity with it. Guy should have been a damn guru instead of an executive suit. "You okay?"

Because it was Jon, Lucas relented. He didn't compromise business for personal pride. "I think I know this girl. If I stumble, watch my back, okay?"

"Always do," Jon said. "Though you've never asked me to do it when a woman was involved. I'm going to have to give her a closer look."

"Just keep your hands to yourself this time," Lucas said dryly. "I'll handle any door opening."

⌘

Jon Forte was laughing at something as she stepped into the room. When Cassandra had reviewed the data and photos for the K&A team on her computer, she'd knocked a lukewarm coffee off the desk. It had doused the cat, whose ire was compounded when she jumped up and trod on the poor creature's tail. It had taken her a half-hour to get Nate back to sleep from the commotion.

Lucas Adler, CFO of Kensington & Associates, college roommate of Matthew Lord Kensington. At first, she'd try to convince herself she was wrong. In that news clipping he'd had much longer hair, fine golden strands just above his shoulders, but streaked with lighter shades from exposure to the sun. Sitting in a board room, he'd looked relaxed as he gave an interview about being part of what had been dubbed over the past years as Kensington's wunderkind. Five young men who'd turned K&A into a global and domestic manufacturing empire out of the unlikely New Orleans base of operations, though they'd moved to this satellite office in Baton Rouge in the aftermath of Katrina. Lucas was key to identifying and pursuing acquisitions of seemingly unprofitable plants, which then had a spotless track record of becoming success stories in the team's hands. When she'd searched for other data about him, her hope she was mistaken dropped like an elevator car with a broken cable.

Lucas Adler was also an amateur cyclist, who'd placed high enough in several marathons to be mentioned in a handful of news stories. He stated he challenged himself to break his own records, always asking more of himself. *Conquering the unconquerable*. The quote tied into his approach to his career, but it sent a thrill of inappropriate excitement through her vitals.

She'd been bullshitting herself on the team review. She'd recognized him in the first photo. The first heartbeat. She needed to put it behind her, once and for all. There was no reason that day should have lingered with her the way it had. She'd put it down to excessive sexual deprivation, even when she found her mind drifting to an analysis of his face, his every expression, the flickers of emotion in his eyes during their brief meet.

The Berkshires had been one of those crazy things. They were both adults, about to be thrown together for several days, the primary players in the start-up plans that would combine the resources of Josh Johnson's industrial hoist system operation with Kensington's. That should be her focus. Not the overwhelming disbelief that fate had delivered this guy right back into her lap. Okay, *not* the best visual if she wanted to concentrate on business.

Lucas Adler. A name to go with the hands, the mouth she couldn't forget. At the time, she'd thought it smart not to allow herself to touch him. Ever since, she'd felt like a kid deprived of candy. She couldn't listen to Foreigner at all without getting achy with need.

So he was great fantasy fodder. She could handle it. Even though his voice still stroked her nerves, running through her head fifty times a day. The way he'd realized she was getting short of breath and immediately moved to help. A man with that kind of hard-on was supposed to be oblivious to a woman's respiratory needs. Then the crowning moment—the way he'd anticipated her bolting. He hadn't stopped her from leaving, but he'd made sure she knew she hadn't gotten away with anything. Damn if that hadn't really tugged at her interest, keeping it piqued.

It was just the perversity of a woman's heart, she knew. She preferred to control all the elements of her environment, particularly men. Yet a man who could overwhelm her, take control of the situation, bring her pleasure and compel her submission, not only terrified her but made her want him so much she couldn't imagine ever wanting anything more. Ridiculous. A dangerous inclination she would never indulge.

Pushing all that away, she stepped into the K&A board room, dominated by one wall of windows and a conference table shaped like a lotus pool. Potted Japanese maples with their delicate red lace leaves were arranged in several places. There were Asian prints on the wall, along with several Samurai blades rumored to be there so that those on the receiving end of Matt Kensington's displeasure could opt for ritual suicide. While the surroundings might intimidate most, they steadied her, reminded her of the job she was here to do. This was her environment, her playing field. She'd given up about a decade of sleep to make it so, and was forever grateful for the chance Steve Pickard had given her, taking the talents of a college intern and throwing her into lion dens like this one. Until she'd built a foundation for her own self-confidence, he'd assured her, over and over, that she had the gift of diplomacy and mediation. As well as an exceptional business acumen that allowed her to grasp the full range of financial, manufacturing, legal and management dynamics that made her an effective problem solver.

She reminded herself she'd had articles written about her as well, one claiming she had almost psychic insight in knowing when to mend fences and when to disembowel. Another noted she was so unflappable she could walk the floor of Congress buck naked, not a hair out of place, to deliver an address on world economics.

She could do this.

When Matt courteously gestured her in ahead of him, she schooled her face into a polite mask.

As riveting as Lucas had been that day, he was more impressive now, dressed for success in a custom-tailored gray suit. The white dress shirt and silver tie emphasized his silver-gray eyes and the gold of his hair. He'd have made any woman's tongue tangle. When he met her gaze across the table, the shock of the contact detonated through her, leaving more than her tongue at loose ends.

It had just been sex. Not even actual sex. Just a sexual encounter. She was repeating herself. Not a good sign.

"I understand you and Jon have already met." Matt was making the introductions as Jon came around the table, followed by Lucas. She could see the athlete in the way he moved. If she put her hands on his chest, she'd feel that hard body beneath the thin shirt. The heat of his mouth had been between her legs, his long-fingered hands bracketing her rib cage, as close and lovingly as the corset she wore now.

She shook Jon's hand, said the appropriate things, and then there was no avoiding it. Lucas extended his hand. Smoothly, without hesitation or hurry, she put her hand into his.

⬗⬗⬖⬖

A tremor. He definitely felt a tremor. Her color was up. Not enough for anyone to notice, but he did. Under a trim blue suit jacket, she wore one of those thin silky blouses. Beneath it he could see the faint outline of the corset she was wearing. This one was strapless, a faint floral pattern in a sheen of silver leaf that added to the embellishment of the shirt. The blouse's neckline showed a modest dent of cleavage, likely because of the lift of the corset. He suspected it might also give him a glimpse of lace and flesh, if he was a cad and strained.

She had her golden hair in a barrette, emphasizing the delicate line of her throat. Pearls with a topaz amulet made those blue eyes even more stunning. Her snug black skirt had a ripple of fabric at the hem that fluttered as she walked. The skirt was just past her knees, so only shapely calves set off by her heels were visible, but the fit of the garment turned her into an hourglass. She had to be wearing a thong to achieve those smooth lines over her pretty much perfect ass.

The whole package screamed, "Beautiful woman—give her whatever she wants."

Matt's team had an unintentional reputation for overwhelming and charming female opponents, to the point most companies didn't even bother sending them anymore. However, it seemed she'd turned that around, realizing that such men might be just as susceptible to an unexpected offensive of feminine wiles. Could she be that clever? As he registered her cool smile, no different from what she'd bestowed on Jon, he thought maybe she was.

Jon cleared his throat, pulling him out of his examination and making him realize he hadn't even greeted her yet.

"What's the matter, Mr. Adler? Cat got your tongue?"

Oh, no, she didn't. She met his gaze with those wide, guileless eyes. But in that startled moment, like the snap of a gun stock locking into place, he had his feet beneath him again. It had been a hell of a bow shot. He almost felt like smiling.

"Would that please you, Miss Moira?" he asked. Then, before she could respond, he arched a brow. "Matt, you didn't have her take the stairs, did you? She seems a little short of breath."

Something sparked in the blue depths, and if they'd been standing on the deck of two opposing ships in truth, he'd have taken it as the warning strike of flame, about to be touched to a cannon's wick. Withdrawing her hand, she turned toward the rest of the team.

"Mr. Kensington, I'm ready to get started whenever you are."

⬥⬥⬥

He'd never really thought about the sheer sensual impact of a corset worn the way she wore it. He was used to seeing it on the outside, a blatant sexual enticement. But the way it hugged her body discreetly out of sight, it molded her posture so that the rounded curve of the buttocks, the long line of her throat, the high position of accentuated breasts, were impossible to ignore. Hell, it made every movement an act of careful, planned grace, if the woman worked with it. Cassandra Moira worked it to the nth degree.

He did listen. He evaluated her strategies, her approach, and was impressed by the level of homework she'd done in the short time period she'd had. She spent little time on the points she'd deduced they agreed upon, then presented resolution options for the more contentious points she'd accurately anticipated. By the time she'd worked down the nearly hundred items they had to handle for this phase of the contract, he'd marked down only ten concerns needing more work. He didn't think he'd ever seen a negotiator do so well, and he'd been actively trying to find things to break her stride.

"If you find this suitable, we probably need to go over the legal points with the Japanese suppliers to meet regulatory requirements. We could videoconference them in tomorrow or on Wednesday."

The regulatory step was an onerous, information-only process that Matt would typically relegate to middle managers, but Lucas inclined his head to Matt. His CEO lifted a brow, a brief flash of surprise in his gaze, but otherwise remained poker-faced as he faced Cassandra.

"That will be fine," he said. "We'll set it up for tomorrow. I do have some concerns about . . ."

As Matt began outlining many of the list points Lucas had on his sheet, he studied her profile, the way she held her attention on Matt. Was her focus a little too intense? Was he deluding himself, or was she avoiding looking toward him? A negotiator would be expected to shift her gaze, gauge the reaction of Matt's CFO to his concerns. But she didn't. Not once.

"I think we can work with most of those," she responded at last. "But—"

"I have a couple more, Matt," Lucas cut in. Normally he would have interjected at the end of Matt's, as Matt allowed a pause for him to do just that, but she'd jumped the gun a little. Another subtle sign of nervousness, unless she hadn't expected Matt to defer to his team.

She settled back, though, apparently unruffled. "My apologies, Mr. Adler. Please continue."

"I agree, most of these can be worked out, but we have a genuine concern about stock prices. K&A is putting a lot into the plant conversion. We want control of the company."

"That has little to do with investment and everything to do with K&A's desire to own the whole world." She underlined the words with a charming smile, laced with the right touch of just-between-you-and-me banter. Now her gaze did sweep the table, pausing briefly on each of the team, before returning to Matt. "But you know you can get your return on this investment, and then some, without owning it. Mr. Johnson wishes to retain his majority interest."

"You have very few willing to undertake this," Lucas pressed. "Josh Johnson is not easy to work with."

"True enough. But 'very few' is still more than one, isn't it? We've indicated our willingness to compromise, meet you halfway on seventy-two points, gentlemen. Your demands have not been unreasonable, and I think we all know everyone stands to make a lot of money. But on this one issue, we stand firm. We will not negotiate on holding majority interest. While I look forward to the pleasure of your company for the next couple of days, if that point is a deal breaker, I shall have to go seek out more flexible—if less pretty—faces."

A text message popped on Lucas's PDA, from Peter, who'd been taking notes at the other end of the table.

Jesus Christ. Is anyone else hard as a rock?

Ben muffled his chuckle in a cough. Matt registered the note with a glance, but didn't change expression as he shifted his attention back to Cassandra.

"We have a penchant for pretty faces ourselves, Miss Moira. Therefore, we'd invite you to stay. You and Lucas can work out the remaining details in here this afternoon."

She inclined her head, though she still didn't look toward Lucas. "It would be my pleasure."

That was an understatement for him. Because he *was* as hard as a rock.

⁂

She wanted to say it would be never-ending torment. Had she pushed so hard because strategically she knew Matt Kensington appreciated strength, or because she'd hoped to escape this? Had she actually been willing to take a dive on this one? If the latter, she was already in deep trouble.

Fortunately, there was no way to know, and in times of crisis, or at least the need to regroup, a woman always had one sanctuary. The admin pointed her the way to the ladies' room on the break. It was the last calm moment she'd have before spending the afternoon with Lucas. She headed toward the restroom without hurry, though she felt like bolting.

She reminded herself this was the very reason she wore the corset under her clothes. Controlled, precise movements, no matter that the mad fluttering in her chest was like butterflies hopped up on crystal meth.

She even leaned up against the door after she was inside, as if barricading it. There were fresh flowers on the counter. White, red and yellow roses. A vanity with a padded velvet chair, positioned against the wall, was supplied with various toiletries. Feminine products, not provided in ugly metal dispensers, but discreet baskets. On the wall, a painting showed a woman sitting at a similar vanity, the curve of her back exposed, for she wore only a towel wrapped loosely around her lower body. Elegant, sensual. Unusual for an office setting, but not a richly appointed powder room like this.

Steve had actually apologized for having to send her instead of Tim, who'd been in Seattle. She was his top negotiator, so she'd been vaguely insulted when he revealed he'd intended to send a man because most women couldn't keep a clear focus with the K&A team.

She'd bet him she would come back with everything Johnson really wanted. She'd done that, won the bet. But she was no longer insulted. If any woman could emerge from a meeting with this group without an elevated pulse and the undeniable urge to have a personal marathon with a sexual aid, she wanted to meet her and find out what libido-paralyzing drug she used.

On the surface, they were just five men. Exceptionally handsome, yes, and confident in distinct ways, with an easy rapport together. They listened to her, responded to her, challenged her as a business equal, refreshing and unexpected in manufacturing environments. But that was part of their seduction, she realized. It went perfectly with the contrast of what simmered below the surface. Being in their presence made her hyperaware she was a woman, as if they were a pack of wolves who'd scented her when she entered the room, stimulating the sexual radar of every gorgeous one of them. God, if she let her mind get away with her, she could imagine them putting her on the table to share her for lunch.

They'd done nothing inappropriate, not even anything overtly sexual—they just exuded sex. It was something even more than that, though. Something that swept her skin with heat and made her shy away from delving too deeply into it. Whatever it was, whatever they were, it called and connected to the base instinct of what she was.

Even the way Peter Winston had asked her if she wanted coffee. Leaning toward her, his gray eyes close enough to distract—storm cloud color, whereas Lucas's were silver—his hand poised just inches from her arm. It made a woman want to lean in, just a bit more, toward the combat-ready physique Peter had, as an active reservist who she knew had already done at least one tour in Iraq. He had an intriguing aftershave, something clean and spicy, though she preferred the musk of Lucas's cologne.

Okay, so there was no denying every single one of them could bait the hook, make himself irresistibly tempting to his prey. Big deal. That, and they fairly pulsed with the unspoken promise that they knew how to please a woman. Body, mind, and soul.

Overwhelming, sexually confident men she could handle. But adding Lucas to the mix was nitro to a system already revving dangerously high. If she could lump him into their extraordinary, pheromone-overdosed clan, then her reaction to him would be no more dangerous than getting besotted by a remote movie star.

But Lucas wrested something else from her. His gray eyes seemed to see deeper, want something *for* her, a key prepositional difference. Hell, maybe she *should* cross the line, take one of the others to a hotel, and dull the edge of the nonsense her mind was spinning.

She wondered if he'd cut his hair shorter for cycling. She'd read up on the sport enough to remember how his legs had been shaved, his chest bare. Of course that made her misbehaving mind wonder if his heavy testicles would likewise be smooth to the touch.

"He is just a man. What the hell is the matter with you?" *Thirty minutes in a field. You didn't have sex, and the orgasm was short.*

"If you just came out of a meeting with Matt and his strategy team, I expect any one of them could be causing that reaction."

Cassandra's eyes sprang open to find she wasn't alone as she'd suspected. She'd glanced at the stalls and noted no feet, but now as she stepped forward, she realized beyond the stalls, around the corner, was a retiring room, complete with a couch, magazines, and a coat rack. This woman had apparently been sitting in there before she'd risen to approach the mirror.

Savannah Tennyson. Matt's wife of just over a year, and the head of Tennyson Industries. Her face and reputation were known to every businesswoman who'd ever aspired to join the ranks of the CEOs of the Fortune 500, because Savannah was one of them.

She and Savannah had similar coloring. Blond hair, blue eyes. Savannah was shorter, but the figure worked with the height. Slim, not as curvy as Cassandra, but she gave Cass the impression of an exotic princess. Refined and remote, though there was a faint smile on her lips now.

Never try to pretend a gaffe hadn't happened. Just move on as if it was of no consequence, and it would be forgotten, because you didn't make a big deal out of it. Moving forward, Cassandra extended her hand. "It's a pleasure to meet you formally, Ms. Tennyson. I'm Cassandra Moira."

"I go by Mrs. Kensington since I married, but you're welcome to call me Savannah." A gleam of amusement crossed her blue eyes. "Now which one of them is driving you to distraction? If my husband has gotten a beautiful woman this agitated, he's going to be in a great deal of trouble."

"Oh . . . no." Cassandra managed a return smile, though remained wary of the woman's close scrutiny. Did everyone at K&A study visitors as if dissecting them under a microscope? Of course, that was her job as well. "I'm afraid I'll have to decline to answer. I'd give up a tactical advantage if I divulged that information."

"So you would. And your statement supports your reputation, which is an excellent one. We'll leave it an intriguing mystery, then. I just walked over from my building to see Matt for lunch." Crossing the room to the door, she looked back at Cass. "You're all done with them for a few moments, I assume?"

"Yes, we finished up the preliminary round. Mr. Kensington has ordered lunch just for Mr. Adler and me, because the two of us will be working out the specifics this afternoon."

"Good, then." Savannah reached for the door handle, just as it was pushed open, bringing her face to face with Lucas. His gaze shifted between the two women.

"Lucas." Savannah glanced at Cassandra, her lips curving. "A good choice."

Cass wasn't going to consider what that meant. She was too busy quelling the desire to grab hold of Savannah's sleeve to prevent her from leaving.

Savannah shifted her attention back to Lucas's inscrutable expression. "Lucas, are you confused about your whereabouts?"

Sliding a hand in one pocket, he held the door so it stayed open, nodding courteously but pointedly at the archway provided by his arm. "No."

"Hmm. I didn't think so." Savannah tilted her head just enough to pass under that human bridge, her body brushing with familiar affection against his hip and side, her hair grazing his elbow above her. As she passed, she gave him a firm poke in the side. "Be nice. Is Matt in his office?"

"Already wondering why you aren't there yet. It's pathetic, really. Ow."

Cassandra blinked as he flinched from the jab Savannah landed in his kidney before she breezed past and continued up the hall, the silky brush of her hose and the rustle of her skirt drifting back. A sound cut short, as Lucas let the door close behind him.

Three

He leaned on the door as Cassandra had when she first came in, but for an entirely different reason, she suspected.

"You're in the ladies' room," she said.

"Obviously." When he took a calculated moment to let his gaze rove over her, she forced her hands not to close into defensive balls. *Relax.* She felt the hold of the corset, remembered the significance of its support and restraint. The structure and rigidity of it, defining the boundaries of what she could and couldn't do.

"So you're an accountant." She gave him a dismissive glance as she moved to the mirror. "Accountants tend to be stunningly uncreative, if useful."

"Really?" Unruffled, he crossed his arms across his chest. "Next time I get my mouth between your legs, I'll take care not to bore you as much as I did last time."

Deliberately, she checked her makeup, hair. She looked fine. Damn good. Nothing to touch up. Everything in place. Pivoting on her heel, she summoned a bland smile. "So you recognized me. I'm surprised, as brief as that shared moment was."

"You recognized me," he pointed out.

"It took a few moments. I probably wouldn't have, except there was a mention of cycling in your bio workup. Next time I'll be sure and screen the men who drop in on me in the woods."

"That might be wise." When he flipped the latch on the door, the click made her heart skip several beats.

"What are you doing?"

"I told you, that day in the Berkshires." Shrugging out of the coat, he hooked it over the edge of a stall.

"I don't recall that day very well." Cassandra fought to keep a note of panic out of her voice. "But I'm fairly sure when Mr. Kensington said we would work together today, he meant in the board room after lunch. Not now, locked in the executive women's room."

"You remember every word I said, particularly what would happen when we met again." Loosening his tie, he drew her eyes to it as he slid it free, the gray and yellow silk. As he moved, he countered what she'd hoped had been a subtle movement to get between him and the door.

The white shirt stretched over his shoulders fit his upper body so well, tucking into the slacks. She didn't dare look below his belt, knowing he'd catch that instinctive desire to check out his groin. He was already seeing far too much. Was he wearing the silver medallion? He was getting close enough to smell him, the light cologne and aftershave fragrance making it hard to resist a deep breath.

"I don't want this. You need to leave. Now."

He came to a halt, several feet between them. She realized then she'd backed up against the counter holding the sinks.

"You're a student of body language, Cassie, same as me. What I see is a woman who's put her hands behind her back." His gaze shifted up toward the mirror. "Grasping the edge of the counter, hard. It suggests tension, and nervousness, but you put your arms behind you. Not crossed defensively in front. As if you were restrained, in order to be open to my touch."

His gaze heated as he made the last step and his hands closed over her breasts, long fingers on the lifted curves, thumbs on the stiff fabric and underwiring of the corset. Her breath caught in her throat and she couldn't help it—she shuddered, moved into that touch, even as she was shocked at her inability to move away.

His reaction stunned her even more. He let his hands slip to her sides, fingers tucking into the intimate crevice just below her armpits, the heels of his hands still pressed against the sides of her breasts. Closing his eyes briefly, he rested his forehead on the crown of her head, his nose brushing hers. "Jesus, can you believe this? When you came in this morning, I thought I was hallucinating. You can't imagine how much I've thought about you, touched you a million fucking ways. Kissed your mouth. Taken you hard, easy, felt you come against my mouth and my cock, until you were exhausted and slept in my arms, all that golden hair spread across my chest."

She'd dreamed of him almost nightly, in much the same way. Hellfire, what were they doing?

"As appallingly inappropriate as that is, I'll let it pass." She tried to slide away from his body, despite the shriek of protest from her own. "It was just a moment. It shouldn't feel like that. If it does, it's because we didn't finish. That's all."

"You think so?"

When she nodded, he considered her, eyes gone dark and dangerous. "Then let's finish it. I prefer having a couple hours to feed on a woman's pussy, making her come six or seven times, but we'll see what we can do with a short lunch break."

"No." She shook her head. "Even if I wanted to, I can't. I . . ." She let her gaze drift significantly to the feminine products basket, even as she despised herself for using the female escape hatch.

"First, you're lying. Second, you think that would bother me?" Lucas moved with her, and now she was in a less favorable position, in a corner formed by the counter and the wall, his body blocking any motion. Though in truth, all he seemed to need were his words and those eyes to keep her standing here, grasping at her fleeing sanity. Oh, God, all those dreams she'd had. He'd had to remind her. Her nails digging into his bare back, his body between her legs, her feet crossed over his hips, his jaw brushing her skin.

"I'd love to know you intimately enough to know when it's your time of the month. When I'd need to handle your breasts more gently because they're swollen." His hands passed over them again. "Know when your stomach might hurt and bring you chocolate to make you feel better, less cranky. Rub your feet." He put his mouth to her ear. "Women at that time are stimulated by the very . . . lightest . . . touch."

Sliding his touch down her arms, he came back with one of her hands and wrapped his tie around her palm, twice. Then he did the same to the other, leaving a length of slack fabric as a tether between them, held in front of her. "Hold the wrap in place with your thumbs in your palms," he said, pressing them briefly to underscore the command. Then he put his arms under her back and legs to lift her, turning toward the retiring room with its inviting long couch.

"No. We can't." Panicked, she started to struggle.

"Cass, easy." As he laid her down on the couch, he bracketed her there with one arm pressed against the sofa back, taking a seat on the edge. "You think the only problem is we didn't finish. I don't know about you, but this is a hell of a lot more appealing than sandwiches. Let's test your theory, get it out of the way. If it's not anything more than that, then what's to object to? Door's locked, and I think you've already seen that my desire for you isn't going to make one minute of this negotiation any different. I'll play fair, if you do. Though with your looks and that fuck-me scent of yours, you already have an advantage."

I can't. I can't possibly handle this. But if she ran, she was as much as admitting it was more. She needed this done with. Maybe he was right. Maybe it would get it out of the way. Was that what he really thought? Why would it bother her if he did?

Sensing victory in her silence, he drew her tethered hands up to her face, fitted the slack of the tie between her parted lips before she expected it, then guided her wrapped wrists behind her head, lacing her fingers so the slack drew taut along her cheeks, stretching the corners of her mouth like a bit. She could get free, but the feeling was of being bound. The gag deprived her of the ability to say anything further, while giving her something to bite down on, as if he anticipated her involuntary need to scream.

Leaning over her so she was staring up into eyes darkened to slate, he delivered words as potent to her as the restraint. "You move your hands, and I'll spank you. You understand me?"

Holy Jesus. She was almost tempted, but she managed to hold on to enough of her pride to shoot daggers at him with her eyes. His lips twisted, but his finger dipped, slipped several buttons of her blouse so the strapless corset was visible. "Beautiful. Try your best to hold on to that control, Cassie. I'm going to shatter it."

He didn't understand how much she *wanted* him to shatter it. She just couldn't afford it. . . . Ah, God. What was he doing now?

He found the side zipper to her skirt and then worked it off her, laying it to the side with as much care as his suit jacket. "That skirt's so tight it should be illegal," he muttered. "You can't even bend in it."

She'd have responded to the slur on her very carefully chosen wardrobe, but he was staring at the tiny thong she was wearing, which barely covered the swollen oblong shape of her pussy. Her half whimper would have shamed her except for the burst of additional fire it sparked in his gaze.

"You wouldn't touch me before. Wouldn't let yourself." He drew her focus to his crotch as he used one hand to cradle what was there, giving her a tempting glimpse of its shape and impressive weight. "This is all for you. I'd like to thrust it into your pussy, inch by inch, stretching you, feel you writhe to take all of me, until I'm in to the hilt and you've got nothing to hold on to but me. You think about that, because today all you're going to get is my tongue. Then you can tell me if that finishes us.

"It was more than a moment in a glade," he continued, lifting his gaze to lock with hers. "When I got back, there wasn't a woman in this city I wanted. Just you. I found that scent you wear at the department store. Honeysuckle's Kiss. It's a body spray. The minute the salesgirl sprayed it on her arm, I recognized it, though the smell of her skin was different. I nearly disgraced myself like a teenager. As it was, I got a hard-on that I'm sure made her want to call Security."

Or drag him into a back room and rape him, Cass thought.

"Don't be afraid of me, Cassie. For God's sake, I knew you for twenty minutes, and missed you for a month. This can't be a freak coincidence. Since you're not screaming for Security, I've got to believe I'm not alone in the way I feel. We both know there's really nothing to prevent you from leaving. Show me something, give me something. Do you want me to stop? You like it better this way, don't you? Bound?"

She could tell how hard it was for him to give her a choice. He probably overwhelmed women on a regular basis. But she had to wonder if he knew how devastating it was to be asked like this.

I shouldn't. But she nodded. She wanted him more than she wanted sanity or the ability to face herself in a mirror, this craving desire to be restrained, overpowered by him. The door was locked. She could give herself thirty minutes.

As if knowing how tenuous her capitulation was, he ripped the thong away, going to one knee next to the couch in almost the same motion. He dragged her up to his mouth, guiding one leg over his shoulder, locking the other around his waist so her heel rode on the curve of his taut ass.

His mouth was even better than she remembered. She'd brought herself to climax over the memory a million times, at least in her mind. Only once in reality, the only moment she could take for herself. In desperation, she'd pulled into a park on the way home, sat in the deserted parking lot at twilight, and fumbled open her slacks. Pushing herself to roaring orgasm in a matter of minutes, she didn't dare to think what would happen if a police officer cruised through.

It was just sex. Just hormones. But that couldn't explain why, in a room of available, beautiful men, she wanted only him. Well, sure, there was the powerful memory they shared. If that was true, once this was over, she'd be fine. But even if she wasn't, she'd take Ben to dinner. It was a goodwill gesture she'd already intended on Johnson's behalf, taking the legal advisor to dinner for all his setup efforts. Since Ben had given her a thorough checking-out, it would send a concise message to Lucas. Tell him that this was it. All she was interested in giving.

Her rapid staccato of thoughts stuttered off into oblivion as his mouth took over her mind. Holy God. She remembered that thought from last time, and all the banked longing that had built up since that day surged against the dam she'd created to contain it, threatening to send the flimsy rationalization that reinforced it spinning away in churning whitewater.

Lucas knew just the right way to integrate the wetness of his tongue with the pressure of lips, the friction of his jaw, the licking alternating with suckling, then just soft, heated breaths, the feather of his lips in tiny, bare kisses. The limning of the labia, a delicate slow entry of the tongue between them. A caress of his nose against her clit, then a firm suction of the mouth over the whole area, tongue going into a swirling, rapid dance, over the labia, the clit, plunging in and out until she was rocking up against his mouth, going insane because he wouldn't let her find a rhythm, dragging her higher and higher.

Keeping her breath controlled through this wasn't going to be possible, but the harder she tried, the wetter and hotter she got. The restraint of her hands galvanized it. She imagined the tie in her mouth would have her lipstick on it. He'd probably wear the damn thing for the next two days, just to torment her. She'd had nothing from the glade but her memory, and that had haunted her for over a month.

He put his hands beneath her, and now, in addition to that oh-so-clever mouth, he began to knead her buttocks, his thumbs playing in that tender crevice between them, causing a motion that rolled the pressure of his mouth evenly across her clit.

The orgasm tore through her, images assaulting her so she couldn't resist it. She wanted to pull him up her body, feel all that delicious weight upon her, holding her down, his cock seated between her legs. She wanted to touch him, close her hands over him, even her mouth. That was something she hadn't thought much about before, but she'd like to drive him crazy like this, feel his balls convulse under her squeezing fingers, the flood of his seed on her tongue. Have the intimacy of it on her skin. Inside her body.

Now she thanked God for that tie, for unless K&A had made their bathroom soundproof, her scream would have brought Security running. As he kept his mouth working her, it became unbearable, but she had the wrapping too tight and couldn't think clearly enough to twist herself free. She made the plaintive cries in the back of her throat, clamping on the tie like she was having a seizure. It felt so . . . good. Almost as good as she wanted it to be, with a man on her, in her, that need for intimacy she couldn't have. But of course, that was the problem with something like this. It led to wanting that.

She was panting, short, shallow breaths, and as he came up her body, his gaze followed the flush across her fair skin from the orgasm, the enhanced size of breasts shoved upward by a corset and heaving with quivering pleasure. His mouth was glistening with her juices, and when he brought it down to hers, he captured her open lips over the tie, teasing her with darts of his tongue over and under it, giving her the taste of herself. She wanted to suck on his lips, and he was kind, at last pushing the tie beneath her chin which, while forcing her head to tilt upward, also allowed her to nip at him. Framing the side of her face with one large hand, he swept her jaw with a thumb.

The slippery fabric made the tie drop down, pressing on her windpipe. Before she could figure out how to deal with the discomfort, he'd slid beneath it, holding it away from her, collaring her throat with those warm, strong fingers.

"Lucas." It slid from her mouth, a plea. As she arched up into him, wanting to feel his chest against her, he obliged. When he put his knee on the couch, he pressed it between her legs and she moaned against his mouth at the rippling aftershock. He kept cradling her face, his thumb remaining under the tie, stroking her throat as he kissed her, tender now. Intimacy. The bliss of the word was a warning, interjecting itself into her consciousness.

"Hold on a second, sweetheart." He lifted off her at last, went to retrieve his coat. As he turned, his gaze coursed over still quivering limbs, making her cognizant of the fact she was lying there in her corset and open silk blouse, her hands still twined behind her head. She could have pulled them free, had thought about it as he walked away, but for some reason didn't want to do so until he said to do it. That should have discomfited her, just like him being fifteen feet away and staring at her in such wanton display, but his expression was suffused with pure male hunger. She couldn't help noticing how enormous he was, pushing hard against the slacks.

"God, I'd keep you like this if I could." Coming back to her, he knelt and put the square of his folded handkerchief between her legs.

She let out a shuddering moan at the feel of the cotton linen. A linen that likely smelled like his light cologne. "What are you doing?"

"Cleaning you. Ostensibly." He cocked his head, that sharp profile turning in her direction, in handsome contrast to the soft feather of sun-streaked hair on his forehead. "I also want to keep your scent close, so I can take it out and enjoy it this afternoon."

"That should be distracting," she whispered.

His lips curved. "All part of my diabolical plan."

But there was quiet care in the way he tended to her, drying her where her fluids had dampened in the crease between thigh and buttock, the delicate pocket between the lips of her sex and her legs. While it emphasized that she was spread open for him in embarrassing detail, his hand, high on her thigh, told her he expected her to stay that way. And she did.

As a slow stroke over the clit made her lower extremities behave as if they could quickly moisten for him again, she almost blurted out that her overreaction to him was because she hadn't had sex in a long time. Fortunately, she caught herself, recognizing the weakness that would reveal. The best thing, just like the faux pas with Savannah, was to say nothing about the earth-shattering orgasm she'd just had and move on to the next step. Which would be freeing her hands, which didn't appear to be functioning.

"Lucas." She tilted her head up, vaguely concerned to see a blue tinge to her fingertips.

"Ah, hell. Sorry, sweetheart." Bringing her arms down, he unwrapped her hands, showing red marks on her palms from her passion. On, crap. Did she have similar red marks along her cheeks, where she'd pulled the tie against her mouth? A quick lift and glance at the mirror showed she was okay.

"Silk is an abysmal binding. Not that safe, really." Easing her to a sitting position, he shifted her onto his lap and began to chafe her hands and wrists, making the blood rush back in.

It was uncomfortable, only because it wasn't. She was sitting on Lucas Adler's thighs, wearing no panties since he'd torn away her thong. The desire to move against the light scratch of wool, against the hard evidence of his unappeased lust, was almost overwhelming, particularly when she saw the flex of his jaw in reaction to the pressure of her bottom. Her heels had tumbled onto the carpet of the small retiring room.

But more than the erotic nature of the position, being held in a man's arms like this was so welcome she hoped the shudder that went through her would pass as just another aftershock, rather than a sign of emotional deprivation.

Clearing her throat, she tried to sound reasonable. "So how much time before the lunch break is up?"

"About ten minutes." He glanced at his watch, then back up at her face, his eyes lingering in that unsettling way. "As beautiful as you are, it will take less than half that for you to put yourself back together."

"I have no underwear."

"No." He traced the line of her temple. "Just think how you can torture me, knowing you're not wearing any. I can hardly walk as it is."

"There is that," she agreed, shifting. "You're giving diamonds a run for their money."

"Sorry. Uncomfortable?"

Yes. Because of how much I want you inside me. Struggling up, she tried to ignore how he put his hands to her waist and helped her to her feet. She moved away and collected her clothes before heading toward the closest stall. She wasn't going to put herself together in front of him. The slow burn of desire, the physical and something far more precarious, was still licking away at her insides. This had been a mistake. "I . . ." She forced herself to stop. "You didn't have me take care of you."

"I love that you think of it in those terms." The possessive gaze moving up her body, starting at her feet and working its way to her throat, was enough to hold her in place, as if he still had some kind of tether holding her to him. "Would you go down on your knees, Cass? Take my cock in your mouth if I commanded you to do it?"

The image made her already shaky legs quiver. She found herself unable to answer without making a fool of herself, more than she had already. As he rose from the couch, she held the clothes in a tight fist at her midriff. Then she realized there was a mirror behind her. He could see her back in the laced corset, her bare ass flared out beneath it. Before she could turn, he had his arms around her, his hands descending to cup her there as he stared over her shoulder. "Gorgeous. Ben would be drooling all over himself. He's a dedicated ass man."

Lucas knew he was pushing the contact on her, that she was trying hard to retreat, but he couldn't let her go just yet. Before she'd moved back to the tile, she'd stepped into her heels again, elongating a pair of already mouthwatering legs. One thigh was revealed all the way to the bare hip on one side, while she held the clothes so the skirt covered her bare mons and most of the other leg. The faint red lines of the silk he'd used to bind her hands were still discernible there. Her breasts quivered, just a bit, from her breath. The blond hair was tousled over her shoulders. She was stunning, and she didn't even know it. She thought she'd fucked up, and she was getting ready to bolt again, even though he knew she'd wanted this. Even when she'd called him an accountant like it was an insult, she'd given him that tantalizing flick of a glance. A challenge. *Take me down. Take me over. Make it worth the fight.*

"Don't say it was wrong." Bending, he pressed his lips to her bare shoulder, smoothed his palms down her delicious buttocks.

"Lucas." She closed her eyes. "I worked my ass off to get where I am. And if you make any jokes about my ass—"

"Shh. Hey." Lucas cupped her face, gave her an even look. "What's between us doesn't have anything to do with your reasons for being here. I'm going to go out there and make you fight for every point."

He made himself give her a friendly, reassuring smile, hoping to ease her fears, when he really wanted to say to hell with the meeting and abduct her. "Are you up for the challenge, or have I scrambled your brains too much?"

Something loosened in Cass's chest. It didn't alleviate the deeper concern, her personal uneasiness with her more-than-sex reaction to him, but she could manage that. Men often lied, but she could tell he wasn't lying about being professional. Unfortunately, the integrity in his eyes made the deeper concern worse. She *liked* him.

"I don't have to fight about it." Tilting her head away, she gave him an arch look. "You're just not going to get everything you want."

"Oh, really?" His gaze lifted to the mirror again. "This is looking pretty close to everything I want. In fact, I'm not seeing a reason to go back to the meeting at all."

She shoved him back, with a tentative smile. "All right, get out now. I want to put myself back together. Then I'll come cut you down to size."

Thinking she'd delivered that line with the proper nonchalance, she stepped into the stall, only to look over her shoulder and see that humor had become laced with fire.

"Jesus, you should see yourself walk in those heels bare-assed, wearing a corset. Sweetheart, you're going to make me embarrass myself. I haven't come in my pants since I was twelve. Care to bet dinner on how things go this afternoon?"

"I have plans," she said, trying to ignore the heat that washed over her from his words, even as her heart began to pound again. "Indefinitely."

When his gray eyes rose to her face, she caught a thrilling glint of danger there. But his tone stayed mild. "Okay, then. We bet something different. We have nine clauses to resolve this afternoon. If I get the balance of what I want, I win. Which means tomorrow I choose a different way to make you come."

"What if I win?" She congratulated herself for not showing any reaction to that, for sounding unimpressed.

He gave her a smile that Lucifer could borrow. "That's up to you. For example, maybe your idea will be to yank me into the men's room for the wham, bam, thank you ma'am sex you act like we both want. Though I warn you, the men's room doesn't have a lock."

"I'm beginning to understand why the women feel *they* need one. I'm not going for it."

"Are you worried you'll lose?"

"That was a pathetic attempt at peer pressure. I outgrew that a long time ago." Even though she closed the stall door, she sensed he was watching her feet shift, the deft balancing act as she shimmied back into her skirt. When she heard a step, she looked up to see him in the stall next to her, looking over the edge.

"That's a sexy little wriggle you've got there. If this business thing doesn't work out, lap dancing might be in your future."

"Now that's just the type of obnoxious remark I expect from manufacturing moguls."

"I figured. Wanted to put you back in your comfort zone."

She would *not* smile. She made herself send him a frown instead, buttoning her blouse. "If I concede to play at all, a game I don't have to play, you've already won."

"But I have something you want. As nice as that orgasm was, what you need, or rather what you think you need for closure, is my cock rammed deep into that tight, wet pussy of yours. My body lying on yours, your legs wrapped around my back while I pound into you until it's all done."

Looking down to hook the top button, she began to busy herself with tucking in the shirt. "I can get that elsewhere, without jumping through your hoops."

"No, you can't. You don't have a man you trust near enough to take you over, force you to let go," he said quietly. "Be honest with me, but don't be defensive. If you don't want me, just say so."

She gave a bitter chuckle, his words scraping raw nerves. "Men always think it's that easy. It isn't about what I want."

"It is, for this. I'm not going to mess with your business here, or who you feel you need to be. But play with me. Enjoy the game." His hand reached over the stall, brushed her hair, his knuckle following her temple before threading through the soft strands. It made her want to tilt into his touch.

Now, who's not being honest? She knew the last thing he considered this was a game. But he wasn't wrong. Neither was she, which meant she needed to concede she couldn't handle it and walk away. But she'd been fighting to win for so long, she wasn't sure how to admit failure. Particularly not right now, when her defenses felt totaled.

She came out of the stall so he no longer loomed over her and moved to the counter, retrieving a brush from her things. "And if I refuse to play?"

"I hound you relentlessly until you agree I'm the man you want to spend the rest of your life with."

"Well, there you have it. You overplayed your hand. If I agreed you were, the game would be over, because you'd run out of here like a scared dog."

At his silence, she raised her gaze to the mirror, and met his. Gray, steady, unflinching.

"Try me," he said.

Putting the brush back into her bag with a careful, precise movement, she stared at it for a long minute. "You attract me, Lucas. I can't lie about that, so no point in trying. I'll take the game you're offering. But no matter who wins or loses"—she found the courage to lift her eyes now, lock with his in the mirror—"when these two days are done, I walk away and you let me. No arguments, no persuasions of any kind. That's the only way I'll agree, because you and I both know I don't really have to agree to any of this."

"Persuasions of any kind? Would you like to elaborate on that clause? In case I'm fuzzy on what—"

She bit back a smile again, despite herself. "I'm not going to orate a *Penthouse* letter for you, *Mr.* Adler." She sobered. "But I will have your word on it. I know you stand by that."

"Deal," Lucas said at last. He didn't like it, but he'd manage the risk, rely on his negotiation skills to get her to change the terms.

"All right, then. Let's get to work." Giving her jacket one last tug to smooth it, she picked up her small makeup bag and stepped toward the door. Before she could reach for the handle, Lucas stepped forward, flipped the lock, and opened it for her. Just as his mother had taught him to do.

It was going to be a hell of an afternoon.

Four

For the next few hours, true to his word, nothing Lucas did or said indicated there was anything but a friendly business acquaintance-ship between them.

It was maddening.

He'd roused a humming need in her body she couldn't seem to switch off now. She resented his apparent ease, slipping back into his corporate mode, even knowing she was presenting the same façade. Only she *knew* hers was a façade. He might consider it dirty tactics, but occasionally she offered a sneaky bit of leg or cleavage, just to see if his eyes would shift, if she'd catch a glimpse of the brutal passion mixed with sensuality she'd witnessed earlier. She didn't.

Matt, Peter, Jon, and Ben came and went at different intervals as needed, supplying answers to questions, insights. As the afternoon waned to evening, they had spreadsheets and faxes, as well as bun-dles of past history on both companies, scattered across the table. Initial contract terms were sketched out on the electronic dry erase boards, and they were neck and neck by dusk. Four to four. They'd both secured things they'd wanted, but in each instance it was clear who'd received the best benefit of the decision.

They kept the admins busy, and she'd contacted Johnson's New York team several times for downloads to Alice's computer. They conferenced with Johnson as well, even bringing Matt in for a spir-ited debate with him where her admiration for K&A's leader in-creased exponentially. He backed the irascible Johnson into a corner, then allowed Lucas to move in with diplomacy to smooth it out, while she protected her client's interests and made sure their over-whelming abilities didn't leave him naked and shivering. She man-aged it, proud and nearly exhausted by the accomplishment, because it took the skills of a chess champion. The K&A team obviously would never need the skills of her consulting group.

The last point involved management of the main plant. As they compared people, it became depressingly obvious who had the edge in experience and skill. It was the K&A man, but Matt was willing to allow Johnson's man to be assistant plant manager.

At eight o'clock, they were all back in the board room, on conference with Johnson. When they were done and the line disconnected, Matt glanced at Cassandra. "I'm glad you felt that was a win-win for all of us."

She shrugged, managing a cool smile. "We want the plant to succeed. Having it managed by the best person, with the resources of the next best candidate at his disposal, can only be beneficial to both parties."

"I'd call this day a draw, which is the best scenario possible." He flashed a smile. "That is, if I can't win."

"Is that what you'd call it, Cassandra?"

Cass directed her attention to Lucas, sitting directly across from her. He'd asked the question with casual interest, while she knew it for the loaded weapon it was. She did and didn't want to take the out Matt had just offered her, and neither inclination had anything to do with professionalism. However, she forced herself to answer based on it.

"No," she said. "It's not a draw. I'd call that one a point for your side, Mr. Adler."

Lucas inclined his head, giving her some small gratification at the flash of surprise, followed by respect, in his face. But what did he have to lose? Of course the bastard could control his lust, despite the fact he'd gotten no relief. After all, he could ravish a woman in his own office if he wanted to do so. Despite his protests to the contrary, he probably had sex on a nightly basis with any one of the women the social registers reported him escorting, another less welcome fact she'd gleaned from the online search.

She would have to accept Lucas's challenge for tomorrow, because her reputation had to stay intact. Everything had to stay intact. The way to beat him was to walk away without a hair out of place, no matter what claw-and-scream-herself-hoarse orgasm he managed to wrest from her. If she could do that, it would be another victory for her self-control. Another notch for her very lonely bed.

Matt and the rest of the team had somehow slipped out of the room, leaving her and Lucas facing each other. Disconcerted, not sure how they'd managed that, unless her mind was deep in places it shouldn't be, she rose, sliding on her jacket.

"Cassandra, you did well today."

"Why, thank you. Your approval makes me all a-flutter."

His lips did that sensual twist, the precursor to a smile. "You'll honor our bet."

"Why wouldn't I?"

"A lot of women would try to back out when they're this scared."

"I'm not scared of you."

As he rose from the table and came around it, Cassandra stayed still to prove it, though her pulse rate increased. The situation called for a catty response, followed by a saunter out of view. A quick saunter. When she looked at him, she recalled tigers on the Discovery Channel about to leap on a herd of gazelles. Those tigers had the same deceptively relaxed movement he had now. It aroused her, just the idea that they might be about to cross blades some more. Fencing, dancing, even board negotiations—they were all forms of sex, done right. But while she'd used sex appeal as one of her weapons, she'd always kept sex out of the equation. With Lucas, she didn't think that could be an option. The challenge in his eye thrilled her.

"You got what you wanted today because it was reasonable. Not because I was female and overwhelmed by the K&A charm."

He kept moving, didn't respond or engage until he reached her. She stood in the doorway. Behind her was a hall that was a short walk to the admin's office. She could hear Matt and the team talking. As far as she knew, they were speaking gibberish, for Lucas laid an arm against the frame, leaning into her so her back came against it, straight and rigid as her own stance.

"I'd agree with that. I'd also agree you're not afraid of me, not on the surface." His fingers touched her cheek, slid along the corner of her mouth, reminding her of the tie's restraint, then on to the line of her chin, so she lifted it. Keeping his eyes on hers, he let his fingers descend, stroke her throat, using one light knuckle, making her lift her chin further. "Underneath, there's so much going on. You're an orchestra. A slight breath, a flush to your skin." His lips were just over her right cheekbone, an inch or so from her mouth, his breath touching her. His body, so close. "You're all about control. Denial. It's enough to drive the man who wants to dominate you fucking insane."

"No man controls me."

"I didn't say control. A man who sexually dominates a woman, who demands her submission, does so to free her. Lets her fully embrace the passion and need locked inside of her."

His finger was cruising down her sternum, moving at the pace of a boat floating down the Mississippi, baking the occupant in a lazy summer sun. He slipped the top button of her blouse. She could hear Matt speaking to Alice, his assistant. Jon, Peter, and Ben were still with him. She should shrug away, slap Lucas's face, but his finger was caressing the cleft between her lifted and compressed breasts, teasing her nerve endings as powerfully as his words.

"Let's test that control." Lucas murmured it. "Lift your chin as high as you can and hold it there for ten seconds. Then you can push me away, slap my face, whatever's going through that incredibly ordered brain of yours."

She swallowed, and his thumb, resting on her larynx, sent him that unsettling message. But she averted her face, tilting her chin so she could see the wall clock in the board room behind them. "Clock's ticking," she said.

Breathe slow, breathe even. Breathe shallow. Stand straight. Don't writhe. Within her laced regimen of behavior, she could handle one arrogant bean counter. What kind of accountant looked like this? There should be a hidden camera somewhere, a TV show prank. What kind of accountant . . . could do . . . *that?*

Bracing his other arm so she was caged between them, Lucas had put his head down and brought his lips to the raised mounds. The tip of his tongue slid into the deep cleft. A teasing lick between the folds, barely touching ultrasensitive flesh, like a raindrop rolling down that tender crevice. His hair brushed her chin, her body somehow now canted into his so she could feel the pressure of it. All she had to do was lift her hands to slide across his broad shoulders, or put them inside the coat, to grip him at the waist. She'd seen that hard, lean body almost naked, knew what was concealed beneath the clothing.

Breathe. Slow. Even. Stay in control.

She pushed him away. Slap, hell. She punched him, though she was careful to choose the jaw and not the elegant nose or sweep of cheekbone.

Fire coursed through his gaze. For a blink, their deceptively civilized surroundings vanished and she thought he was going to wrest control from her, master her in truth. Take her down and fuck her right here on the carpet as a double-edged punishment. God help her, her response to the thought, the shameful need which she could feel trickling down her thigh, was just there waiting, making her even weaker.

But he brought himself under control. One corner of his mouth lifted. "Nice jab. So who do you think won this round?"

She wanted to touch where his lips had been on her breasts. She thought if she did, she would come, just from bringing their two energies together like that. Her pussy was beating insistently, as if it had its own heart. It knew exactly what it wanted, unlike the higher, supposedly more sophisticated, organ.

"I pushed you away in ten seconds. I'd say the round is definitely mine."

"I'll let you have that, because I wasn't watching the clock." He leaned back against the opposite side of the doorframe now, which put her standing between the stretch of his long legs. "But if you make yourself come between now and the next time we see one another, the round will go to me. Because I'll know whom you're thinking about as you've got your fingers in yourself. You won't use a vibrator."

"Vibrators are far more efficient to deal with a passing urge," she said, tossing her head. "Basic need fulfillment."

He nodded. "They are. But you'll use your fingers, sink them deep in your pussy, because you'll want the warmth of human flesh. Because you'll want to imagine it's me."

"Get over yourself," she advised, and stepped, graceful as a gazelle, over his polished shoes. As she headed down the hall, she knew she was fortunate not to have tripped and fallen, since her legs were less than steady.

"Cassie, your blouse."

She gave it a dismissive glance. He'd opened one additional button, so only the leading edge of the satin cups of the corset was visible, though of course, what was most noticeable above that were her breasts, the glimpse of cleavage considerably expanded. Still, it wasn't porn, white trash level. It was as much as she might show if she was headed from the office to a night club to meet clients. It was way after five, after all.

"I don't have a problem with your boys getting the same view you got, seeing as they're not going to get a piece of it either."

Shouldering her briefcase strap, she kept going. And was brought up short one step later as he clamped down on her arm, turned her so her back was flat against the wall. His eyes might have beautiful doll's lashes. He might be an accountant. But the dangerous expression in his face left no doubt he was a man, and a lot bigger and stronger than her. It made her breath catch in her throat, a sound of desire, and of course, damn it all, he saw it.

"You like the fact I can overpower you, don't you, Cass? That I don't let you get away with your freeze-out routine."

"Get off," she snapped. Even as it occurred to her that control was a very fine line when one was in the ring with a lion, with no whip or chair in reach.

"As far as your blouse goes, *I* have a problem with it." His fingers brushed the tops of her breasts, making her bite her lip, which did nothing to control the shiver still rocketing through her. Sliding the button closed again, he smoothed his hands down the front of the blouse, over the tightly bound curves, her rib cage, to settle on her hips. He brushed his lips over hers. "Do you smell yourself on my mouth? Just a faint trace from hours ago?"

When she closed her eyes, his lips moved to her nose, her temple. "You like the challenge of me, Cass, but you're afraid to enjoy it. You don't want there to be anything in your life you can't control."

"I'm not a child, Lucas. There are things beyond my control. Beyond anyone's control."

"But not your reaction. That's what the corset's about. To remind you that the rest of the world may be out of control, but you never will be."

Cassandra opened her eyes, stared up at him. "Is that what you enjoy, Lucas? Kicking in people's doors, just to see if you can? I guess destroying mine gives you a real charge, doesn't it?"

His brow creased. "Cassie, what—"

"My name is Cassandra, you arrogant ass." She pushed him, hard enough that she was able to take advantage of his surprise and jerk away. It may not have been the smoothest retreat, but it was a swift one. She made it to the relative safety of the admin area before he could catch up.

She was safe from him here. She just wasn't sure if she was safe from her vibrating body, her own dark urges, or her aching, confused heart.

Matt was signing some documents his admin had apparently left for him at her desk. Peter was sprawled, relaxed on the couch, tie already loosened, while Jon stood talking to him.

Steady. Next chess move. Remarshalling her strategy, Cass painted on a cool smile, extended a hand to Matt. "I'll look forward to seeing you tomorrow, Mr. Kensington."

He straightened and took it. She ignored the gooseflesh that his brief grip sliding over her skin gave her. Her hormones were in overdrive and Kensington was just too damned attractive. Like all of them. Despite the pheromones that radiated from his every gesture, she was pleased that at no time had she detected anything suggesting he wasn't entirely faithful to his wife. Of course, ironically, that would just enhance his appeal to women.

"And you, Miss Moira. Though you're welcome to call me Matt."

"Thank you, but I find it best to keep business relationships on that level. It ensures professionalism and keeps our minds on getting the job done."

"It certainly does," he responded with a cryptic smile.

Turning, Cass found Lucas in the hall doorway, hands in the pockets of his slacks, tawny hair falling over his forehead, enhancing the intent eyes. Tear the dress shirt open down the front, loosen the tie, and he could be a calendar pinup. A package that screamed sex, particularly the way he was studying her, calculating the meaning behind her every word and movement, figuring out how to dismantle everything she'd tried to build for herself. Oh, yeah. She was going to have to hang in there, keep matching him, even as there was a part of her that wanted to run away or worse—not fight at all. Then she recalled his infuriating words about her, about why she wore the corset.

Think you know everything about me, Lucas? See if you predicted this.

She turned to Ben. "Mr. O'Callahan, will you let me take you to dinner? Mr. Johnson would like to show his appreciation of your expeditious handling of the legal obstacles."

If Ben was surprised by the offer, he didn't show it. Giving her a sexy Irish smile, he plucked her light overcoat off the coat rack by Alice's desk. "A business dinner that doesn't end up on Matt's tab. How can I refuse?"

She nodded. As he helped her into the coat, she delayed freeing her hair from the collar. As she expected, Ben loosed it, his hands sweeping it from beneath, knuckles brushing her neck as he let the clipped tail tumble down her right breast. While his touch produced an erotic ripple on her nape, she resented that the power of it seemed to come from the memory of Lucas's lips there, the way he'd pushed her into climax a month ago.

"Just dinner," she added with a smile. "I don't mix business with pleasure. While we're doing business, of course."

"Ah, a carrot to get this deal closed as quickly as possible. I love a manipulative woman. I'll see if I can get Lucas and Matt to hurry this all along, so I can find out if you're bluffing." Ben grinned.

"Good night, gentlemen." She allowed him another practiced smile, the right amount of distance and warmth combined, promising nothing, and nodded to Matt, Jon, and Peter. Then she shifted over to Lucas. "Until tomorrow, Mr. Adler."

"I'd appreciate it if you were here at eight. So we can take care of the preliminary details we discussed. Don't be late."

She noted the clipped edge to his words, and how his attention was on Ben's hand, resting at the small of her back, a bit low. If his little finger dropped a millimeter, she suspected it would be on the top of her buttock. Giving her the temptation of more, with the most discreet of contacts. They must practice this. Keeping business and pleasure separate on the surface, but making it impossible for a woman to conduct the former without thinking of the latter.

She shrugged, nodded. Later tonight she'd dissect her strategy for tomorrow. For now, she just wanted to be away from him, where her pussy didn't vibrate like a damn dinner bell every time he spoke, or leveled those eyes on her. Of course, that made her remember his earlier offer of dinner. What would it be like to take him to dinner, then take him home? Wake up with his smell around her, her face buried in his throat, body resting against the hard chest? Feel the cool metal of his medallion against her temple?

Maybe in this situation, cowardice was disguised wisdom. Maybe she *should* be late tomorrow.

❦

As Ben guided her out the door, he threw an enigmatic expression over his shoulder. When it closed after them, silence reigned for a long moment. Peter glanced at Jon. Jon looked toward Matt, who was studying the stone passive face of his CFO.

"If you wait too long, Ben will drive off with her," he observed at last, sitting down on the desk.

"No, he won't. He'll stall at his car, if he values his balls." Lucas directed his next comment toward Peter and Jon. "I may have need of the three of you tomorrow on this. If you can wait a few moments, I'll come back and explain the details shortly." His gaze shifted. "Matt, it's probably best if you're not privy to it."

"One of the very few drawbacks to being married," Matt noted, but shook his head. "I'll take the risk. I'd like to hear the discussion. We'll wait on you. I assume you'll bring Ben back up with you. Intact, if you don't mind."

Lucas gave a feral smile and slid out the door. Once out of sight, he took the stairs, glad for carpeted hallways to mask the sound of sprinting feet. As well as for the shape he was in, so he wouldn't be wheezing like an asthmatic once he got to the parking deck.

As he expected, Ben did have her at his Mercedes McLaren Roadster, in its assigned place in the parking deck. He was propped against the car door, about two steps too close to her as he gestured through the opening of the parking deck at the building across the way. Probably explaining how Savannah worked at that building, or some other smooth lawyer talk.

There'd been no prearrangement to Ben's delay. Lucas knew he'd still be here, just as he knew what was said about the five of them, both informally as well as in the many articles that had been written. That they were in tune with one another like a wolf pack. However, someone else had called them the Knights of the Board Room, because they had an unbreakable honor code when it came to business associates, community giving. But the code was much more personal than that. Ben knew Lucas had marked Cass as his. As well as he knew what her power play was about and, being a gentleman, had played along. A little too enthusiastically for Lucas's tastes, but then Ben did like to yank his chain. Lucas made a mental note to have Jon mix up the numbers this month so it looked as if Legal was about 200 percent over their annual budget.

"Lucas," Ben straightened from the car, arching a brow. "Is there a problem?"

"Matt needs us all upstairs. Something just came up at the Seattle plant. I would have buzzed you, but your cell apparently doesn't work in the parking garage."

"I think I must have turned it off. Wanted to give my full attention to a beautiful woman." He turned to Cassie. She was doing an excellent job looking unperturbed by the disruption. Good enough that Lucas wanted to toss away the briefcase she was holding in front of her and lay her out on the hood of Ben's disgustingly expensive car. Wipe every act off her face except the truth of her own desire and sexual nature, a match for his own.

"My apologies. Some other time." When Ben picked up her hand and gallantly kissed her knuckles, his hand curled over her wrist and palm so that as he pulled away, his fingers slid along her pulse. It never failed to elicit a shudder, and even Cass was no exception. It had to be an involuntary reflex, Lucas reflected darkly. Kind of like smashing a hammer into someone's knee.

He gave Ben a tight, I'm-going-to-kick-your-ass smile, which Ben returned with an anytime-you-feel-lucky glint in his eye.

As Ben left them, Cass reshouldered the briefcase strap. "Well, then, I'll just catch a cab and head back to the office to get my car." She was keeping an eye on Ben, trying to move past Lucas, for he knew as well as she did that she didn't want Ben to get out of sight.

"You didn't mention your evening plans were with Ben, when we were in the restroom." While he made the comment mildly, when she shifted, he moved to block her. "Though I admit I did keep you a little preoccupied. I'm also surprised you didn't offer me dinner. I worked at least as hard on the financial piece as Ben did on crafting his usual bullshit."

"Taking Ben to dinner is a business courtesy you should understand. And I've offered you as much as I'm going to." Her eyes flashed blue fire. "You're pushing it, Lucas."

"Funny, that's what I was going to say to you." Then, going with inexplicable fury instead of reason, he trapped her against the car, closing his hand over the briefcase. Yanking it away from her, he dropped it to the asphalt as he cupped her head and dived in, covering her mouth with his.

He was vaguely aware of the chirp that cut short the startling blast of an alarm. Ben, probably at the elevators just around the corner, had been astute enough to hit the security alarm just as Lucas pushed against her, hard enough to rock the light-bodied car. Okay, maybe he'd only show him as 100% over budget.

So she didn't want to touch him. She didn't want to remove the corset. She was doing everything she could to manage the situation, control it. Taking Ben to dinner, letting him flirt with her, just to tick him off. Well, she was touching him now, from chest to groin, and Lucas pushed himself against her harder, yanking at her skirt so he could pull one of her legs up and around him, put himself firmly against her bare pussy.

She made one of those maddening noises in the back of her throat, which he answered with a triumphant growl of his own when she let loose and kissed him back, her hands sliding along the short hair of his skull, nails digging in.

Too soon, she stiffened, tore her mouth away. "Just because my cunt says yes, it doesn't mean anything."

He jerked her head back so he could stare into her face, make her meet his gaze. "How about your racing heart? The breath sobbing in your throat because you won't let yourself draw a deep, real breath? Just *when* do you take the corset off, Cassie?"

"I'm Cassandra, not Cassie," she snapped the reminder. "Cassie is a girl's name. A little girl."

He remembered Savannah saying once that men were always boys when it came to the women they wanted. And a woman's heart pounded like a girl for the boy she wanted. He wanted to believe that was why Cass's was pumping madly for him.

"You're my girl." He changed the hard grip on her hair into something different, loosening the barrette and letting it ping off the side of the car as he stroked his hand through the thick pelt of it, moving his thumbs over her lips. Her hands gripped his forearms, conveying uncertainty with the switch to tenderness. She was rigid, ready to stave off an attack.

Rocking up to his toes because of her heels, he put his chin on her head, emphasizing the difference in heights. "See. My little girl." He could feel the softness of her full breasts, straining over the hold of that ribbed cage she'd designed for herself.

"Idiot," she muttered. "I'm not little. I'm tall."

"But you didn't deny the mine part."

"It didn't dignify an answer."

"Or maybe you liked the sound of it."

She pushed back from him then, her expression sobering. "Lucas, I told you, I'm not going to deny we have some chemistry. Hell, if I can arrange my schedule, you might even talk me into checking into a hotel room for a few hours tomorrow to get it out of our system, split the bill, but that's it. The finish line."

Did she realize he could read her? That her eyes told him how much more she wanted? What she wouldn't give herself? Pressing his body against hers again, this time he laid a hand on her throat, thumb passing over the sensitive network of bones and thudding arteries there. "Don't write a good deal off before it even hits the table, because you're afraid of how it might change things in your life."

"I don't have room for you in my life, Lucas. If you really knew me, you wouldn't want to be part of it anyway."

She bit her lip as if she hadn't meant to say that. But Lucas tilted her chin up. "I don't know it all, but I've figured a couple things out. You've worked hard on it, so it doesn't come through often, but there are some inflections in your speech which suggest you came from a poor Baton Rouge family." At her stunned look, he raised the hand wearing his Yale class ring. "Linguistics was part of my studies. I'm guessing that's why you don't like being called Cassie. Maybe the last time people called you that was when nothing was expected from you but becoming some drunk guy's Friday night punching bag and breeder."

Muttering an expletive, she tried to pull away, but he gave her a little shake, commanding her attention again. "The five of us come from diverse backgrounds. But the one thing we all respect is a person who worked her ass off—your own words—who didn't whine and ask for handouts, but managed to make a success of herself.

"I'd love to hear your story," he said sincerely. "I'd love to get to know you. Whether you want to admit it or not, it *wasn't* just sex. You think every guy gets the privilege of stumbling upon a gorgeous woman stretched out on a Harley in nothing but a corset and panties? And then has her show up in his conference room a month later?"

She made a desperate sound. "That doesn't make the problems any simpler."

"Well, tell me, then. If it's something I can't handle, then fine. I'll take you up on the wild monkey hotel sex. But I'll pay the bill. I'm old-fashioned that way."

She blinked, then let out a chuckle that disturbed him with its note of weariness. "You're better than I expected you to be, Lucas."

"I assume you mean in terms of kindness. Not my overwhelming sexual prowess."

She gave him a narrow look, but then averted her glance. He noted her swallow, her sudden discomfort. "About the restraints and all, earlier. I mean, I do fantasize, but that's not really me."

"Yeah, it is." Guiding her face back, he made her hold his gaze. She belied her own words with the tremor that went through her at the demanding touch. "You're just embarrassed by it. Don't ever apologize for the way you like to be pleasured. I'm very much a Dominant when it comes to sex, if you hadn't noticed. You think I don't recognize a compatible match? I won't let you lie to me about that. It is what it is, and we'll let that unfold the way it needs to. All right?"

When Lucas straightened, he felt somewhat heartened by the pensive look on her face, the hint that she was feeling less defensive and just more confused. However, he had to quell his desire to hold on to her too long, to try and drive the worry out of her eyes. Taking out his cell and punching in a code, he added, "I'm summoning our limo pool. They should be out front in just a second. I'll escort you to the lobby and you can take that back to Pickard's. The driver will drop you off by your car and make sure you get on your way home safely."

"I don't need that."

Pocketing the phone, he took her arm in a firm grip to guide her to the elevator. "It's late."

"And you don't think I'm capable of taking care of myself?"

"On the contrary. Which is why I expect, if you weren't trying to prove something to me, you wouldn't be contemplating taking an unnecessary risk. I like taking care of you. Is that so bad?"

"I should have run you over with the Harley. And rolled over your bike for good measure."

"Now that's just pure spite," he said, but found he had a desire to chuckle. Particularly when he noted a tiny curve at the corner of her luscious mouth as well.

<hr>

When he returned to the board room, Matt cocked a brow. "So, did it go well?"

"Well, she called me an arrogant ass earlier."

"Always a good sign," Jon noted.

"Or tomorrow she's going to bring a Taser and use it on your testicles," Peter observed.

Lucas glanced at Ben. "You were laying it on a little thick down there."

"Well, I was going to slap your ass as I went by and say 'Go Team,' but you weren't wearing those cute black shorts that drive me wild."

Lucas rolled his eyes, but he proceeded to lay out what he had in mind. When he was done, he had the attention of every man at the table.

"And you think she'll agree to this?" Jon raised a brow. "You've known her, what? A total of one day?"

"We had a connection. She won't know about you all, until the rest is in process. That's the point."

"A thousand." Ben thumbed a poker chip out on the table. "I call a month from today."

They all carried a pocketful of the plastic chips, and now Jon put out the same amount, along with a five hundred chip. "I'll raise that bet and say five weeks. She'll make him work for it."

"I think she'll really make him work for it. Six months." Matt tossed three chips into the pot. "Three thousand, gentlemen."

Lucas frowned, reaching for his chips. "What the hell are we betting on?"

"When you'll get her to agree to marry you."

"What?" He might have choked on his coffee if he hadn't just swallowed it.

"I think it would have been safer to bet on when he'll get a commitment," Ben observed.

"Nah." Peter sat back. He'd changed into jeans and T-shirt. His pose, his hands laced behind his hair, displayed a tattoo around his impressive bicep, the DON'T TREAD ON ME serpent flag. "When Lucas moves in to close a deal, he makes it permanent. He won't give her the chance to find out what kind of trouble she's in."

"She probably won't have him," Ben commented. "I've seen him in the shower. He doesn't have a lot to bring to the table. Since it looks to me she can shrink a horse's schlong down to the size of a mouse's dick with a few sharp words, he's already starting out with a handicap."

"Says the guy with the horse's schlong. That's why you prefer ass-fucking, Ben. If women saw you coming at them with that thing, they'd run screaming," Peter remarked.

"You know you want it, you pussy."

"Truly spiritual and earth-shattering sexual practices have nothing to do with genitalia size," Jon pointed out.

"The lacings on that corset are tight for a reason, aren't they?" This came from Matt at the end of the table, quelling the banter. He was partly in shadows, now that they'd dimmed the overheads to make the most of the nighttime city view.

"Yeah. Which is why I'm calling on all of you." Lucas tossed in his chips, matching Matt's bet. "I wanted to do it slow, easy, but if I don't get her tomorrow, I might lose her. I won't take that chance."

"Well, we've all known the type of woman who's walled herself up in her own castle, never realizing she's made herself the prisoner." Jon glanced toward Matt, then back toward Lucas. "Is she wild enough to handle—"

"No," Lucas said decisively. "No. She's first class, and I want her treated that way. This has the potential to scare her to death if we don't do it right. It's got to be gentle, but take her over the edge."

"Lucas," Matt said, drawing his attention. "No one here would treat her any other way, whether or not she's special to you. You know that. If your gut tells you the deal has to be an aggressive take-over, just be sure to weigh carefully what it is you want from her when the deal is done."

Lucas nodded, sat down, and stared at the table. "This is crazy." And then he told them everything. How he'd met her.

When he was done, the room was silent for a long moment. Then Jon spoke.

"Lucas, there's no point in fighting it. Things like that just don't happen. I don't care how skeptical you are, when Fate punches you in the face like that, you better take what She's offering."

Lucas gave him a wry smile. Peter nodded in solemn agreement, and Ben, for once serious, gave him a straightforward look that made the vote unanimous. The bond he had with all of them gave Lucas the courage to accept it, to feel the truth of it sweep him with unex-pected pleasure . . . and fear. He turned his attention to Matt. "I thought if it ever happened, I'd just be in the gate at this point, not sure how far I want to run the race. But I want her more than I've ever wanted a woman." Than he imagined ever wanting a woman again.

"You just know," Matt confirmed softly. "You know it's the deal you want forever."

Lucas nodded, and then, his lips firming, he reached in his pocket, drew out the rest of his chips and added it to the pile. "Tomorrow."

Grins swept the table, and then Ben cocked a brow at him. "Well, I guess there's no time to enhance your equipment after all. I was going to suggest a guy who could pimp up your rod—and I ain't talking your car."

"Oh, Jesus Christ. This from the lawyer whose car personifies the biblical quote about rich men and the eye of the needle."

"That car is going with me to Heaven. I don't care what I have to fit it through. I'm just saying, Cassandra is a fine-looking woman who deserves the best. One more second, and I'm sorry, man, I could have had my hands all over her ass. I'm only human. Jesus. If you need any help at all—"

"I'll know where to find you. In the meantime, put it on a choke collar."

"Lady on deck," Peter warned, glancing left to see Savannah coming down the hall. "Clean it up, gentlemen."

Lucas rose with the rest of them as Savannah entered the room, but underscoring the subject, he saw the way her gaze immediately went to Matt, and how his dark eyes softened on her face.

Feeling his heart twist at the sight, Lucas suspected by the end of tomorrow he was either going to be the luckiest son of a bitch ever, or he'd have lost the deal of a lifetime.

Five

She wasn't late, but she didn't come early either. Still, Cass wasn't surprised when she reached the executive floor that the admin directed her right to Lucas's office.

"Mr. Adler said he wanted to meet with you prior to the video-conference."

"Of course," she said.

She'd stopped in the lobby ladies' room to ensure she was well put together. Today she'd worn the black, wasp-waisted boned corset, the most structured of her collection. It nipped in and was tightened to the point a man's hands could span her waist . . . if she let him that close. While she'd originally intended to give her body as well as her mind the message of self-control, she'd chosen clothes to shred Lucas's. A strategy she realized might be unwise. But here she was.

The deep pink cashmere sweater with pearl buttons down the front had a modest scoop neckline, but since the shoulder straps of the corset shaped her breasts, it clung precariously to smooth, high curves. The attached narrow ribbon collar fastened at the throat, held with a cluster of delicate seed pearls, which drove the eyes to the expanse of flesh beneath that strip and above the sweater's neckline.

Her straight black skirt stopped at mid-thigh. She had her hair arranged in a twist that spilled down one shoulder again. He liked her hair, she could tell that, so she'd given him a teasing amount of it. Then she'd selected stiletto black heels that should make her five-eight much closer to his six-three height.

It was probably his damned German ancestry that gave him that imposing stature. Adler. German translation, eagle. Sharp-eyed, swift predator. Able to steal away the breath when seen up close. When she'd thought that through this morning, she'd realized anew she couldn't go into his office with the assumption that winning meant resisting him. Winning meant getting through the day and sticking to her resolve to walk away when it was done. He'd promised he'd honor that, but she wasn't so naïve as to think that he wouldn't try to get her to change her mind.

She'd also accepted that having sex with him was inevitable. If she could goad him to lose all control, ravish her on the floor, and she could walk away, she could still consider it a win on her side. What woman could feel she'd lost if she was sexually sated? So she didn't have to rely on ice cool calm as the foundation for today's game, which gave her a sense of recklessness she typically didn't get to indulge. She'd go in edgy, taunting him with what he couldn't have beyond today. Then she'd wait to see if he could take her down, and allow herself to enjoy the challenge. Even if he overwhelmed her, it would be like indulging in a day of chocolate, knowing that tomorrow she'd have to return to a sensible diet.

Of course, she couldn't ignore the voice in her head suggesting that, after the mother of all hot fudge sundaes, it might be difficult to convince herself she would eat salads for the rest of her life.

His door was open. As she stepped in, pushing the disturbing thought away, she saw he was on a call, wearing a headset. He waved her in without glancing directly at her, giving her the chance to look at the man and his office unexamined. She took the brief reprieve as a gift.

Same gray suit today. Silver cuff links, white dress shirt beneath. His tie was black with a thin blue stripe through it. He hadn't yet tied it, but there was a tie pin, which appeared to be a silver bicycle. Likely a gift from a young family member, she thought.

Corner office with lots of windows, of course. The early morning sun was turning the sky rose and gold on the Mississippi, outlining downtown Baton Rouge in a soft, midmorning light she particularly liked, more than the more urban-looking afternoon sunlight, which somehow always reminded her of the pollution and other things stirred up during a city's daily bustlings.

He had the bike she remembered on tracks, perhaps for workouts when he couldn't get free of the office. A large rock fountain in one corner gurgled and splashed water over smooth stones in a pleasing display. She walked the perimeter, indulging in a slow, casual perusal out the windows that took her behind his desk, between his chair and credenza. Sleek flat-top monitor, keyboard tray neatly tucked beneath. He apparently liked those silver puzzle things. They were scattered over his desk, a lot of them the metal bicycles that could roll from one track to the other to prove some law of physics. A family photo. Parents, she could tell. A sister with a feminine version of Lucas's good looks.

The office was very sparse, but it didn't feel impersonal. The fountain, bike, and picture were carefully chosen. He didn't collect or display carelessly. There was a sofa, chair, and coffee table arrangement, minifridge and microwave. Printouts scattered across the table suggested it had been a late night for him. Had he gone home, or was that closet she spotted holding extra clothes?

While he was on the phone, she had an advantage. He was apparently just going over a point of tax law with one of his offshore counterparts. He'd turned slightly toward her and was now taking a more thorough look. In a moment of abandon, the same feeling that had gripped her when she chose the clothing, she stepped into the narrow opening between him and the desk, took a seat on his knee, and began to tie his tie for him, sliding the silk strips through her fingers.

It was worth the surprise on his face, even as it was a tremendous effort to keep her expression casually amused, while she performed what she realized quickly was a very domestic task. Something Savannah might do for Matt in the morning.

She tied the tie, straightening his collar to adjust the accessory beneath it, so when she folded it back down, her nails were grazing his hair, the curves of his ears. She had no idea what he was saying to the offshore manager, because all she could think about was the taut muscle in his thigh, beneath her bottom. His fingers grazed her back, as if he intended a grip to keep her there. While she didn't look into his face, she felt his regard as if he were branding her flesh, making it his.

A quick tightening, an adjustment of the pin, and she was done, demonstrating she was as efficient with a tie as he was with a corset, a quid pro quo. Keeping control of herself, she rose and moved out of his reach, passing behind his chair. But as she did, she let her hand slide along the top, brushing his shoulders and across his neck with her long fingernails, raking lightly. He turned to follow her direction, but she pretended to ignore him, already moving on to look at the wall art. Black-and-white photos, a cyclist's perspective of the environment in which he trained. Speed, blurring techniques, but also nature scenes, a bike poised on the edge of a canyon, as if the rider were contemplating making that leap, being limited by nothing, like the Bob Seger song title scrawled across the bottom in someone's handwriting.

Roll me away . . .

She didn't find evidence of a limousine liberal here. He obviously liked having the money to play, liked to work hard for that money, and so didn't have guilt over the having of it. He also gave generously to others. After she'd checked homework, gotten everyone fed and tucked in, Nate fast asleep with stories of adventurous bears, she'd done some more searching and confirmed what she'd already heard about them. The K&A team were well known both for their corporate and individual giving. In fact, rumor was that they ran bets among themselves all the time for the most peculiar things, and whoever won got to donate the proceeds to the charity of his choice.

She passed his weight training set, then reached the closet. As she opened the door, she knew she was in his line of sight, but she continued to ignore him.

Several suits, which meant he could have been here all night. A four-drawer unit built into the closet was likely for toiletries, socks, underwear. What kind did he wear, and did she really dare to look, with him watching her? Her lips curved, satisfied, as she heard him correct himself on a fairly straightforward calculation. *How do you like having* your *focus disrupted, Lucas?*

But as she reached out and fingered the suit, discarding the gauche, prurient idea of checking out his underwear preference, she did move a couple steps forward so she could inhale the cologne-and-Lucas smell that lingered on his clothes. It wafted over her like a caress all its own that tingled along her nerve endings.

Her father had worn a suit to work, she remembered, before he'd disintegrated into a worthless drunk. She recalled how she'd seen her mother and father in the kitchen one night, right after he got home. Her mother had run her hands beneath the coat to link them around his waist, pressing her face into his shirt. He'd teasingly enclosed her in the extra folds of the coat before nudging her head up for a kiss. They'd been so young. She'd been so young. It was one of the few good memories she had of them. It made her wonder what it would be like to do that with Lucas. Slide into his embrace, be surrounded by the comforting smell of broadcloth and aftershave, all the trappings of a businessman in charge of his destiny, at the top of a castle with thirty-nine floors.

She suppressed the urge to bury her face in the suits, hug them to her like some cliché movie heroine, but of course, every woman she'd ever known had that impulse, to smell her man's clothes, wear his shirt. The man she loved. Or was falling in love with.

It was a cold shower reminder she was playing a dangerous game, because her heart was involved in this, ridiculously more than it should be. Play games for a couple days she could do, but she couldn't go places like that. Too many competing responsibilities.

Closing the door with a snap on that nonsense, she moved on to the fountain, delighted to find koi with long white and orange whiskers. Three of them, swimming lazily over shells and rocks that might have come from a variety of his travels. At the bottom, a small metal treasure chest opened and closed, revealing plastic pearls, uncut gems, and gold doubloons that spilled out on the skeleton lying beneath the weight of the trunk. She wondered if that was to remind him money wasn't everything.

As she leaned over to take a closer look at the fish, she knew the tight skirt would be inching up, up until he glimpsed the lace at the top of her thigh-high, the strain of the fabric over her hips. Settling one hand on the rock ledge, her pink nails tapping the stone, she reached forward with the other to try and coax the koi to nibble at her fingertips. One of her shoes left her heel as she stretched forward. She stifled a chuckle when Lucas asked the caller to repeat himself.

A moment later, she drew in an exhilarated and startled breath as his hand slid around her waist, the other catching her hair as he turned her in his arms, holding her over the water, his knee braced on the wall just inside her thigh.

When he'd turned her, she of course had to catch on to his shoulders, though his hand went to the center of her back, holding her securely.

He was still on the phone, the headset having made it possible for him to cross the carpeted office on silent feet. Now, as she heard the tinny distant voice of the caller, he tilted her head back with a thumb, denying her hungry, parted lips to kiss her throat just below the line of her jaw. Her fingers tightened on his shoulders, feeling the hard biceps flex against her forearms.

When he lifted his head, his gray eyes were molten steel, his mouth wet. This close to the water, her face had been misted by the light spray of the fountain, though it did little to subdue the heat he'd stirred. She realized his courteous hold on her hair was to keep it from trailing in the water. So careful with her, even as he wrecked her defenses with ruthless abandon.

"That'll work, Joel," he said. "I've got a visitor. I'll get back to you later on the rest."

Then he dragged his mouth lower, nuzzling beneath the pearl and cashmere collar around her throat, and clamped his lips there. Suckled, hard.

High-voltage lightning speared down her belly, straight to her pussy, her nipples becoming aching points. Somehow, she now had the stretched-out leg wrapped behind his calf in automatic reflex. He gripped her hair harder, curling his other arm around her back, hand braced between her shoulder blades.

When he lifted his face, her breath was shallow, quick. He examined her neck, then nudged the fabric back in place, hiding it. "I think you'll carry that mark awhile."

"A mark of ownership?" While she tried for a mocking tone, her voice quivered at the look in his eyes.

"As you like." Cocking his head, he gave her a leisurely perusal. Because he'd taken all her weight and balance, she realized she was in this position as long as he wanted her there, unless she wanted to attempt an ignominious wiggle that could land her in the pool with the koi. So she relaxed, as much as was possible, trying not to be impressed that he seemed to have no difficulty bearing her weight like this.

"Do you think you could use all this manly strength to let me up?"

"In good time. Good morning." He flexed his fingers against her back, stroking the line of the corset. "This one is new."

"Mr. Adler, I know you're not making a comment about what's under my sweater. That would be sexual harassment."

"A simple fashion statement only, Ms. Moira. Being a sensitive male of the modern age, I'm capable of discussing women's clothing choices. And crying."

Cassandra challenged any woman to stay unaffected by the sexy humor in his gaze. His voice lowered, taking on a husky note. "But if I'm already in trouble, I'll risk it all by saying I can't decide which part of you it enhances the most. The curvy ass, which I very much liked having on my thigh, or your tits, sitting up so high over that absurdly tiny waist that they jiggle with every breath you take."

"Crude," she responded with a sniff. "Women don't appreciate that."

"Not until they're good and hot. You walked in here soaked for me, and your nipples are already hard. Aren't they? Tell the truth, or I'll find out for myself."

"Just because my body has an involuntary attraction to you, which you know damn well any woman with a pulse would, doesn't mean anything," she said loftily.

"Like you and Ben flirting?"

"Exactly."

"Did you go check out his office this morning? Smell *his* suits?"

The flush in her cheeks was gratifying, but her words gnawed at

Lucas's gut. As hardcore evidence went, he knew he didn't have much to justify a deeper attraction. While another man would understand that it was different when sex gnawed at him like this, a woman would just think he couldn't keep his hormones under wraps. She didn't realize that sex at this level for a man was the need to possess, to claim. To keep.

This was beyond hunger. This was evisceration, begun when he heard the first note of her voice as she came down the hall. Then, put this outfit on top of it . . . Jesus, she was trying to kill him.

Down, boy. All in time. You have a plan. Stick with it.

Easing her to her feet, he covered his reluctance to release her by straightening his cuffs. "So, if it's just sex, I assume you're still willing to take my dare."

"As long as there's no interference with—"

"Business. We settled that yesterday. However, ultimately, I think that depends on you. Your infamous control, that is."

She narrowed her eyes as he continued. "This meeting will be a couple hours of Ben droning on with a Japanese lawyer about worker standards and listening to the appropriate report from the Japanese team on the other side."

When Cass shrugged her shoulders, it felt as if they were weighed down by the ropes of tension drawing taut in her stomach. "I know that. Are you proposing to liven it up?" Her alarm mounted at his expression. "You're joking."

He moved to the door, closed it. "Go over to my desk. Put your hands on it and spread your legs."

She told herself she hadn't heard him correctly, though the way the corset's boning constricted over the trembling of her lower belly told her there was at least one part of her anatomy that had heard him, loud and clear. "No."

Lucas left the door, but while she tensed, he simply passed her, giving her a tantalizing whiff of cologne and male heat, before going behind his desk. He removed a blue velvet box from his desk drawer, a box with a white satin ribbon around it. The color of surrender, she thought.

"You know what I remember about that day in the forest, Cass?" His voice was doing insane things to her nerve endings, stroking them, arousing them, making her want to go to him, do anything he said. She forced herself to hold her ground, latching on to an absurd anchor. A children's book she and Nate had read together, of all things. The young peasant heroine had overcome overwhelming trials and tribulations to rescue her brother from an evil witch. But that witch had a donut-hole-sized wart on the end of her nose and a harsh cackle, not the patrician features and velvet voice of a golden Egyptian prince.

"I remember how you put your hand under the pack cords. It was uncomfortable, the way they cut into your flesh. You don't mind a little pain. It all increased your excitement. The moment I restrained your hands yesterday, you went from hot and wet to full flood, trembling on the edge of climax. You crave dominance, but you don't think you can allow it in your life and protect what you're responsible for protecting. Or honor what you've made of yourself. You couldn't be more wrong."

Lifting his gaze from the box, he locked it with hers. "The strongest women in the world have the hardest time surrendering. They don't realize when they do it with the right man, the one who cherishes them, it's the most beautiful gift she could ever give him. Her trust. Trust me, Cass, and do as I say."

The last thing she wanted to do was capitulate to this, whatever this was. Yet it hadn't stopped her from goading the situation with her provocative walk around his office. He got her so charged up. If she put a hand over where his mouth had been on her throat, she was sure she'd feel a resulting contraction between her legs. Her body trembled in reaction to her thoughts, and she could tell his shrewd eyes saw it, the way he'd already seen so much. Somehow, she managed to raise her chin anyway. "The answer is still no."

"Okay, then." When he came around the desk, she wondered if she should bolt or hold her ground. Then he startled her by dropping to one knee, so close it brushed the outside of her leg as he ran his hands down her calves, his palms whispering over the nylon silk of her sheer stockings. He set the box beside him. "Stay still for me."

As she tried to think of a way to respond, her eyes full of his broad shoulders, the crown of his head almost level with her breasts, his hands glided back up her legs, past her knees, along the outside of her thighs and right under the hem of the skirt. She bit her lip at the welcome heat of his hands, all the more unsettling because they moved with swift precision up to her hips, his thumbs hooking into the thong panties beneath the molded edge of the corset and bringing them back down over the lace thigh high.

Black satin, a simple design, no embellishment. As he ran them down to her ankles, his thumb stroked over the wet crotch panel. He looked up into her face. "Step out of them."

Cassandra let him guide her hand to his shoulder, nudge her into lifting one foot, then the other. She should be saying no, refusing him. When he slid the panties into his coat pocket, she wondered if he'd ever give them back. Or if she wanted to imagine him with them, like the handkerchief.

"Men like to sniff women's clothing as well," he informed her. "Just different items."

Then he untied the ribbon on the box and lifted out what also appeared to be some form of thong, only this one appeared to be of latex.

"Keep holding my shoulder."

"Lucas, I can dress—"

"I'm doing this part. Hold my shoulder so you don't break your neck on those killer heels, and hush for a minute. Your only responsibility is to let your mind go wherever I want to take it."

She might have pretended affront if she hadn't just allowed him to remove her underwear. Stepping into the new garment, she had to press her lips together hard as he slid them up the same track again, barely able to stifle an aroused gasp as he adjusted them in the crease of her buttocks with shocking intimacy, fingers brushing her rim, then over her clit, making her hips jerk.

He rose, taking her hand from his shoulder but holding it against his chest. When she curled her fingers into the soft linen, she felt the shape of the man beneath. "What you're wearing is a type of vibrator.

There's a bullet against your clit. It has an adjustment that can drive you to climax in a matter of seconds, as well as multiple other speeds to keep you wet, building you up slowly for a deeper, more satisfying release, depending on how patient I am." His forefinger stroked hers, just a slow glide from the nail, up over the knuckles, back to the hand again. Amazingly, her pussy was reacting to just that motion, throbbing in rhythm with his finger's movements. "There are also sensors in the back strap. It will feel like my fingers are teasing your rim, adding to the sensations."

His gaze lifted. "Knowing your propensity for form-fitting clothing, I didn't bring the nipple teasers. They cover your nipples, and through a combination of oil, heat, and tiny electrodes, simulate a man's mouth, suckling you. I'd love to see you wearing them under this sweater, nothing else, and then take them away when your nipples are large and erect, pushing against the fabric. When you walked toward me, your breasts would move with that firm little quiver from every slight movement, your thighs rubbing the lips of your cunt together. I'd have you so worked up, you'd come, just from that walk. But I'd make you keep walking while you came, and if your knees gave out, I'd catch you."

As he kept up that torturous, teasing stroke of her one finger, she thought she was going to come just from that, the seduction of his words.

"So you're going to turn this on during the meeting." She was proud of her ability to say it in a reasonable tone, even if her attempt at incredulity sounded to her own ears a bit breathless.

"Yes. Different amps, different times. It's silent." He took a small ear wig out of the box and settled it in the shell of her ear, sweeping her hair forward to cover it. "And I know you're too proud, but this is where the taking care of you part comes in, when you submit to a Master. If you can't stop yourself from coming, if you're afraid you'll reveal what you're experiencing to the others, just shake your head at me and I'll stop."

Why hadn't she locked her bedroom door last night and taken

care of this edge, about fifty times or so? Maybe because Nate and Talia had been sleeping with her, Talia having another of her nightmares, Nate's asthma acting up a bit.

"Master? What does that mean?" She tried for sarcasm this time, even as her body seemed to know exactly what it meant. Because it had shifted into defensive mode, backing up without her permission to do so, her limbs trembling. If she hadn't been wearing the corset, he would have seen her nipples as large and proud as he'd suggested. "And I thought your intention was to make me come, not sexually frustrate me."

When his hands closed on her hips, just below the tight cinching of the waist, gripping her hard there, it drove the breath from her. Despite herself, both hands ended up on his chest, curled into the shirt, her forehead pressed to his shoulder, trying to get a grip on herself. What was the matter with her?

"Don't faint on me." His voice held tenderness, laced with something far more serious, inexorable. His hand passed down her back, an easy, soothing stroke that she wished was finding skin, rather than the hard shell of the corset. Her fingers tightened on his shirt, feeling the slope of iron pectorals. "You know what I think, Cass? Ask me. Speak to me."

"I don't want to. W-what?"

His smile pulled against her cheek, but from the stillness of his body, she didn't think he was any more amused by her petulance than she was. "Somewhere along the line the corset became about something more than your need to control your life. The binding of the corset was the substitute for a lover's restraint, holding you, gripping you. The way it pushes your breasts up so high, like hands cupping them. You're waiting for release from the one man who can also release you from the corset, who will replace its restraint with his own. Your master. Your lover."

"Sounds like a chauvinistic delusion," she muttered faintly. "Dog collars and leashes."

"Most of those who crave dominance or submission can't walk

around in leather cracking whips, Cass, or hang out at underground clubs. They're people like you and me, and it's a need as old as the need for love. In all its crazy, perverse forms."

Lifting his head, he tilted her chin to caress her lips with his thumb, that romantic gesture he did so well, his other fingers tugging on the hold of the cashmere ribbon collar. "Don't bolt on me. Not from the truth. If it helps, tell yourself you're pretending, that it's all role playing, an exciting sex game. I've put that vibrator on your clit because I want you to sit in the board room, surrounded by the K&A team. I want to watch the rigid way you hold your body, even more than the corset requires, because you'll be fighting not to come. It isn't about you begging me to stop. It's about feeling safe enough to beg permission to let go. And I will let you release before the day ends. On my terms."

As she did indeed think about bolting, he lifted a brow, the gray eyes sparking with a mesmerizing mixture of desire and resolve. A challenge. "You walk away at the end of the day. That's our agreement, right? So what do you have to lose? Now—" he changed gears smoothly—"one other gift. I thought they'd go with the theme of today's meeting."

His touch eased, became a stroke down her arms. When he opened the other side of the blue box, she was looking at four bracelets. Cuffs of beaten silver, beautiful in their simple purity, the edges smooth and rounded. On each there appeared to be Japanese characters.

When he snapped them closed on each wrist they were a snug fit. Then he knelt and put the other two, which were thinner, on her ankles. She hadn't worn any jewelry except a pair of silver earrings, so the anklets and bracelets added an exotic touch that felt exactly like she suspected he intended them to feel. Unbidden, she somehow imagined herself as a slave bought at auction, her master putting on the symbols of his ownership with strong, caressing hands that also said she was his. That he would care for her, cherish her. And she would serve him however he asked.

His gaze rose, paused on her throat then, the mark they both knew was there. "Believe me, I was tempted to get you a collar," he said, low. "But one step at a time. You ready?"

Cass started out of the fragments of fantasy that had taken over her head, returning her to this corporate office, the Baton Rouge skyline, and the reality of who she was, what her life was. She shook her head, started to back away, though he'd retained one of her hands. "I've stepped over a line I never really should have crossed. I can't, Lucas. This is too much." She tried to unlock a bracelet, found she couldn't locate the mechanism.

"Cassandra." He stopped her. "Answer me this. Are you aroused?" She looked away. "You know I am. But—"

Guiding her face back to him with a hand she couldn't shake, he held her there. "Your cunt is wet because I want it that way. I'm going to work you throughout this meeting until you can't do anything but think about how much you want to come, because that's what I want, too. And you're going to submit to it, because your body and your mind need a Master to really let go. Maybe even your heart. For the next two hours, you obey me. Can you trust me that much? Because that's what this is about. You're very intelligent, Cass. You know a woman gets the maximum amount of sexual pleasure when her mind is as engaged as her body. That's the focus here."

For women, the physical and emotional both were key to great sex. Just sex. She *did* know that. So did he. So was she overreacting? Everything was still within the parameters she'd set. And what had he said? Pretend, if it made it easier. She wasn't an idiot. There was a double-edged sword there, and he wanted more from her than she wanted to give, but she was in fact so turned on she couldn't think straight. She *did* want to trust him. For the first time in a very long time, she wanted to trust a man not to hurt her, break her.

"I don't let go of control to anyone."

"You will to me."

Last night, in imagining what he might have planned today until she was aching and wet, she'd told herself this was the ultimate test of control. She wore a corset every day of her working life to remind her how important it was to hold the reins, remain even-tempered, clear-headed. What more ultimate test could be devised than one that tapped into one of her more private fantasies? Should she deny herself, just because one man was intuitive enough to ferret them out and she was embarrassed?

Straightening and stepping away from him, she arranged her clipped hair properly on her shoulder, smoothed her hands down the front of the form-hugging sweater. "Shall we go, then?"

His fierce gaze grew even headier as his full lips lifted in a smile. God, like she needed a reminder of what he could do with those lips. Retrieving a folder from the desk, he opened the office door for her, gestured her to precede him.

As she stepped out the door, the feeling returned. Like she was something entirely different from Cassandra Moira, negotiations specialist from Pickard Consulting. She had decorative cuffs on her wrists and ankles she couldn't remove, and was wearing a sex toy that was teasing her clit and anus with every sauntering, pendulum stride she made. A stride dictated by teetering heels and a wasp-waisted corset he'd run his hands over appraisingly as if he'd laced her into it himself. She did feel like a nameless, exotic sex slave, being brought by her màster to a public forum for display. It gave her a shiver of erotic longing that shocked her, even as she knew he'd promised nothing that happened in the board room would be known to the others.

Oh, hell. Enough with the fantasies. He'd promised her release, but she wasn't fooled. This part was about control. He wanted her to shake her head at him, ask him to stop. Depend on him for control of her own body. Her mind told her she wouldn't let him win, while her body and soul clamored for just that. She wanted this claiming, far too much.

Six

"Good morning, Miss Moira." Matt pulled out a chair from the long side of the lotus-shaped conference table. "It's good to have you back among us. There's coffee and some muffins if you need anything."

"No, I'm fine. Thank you." Cass noted Jon and Peter were conferring on some point at the end of the table, though both rose with pleasant nods when she entered, taking their seats only after she did. Ben gave her a friendly smile and a wink, though he was on his cell in the corner.

"Lucas, they've got you set up in the audiovisual booth over there, if you want to check it and get ready to run your stat sheets." Matt gestured. "The mic's open so you should be able to hear us, and just hit the speaker if you need to change anything."

She'd wondered about the ear wig, but now it became clear. A set of panels had been removed one wall, revealing a glassed-in equipment room that apparently controlled the high-tech audiovisual aids Matt and his team had available to them.

It was also strategic. She could imagine during videoconferences that Lucas's positioning in the booth would allow him to make observations about the meeting to Matt privately, through something like her ear wig. Which meant Lucas could talk to her during this meeting without anyone else hearing him. He'd just added another weapon to his arsenal.

Lucas left her with a courteous nod and a lingering touch on her shoulder. "Enjoy the meeting," he said. She took his words as the threat she was certain they were.

As she got herself settled, trying to relax and not think about when he'd turn on the device he had seated so snugly against her most intimate places, the windows were darkened. Nine of the twelve screens on the opposite wall became one image. When it flickered, they were looking into a conference room a world away. She noted the circle of five Japanese managers, with a female translator there to interpret nuances of meaning if needed, since she knew all of them spoke fluent English. As Matt thanked them for extending their workday, since the time difference in Tokyo made it evening there, Lucas apparently decided it was the perfect time to test her reception.

"Cass, do me a favor." His warm voice was so clear, it was as if he were right there next to her. "Spread out your notes the way you want them, then place your ankles against the front legs of your chair. Lay your arms on the armrests. Make sure you're comfortable that way."

She wondered if he was going to tease her with further fantasies, tell her to imagine that she was bound and not move her hands. She could agree to that, for if they were already curved over the ends of the chair arms, she wouldn't have to embarrass herself with an obvious need to grip something for calm. Complying, she glanced toward the glassed-in booth. To all appearances, he was absorbed in setting up the presentation.

A faint vibration shuddered through the wood under her arms and behind her calves, a barely there impression gone before she could analyze it, but Lucas supplied the explanation. "You're going to find you can't lift your hands or ankles now. There are powerful magnets in the bracelets, matching those embedded in the chair."

Alarmed, she tried, discreetly, and found he was correct. "Let me go," she said between her teeth, in a whisper.

"No. I want you restrained, your legs open so you'll feel the stimulation that much more intensely. Don't worry. If someone asks you something and you need to move, I can release you instantly. And so you're not focused on that . . ."

No. She knew he was going to do it, but still, she wasn't ready for the sensual ripple over her clit, the tickling featherlike sensation along her anal rim that made her want to squirm.

"You're beautiful, Cassie." That voice continued, soothing but ruthless as he'd promised, teasing her mind. "Sitting there, so straight and elegant in your corset, your hands on the arms of the chair like a queen. You've got a light flush on your neck and cheeks from your irritation with me, your nervousness, but also from the stimulation between your legs, the feel of the panty stroking your pussy. Do you wish it was my tongue? I do. If I get you alone today, I'm going to hold you down and eat my fill, until you've come in my mouth. And then I'm going to put my cock in there, fill you deep and hard . . ."

She lifted helpless eyes to him. He had his head down, checking his notes, his lips barely moving. She needed to see his eyes, know that he was with her. Strange that she told him she wanted it to be just sex, but she needed the sense of connection.

He stilled. "Cass?"

Had she said his name? She stole a look down the table to where the other members of the team were busy with Matt. "Look at me," she whispered.

When he lifted his head, she wasn't sure what she was seeking, but she found it in the riveting focus on her face, his tautly held jaw.

"You're okay, Cassie. I'm here. I'm only going to bring you pleasure, I promise."

Glancing down, she pretended to look at her notes. "Why are you doing this?"

"Because you've had this fantasy. Of someone mastering you, of the possibility of being watched while you're pleasured."

"Fantasy and reality are two different things."

"I'm going to make the reality better than the fantasy."

She shifted, pretty certain he'd already accomplished that. Her movement resulted in a wave of sensations that gave her an irresistible compulsion to rock. As she swore softly, she saw the desire increase in his gaze.

"I want to take you to lunch after this. Lie you down on my bed afterward and make love to you for hours. When you're tired, you'll sleep in my arms. I'll feed you from my fingers."

"Stop it," she muttered. "What do the symbols on the bracelet mean?"

"What do you want them to mean?" When she didn't respond,

he pressed on, the voice in her ear relentless, temptation itself. "Pretend, Cassie. Pretend that you don't have to worry about what happens when you walk away from here. Pretend like you have time to do whatever you want, with whomever you want. What do you want them to say?"

She wanted them to say things scribed by adolescents on beaded bracelets when feelings ran so close to the top, so hard, furious, and bright they burned out quickly, the bracelet cast away, forgotten. It was ironic, considering those feelings were felt far longer when one was older, deep enough to scar. By then fear and doubt made them impossible to say, restrained like her body in the corset.

Business precepts didn't necessarily translate to personal relationships. But both she and Lucas were in the business of knowing people, sizing them up. Apparently Lucas understood her well enough after no more than a day, plus one stolen episode in a forest, that he'd coaxed her into this, holding her on a taut line between mortification and mounting arousal. The world was full of fools. As she met his intent look, she knew she must be one of them, because she'd never wanted to put herself in someone's hands like this, believe in him.

"All right, let's get started." Matt dimmed the lights further, took his seat at the head of the table, and they initiated the conference. Above the one image, the top three screens shifted between individual members of the Japanese team as they spoke. She tried to balance the distraction of her straining body by identifying each and reviewing in her mind what she knew of them. The translator was a typical Asian beauty, elegant in a form-fitting pale green business suit, her obsidian eyes thickly lashed and sharp. Her long dark hair was bound in a heavy jeweled net, low on a slim neck.

As Ben ran down the points, the lawyer on the Japanese side began to respond, checking different facts as they went along. All standard due diligence for the paperwork they'd sign later today to put everything in forward drive. Ending this. On Wednesday, she'd be on to the next job, as would Lucas.

"Getting bored, Cass?" That soft whisper, and the vibration started to increase.

The financials were up on the right wall screen for everyone's review. She managed to process a question Matt posed, then follow Ben's response. Jon and Peter were studying the numbers, Jon making some clarifying points regarding engineering impact. Her fingers were tight on the chair arms, she realized, her toes curling in her shoes as her thigh muscles grew taut. She couldn't close her legs, not with her ankles held by those slim cuffs. Thank goodness it was all below the table surface. She remembered the way Lucas had looked at her neck, as if he'd wished he could put an actual collar there, like these bracelets.

The "just sex" mantra was getting forced. Even as she told herself that was what they'd shared so far, the truth was he'd used sex to crack open a layer beneath. He'd taken their sexual interactions behind her battle lines into some deep emotional territory. Her current situation merely underscored it. This wasn't a quick spontaneous screw from a bar pickup.

It was absurd. She'd just met him. Of course, she knew that emotions weren't based on fact finding, data gathering. On whether a man preferred OJ or tomato juice in the morning. Hockey or baseball. If he left his socks on the floor or wanted to go camping on a holiday. She'd always wanted to do that. How would he feel about doing it with five kids?

Ah, Jesus. Just focus on this, Cass. Even if he cracked her like an egg, she'd have to settle for just sex. Great sex with a gorgeous man, maybe even a nice dinner, and she'd walk away. How could she complain about that?

"Looks like I'm going to have to work a little harder to keep your attention. Think we'll make this . . . adjustment."

The ripple changed to a sporadic undulating stroke. With her own moisture limning it, holy saints and angels, it felt remarkably like . . .

"It feels like a tongue, doesn't it? Imagine it's my tongue, lapping up your juices, my fingers playing around your ass, making you wiggle and squirm on my face, rubbing yourself there. Your scent. You're trying not to rub your ass against the chair, trying not to rock, though you want to, so badly. You want to pretend it's me. Want it to be me."

She tossed back her hair, trying to look casual, indifferent, and of course, that jolt of motion sent a response rocketing through her clit, down her thighs, up the center of her body. The corset was so tight it made it more intense, increasing the aching pressure in her stomach, her chest. Maybe it was good he'd spread her legs like this, for if her thighs were closed, the urge to squeeze them together, bring herself to climax, would be nigh unbearable.

The toss had become a fractious roll of her head onto her shoulders as a result of the wave of stimulation. At Matt's glance, she forced herself to make it look as if she were just stretching a stiff neck, even as her hands held their death clamp. She was going to lose. She was going to have to tell him to stop. But it felt so damn good, she didn't want to stop . . .

Focus. Her lips parted to give her more air. When had her senses sharpened so significantly? She could feel the moisture of her own lips from the cream lipstick she wore, the gloss over it. With a corset, the faintest breath pillowed breasts high on the chest, left them perched quivering there like soft doves, aching for a stroking touch to soothe them. She could feel the air on them, the touch of every molecule, it seemed. Then, between her buttocks . . . she'd never been much for anal play, but maybe that was because she didn't know it could feel like this.

"Liking the way that feels between your cheeks, Cass? Wait until the first time I put my mouth on your rim, tease it with my tongue. You might be shy about that, but you'll come apart when it's done to you. I want to see you shatter. Look at Saayo, the translator, now. How beautiful she is. Like you."

Did he have a damn implant in her mind? As the legal advisor's drone died away into complete gibberish, Cass realized Saayo's posture seemed like her own. But while her arms were beneath the level of the table like Cass's, they were not on the chair arms. Her limbs were making slight movements as her lips, a shiny burgundy which complemented the flawless Asian skin, pressed together in arousal, obvious to someone who was a mirror image of it. A quick glance at the other screens showed the Japanese men were all adjusted toward Saayo, serious faces intent.

No, it couldn't . . . she knew the men in this frame. She'd researched them last night. Part of a cartel who managed K&A's distribution over there, a group of dedicated men known to become suitably aggressive when needed to get shipments out of some of the more questionable ports of call. But reputable men.

"They have one camera positioned beneath the table. You'll notice their gazes keep moving from her to a wall beyond our view. They have a screen there, showing that camera's feed. They've provided me the patch to it in here. She shaves her pussy, and she's got a clit piercing. Her fingers are buried in herself. They have a little bet running with her as well. If she doesn't come before the advisor gets done, then they'll each have their turn, fucking her on the table when the meeting is done."

"You set this up," she managed under her breath as Ben asked a question.

"Everyone knows the regulatory check is as dull as dirt. I thought you'd enjoy the entertainment."

"Does Matt know what they're doing?" She said it in a whisper, not even sure if she'd spoken loud enough for him to hear her.

"They all do. And that's not all. Every man at this table also knows what I'm doing to you."

Her mind froze in shock. She wasn't sure how much time passed before she snapped out of it, but then her gaze shot around the room. All four men were still apparently engaged in the screen.

"They can smell you, the lucky bastards. See Jon over there, Peter, and Ben. They all know what I'm doing to you. They want you, so badly. What if I commanded you to let every one of them fuck you on this table? I could let all three take you at once, since I know you hate to get behind schedule."

Her pulse leaped, as her body quivered in a state perilously close

to the edge. She was holding on by a rotting branch just above a waterfall, and she was sure he knew it, for he kept on, doing his best to
push her over with his seductive voice.

"Did you know that we did something similar with Matt's wife,
Savannah? That's how we got her to agree to marry him. She was so
knotted up in her emotions, but we all knew she loved him. So one
night, we bound her on a table like this one. We each teased her to
climax, over and over, until she was insane with it. Our restraints
freed her feelings, and she surrendered to them. To Matt. They were
married that same week."

"Lucas . . ."

His timing for such a shocking revelation was impeccable. She
was so aroused, so close to climax, she couldn't deny the dark temptation of such a scenario, for herself or Savannah. He'd not only stolen her sense of reason and grasp of what was proper or not, he'd
picked up on her fantasies perfectly.

Now they turned toward her, the irresistible Knights of the
Board Room. The article reference came to her now, and it seemed to
fit, men with a code of behavior, a connection beyond words. Irresistibly powerful. As their intent gazes landed on her, she realized Lucas
must have given them the same ear wigs, so they'd been hearing everything he'd said to her. She also noticed Matt had quietly excused
himself, so she was on display before just the three of them, Ben,
Jon, and Peter. Saayo's breathing was heavy enough now to be noticeable over the speakers, but the Japanese advisor didn't stop. The intriguing detachment of it elevated her own response even higher.

As Cass looked up, the woman locked gazes with her. The Asian
woman's lips curved in a half-smile, her eyes warm, yet distracted,
close to the same pinnacle as Cassandra.

"How would it feel," Lucas mused, "the two of you tied to each
other? Your legs scissored together, hips close so that as she played
with her pussy, her knuckles would barely brush your cunt. Your
arms would still be bound, behind your back. You'd have to lie
there, writhing, feeling only that occasional brush of her fingers, the

vibration against your clit and ass. We'd all be gathered around you, watching, wanting you both, wanting to fuck you both.

"Look at Ben. If he'd taken you home last night, he'd have wanted his dick buried deep in your delectable ass. Peter would spend hours suckling your breasts. Jon's specialty is making devices that can keep you in the throes of an orgasm for well over an hour. The chair and bracelets are his invention."

He paused, letting those words sink in, then gave her the answer to one of her questions. "The symbols on the bracelets are Trust and Surrender. And Love. They're intended as a gift, sweetheart. Not a punishment."

She swallowed, not sure if she was going to panic, scream, cry, or climax. Her body shook in a paroxysm, drawn and quartered between all of them. While there was no need any longer to disguise her reaction, still she tried, but he was going to be merciless with her. Her mind was full of his voice, Ben's unreadable green eyes, the singular focus in Jon's face, Peter's undisguised absorption with the way her breasts were moving. That first day, she'd analyzed the sexual undercurrent, the way they emanated sex, their ability to take over a woman's senses without any overt attempt to do so. Now here it was unleashed, and it pressed on all sides, their desire for her making it almost impossible to breathe, to do anything but feel the pounding want between her legs, the ache in her throat and chest.

"I know you're worrying your reputation is ruined with them. It isn't. Trust me on that. Your beauty and intelligence, and the desire you show us now—it's a gift to any man breathing. We treasure it. So tell me what *you* want, Cass. Do you want me to stop all this now? Do you want me to release you, let the three of them spread you on this table, please you until you lose consciousness?" Another pause. "Or shall I let you climax just for me, while they watch?"

At that, the speed of the vibrator jumped. Her body arched against her bonds, her knees jerking. Self-consciousness was abandoned, for even if she'd reached for it, it was already far beyond her grasp. The screen Lucas had described was now up, a close-up so she could see Saayo's fingers dipping into her wet pussy, fucking herself, tugging at the silver ring of her clit piercing. Cass could hear her cries building. In the screen that showed the translator above the table, one of the men next to her had put his hand beneath her neck, supporting her.

Think, Cass. She tried to force an eye of calm amid the hurricane of her body's spiraling response. Last night, she'd used Ben to erect a barricade between them. Unsuccessfully, but this time it was Lucas who'd handed her a similar weapon. Since it was disguised as his own strategy, he might not realize until too late that he'd rearmed her.

Each of the men in this room could stimulate her body. It was the same game as always, even steeped in sex. Backed into a corner with two choices, you chose the door that left you the most control. Give the enemy the bailey, in order to protect the keep. Once he had what was there, he might be satisfied. So she'd sacrifice control of her body in order to protect her heart and mind. The assault of her flesh had seriously weakened the inner gates, but if he was like most men, he might not realize there was a gate to breach beyond the one to her flesh.

"What if I said . . . have them take me . . . on the table? Would *you* want that?"

It had taken a supreme effort to say the words, but she managed to stave off her body's roar for release long enough to fire the challenge, send Lucas a glazed but defiant look. As he locked gazes with her, his face going inscrutable, Ben gave a low whistle. She heard a trace of Ireland in his voice, brought out by a palpable wave of pure male lust. "If you don't want her, Lucas, I'm taking her. Even with you scrambling that marvelous mind, she's calling your bluff."

Lucas's eyes flickered. Then his mouth lifted in that slow smile. She knew then she'd lost. Or won. She didn't know anymore. Regardless, the bare movement of his sensual mouth shoved her against the gateway of her own control and, despite all the physical stimulation, was the true last straw. She began to go over. But he was too intuitive. He eased back on the vibration, a near miss. "I won't let them have you, Cassandra. But I will let them give you pleasure. Peter?"

Her gaze tore away from him and went back down the table, where Peter rose from his chair. His corded neck and broad shoulders would be intimidating, if not for the kindness in the storm-cloud eyes. His physique was obvious under the crew neck sweater he wore. Of all the K&A team, he alone wore a pair of jeans, having come from one of the plant operations this morning.

"If I may . . ." He slid her chair out, moving her effortlessly, and then knelt between her spread legs, so tall that he was still eye to eye with her, his shoulder span shadowing her body. As he leaned over, she saw he wore a small gold Saint Christopher's medal. Maybe that was part of their unique relationship as well, sharing the same type of jewelry.

She pushed down the hysterical and irrational burst of humor. *Stay on course.* She could do this. She could. Follow the body, not the heart. Just the body. It was easy enough to follow the urges of the flesh, if you kept it light, easy. Except nothing about this was light and easy. This was as over-the-top as it got, and it was her own fault. She'd kept it bottled for so long. The moral outrage she should have felt at all of this, that should have quelled any desire she had, was absent. She longed for release, oblivion, enough to hang on to Lucas's words, trust him. This had gone too far for her to do anything else, relieving her of any responsibility. So she told herself.

"Tear it open," Lucas said, something raw in his voice. "I'll buy her a new one."

"No—" But Peter had already laid his hands on the lower section of the sweater and ripped it, several pearl buttons bouncing off across the floor. The physicality of it made her gasp, the pull of the slim collar around her throat that remained intact. Her reaction rocked her breasts in a lascivious display above the tight corset before his appreciative gaze.

Cass turned desperate eyes to Lucas. "I never said what my choice was, of the three you gave me."

"It doesn't matter. I'm interested in your opinion, but the decision is mine. Isn't it, Cass?"

Captured by the intensity of his face, the implacable line of his mouth, slope of royal cheekbones, she knew it was. Had what they called magic in past ages simply been this? A knowledge of a person's soul, so honed that he knew things about her that she'd refused to admit to herself? There was no way she could admit to it, even after he laid it so bare here. But he anticipated such lines in the sand, and knew just the right form of sugar to sprinkle over them, making them disappear as if they'd never existed. At least for now. "Pretend I'm your Master, Cass. You lose nothing by giving in to your own pleasure here."

Just like the day she'd left the glade, wishing she could tell him she wanted to stay, she wanted to trust Lucas beyond pretense. If she really could, maybe it *would* be worth all of it, the two of them hurtling down whitewater rapids together, laughing their asses off like kids as they whirled in the frenetic, dangerous current, willing to be pummeled and tossed to feel like this. But she couldn't.

Peter's hands were on the corset bodice, feeling along the edge of the straight, tight hem. His thumb passed over the hard point of the nipple, visible through the straining satin, so close to the edge of exposure. She arched, crying out.

The problem was, she *wasn't* pretending. She was defiant against his Mastery only because she wanted him to earn it, not because she wanted to refuse it. *Make me believe I can trust you.* She wanted to see the fire teased to raging in his eyes, wanted to explode under the touch of others while he watched. All the wild parts of her she'd wanted to indulge but hadn't were here now. Parts that had been coming out in brief bursts, like the day she'd thrown her leg over a Harley and run for the forest.

She was so goddamned tired of being careful. Logically—if she had any tendrils of logic left to grasp in her turbulent mind—they had as much to lose from this scenario as she did, if it went beyond this room and whatever odd relationship they had with the people on the videoconference.

"Suck on her, Peter." Lucas's eyes dared her to look away from him now. Saayo was starting a moan that sounded as if she were sliding into climax. But not quite there yet. The advisor was finishing, which meant each man would be taking her on that table tonight, fucking her as he pleased.

Peter had large hands, and when he cupped her breasts, squeezing them, she gave a hard, guttural groan at the relief it brought. Another sweep of those thumbs, against nipples so sensitive she felt a renewed flood of moisture between her legs. Then he unhooked the top two or three hooks of the corset, just enough to free the nipples, so he could put his mouth over one.

She cried out again, and Saayo's dark eyes were lost in the same way, both of them giving up their minds to pleasure. Peter had short hair, just a step above the military cut, and it tickled her skin, his temple brushing her, along with his heated breath. Just like Lucas's expertise in another area, apparently Peter knew women's breasts better than they did themselves. When he paused to strip off his sweater, the black T-shirt beneath revealed a mesmerizing flag and serpent tattoo that held her dazed attention, the way it undulated with the movement of his packed muscles, the strong flexing lines of his shoulders and back.

"Lucas," she gasped, yanking against the cuffs again. "Lucas."

"She needs something to do with her mouth, Ben." Lucas's attention tilted to their legal executive. "Occupy it with yours."

"My pleasure." Ben approached from her left. He gathered up her hair in one hand, using that to tilt her head back, make her look up at him, up the line of his sculpted body. As he spread the golden-white strands over his palms, he gazed at it, and her, reverently. "God, you're beautiful," he murmured.

She would have replied, but Peter moved to the other nipple, both hands still cradling her, and she cried out again, her fingers digging into the chair arms. A convulsive flick of her gaze showed Saayo below the table again, only now she could see they had her legs tied as well, only wider, to the chair legs of the two men on either side of her. Each had a hand high on her thigh, adding to the sensation of being held open. A series of symbols were tattooed on the inside of the one thigh. Cass realized two of them were the same as those on her bracelets, but her mind couldn't process which two they might be, or what the others might signify. Though that dark part of her that Lucas had tapped knew intuitively it was some mark of ownership, that Saayo willingly belonged to at least one of the men in that room.

Ben had wrapped her hair around his broad palm again and was descending, his firm mouth, green eyes coming down, his grip strong, sure. Not hurried. She was overwhelmed by the sensation of being desired, of their need to savor her, one luscious bite at a time. As if reflecting her thoughts, Peter nipped at her. She screamed at the resulting wave of sensation that took her over. Then there was the heat of Ben's breath. His kiss would be like everything else here. Pure blow-the-top-off-her-world fantasy.

But not bliss, not a resting place for her heart, which was what Lucas's kiss had seemed to offer. She couldn't risk herself on the illusion or the truth of that. But this, Ben's kiss, this was just the physical. What she knew was safe. What she could accept.

As Ben's hand cradled her jaw, his thumb brushing her cheek—yes, they all definitely knew how to make a woman melt—she surrendered.

She averted her face.

Seven

She pressed her face into her shoulder, her breath fast and shallow, tiny whimpers coming from her throat just above Peter's ministrations, her body jerking in preorgasmic spasms. She couldn't tell Lucas she needed to stop. Not because she was about to climax, but because she was about to plummet over a far worse precipice.

But at that gesture, Peter sat back on his heels and Ben straightened, signal apparently received. When Saayo came to climax then, a long, yearning cry, the shuddering thrill of it rippled through her own pussy, her body jerking again as Peter gently rearranged the corset cups back over her breasts. Ben threaded a hand through her hair once more, a stroke of reassurance as he leaned over her and laid her hair comb on the table. Then, unexpectedly, he eased her sweater off one shoulder. She trembled as she saw him register Lucas's mark on her throat, a moment before he placed his lips on her bare skin, several inches away from that possessive brand. Then he eased the fabric back in place and withdrew.

She closed her eyes. What had she done? It was a game. Only a game. She'd scoffed at the idea that emotions like this could exist after just meeting someone. But she'd just turned from the penultimate sexual experience. Where Peter's lips on her breasts and being watched by a group of near strangers while she was brought to climax had been, remarkably, something she could handle, the intimacy of lips, of Ben's mouth, was not. She was far too aware that if it had been Lucas's mouth, she would have been okay.

"Cassie, open your eyes."

She didn't know how long she'd kept them closed, but when she raised her lashes, she found the room silent, the videoscreen dark. They were alone and Lucas was standing before her. He studied her, unsmiling, leaning against the table only a couple feet away. She had to tilt her face to see him, and the disadvantage, while uncomfortable, didn't match the abrupt, inexplicable desire she had to go onto her knees before him, take him into her mouth, serve him. For her own comfort. Something was wrong with her. She was tired. Too tired.

"Sshh." Instead, he dropped to one knee before her and laid his hand on her cheek, much as Ben had. She shuddered with emotion, beyond mere physical reaction. "I'm going to make you come. Would you like that?"

She nodded. "Would you have . . ."

He offered a strained smile. She had such a desire to reach out and feather her fingers through that scattering of blond hair across his high forehead, trace the thoughtful lines that had formed there. "I didn't expect it to become that intense," he admitted. "Though I suspected it was possible. I knew there was more between us than sex. You're an incredibly hot woman, Cass. Makes a man who wants you do crazy things. Obviously." That tug of a smile again.

"The answer is no, though. I would have stopped Ben a second before he kissed you. I didn't want to see his mouth on you. Or let him touch you. Maybe Matt and I are different, or maybe it's that our relationship to Savannah and him is different. He's . . ."

"He's the leader. Like a king to his soldiers. You all serve him, in a way."

"Sounds pretty ridiculous in the modern world, doesn't it?"

She glanced down at her bonds, experienced a weary but wry smile herself. "Can't really speak to that. And Peter?"

"Well, Peter's different." Lucas lifted a shoulder. "He has this thing about breasts. You can't really deny him a taste. It's like denying a puppy a treat or something. He gets the soulful eyes going, and you just feel like shit."

She coughed, a surprised laugh, but then she had to swallow it, for he surged up and seized her mouth with his. So forcefully, he knocked the chair back, pushing it off its front legs into a tilt against the table, his hands clamped over her wrists as he leaned over her.

She used his mouth to breathe, because her breath was gone. Catching her hair, he moved down her throat, adding another bite to that sensitive mark, tongued the cleft between her breasts as she whimpered anew, and then he dropped down again, keeping the chair tilted up with one knee beneath it, his gaze zeroed in between her legs.

The panty detached from the side, and he slid it out from under her, tossing it to the side. "If you come, it's going to be my mouth, my hand, my cock. You understand? No offense to Jon's wizardry, but I want your response to be because of my touch, always."

She nodded, trying to ignore the last word and the butterflies it gave her. "Please, do it now. All I've been thinking about is your mouth there." That and his cock, but she knew that was truly the point of no return.

The flame in his eyes was as gratifying as she'd feared it would be. Unzipping the back of her skirt, he pushed it up and out of the way before taking hold of her hips, cupping her buttocks, and lifting her to a different tilt. His golden hair brushed her thighs as his tongue slid into her, his mouth sweeping over her clit and labia.

She expected to come just at the thought of his mouth on her, but he surprised her with his knowledge of a woman's body again. Slowing the pace, teasing the hypersensitivity of her engorged flesh, he indulged in brief touches, tantalizing licks, nothing rhythmic or too much, so he actually took her down a notch. The searing pain of a raging burn changed into a swirling, slow yearning that began to build, not like a tornado, but a tropical storm, its advance slow but unstoppable. He held her on that point, spiraling up, until tiny cries were coming from her, pleading, as time ticked away and she knew her mind was lost forever. She'd become all sensation, nothing else.

At length, he pressed his lips to her thigh, making her register the fact she was shaking all over. "If I was in your bed, Cass," he whispered, "I'd lace you into your corset every morning, making it as tight as I pleased. You'd wear it at my pleasure, and you'd wear it to remember you belong to me. That's one of the main reasons you wear it now, isn't it? Imagining that you wear it for a man?"

A quick jerk of her head was all she could summon. No point in denying anything, for everything but truth was stripped away. She hadn't really acknowledged the truth of it herself until he showed it to her. A man she was all too willing to allow to master her. His eyes flashed. "So there you go, then. You don't think it's just sex between us anymore, do you?"

"You . . . know lots of things about women," she hedged. "All of you."

He nodded. "We do know lots about women. Enough that we know every one of them is a mystery, and those mysteries overlap, give us an avenue into the heart of the next treasure to unravel. But you're different. You're a mystery, Cassie, but from the moment I saw you in the glade, I knew there was a part of you that was open to me uniquely, clear as the blue sky, like your gorgeous eyes. So full of arousal, so worried. You're meant to be appreciated and cherished every day, just like that sky. Doesn't matter to me whether it's cloudy, sunny, or storm dark. You know me, too. The same way. That's why you make me crazy like this. Time has nothing to do with it."

Lowering his head, he put his mouth on her again. Sliding his hands beneath her hips, he began to move her in a rhythm against him, fingers teasing the cleft between her legs again, reawakening all the nerves provoked by the earlier vibration.

Her head dropped back, snapped forward, the only part of her that could move with abandon, and she thrashed with it now, her blond hair sweeping over the satin mahogany finish of the table. Her movements whipped some of the strands across her mouth, then they fell away again. Unbidden, she imagined what it would have been like, having them all in here watching Lucas do this to her, claim her this way, with his mouth, with his ability to bring her to climax. A fantasy with a medieval flare to it, the bedding of the bride.

Marking his claim upon her as Matt had done Savannah. She pictured it as a dark and stormy night they had done that, the room dim like this, filled with the watchful stillness of aroused men, a woman's rasping breath like Saayo's, one man's eyes watching her every movement, knowing just when to move in and take her up to screaming climax before them all, calling his name.

Maybe an hour or two ago she'd have been flummoxed by this, as well as by Matt's relationship to his wife. She lived in a modern world where female independence was so strategically critical, and yet now it fit, made sense to her in a way that was entirely illogical, inexplicable. She'd say it was hormones, but he'd just given her an example that it wasn't. Not only in her desire not to be kissed by anyone but him, but in the apparently successful marriage between two people highly respected in the business world.

"First time in my mouth. Next time for my cock." Raising his head, he dug his fingers into her legs. "You *will* have lunch with me today, and then I'm going to take you somewhere, fuck you, and make you completely mine."

"Yes. Yes." She couldn't think about all the reasons that wasn't likely to happen. She just needed him now and she, the paragon of business integrity, would lie, steal, cheat—hell, maybe even kill, if it was some psycho criminal who deserved it—to have him consider her his, to belong to him, heart, soul, and mind, for at least these few minutes. She'd give herself this, even if it tarnished her to do it.

He held her gaze, though. "I won't let you lie to me, Cassie. It will happen, even if you try to back out."

She'd never heard more reassuring words, even knowing he'd likely be the one backing out. "Please, Lucas."

He nodded, lowered his attention again, and his mouth breathed on her.

"Oh, God." She strained against her bonds.

"Beg, Cassandra. Make it dirty. Ask for it the way I know you want it."

"Please . . . make me come. I want my pussy, hard against your face. I want to see my come on your mouth, your cheeks, know that you've rubbed your face all in it. I want your tongue fucking me."

And she let out a cry as he did just that, working into her, teasing her inside and out, his fingers tight, bruising, yanking her forward against her bonds to shove her against his face, making the chair rap against the table once before he let out an oath, pressed a control beneath the chair, freeing her arms. But she didn't want to be free.

Picking her up under the arms, he lifted her as if she weighed nothing, brought her down on the table, guiding her arms above her head. The magnets in the restraints clamped to each other as he crossed her wrists and left them there. Pulling her hips off the end of the table, he returned to his penetration of her, the wild licking of her clit and labia in a way that seemed to have no rhyme or reason but was bringing her to a sure, spiraling release.

She screamed long, her hips beating on the table, the world flashing with spots and colors. As she fought for air, she welcomed the stranglehold of the corset, of his restraints, of the brutal force of his hands. Her breasts were generous, milky white overflowing curves that drew and held his fascinated gaze. If things ended between them, as she knew they would, it would be months, maybe years, before she got it out of her head, the idea that he'd placed there. That the restraint of the corset was his restraint upon her. That she wore it for him. For the hope of a man like him.

She'd seen the fetish sites, her fantasies depicted in such a demeaning way she'd never allowed herself to think of it as more than a guilty private depravity that crept in when she sought to relieve her own frustration. Even then, in the aftermath, she'd passed it off as a typical woman's desire to be ravished by a forceful alpha male, nothing darker and needier than that.

But Lucas had opened up a different take on that world, one that could exist in the real world, that was gilded with the light of her true desires. In that world, he could stake his claim and not only bring her this kind of ecstasy, but give her a shelter in the storm. Those embarrassing trappings of overly made up porn actresses with whips and leather corsets fell away from what it really meant. Protection and devotion, surrender. Belonging.

Trust, surrender, and love. The bracelets. Oh, God, she was losing her mind.

She wasn't sure if she lost consciousness, but she might have. All she knew was when she tuned back in, she was no longer on the table. Lucas was on the floor, sitting on the cushioned carpet, his back against the wall. He was holding her in his lap, toying with those three open hooks of her corset, making brief caresses of her nipples that increased her trembling. He'd rearranged her skirt, though, and her shoes were neatly paired next to the two of them, waiting for her.

As he looked down at her, his eyes were filled with so many things, she found she couldn't think of what to say to him. With her emotions in a jumble, her mind fled into the refuge of numb shock.

But he spoke first. "I believe you have to let me take you to lunch now."

⊰⊱

He wouldn't let her throw herself out the window instead of walking through the admin's office, where she could hear the other men talking. Since her sweater was stripped of buttons, he removed his dress shirt, under which he wore a white T-shirt, and put it on her, rolling up the sleeves. Though too large, worn over her dark shirt, it gave her an Annie Hall look her that was reasonably fashionable. She was coated in his scent. He wouldn't let her have her hair clip back, for he told her he wanted the corn silk of her hair spread out on her shoulders. As he examined her, he let his finger dip into the neckline, unbuttoned to the point he could tease the cleft between her breasts, the top refastened hooks of her corset.

"You shouldn't look like you won the war." She was proud when she found her voice at last. "Just a battle."

He'd told her she was different than other women he'd seduced. She was determined to act like it, even as she refused to let herself acknowledge the jealousy she felt about those others. It was misplaced, regardless, for she likely owed his incredible expertise to practice sessions with them.

"I'll look forward to any battle with you." His eyes were warm and distracting as they coursed over her, but then he surprised her by removing the bracelets with caressing hands. As he dropped to do the same with the anklets, he must have seen something that betrayed her surprisingly bereft reaction, for he dropped a kiss along the inside of her knee, making her shiver. He rose. "They're yours, sweetheart, but you have to ask for them back. And when you do, it will be because you've accepted you're mine. Let's go."

Whether it was the shock of digesting those words or the fact he'd reminded her she was about to go back in front of the team, she didn't realize she'd planted her feet until she rocked against his tug on her hand.

Since she was wearing the tall heels again, he was courteous enough not to yank. But he turned around, put both hands on her shoulders, leaning in so she had to meet his gaze and smell her own scent on his firm mouth. "Cass, this won't be bad, I promise. When a woman embraces her sexual desires, it doesn't place a mark against her intelligence or our respect for her. We don't share the crude and immature way our society views sex."

"Sure you don't." She struggled to find her tongue. "A bunch of guys—you're all above that."

A flash of teeth. "I didn't say we don't appreciate a naked female. But we appreciate her differently. At one time, most of us were as typical about it as you'd expect. But Jon taught us an alternative perspective. It's a sacred act, a gift you've given us tonight. C'mon. Trust me."

With a little more coaxing on the same line, along with a half-teasing threat to just ravish her on the floor if she didn't move her ass, he was finally able to get her walking toward the front office area. She told herself the whole way she wouldn't bolt, though not doing so was one of the hardest things she'd ever done. Which, considering her past, was saying a great deal.

When they stepped into the room, her heart jumped into her throat as they all turned. However, Peter was closest, and he stepped to her immediately, drawing her away from Lucas and astonishing her with a strong-armed, reassuring hug, his body a hard bulwark against any shame or guilt. Absurdly, almost like a big brother. As he eased her back, he grinned down at her, as if the two of them were part of a planned conspiracy. "That was the best damn regulatory review I've ever attended. Think we should do that more often."

"In your dreams," Lucas said dryly.

Jon came next. Kissing her hand, he gave her a pleased, gentle smile. "When you feel comfortable about it, Miss Moira, I'd like to know how the device and the chair worked for you. I know it's no comparison to Lucas's devil-blessed mouth, but I like to improve my work."

"Sure," she said faintly. He squeezed her hand. Ben had drawn close, giving her a friendly, concerned look. They were grouped around her, Lucas at her back. Amusingly, she felt adopted, in a very nonsibling way.

Being the oldest sibling in her own family, she knew what it was to offer reassurance and protection to others, guidance, shelter. Just like the remarkable idea of Lucas's feelings for her after such a short time, this had an intuitive feel to it, a relationship meant to be, waiting out there in the collective consciousness until they were brought into the same room, under these unusual circumstances.

"You all seem . . . very comfortable with this." She groped for something to say.

Ben took her hands then, pulling her to him. He gave her a hug, too, though his hands wandered over her with regret, until Lucas made a warning growl in his throat that did remind her of wolves. Ben lifted his head, his eyes twinkling. "You need to know we don't make a habit of ravishing our female associates. You're a special case. As Lucas told you, Savannah has been the only other one. I'll let you draw your own conclusions from that."

Then he stepped back and she saw Matt Kensington sitting on the arm of the couch, watching them all. When he rose, holding out a hand, Lucas's hand touched her back, a reassurance as she moved forward, putting her hand with only a slight hesitation into Matt's.

"With the exception of my own wife, I've never met a more clever businesswoman. If Steve Pickard didn't have my utmost respect, I'd steal you from him. Plus, I can tell you have an integrity that can't be bought."

"No, sir. Mr. Kensington."

He nodded, squeezed her fingers as well. The hawklike dark eyes studied her, his sensuous mouth in a thoughtful line. She'd tried not to notice those things too closely, given that he was married, but now she noticed it all, including his commanding grip, telling her what kind of animal she was dealing with. She saw it, too, in the way his gaze flickered when she addressed him formally.

As it dawned on her, she looked around her, saw that same brand of sexual dominance stamped on every one of them, even the gentle Jon, and comprehended another element that gave them their understanding of one another. It was a heady combination, one that made her more cognizant of how she'd been drawn into the fantasy so easily. But that underscored it had to be a fantasy, a few stolen moments. If she was wise, she'd start shoring up her defenses.

"I feel like the cheerleader who gets protected by the whole football team," she ventured. "Not sure whether to feel offended or just amused."

She couldn't deny the gratification she felt at Matt's smile, though. "We are unapologetically male, Cassandra. I look forward to seeing you bust Lucas's balls regularly. He needs it. Arrogance is an unfortunate trait."

"Really?" She arched a brow. "It's so fortunate, then, that the rest of you don't goad him by example."

A feminine chuckle showed Savannah in the doorway. "Truer words," she said lightly.

It *was* like a family gathering, one that made the low-level yearning simmering in her gut expand to a more painful size. This sense of belonging wasn't for her. She couldn't keep it.

"I need to go," she said abruptly. When she noted her briefcase was next to Matt, he beat her to it, but simply handed it to her. Though his smile had given her a rewarding sense of pleasure, his quiet and shrewd expression now was something she avoided. She cleared her throat, drew herself up, and swept a glance over all of them, lingering on none. She didn't turn to face Lucas yet, still a weighted presence behind her.

"I . . . this has been a profound experience, for certain, but obviously my work is done here. The remaining paperwork can be tied up via fax and e-mail. Thank you, Mr. Kensington. Mr. Johnson will be very pleased."

She nodded blindly to the men, moving through them, hoping none would shift to stop her, somehow wishing they would. A corset was no protection against these kind of forces. In fact, it was a damn liability.

When she reached Savannah, the woman's expression, like her husband's, held a knowledge that terrified Cass.

"I know just how you feel," Matt's wife murmured, with a poignant smile. "Run. He'll catch you for certain, but make him work for it. Let him prove what a wonderful man he is, so you'll never doubt it."

"It's not him I doubt," Cass said without thinking. Then shaking her head, she fled, as she heard Savannah give her the blessing of a head start.

"Lucas, I need to ask you something . . ."

Eight

She had a problem, though. While a life-changing orgasm could make her merely short of breath, her own emotions could apparently make her hyperventilate. Why did this have to happen now? She'd avoided this type of thing for so long, blown off any attempts to get below the surface. Work, making money, taking care of the kids, that was what came first.

Matt was on the top floor, of course, so she hit several buttons in the elevator and then got off on the fifteenth, fleeing to the stairwell. She went down a couple flights before she sank down on a middle step and fought for air. After spending twenty-four hours with this group, any other idiot would have removed the damn thing. Changed into a sports bra that allowed an Olympic runner freedom to drink in gallons of oxygen. It was a good lesson—the weapon that gave you an advantage in a world of mildly aggressive dogs could be turned against you in the company of a pack of sleek, sexy predators.

Her mind was a mess. She'd be hard put to outthink Nate, her five-year-old brother, let alone someone as sharp as Lucas. But she would try. He had a high opinion of her bravery, so if she went the coward's way, maybe she'd give him the slip. She waited, heading down to the lobby after about ten minutes, figuring he would think he'd missed her. He knew where her office was, of course, but that was her turf. He'd have lost the strategic and tactical advantage. Maybe now was the time to take that week of vacation she'd been thinking about. Take the kids somewhere camping.

Maybe the remote mountain ranges of Tibet.

She had to be wearing his shirt, feeling its heat and scent against her flesh, every movement of the fabric like his touch. She thought seriously about stripping it off, leaving it lying on the stairs and stomping through the lobby in just the corset and skirt. But it was a fall day outside and she wasn't foolish enough to risk the cold, since she'd also left her coat behind. She'd get another.

When she got to the lobby level, she slipped off the heels and stepped out the stairwell door onto the slick tile floor. Her legs were still shaking, down to her quivering ankles. She wasn't going to risk making more of a fool of herself than she already had, but Lucas had been right. She hadn't felt decimated in their eyes. Only in her own.

Of course, there he was, like a promise. Sitting cross-legged on the floor in his cotton T-shirt, untucked over his slacks so she couldn't help thinking about running her hands up his flat stomach beneath it. He'd shrugged the suit coat over it.

The stairwell door closed behind her as he lifted his gaze. "Why didn't you just come up the stairs to find me?" she asked.

"I figured it's like the women's restroom. That sanctuary rule you all have." When she raised a puzzled brow, he clarified. "If a lady goes somewhere by herself, you give her a few minutes. Particularly if she seems to need it. Then, there were all those stairs." He gave a mock shudder. "Exercise. I might get sweaty."

Back in the glade, his body had looked like it was oiled under the touch of the sun. She shoved the distracting image away. "Wasn't I in the restroom yesterday?"

"Sometimes a woman doesn't need sanctuary. Not that kind."

"Oh." She narrowed her eyes. "And you're a good judge of that, are you? You're insufferably irritating."

"Not arrogant?"

"Arrogant men like being told they're arrogant. Romance novels have made them think that's a good thing."

A trace of humor went through the serious gray eyes. "I owe you lunch."

"You don't owe me the meal. I pay, because you won."

"No, I didn't." Rising, he brushed off his slacks. "Because I hurt and upset you."

"So let me out of it, then."

"No. You don't need that."

"Of course I don't." She closed her eyes. When she opened them, he'd taken a step forward. Maybe two, for he was directly before her now. When he looked down at her bare feet, her painted red toenails, her hand tightened on the straps of her heels. "Your floors are terrible. I'm surprised you don't have lawsuits."

"They're pretty, though. Ben makes threatening lawsuits go away. I think he has connections to the Irish mob. Either that or he takes plaintiffs out and drinks them to death."

She stared at him. "You completely overturn my world, transform a business meeting into a . . . I don't even know what to call it. A chessboard to accomplish getting up my skirt, and now charm and humor are supposed to work."

He looked toward the ceiling, pondering. "Fairly good summation. At least everything except it being all about getting up your skirt. Though that was a pretty good side benefit."

When she made a sound between a snarl and a sob, he caught her arms. Unfortunately for her, fortunately for him, he hadn't forgotten the strength of her right hook. He pulled her against him, holding her there as she struggled. "Let go."

"Cassie, listen. Stop it and listen, will you?" When he gave her a little shake, she wished she still had on her heels so she could have punctured his foot. But when she looked up in his face, she didn't see anything that suggested he was making light of the situation. Far from it.

"You've got some formidable shields, and I'm not going to apologize for using the resources I have to get past them. Because you know as well as I do that what's upset you has nothing to do with me getting up your skirt. If that was the case, you never would have stopped me a month ago. It would have been a fun fuck, and two adults would have gone their separate ways.

"But I got in. In just those few minutes. So you're scared shitless about what I'm going to find now that I'm there. Which means it matters to you." A grim smile touched his mouth, though his eyes remained hard. "Which also gives me hope that this is more to you than just getting into *my* pants."

She fixed her attention stonily on his chest. "I had it all planned out. I was going to use you and cast you aside."

"Like yesterday's *Wall Street Journal*." Lucas sighed, gathered her in, letting his chin rest on top of her head. "You know, some of those articles are good reference material."

As she let out a muffled snort, Lucas rubbed his hands up and down her back. "God, I want to get you out of this damn thing, feel your skin."

She couldn't agree more, but she drew back. "Lucas, let me put on my shoes."

"No, you're right. You'll break your neck in these."

"I'm not walking into the K&A lobby with the CFO in nothing but bare feet."

"Okay." Letting her go, he pulled off one loafer and then the other as she watched, nonplussed. He considered his black dress socks. "We had a sliding contest down here, late one night."

"A what?"

"Sliding. You run fast and then slide in your socks across a slick floor? We had a bet on who could slide the farthest from a certain point. Kind of like shuffleboard, with people. Then we did all sorts of crazy acrobatics. We had an audience of homeless people standing outside the window, staring at us before it was all over."

"Who won?" Cass asked, for lack of anything else to say, her mind torn between the intensity of their exchange only a breath ago, and the whimsy of seeing the K&A team play like boys in their own lobby.

"Peter. Damn mutant cyborg. He can run the fastest. I guess that's a good thing, since when people are trying to blow you up or put bullets in your ass, being fast is important."

She shook her head. "You're insane."

"We're human, Cass. That's all. We're all kids playing grown-up. We do the best we can."

Taking her hand and holding his shoes, he walked into the lobby. She thought about digging in, but the floor was slick enough he'd probably haul her forward like a sled dog, so she went along with him.

Traffic flow was always steady through the K&A lobby, and today was no exception. Some of the faces were known to her, but somehow with Lucas holding her hand and moving along as if it was the most normal thing in the world to be padding across the floor in his socks, her in stocking feet, she was able to assume an almost nonchalant air.

As the receptionist gave them an amused glance, they won a snort from the security guard, who obviously knew Lucas. Then they were past, heading for the revolving door. "You're shorter this way," he commented. "Petite, like a doll."

"If you say Barbie, I'll sweep your legs and crack your skull on your pretty shiny floor."

"Ouch. Kung fu Barbie." Laughing, he dodged her shove, came back, and claimed her hand. "There's the biker chick who stole my heart." Guiding her into the revolving door, he took the same section, crowding her until they emerged into the crisp fall air that nevertheless was full of sunshine. When she started to put on her shoes, he shook his head, pulled her out of the flow of foot traffic. "Feel the warmth through the concrete."

"My stockings will tear. And the rest of me is a little cold."

"I swear, you're as bad as working with metal. A man has to fire you up to get you to bend." Gathering her against him, he wrapped her up in the open panels of his suit coat. "Now, feel the heat through your soles. Doesn't that feel good?"

Cass resisted the urge to bury her face into his shirt, rub her cheek against his chest beneath the stretched cotton. Instead, she tipped her head back to look at his eyes, narrowed against the glare, the sun forming a halo limning his golden hair.

Yeah, right. Definitely a trick of the light, that. "Yes," she admitted, glad he didn't know what felt so good to her. The strength of his arms, his body pressed close. The coat around her, the way she'd imagined.

"Here comes our limo, to take us to lunch." At her arch glance, he shrugged. "What's the benefit of being a big shot at K&A if you can't use the limo pool for lunch?"

"You don't have a car?"

He grinned. "You saw it in my office."

"You ride your bike to work? Where do you live? Are you insane?" She looked at the busy downtown traffic.

"It was about ten miles in New Orleans. Here it's about fifteen. It's a good way to start the day. I do have a car," he added. "I only use it when I have to. Green footprint, and all that."

"Glad to hear it. Because I'm not going on a date on handlebars or pedal pegs."

"Progress." He smiled, holding her closer, his hands low on her hips. "You're calling it a date."

Cassandra didn't want to be so comfortable in his company. She needed to be out of sorts with him, convince herself she felt used, exposed, forced to an unwelcome vulnerability. But she wasn't in the habit of lying to herself. She could avoid what she didn't want to think about, though. So for the time being she decided not to dwell on the fact he'd made her do the unthinkable. As well as left her with a frightening need for more of him.

In the limo, he slid an arm along the back of the seat, giving her a loose sense of being encircled, particularly when he toyed with her hair, coaxed her with amusing guile into leaning across him as he pointed out a landmark of interest. When she leaned back, she found his arm settled on her shoulder, holding her closer.

"I said lunch," she said. "Then you said I could walk away."

"Is that what you want to do?" he asked. "Walk away? Why won't you give this a shot, Cass?"

"I don't really have a choice, Lucas. My life has no room for something like this. Much as I might want it." She needed to give him that, but she almost regretted it because the softening of his expression made her wish fiercely she had more to give him.

"There are always choices. Let's at least talk about what the obstacles might be. Let me get to know you," he insisted. "I want to know you."

"I can't—" Thank God, her cell rang, but then she saw the caller ID. *No, not right now.* The timing couldn't be worse, or more ironic. She told herself to ignore it, even as she knew she couldn't. Any more than she could cover the questions it would raise. Suppressing a desire to scream, she opened the cell.

"Yeah, George. How long ago? You should have called me." She bit her lip. "Yes, I know you're busy. No, I'll come get him. Yes, I will. Damn it, George, we've been through this. I can't." She shook herself. "I'll just be there in a minute, okay?"

When she got off, Lucas's eyes were on her face. Miserably, she averted her own, looked out the window at a world where the sun had dimmed, and everything she'd just done and enjoyed was laced with bitterness. "I'm going to have to skip lunch. If you'll stop, I'll get a taxi."

"Cass. Tell me what's going on." Tiredness had taken over her features the moment she looked at her caller ID, and there was a pain in her eyes Lucas wanted to erase. He touched her hand, but she drew away, shook her head.

"My brother has some problems. He got picked up. Again. I need to go get him."

"This is one of the reasons you think I shouldn't get involved with you." When she pressed her lips together, he sat back, suppressing his own frustration. "Max, take us to the District One police station, will you? I assume that's where he is?"

"What?" Her gaze snapped to him. "I don't want you involved in this."

"Tough. Now tell me what we're dealing with."

"*We're* not dealing with anything," she said sharply. "I'm just going to get him. This is my business, Lucas. There's no need to involve yourself."

"No need at all, if my interest was only in your beautiful body and eager pussy." He'd pitched his voice low, but it still made her attention jerk toward the driver then back to him, her face burning.

"That's not what I meant," she hissed.

"Yeah, it was. You like men, Cass, but you view them like pets.

You can only count on them for certain things, and you're wholly responsible for taking care of them. Which, for what a dog or cat provides us, is a wonderful symbiotic relationship. When you apply that to a human, it's way too much work."

"Don't you analyze me," she warned. "We're not in a board room now. I can make Max stop this limo, tell you to kiss my ass and go on my way."

"We're almost there." Lucas studied her. "I'm not trying to threaten you, Cass."

"Yes, you are," Cass retorted. She tossed circumspection out, since he already had. "Okay, we can do sex. Hell, I'd be happy to fuck our mutual brains out. You're the first man I've met in a while that might actually do the trick without taking too much time out of my day and still be satisfying. But my cunt is not the gateway into my life."

The limo veered, a quick brake. Lucas sent a grimly amused glance toward the front. "All right up there, Max?"

A cleared throat and the driver, a man who looked to Cass like he also served as a bouncer, spoke. "Er, yes, Mr. Adler. I'll just, uh, raise the glass. I'd like to listen to some music."

"You can stop right here, Max, and let me out," she ordered.

Max shifted his gaze to her in the mirror, then back to the road while Lucas sat silently. "All due respect, ma'am, but we're in a section of town now where I wouldn't kick my worst enemy out of the car, let alone a young lady. Mr. Adler isn't going to allow it anyhow."

"I see the whole unapologetically male thing extends to your staff as well," she said through gritted teeth as the glass scrolled up with a quiet hum.

"You have more kids at home," he said gently. "Don't you? Are they yours?"

"How did you—"

"Because I'm as good at this as you are, and that was a rotten attempt to freeze me out. Now, are they yours?" Despite his indication that he was aware she was being defensive, the temper in his expression said he wasn't going to let her insult him again without consequences. Cass wasn't sure she could handle his idea of retribution right now.

"Yes. Siblings," she stated stiffly. "Five of them, from ages five to sixteen."

He blinked. "Your parents—"

"Are no longer part of the picture. Haven't been, for a long time." She shook her head, looked out the window. "Please stop, Lucas. Please. Just . . . stop."

Mortified, she had to blink back tears. She could already feel the weight of what she was about to do settling in the pit of her stomach. She'd spent too much time in fucking hospitals and police stations. If he said one more word, she was going to lose it.

Instead, she stiffened as his arm settled on her shoulders. To her surprise, he didn't say anything further, just squeezed lightly, a reassurance, his hand stroking her upper arm. A soothing she'd be crazy to take. Like lying down for one minute at home when she was so tired, or taking one more bite of chocolate, things she'd taught herself not to do. But Lucas had undermined some of her normal defenses, to say the least.

"If I put my head on your shoulder for a moment, will you be quiet and not say anything?"

In answer, his hand molded itself to her temple, easing her down. He kept it there, just stroking her as the limo made its way through the traffic toward the police station.

⋙⋘

George was the uniform who worked the beat where Jeremy most often was picked up. He'd known her for some time, one of the cops who'd been called to the house for domestic disturbances involving her mother, sometimes her father. So when Jeremy got picked up, he usually tried to keep him from being processed, giving her the chance to come retrieve and talk some sense into him. Occasionally, he'd suggested that shipping Jeremy over to the East Baton Rouge holding facility to cool his heels might not be a bad idea. But they'd been that route before and she wouldn't do it again, not when she had a choice.

She'd asked Lucas to head back to his office or, at the least, to stay in the car, neither of which he did. So he was a quiet, unobtrusive shadow behind her as she went through the far-too-familiar routine.

"I'll send him out front," George said, giving Lucas a quick cop assessment. "You can head him off before he takes off."

"Thanks."

He nodded, gave her a pitying look she hated, particularly with Lucas there to see it, too. Turning without another word, she headed back out, aware that Lucas held the door for her, his fingertips grazing her lower back as they left the station. She moved a few steps down the sidewalk, and took a seat on a bench. Lucas stood beside her. She wondered why he didn't sit down, then realized he was blocking her from the chill wind that was sweeping garbage along the sidewalk. He put his jacket around her, made her put her hands through the sleeves without making her talk.

That simple kindness could have broken her, but fortunately Jeremy came out the front then. He saw her immediately, of course. She always came to get him.

It was hard to comprehend everything that passed over his face. Derision, hunger, need. Waste was what she usually saw. Features too gaunt, the eyes burning or distant and vague, depending on whether or not he was still riding his latest hit. He'd inherited their father's height and good looks, as well as the addictive personality that had made her daddy a drunk. Unfortunately, the height and addictive personality were all Jeremy had left. Her twenty-four-year-old brother had the face of a man thirty years older. On the last visit, she'd heard one of the uniforms mutter to George, "She won't have to waste her time on him much longer. We'll find his body in an alley soon enough."

She couldn't argue with the truth of that either. But she couldn't give up on the brother who'd gone from recreational drugs in junior high to hardcore abuse in order to blot out what was happening at home.

"Rescued by big sis again." He spread his arms out as she approached him, noting his calculating look toward Lucas and the limo. "Glad you could fit me in before your big date. Going to the prom?"

"You're looking worse, Jer. Why don't you let me take you somewhere, buy you some lunch?"

"Got things to do. You can give me the cash, though. I'll pick something up at the deli. Since you've got funds to spare."

She shook her head. "You'll just buy another fix. How are you buying your drugs, Jer? You know, possession is far different from dealing. You could—"

"Go to prison for a long time. So much worse than my life now."

She knew better than to engage, but then again, these brief minutes every few weeks were the only chance she got. "You chose this life. You can choose something different. Let me take you to get a sandwich. We can talk about it."

"At home?" The thread of hope behind the derision ripped her heart out of her chest, but she maintained a neutral tone.

"You're not allowed to come there. Not as long as you're strung out. It hurts Marcie and the others too much. Jessica really misses you. If you'd just let me get you into a program—"

"Been there, done that. Don't give a shit," he said bluntly. "Fuck off, sis. Don't need help from someone with a silver spoon stuck up all her holes but nothing to give her brother. Maybe that's your problem. If you'd given me more of a chance to be the man of the family, rather than taking on the role yourself, then maybe I wouldn't have turned out like this."

"I was the oldest, Jeremy. You know I—"

He cut her off with a sharp gesture. "I'm only two fucking years younger than you. But you had to run it all, do it all, make me feel even more like a screw-up."

She really did know better, but her nerves were frayed, firing her temper. "I tried that, remember? While I was trying to get my degree, you invited your creepy friends over to shoot up. You remember how one of them tried to rape Marcie when she was thirteen?" Cass stepped into him, bumping his toes. He stank. God, when was the last time he'd bathed? "Or were you too stoned to remember your sister screaming for your help?"

"Back off," Jeremy snarled, shoving her back, curling a hand into a fist. And found that hand caught, his body yanked around, hard gray eyes inches from his face.

"I don't care if she is your sister, you don't hit girls," Lucas said evenly. "And you sure as hell don't hit her."

"So she finally got herself a boyfriend. I was beginning to think she prefers pussy, only she's so cold you'd have to use a hairdryer to get anything up her cu—"

Lucas hauled him up onto his toes. "Finish it, and you'll be on your ass picking up your teeth. She may see her baby brother, but I see a piece of shit. You shut it, or I will shut it for you."

Cass had frozen. In her anger, she'd almost forgotten Lucas was with her, at her back. Cold, controlled, his eyes like steel. Her brother was enough of a street creature to know when the odds were against him. He shut up, though he glared.

"She weighs nothing, comes up to your chin, and you were about to hit her with a closed fist. Jesus." Lucas thrust him off, away from Cass, hard enough to send him stumbling, and she didn't miss that he positioned himself between them. "If nothing else, that should tell you that you need help. You're absolutely right. She does need a man to help her lead the family. Get into rehab, stick with it. Admit you need your family's help. That's what a real man would do."

"Jeremy." Recovering, Cass stepped around Lucas. "Please, let us help."

"Fuck off." Jeremy took off at an awkward run, his limbs uncoordinated so he stumbled over a couple cracks on the pavement, but kept going.

She almost gave chase, then felt the gentle but firm restraint of Lucas's hand. Pulling away, she rubbed her forehead, counted to ten. "I'm not in the mood for lunch anymore." She didn't think she could bear to look at him, but then Lucas touched her face, surprising her such that she looked up at him.

"I'm sorry, Cass."

"No. Nothing for you to be sorry about."

"Yeah, there is." He looked down the sidewalk, where Jeremy had stopped, backpedaling when he realized they weren't following. He shot a middle finger at her, shouted something intelligible, and then turned, striding away among a largely apathetic crowd who recognized a junkie when they saw one. "That's something for everyone to be sorry about."

Moving farther from his comfort, she stared at a homeless person propped against the side wall of a storefront, sheltering from the wind. "I live in a safe, beautiful house. I have a security guard and a gate. Specifically so he can't be there."

"Has he been through rehab?"

"Twice. Ditched it both times. I had to make sure he couldn't get to the girls and Nate," she added, a steadying reminder. She wouldn't let Lucas see her fall apart over this. More than that, she wouldn't do it to herself. "They'd fall right into his traps, his sob stories. But I keep . . ." Her voice trembled again, despite her attempt, but she steadied it with a fierce shrug of her shoulders. "Well, that's that, then."

"No. What?" He took her by the shoulders, wouldn't let her go when she pulled. "Tell me, Cass."

"I keep telling myself not to think of him as my brother anymore. Because he really isn't, not anything like what I remember. But he is. He is." And she couldn't help it, the tears were coming, the sobs, and she couldn't stop them. "Sometimes I just want it to be over. I want to grieve him all at once, rather than these bits and pieces."

Appalled at the words she'd said, bitterness gave way to something else. *Oh, God, I can't do this here.*

At her look of total panic, Lucas simply picked her up off her feet, right there on the sidewalk in front of the police station, and strode back to the limo. Cass wanted to protest, but she couldn't. The tears were overwhelming her. This was Lucas's fault. This whole well of emotions he'd opened up in her today and yesterday, it was spilling out now, in the place she could least afford the show of weakness.

As they approached the car, she remembered he'd sent Max off to find some lunch, but her gratitude for that did little to ease the pressure inside her. When he slid her into the second seat and got in, she struck out at him, intending to castigate him for treating her like some weak-kneed female. Only somehow she ended up clutching the T-shirt instead, gripping it hard enough to rip, as she tried to pull apart something other than her own insides. He folded his arms around her, brought her against the cotton.

"Goddamn it, Cass, let it go. Anyone can tell it's gnawing at you like a cancer. I'm not going to hold it against you."

She broke. Sobbed out the frustration and misery. She couldn't remember the last time she'd cried about it, because it hurt so much to do it. His hands were between them, pulling the borrowed shirt free of her skirt, as she hiccupped painfully. Now he reached beneath it and unhooked the corset, all the way down, just one of the ways he was easing the combustible emotions pouring out of her. She didn't try to stop him, though in hindsight she doubted he would have let her this time. His hands slid in under it, replacing the stiff stays with heat, the welcome touch of his fingers, molding over her bare rib cage, becoming a different form of support as she gulped in the air she needed for the sobs.

By the time she eased up, she was sure she'd turned her makeup into a raccoon's mask, but embarrassment was getting to be a lost cause with him. Repairing the damage to her pride wasn't worth the effort.

"Shh." Lucas was murmuring to her quietly, she realized, and had been doing so for a while. As she pushed herself up, trying to avert her face, he drew her back, wiping her eyes with the fresh handkerchief from the pocket of the coat she was still wearing. When she tried to take it, do it herself, he let her, but he kept her within the curve of his arm, stroking her hair, his other hand settling on her hip, holding her in a secure circle. He pulled the corset out from beneath the shirt, away from her body, and folded it on the seat beside him, out of her reach. "You don't need this. Not with me."

Exhausted enough not to argue, she leaned into him. Her breast mashed into his hard chest in a comforting way. There was nothing between them now, on several levels. She'd just revealed far too much to him, and there was an ache inside her she was tired of feeling. His body was solid heat, and the steady drum of his heart was a counterpoint to the erratic beat of her pulse. It reminded her that there was a way to assuage the loneliness and despair of all of it, at least for a few minutes. The way she'd wanted him to do from the beginning.

Surging up, she found his mouth with her own, awkwardly enough she thought she might have cut his lips with her front teeth. However, as she locked her arms around his neck and straddled him, she tossed aside control or finesse and demanded from his mouth what some deep part of her was sure only he could provide. No logic or rationality to it, those two things she'd always allowed to guide her life. She willed him to know what she wanted without words.

His hands slid under the shirt again, caressing bare skin marked with the impressions of the tight corset. Finding them, he spoke against her mouth, a soft admonishment as he stroked abraded skin. But he also brought her closer, and the first time both breasts touched his chest, she moaned in his mouth, her hand dropping down to push his jacket out of her way so she could feel him beneath his thin shirt. Cotton felt so good when it was fitted over a man's firm, hot skin, imbued with his scent. His arms circled her back, letting her feel the imprint of his fingers on her flesh, learning the curves of her, learning where she liked to be touched. If it was Lucas, she didn't care where, just that he touched her. She ground herself against him, against the unyielding hardness of his cock.

"Cassie," he said, his voice harsh as he wrapped his hand in her hair to hold her back a necessary inch, though his eyes were full of reassuring desire. "We're in front of a police station. We can't do this here."

"The windows are tinted. I need you to make me come. I need to come, and only you . . . I only want you to do it. Make me do it. Here. With you inside me. Not any other way. I want you to just fuck me, the way you've been wanting." She wanted to be taken, swept away. Wanted to smell him and the vehicle upholstery, his suit, bite his irresistible mouth as he slammed her down on him.

As she curved her long nails, stabbing him through his shirt, her eyes were half-wild, like a feral cat. Lucas suspected she wanted the wildness, all the world narrowing to just that and not any of the other nightmares she was facing.

"I don't want to just fuck you, and you know it. That's not what you want either." He caught her wrists, holding her. "Cassie, look at me. I want to make love to you. Take you into my bed and keep you there a few decades, savor every inch of you. Make you scream yourself hoarse, and mark every part of you as mine. Make you want to be mine."

"No." She shook her head. "That's not what I want."

"It's what you need." He made himself soften the words, though he kept enough steel in his voice to hold her attention, mindful of whom he was dealing with. "In a few minutes, Max is going to be back. He's going to drive us to your home, and that's what we're going to do."

"I haven't agreed to that." Her expression fired, but he saw fear behind it.

"You want me enough to take it how you can get it," he said shortly. "This is the offer that's on the table. You willing to take the risk that I'm right? That it will be hell and gone from just fucking?"

She stared at him, and her big blue eyes, the need in them, almost broke his resolve. He'd take her any way he could get her, too. Wasn't that a hell of a discovery? If another tear fell, he'd be a goner.

"You . . . can't. My sisters are there."

"Okay, then." Taking a deep breath, he considered that new variable, an obvious one that had been clouded by lust. "Then we go spend the afternoon with your sisters. I'll figure out an option for the evening. You keep some energy in reserve."

She nodded, her mind in obvious confusion. "Lucas, with them in the house, we can't—"

"Cassandra." He framed her face in his hands, held her captive. "I've had enough of playing games about this. You hear me? When I take you to your bed tonight, it won't be blatant or inappropriate, but I'm going to be there for breakfast. I'm going to become part of your life, and theirs. We're going to see where this takes us. You deserve something for yourself. I'm that something. What better example could they have of what sex is supposed to be about, than a guy who's head over heels about their sister? Someone who is willing to stay for breakfast?"

She shook her head, trying to pull away, escape. "Lucas, you know I have absolutely no way to process the logistics of any of this."

"I'm the bean counter, remember?" He smiled, though he wanted to bring her back to his chest, if for no other reason than her generous breasts and the aroused nipples beneath his borrowed shirt were going to make him let go of any resolve at all and fuck her brains out in the backseat until the violent rocking of the car gave them away and they spent the night waiting for Ben to come make bail for them. "Let me deal with that. Don't let it be about consequences, worries, or how the world can suck and things go bad. For once, just take it." He gave her a fierce look. "Take the moment and see if it can lead to a lifetime."

"I don't know," she said uncertainly at last, so unlike herself that he wanted to hold her tight, in comfort this time. But he knew you had to close the deal before the opposition backed out. The most important thing was the signature on the bottom line, and the kiss he crushed on her lips now, bringing those delicious breasts back in contact with him, was a definite signature. With a flourish. So definite that he couldn't help crushing all of her to him, pressing the hard weight of his need between her legs, eliciting a provocative whimper from the back of her throat.

"I want to go home," she said again, gratifyingly breathless. "I need to see the rest of my family."

"Okay. One condition. You tell me about them. About you. Give me that."

When she started to shift, he adjusted her so she was no longer straddling him, but he kept her cradled in his lap. More important, it allowed her to stare out at the parking lot, the dismal landscape of the police station, rather than at his face, which he knew might help her talk about what was obviously difficult. But he linked his hand with hers, a simple sign of intimacy and support he hoped would help. She squeezed down on his fingers, and just when he thought he'd have to prod some more, she spoke.

"My mother was mentally ill." She gave a hopeless laugh. "The diagnosis just depended on what drug cocktail they fed her. By the time I was fifteen, I was caring for the kids. She stayed in her bed all the time. My father was okay when I was little, but then he let his alcoholism get the best of him and became a here-again, gone-again presence. Only came back long enough to get her pregnant and then take off again. Which of course would screw up her meds schedule. One of the nurses took pity on me, told me about a birth control that wouldn't adversely interact with her drugs. I got it from a clinic, saying it was for me, and put it into her food after that."

Lucas hoped Max wouldn't return too soon. It was an odd setting for it, but he found himself blessed by this quiet moment, just the two of them, her opening up to him at last, trusting him. "How did you get to Steve Pickard?"

"In high school, I was doing early college coursework for a business degree. Did an internship with him. He learned about my situation, and instead of seeing me as a liability, he groomed me. He took more than a chance on me. He saved me, and my family."

The truth of it was obvious from the emotion that crept in her voice. Lucas made a mental note to put Pickard Industries at the top of the list of those who could ask K&A for anything.

Cass was silent a moment, remembering when Steve had cornered her in a cubicle, a defensive seventeen-year-old, and told her he was going to pay for a part-time nanny to allow her to expand her studies, go to a local college for her degree. Before she'd been able to reject it, he'd told her flatly that she was an investment. "You're a damn teenager, raising a bunch of kids as if they were your own. I've heard you on this phone every other day, handling social workers, police, doctors, nurses, your own fucked-up parents. You've done all that, managed to keep your family together and worked this job, balanced it with school. Anyone who has those skills has the makings of the best negotiator I can buy."

He'd been a frequent visitor at her home ever since, particularly at holidays. He'd become a grandfatherly figure to Nate, taking him out on trips, doing guy things. Otherwise the little boy would have been raised only by females, since she'd obtained restraining orders against both his father and older brother, with George's help.

"You've denied yourself relationships to protect them."

"Yes," she snapped, defensiveness surging forward again. "That's what you do when you have kids. I have four sisters, Lucas, four very pretty sisters, not that that matters, from ages eight to sixteen."

Catching her chin, he forced her face up. "You don't think I—"

"No. *No.*" She recalled herself enough to close her hand on his, realizing his comment had been an observation, not an accusation at her prolonged silence. "I know you would never. But the news is full of women who let their personal needs interfere with their first responsibility, to their children. And these girls and Nate have dealt with so much. They require a stable influence in their life, one person who puts them first."

"You're right. They do." He held her gaze. "Part of teaching kids about life is letting them see a healthy, loving relationship between two people that includes them, doesn't leave them out. But it should also teach them they don't get to be number one in *every* situation. Life is about give and take, sharing. Their big sister deserves a life, too, if she's busting her ass to give them everything they need."

She rubbed her forehead. "Lucas, I'm just not sure—"

"When did the corset come into it?" He glanced toward the garment, still folded on the seat, but then brought his attention back to her neckline. Because it was his shirt, he didn't need to slip a button to let his finger play along the curve of her breast in the opening, using a silken lock of her hair to tease the skin. Cassandra was mesmerized by it, the intent way he looked at her body. At her. She swallowed.

"You're trying to distract me."

"Is it working?" His eyes were even more silver in this light, she noticed, his brows a tarnished gold. No man should have a nose that straight, which now coaxed the trail of her fingertips, down to his lips, which pressed against them, a lingering kiss as she drew away, considered him.

"There were some really rough days," she relented. "Fighting with social workers, my mother's doctors, the police, when Jeremy acted up. Trying to keep my dad out of our lives. One day, I just lost it at the family services office. When I was screaming and crying, some part of me stepped outside myself, took a hard look. Not just at me, but the people around me. I realized I looked just like everyone else there. Run down by life, my behavior and my appearance resulting in a complete lack of credibility. I started paying attention to people who commanded respect, how they handled themselves and spoke, and realized it had nothing to do with money. It had to do with confidence and self-respect."

"And the corsets?" he persisted. "How did that happen?"

She colored a little. "If you laugh, I will smack you."

He forced a smile. "I won't laugh." In truth, Lucas didn't feel anything like laughing.

"The night after that happened, I couldn't sleep. I caught one of those black-and-white movies based on a Jane Austen novel. Looking at the women in corsets, I realized how constrained and elegant they had to be, and figured the outfit helped them maintain that composure. During that time period, everything had a required behavior, so they probably felt like screaming, too." Humor flickered over her soft mouth, then she glanced at the corset. "The first time I bought one secondhand, I felt silly, but when I put it on, I didn't. Controlled by that garment, I was in control of myself. People don't challenge people who approach things calmly, prepared to answer hard questions without making it personal. But you're right." Her gaze moved to his face, his strong neck, the breadth of his shoulders, feeling the controlling power of his arms around her. "It can become about something else."

She trembled a little in his arms when his expression heated at her words. "So here I am. Me and the part-time nanny, Mrs. Pitt, raised the kids. I got my degree, built my reputation in the firm, and now earn a salary that took us out of the corporate housing Steve made me accept, foiling my stubborn pride with concerns about the kids' safety, and into a seven-bedroom in the Lakeshore area."

Lucas whistled. "Pretty amazing accomplishment. Lakeshore."

"You bet your ass."

Lucas saw fire flicker in her again with the words. While he wanted to be the one to absorb her tears, give her comfort, he was glad to see the spark return. Fanning the flame, he brought her hand to his lips to tease her knuckles with his mouth, liking the way she focused on it, her mouth going soft, giving him all sorts of ideas. But he had one more difficult question. "Where is she now, your mother?"

"She died, several years ago." When she tried to draw away, he tightened his grasp and she lifted her shadowed face to his. "Got into her pills and OD'd. I blamed myself for that. I kept her at home instead of a facility because I thought that was what she needed, but we couldn't watch her the way they could have. Anyhow, I had to let it go, because I just don't have time to think about it, you know?"

And can't afford where the emotions would take her, Lucas thought.

"I couldn't save her, and to be honest, I don't know if she wanted to be saved." She drew an unsteady breath. "So that's it. I come with five kids who command the lion's share of my attention, along with my work. A romantic dinner will get interrupted by a crisis involving Cheerios being superglued into someone's hair. Sex is something you book in advance or steal five minutes in a park like a pair of teenagers, because there's little privacy at home. And I won't bring a man into their lives unless he's wanting to be part of it, not just wanting to have me." On this her chin firmed, eyes resolute. "I may not be able to say no to the sex you're offering, but I can't take it near my siblings. They latch on to an adult male far too quickly. I'm not saying that if you walk through the door, you're agreeing to a life commitment, but you've got to care and think it's possible."

"I'm more concerned as to whether you think it's possible." He touched her face. "Because I do. I am sorry, Cass. About all of it. Especially your brother. You feel like you've failed because you can't save him yourself, but to me, it sounds like you already saved five other lives. I was right, what went through my mind that day, when I saw you in the Berkshires."

When she raised a curious brow, he drew her back to his mouth, pausing just before their lips touched. "I told myself, 'Lucas, you've just found the most amazing woman you'll ever meet. Don't let her get away.'"

Nine

Cass's Lakeshore brick home had a welcoming style, with potted plants on the front porch, a circular driveway, and a wide lawn. It was positioned in a quiet neighborhood laid out well for children playing, people walking pets.

After they went through the wrought iron gate, Cass nodding to the security guard, Lucas saw a teenager on the front stoop doing homework, while a little boy of about five years worked his way around the driveway on a bike with training wheels.

As the limo pulled to a halt, the teenager got up, a brown-eyed girl with Cass's blond hair. Pretty enough to already be attracting men's eyes, she could use an older brother looking out for her. That was his first thought. Of course, something about this girl's firm chin and direct gaze, so much like her sister's, suggested she wouldn't take kindly to that idea.

When Cass got out of the car, Lucas understood why she'd wanted so much to go home after the ugliness with Jeremy. She'd barely dropped to one knee before Nate had launched himself off the bike and at her, wrapping his arms around her neck.

"Mommy!" Lucas's surprise at the address was distracted by the child's grin, competition for the brightness of sunshine. He was a younger, far less haggard version of his brother. After a brutal squeeze, he released her to gesture to the bike. "I'm riding. Marcie says I'm doing good."

"You are. I saw, coming up the driveway. Nate, Marcie, this is my friend, Mr. Adler. He works for K&A," she added to Marcie.

"You're one of the *wunderkind*." Marcie gave him a shrewd assessment. "The CFO."

"Your sister's mentioned me?"

"Oh, yeah. She——"

"I mentioned all of you." Cass shot Marcie a narrow glance. "Marcie is already studying business."

Marcie gave her an odd look, but then shifted her attention back to Lucas. "I looked you up on the Internet. Really clever business model presentation to Harvard Business School, by the way. But where does Matt Kensington find you guys? Vegas strip shows?"

As her sister made a strangled sound, Lucas bit back a grin. "That's an HR recruiting secret," he commented gravely. "I trust you won't betray our confidence."

"Marcie." Cass sent her a quelling look. "Where's everyone else?"

"Out back. Nate just wanted to be here when you called and said you were coming home."

"Mommy, look." Nate rattled past again.

As Cass smiled at him, she murmured to Lucas, "Nate's always called me Mommy. I'm the only mom he's ever known."

Any other time, she could have managed that without the quaver in her voice, but it had been that kind of day. As she felt Marcie studying her, she cursed Lucas's intuition when he discreetly opted to fall in step with the little boy, moving out of earshot.

"It was Jeremy again, wasn't it? You have the pinched look."

Cass lifted a shoulder. "I picked him up, he's off again. Let's not talk about it, okay? Not in front of company."

"Looks like company that stuck with you through it." Marcie sent a more thoughtful look after Lucas, but then shifted to an examination of her older sister's appearance. Cass pressed her lips together under the uncomfortable appraisal, determined not to say a word to explain the man's shirt and suit coat loose over her skirt. A suit coat that matched Lucas's trousers. Thank God she had it, though, or the bright sunlight would have shown she wore nothing under the shirt.

Surprisingly, however, Marcie held her questions while Cass focused on Lucas. The little boy was jabbering at him. When he made a wobbling turn, Lucas's hand steadied the seat of the bike as they continued their circuit.

"Holy God, Cass," Marcie said at last. "I saw the pictures, but I didn't think they made them that pretty without wings. Or airbrushing."

"You should see the rest of the team," Cass relented. "They're just about as bad."

"Just about? So you think he's the cutest one, then?"

"Objectively, I'd have to say so, but it's mere degrees."

Marcie tucked her tongue into her cheek. "That Ben O'Callahan looks more my type."

"He's probably about fifteen years older than you."

"So? If he was immortal, like Superman, it wouldn't matter. Ours could be a timeless love. Do you think they do internships? I could try to trap him in the mailroom or something."

"Oh, God." Cass elbowed her sister. But her tensions were easing, being here at home. Marcie could drive her crazy, but teenage silliness like this helped Cass more than her younger sister knew.

If she entertained for even a moment that Lucas could become part of her life, she knew that would mean the *wunderkind* would become part of it as well. Thinking of Ben around her sister almost made her laugh. She knew he'd flirt, making Marcie feel pretty and special, but fend her off appropriately, taking on a big brother role.

It made her wonder if the Knights of the Board Room nomenclature had come about because of what women's intuition detected about them. They were decent, honorable men. She'd directly experienced it when they stood around her in that tight circle, an unsettling memory under the circumstances, but she couldn't deny it had been a warm one, strangely similar to the welcome of Nate's greeting.

Unconditional acceptance.

"He's the cyclist, isn't he?" Now Jessica, her twelve-year-old sister, was on the porch, wearing knee pads. "Does he know anything about bike chains? Mine came off and something's bent, so I can't get it back on."

"How did it do that?"

"When I fell off. I was trying to turn on the ramp—"

"Where is your helmet? I told you that you're not allowed to do trick riding unless you've got it on. Marcie—"

"She had it on last time I saw her. I can't watch her every minute." Marcie fired up.

"I told you when Mrs. Pitt had to cut back her hours, you could watch them in the afternoon and I'd pay you for that. You said you could handle it." Not for the first time, Cassandra wondered why she could defuse arguments efficiently in a board room, but at home one irritation could set off a firestorm. And this was an ongoing one between her and Marcie.

"It wasn't her fault, Cass—" Jess jumped into the fray.

"Ladies. Someone mentioned something about a bike chain?" Lucas stood to their left, a steadying hand on Nate's shoulder while the little boy, his expression uncertain, looked between them.

"He knows how to fix it," Marcie said before Cassandra could head her off.

"Marcie, he's wearing a suit. He's not here to—"

"Do you wear a helmet?" Jessica asked hotly. "I've seen pictures of people your age, when they were little, and they didn't wear helmets."

"Nope, we didn't. Not way back then," Lucas confirmed. "We had bigger things to think about. Like dinosaurs and the ice age."

Jessica narrowed her eyes, undeterred. "So you didn't need them."

"No, of course not," Lucas agreed. "Overprotective, overrated"— his head jerked, a tic, twice, before he continued without blinking an eye—"hogwash." Making a wall-eyed look, he feigned a stagger around Nate's bike. "Not a problem at all. Your sister's been kind enough to wipe the drool off my chin when I can't seem to control it. Brain damage, you know."

Jessica tried to look unimpressed, but Lucas was far too handsome and charming. In a matter of minutes, Cass saw him win the girls over. Any woman whose hormones had kicked in would be powerless against him, she knew.

"Will you fix my bike chain?" Jess asked.

"Sure," he said. "Just give me a minute to make a phone call, and

I'll be right there." He glanced at Cass, moved back toward the white limo.

As she watched him, she realized he made the perfect prince on the white horse. The way he moved toward the car, the sunlight glittering across his hair. Broad shoulders and muscled arms. Cass remembered the fairy tales, and couldn't help the twinge, despite her appalled response to it. She didn't need rescuing. She'd rescued them all on her own. She wasn't insolvent, not by a long shot. She had college tuition covered for Marcie. Her own 401k. A home.

So why was it he made her feel rescued with just a smile, a look of those concerned eyes? God, she needed to get rid of him.

When she turned around, her sisters burst into giggles, apparently having caught her staring after him like a lovestruck moonbat.

She definitely needed to get rid of him.

≈≈≈≈

Instead, he stayed for the next several hours, sending the limo away. He fixed Jess's bike in no time, with only one trip needed to their well-organized tool shed. Cass sat on the back steps nearby with Marcie and let her sisters and Nate take over conversation with him, knowing she was testing him, knowing she shouldn't be giving him that encouragement. But damn it and big surprise, he *was* good with them.

In contrast to his frank affability with the outgoing Jess and confident Marcie, as well as his more male interaction with Nate, he was quiet and patient with shy ten-year-old Talia, letting her approach at her own pace, become part of the group of girls without saying much. Next thing she knew, he was talking to her about the book she was carrying, coaxing her to tell him about it while he tuned up Jess's gears.

Then there was eight-year-old Cheryl, whom they called Cherry. She and Nate took right to him. Cass never brought men home, hadn't allowed herself a relationship where it even crossed her mind. Should she let the kids hope for anything? Just because she didn't allow herself hope? Damn Lucas for making her think about it like that.

When he came back at last to sit beside her, the two of them watched the kids bike around the backyard, and he asked her easy questions about them. As she responded, he leaned back, his arm braced behind her on the concrete stoop, making her want to rest against it, but she resisted, not sure if she wanted the kids to see that.

As if he'd read her mind, he nudged her arm. "Lean back." When she frowned, he tugged her hair. "You know my ride left, so you'll have to put up with me."

"You have a working thumb," she retorted sweetly. "I'm sure an amorous, lonely housewife will pick you up. You could become her afternoon fantasy."

"Sorry, already booked." The kids had reached the end of the yard and were exploring something they'd found by the fence. Before she could anticipate him, he'd captured the back of her neck and drawn her to him, holding her fast for a sweet, teasing kiss. Because the kids were distracted, it wasn't outrage that fueled her token attempt to push him away, which just resulted in her hands latching into the front of his grease-stained shirt as he deepened the kiss, made her stomach flutter and knees quiver.

When he raised his head, his eyes alone were enough to keep the fire leaping through her bloodstream. His hand was very appropriately on her waist, but the fingers hidden from view were curved over a buttock, stroking, making her crave him to go lower, palm her there.

"I'm going to be *your* fantasy tonight, Cassie. All afternoon. In a few minutes, some very accomplished childcare providers will be arriving to take your kids off for the evening. Matt, Savannah, and the guys are going to take them to the movies, followed by dinner at a playhouse and arcade, and then back to Matt's place for a slumber party."

Before she could get over her shock to protest, he continued, tightening on her waist. "While they're safely being entertained, suitable to their ages, I am going to take you to your bedroom and entertain you in a manner suitable to your age. I'm going to make love to you through the night, so when there are circles under your eyes tomorrow, it will be for a better reason than working on late-night paperwork. When Matt and the team bring the kids back here, I'm going to make you sleep in and fix your kids breakfast." His eyes held her in place. "I'll bring *you* breakfast in bed."

"I don't know," she said at last. She swallowed. "I'm feeling overwhelmed. I'm not sure that's good, Lucas."

Spearing his fingers into her hair, he pressed the heel of his palm to her jaw. "It *is* good. It wasn't a no."

"It wasn't a yes." When he grinned, she scowled. "Teach me to get involved with another negotiator. Glorified bean counter."

She shook her head, pushed away from the stoop, crossing her arms under her breasts, feeling the impending evening chill. Marcie had taken the kids around to the front, and she wondered now if her sister had picked up the tone and done it with calculated intent. Having the chess pieces rearranged before she could even get a handle on the game was something she didn't like, and she didn't want him to think she'd accept being treated that way. "You know, you can't call in a babysitter every time you think there's something you'd rather be doing. That's not the way this works. I haven't had time to think this through. And tomorrow is a school day."

"Hey." As he rose, she backed up, not wanting him to touch her again. "I just wanted the first time between us to be special. Not hurried. You deserve that. And Marcie told me tomorrow is a teacher's workday. I did check on that first." He closed the distance between them in a quick step, caught her shoulders. "Cass, look at me."

At the command, she raised her angry, uncertain gaze. "I am not your drunk dad," he said. "If I'm falling for you, I'm falling for the whole package. I had a blast with the kids earlier."

"They're not always a blast."

"Really? I find that hard to believe." He gave her that little shake. "Give me some credit."

"You've only known me a day. You can't commit your whole life to this—"

"No, of course I can't. Stop it." He held her fast. "But I can say I'd like a chance. You can't deny yourself love, the possibility that I could be part of this family, for fear that I can't."

"These kids can't be jerked around anymore. I won't allow it just because you—"

"If you go with the 'just because you want to fuck me' line, I *will* smack your ass," he said, and the steel in his gaze told her he meant it. "If that's all I wanted, I never would have come home with you. Cass, I have a sister. A divorced sister with two kids who had to live with me nearly two years when he cleaned her out of everything, the bastard. I understand the issue, and I love those kids like my own. I took over as the male role model in their life during those two years, and they still look to me that way."

"They're doomed," she said after a long moment, struggling with it.

"Don't I know it." His touch eased. "You and I have moved fast, way fast. I know that. But look at me. Look at my eyes, everything you know of me, that you know of people. Use that intuition Steve pays you so much for. If we don't work out, which I have a very good feeling is not going to be a problem, I will be as careful of the kids' feelings as I would hope to be of yours. You don't have to be so god-damned tough about everything."

She wrenched away, crunching through ankle-deep dry leaves in the yard. "Don't you get it, Lucas? It's not about that. Most women aren't tough. We're tired, we're lonely, we're afraid of failing to live up to what's expected of us. While we're looking for the one person who will accept us for ourselves and love us anyway, we're already too walled up to show him who that is. You can't let down your shields. No one can."

"You can with someone who loves you."

"Yeah, and those people come with big neon signs on them that say, 'You can trust me, I will love you through thick and thin, you can count on it.'" She backed away some more, wishing Marcie hadn't taken the kids out of earshot, wishing Lucas hadn't taken off her corset, because words were just bubbling out of her, no filter, no restraint. He was making her need to say them, standing before her, all the possibilities she wanted so much. "There are things I've said in my head I can never say to anyone. Sometimes I'm so tired I don't want to get up ever again. Sometimes I need sex so badly I've brushed against a corner of the kitchen island and made myself come by accident, and had to cover it as a fit of coughing with the kids." She laughed bitterly. "I got them on track, I pay the bills, I've earned my education and reputation, and somehow I feel like all I've done with my outstanding accomplishments is build myself a great big public cage. And when that becomes too much . . . Ah, Christ."

She turned away, but couldn't deny his comfort when he slid his arms around her waist, held her against him, speaking into her ear. "When that becomes too much, you go to a glade in the Berkshires and give yourself twenty minutes of sanity. Everyone feels that way sometimes. But from where I'm standing, you still have a pretty damn good life, you know? You're fucking amazing, everything you've done. You're just missing someone to share it with, sweetheart. Not just to help, but to share it. We tend to make situations that come with big emotions into something complex, but they're usually not. Life sucks sometimes, and you need someone who can stand with you. Everyone needs that."

Through a tear-streaked face, she looked up and found his gaze full of a miraculous tenderness. "I haven't cried in forever, and here it is, twice with you in one day. That can't be a good thing."

"On the contrary, I think it's a very positive sign. Hell, Cass." Turning her, he put his forehead against hers, molded his hands to her back, letting her feel the strength of his touch through his shirt. "I don't know what love is, any more than the next person. But I know when I look at you, every part of me is hoping like hell this is it. So risk it, okay? You've risked so much to get where you are, you're starting in a position of strength here." Lifting his head, he quirked a brow. "After all, I am a major catch. And I'm completely gone over you."

"And so modest." She sniffled.

"Well, first rule of negotiation, sweetheart. Start with the strongest points. Don't want to scare you off with my bug fetish or the bodies in my basement freezer."

"Bug fetish?"

"Typical woman. Her eyes go all big over the bugs, rather than my side career as a serial killer."

"How big? Are we talking spiders? Spiders are not bugs."

Laughing, he pulled her to his mouth and silenced her in a way that forced bugs out of her head.

She pulled back. "The kids."

"Gone." At her stunned look, he had the grace to look sheepish. "I'd already talked to Marcie. She took them in front when I knew the limo would be there."

"And you just assumed——"

"Yeah, I did." He looked down at her. "You know they'll be safe with us, right?"

"That's not the point. I handle my life. Their lives——"

"No question, no argument. But tonight is just for you. You won't give yourself that. I did. You and I both know you're using them as a shield."

When he closed his hands on her shoulders, bent his knees to force her to look into his face, she closed her eyes. "Lucas, I *can't*. I get sucked in. For so long, I wanted something like what you appear to be, so much . . ."

You're the Holy Grail floating over the yawning Abyss. With desperation, she thought it must be the Knights of the Boardroom reference making her think in King Arthur analogies. "Those kids can't afford a leap of faith. I'm what they have, and in order to be there for them, I can't risk any cracks. You're a potential earthquake."

"I think I'm flattered. But why am I an earthquake?" Somehow, while her eyes were closed, he'd backed her up against the stoop. As he posed the question in her ear, his arm circled her. Gently, so gently, with his other hand between them, he began to unbutton the shirt, tease her skin.

"Because I need you too much. Something like you. You'll leave. You all leave. Your cocks and minds get bored."

He paused. Cass realized she'd meant to say "want," but they both knew a slip of the tongue like that was rarely a mistake. She couldn't take it back, couldn't cover it.

"Stop thinking. Just for five minutes, shut it off. Look at me." His expression now was one that made something flutter in her lower belly. He nodded. "Very few men would know that the avenue to *your* heart is, in fact, through your body, Cass. Through your submission. So the irony of it is, by taking your body exactly where it needs to go, I'm going to convince you that my heart and soul are *never* going to be bored with you."

She caught at the shirt as he slipped the last button. There were no close neighbors, but that wasn't why she clutched it. He put his hands over hers, began to pry her fingers away.

"I can't." Her whisper was broken. "I can't say no to you, but I can't do this."

"You're not your parents, Cass. Either one of them. You're you. And you *can* do it." He coaxed one set of fingers to release, then the other. Holding her wrists in one hand, he spread the two sides of the shirt open, revealing the flat line of her stomach, the crescent shapes of her breasts. "Beautiful," he murmured. "Mine. Stand still."

Turning her, he took the coat off her shoulders and then the shirt, laid them on the stoop. The skirt came next, slowly sliding over her hips, followed by the panties and stockings, so she now stood naked before him while he was still fully clothed. When she shivered, he put the coat back over her bare shoulders.

"Should we go—"

"Not yet," he said. Then he sank down before her, hands holding her hips as he studied the column of her throat, the shape of her breasts, the line of her rib cage and abdomen. Her hips, the roundness of her buttocks, the vee of her sex, a soft pelt of hair, smooth and trim. He studied that the longest, and aside from the self-consciousness, the slight sense of embarrassment, it aroused her almost to the point of pain, the way he examined her. Her hands clutched his shoulders, then slid forward, seeking the line of his jaw. Catching her fingers, he sucked on them hard, strong, before pulling free, staring up at her. "Mine," he repeated. "Mine to protect. To cherish. To love. To grow old with, if we're blessed."

She shook her head. "Don't," she whispered. "Don't ruin it."

His eyes darkened and he bent his head, his arm curving around her to hold her in place with a hand on one hip as he brought her into him.

Cass sucked in a breath, clutched him harder as his mouth found her and he spread her stance a little wider. She had to rely on him to hold her steady, because her ground had become unstable. Oh, God. That mouth. Before, she'd been anchored to a chair. On her back, a table, a wall. Now the lightness of the friction as he manipulated her, let her body buck and convulse naturally, made the feeling even more maddening, a dance against his mouth. The wind moved the fall leaves, bringing her the smell of seasonal change, of grass mowed recently, of the lake.

"You're so wet for me, sweetheart," he muttered against her flesh. "Give yourself to me. Let yourself be swept away by a man's desire for you."

His tongue parted her, teased her, teeth scraping the clit as her breath rasped in her throat, her fingers digging in, the nails scraping his flesh, if he'd let her get to it.

"Feel you," she gasped. "I want to feel you."

"In due time. I want you mindless first."

He thought she could think now. Catching her fingers in his hair, she pulled hard as he kept up his artistry upon her slick lips, tasting her, penetrating her, sliding over every sensitive nerve, his tongue doing flexible things a snake would envy. She wanted him.

"Want to come, with you inside me. Now."

"Not this first time," he said, without mercy, and with a rake of his teeth he sent her free falling, both hands tearing at his shoulders, her bare body convulsing over him, nails digging into his T-shirt and the hard back muscle beneath as he held her hips fast, worked her against his mouth. His rough jaw rasped her thighs, his fucking of her with his mouth mixed with the wet sounds of pleasure as he lapped her, took her juices into him in a way that sent powerful aftershocks ripping through her. He held on to her throughout.

When she tried to straighten, her body felt weak. She wasn't sure if her legs would hold, but he'd already anticipated that, rising to lift her off her feet. He was still fully clothed, even down to his shoes.

"Tell me where your bedroom is, Cassandra."

Ten

It was a quiet, dim place, the sun almost gone for the day. Through the sheer panels at her windows, he saw the shapes of the trees in the yard, while in the room there was the outline of a high tester bed, piled with pillows. A dilapidated stuffed bear was there, probably left by one of the younger children, as well as a scattering of children's books on the floor. Clothes she'd perhaps discarded this morning rested on the back of the chair. He could see the domestic scene, her trying to get ready for work, giving them all some attention before she left. There was a scattering of sticky notes on the desk and the computer screen, work waiting for her after everyone had gone to bed. A TV, some books piled up next to it. The clutter of a busy woman.

His heart too full to speak immediately, he laid her down on the mattress, that beautiful bare body that had him so primed for her it was difficult to walk.

But then, as she watched him, he collected the children's books, the work papers. He put the papers on the desk, the toys outside in the hall, setting the bear on top before shutting the door.

"This is your room, Cass," he said, turning to her. "Just the woman tonight. Do you have any wine?"

She nodded to a minifridge in the corner, the stand of glasses up on a shelf. "Like an evening glass of wine, do you?" he observed.

"Sometimes."

"Me, too." He went to it. As she began to shift, he half turned. "No. Stay there."

"I feel uncomfortable, naked like this when you're not."

"This is the way I want you. Would it be easier if I tied your arms and legs, fed you the wine from my own lips? Blindfolded you, so all your senses are focused only on your body? What I do to it?"

She pressed her lips together. "I want to see you," she whispered. "I want to touch you."

Moving to her player, he turned on music. A smile curved his lips as Foreigner's "Waiting for a Girl Like You" came on. "I'll tie you another time, then," he responded. "But right now, you'll lie back on your pillows, high enough that your back is arched, your breasts tilted up. I want your legs spread so that I can see how wet your lips are. If I've a mind to feast on them again, they'll be ready for me."

He waited, his gray eyes holding hers in the soft light, the long slope of his jawline made dark and sensuous in the shadows. He hadn't said "pretend" this time. Hadn't given her that out. From the look on his face, she knew he'd meant what he said. *No more games.* No more denying what she desired, the dark way she desired it. She found herself sliding up the pillows and leaning back so she was in the position he'd ordered, her breasts in such wanton display she almost blushed. For all her experience in business, her knowledge of what went on in the bedroom, her couplings had been perfunctory, an exercise in mutual needs being satisfied. She'd never had a forceful or demanding lover, let alone a Dominant who could make her want to please him like this, to raise the potential threshold for herself. Seeing the look in Lucas's eyes, just a little dangerous, telling her he might not brook a refusal, brought a delicious thrill. It also made her a little embarrassed to open her legs, but when she did it, the fierce desire leaping in his eyes was reward for her bravery.

"You're dripping for me again. I'll have to come take care of that."

"Please," she whispered.

He set aside the wine, and glory be, he carelessly pulled off the T-shirt. He wore the silver medallion he'd had on that day at the glade, so as he put one knee on the bed and leaned over her, she reached up. He stilled, letting her fingers close around it.

"It has an inscription." She studied the engraving, a cross, the burst of sunlight behind it. " 'The right hand of God.' "

"Savannah gave each of us a wedding gift, a groomsman gift, if you will."

A smile touched her lips. "I wouldn't have expected her to have a wicked sense of humor."

"Oh, yeah. She's just reserved at first." His voice gentled. "She never really got to love anyone, until Matt. And us."

Cass raised her gaze to his face. "So you all love her."

"Entirely. She's family. And no"—his fingers threaded through her blond hair, bringing it forward across her mouth, a whimsical gesture—"you're not a surrogate for my best friend's wife. I just happen to have a thing for good-looking blondes. But I'm partial to the ones who ride Harleys and have rapier-sharp business sense. Savannah doesn't have a motorcycle."

"But you wear this, under your clothes."

Nodding, he closed his hand over hers on it, where her thumb was stroking the metal, and his flesh beneath it. "She had it blessed. She worries about me, biking in traffic. It makes her feel better, knowing I have it on, though I always tell her she's going to have to fire the priest if I do get run down. She says that'll just prove God knew I was too much of an idiot to waste the effort. I like wearing it. It reminds me of my connection to them. They're as much my family as my blood relations."

Taking her hand then, he pressed his lips to her knuckles and then eased down on her, still wearing the slacks. However, she wasn't ready to complain, as for the first time the bliss of his bare chest came against hers, the coolness of that metal. Reaching up, she gripped his neck, pressed her lips there, tasted the metal chain and heat of him as she'd wanted to do that first time. Her arms slid behind his back, holding him as she licked and kissed his muscled skin, her hands pressing into the hard lines at his waist, the rise of his buttocks, his slacks bunched under the grip of her fingertips. She was so hungry for him. The need just surged up in her, as if by lying between her legs, against the core of her, his heart to her heart, he'd cracked something open so wide inside her that only tearing into him would help alleviate it.

The music selection had changed to "How to Save a Life," by The Fray, a song too poignant, too close to the way her heart felt.

As he caught her hands, lifted away from her, and used that hold to keep her to the pillows, she tried to follow him. "Lucas, I need you now. Inside me. Please. I feel like I'm breaking. I want you to do everything you said, but for this second, please . . ."

"Okay," he said softly. He rose from the bed, finally removed his slacks and the snug dark cotton shorts beneath them.

She'd seen him with the bike shorts, which had made him all but naked, but now, to see the slim line of hips, the erect cock, rising high and hard, moisture collected at the tip, the lines of his thighs, he was—

"Beautiful," she said softly, and meant it.

His mouth tightened with emotion and he came back to her, taking her hands. "That's you, Cassandra. The most beautiful thing I've ever seen. Do I need to wear anything?"

"I want to say no, but . . ." She shook her head. "No one's been in my bed in a long time, or been this close. Actually, no one's ever been this close . . . emotionally. I'm sorry."

Picking up his slacks, he took care of it and came back to her, settling between her legs, looking down at her, his lips a sensuous curve. "You don't have to say you're sorry for not being with other men. I don't want anything between us either, but we can come up with something that makes that possible another day." His gaze sparked. "In the meantime, this is a prototype from one of our acquisitions, supposed to be the thinnest yet. The strongest and safest ever. You can do a product evaluation for us." When his broad head nudged her, she let out a shaky breath, aching for him, wanting him, but paralyzed by the weight of her own need.

"Okay," she agreed, but when Lucas saw a glistening tear at the corner of her eye, the gentle humor intended to ease her tension fled. Bending, he pressed his lips to it and laid his weight back upon her body. So many willing curves and fine limbs, the silk of her hair. His cock leaped eagerly, but he knew the advantage of anticipating. Plus, he wanted more than anything to eradicate the tears, even willing to set aside his own lust forever if he could keep just one from marring her perfect cheek.

Yeah, he was a goner. No doubt about it. "What's the matter, sweetheart?"

"I want you so much, but I'm afraid." Cass looked away. "People change, Lucas. You think you'll always have them, always love them, and then they change. Every time you open your heart, it happens. And this time, I'm not risking just *my* heart."

Hadn't she learned a long time ago that a family member could turn into someone who wouldn't love her? Or become the type of person *she* couldn't love anymore?

"You never want to lose control. You never want to have the un-expected happen to you. Cass." He tightened his grip until he was sure he had her attention. "I swear to you, on everything that I am, everything that I value, I will not fail you. I'm here, feel me." He pressed against her, effectively riveting her. "I'm not going to stop there. I want to be all the way in you. In your heart and soul, so you never doubt me."

"I want you so much I feel like I'm going to break. And I can't believe I'm saying these things to you."

"I know." As she buried her face in his chest, gripping him, obviously not wanting him to see her expression, Lucas realized the best negotiators knew when it was past time for talk.

Pressing his lips to the top of her head, he kept his arms wrapped around her back and thrust home, deep. The tightness of her channel underscored the truth she'd told him. It had been a while, and he was fiercely glad for it. She stretched for him, her hips tilting up, her mouth open in a cry against his chest, her teeth scraping his flesh as he plunged, hard. Her legs wrapped around his back, gorgeous flexible thing that she was, and he rammed into her again, going with a more aggressive attack because he knew that's what she needed. Every defense she'd thrown up, the fortress she'd built, she needed them shattered, because she had to be absolutely sure she could trust him, not only to reach her, but to stand with her. Protect her, love her. She needed a guarantee, even though he knew she was smart enough to realize there wasn't one. She was just enough of a woman to always hope there might be one. He could almost feel her desperation in this dark room.

It was time to drive her mind out of the equation, because sometimes the heart needed to make the decision. Lifting his upper body, he drew her away from him so she was lying back on the pillows again, those delectable breasts just there for the tasting. He went to work on them, pleased to erase the unique lingering mint smell of Peter's mouth with his own, taking a nipple into his mouth, sucking as she contracted on him, her fingers raking his back. One hand found his buttocks, exploring, pleasing herself with the feel of him. As he lashed the nipple, kneading the breast with his hand to roll the peak in his mouth, her fingers dug in. He surged into her harder, thrusting deep. He wanted her sore, sated. Her body was trembling, flushed, and he worked his tongue in between her breasts, holding the generous curves together so he was emulating the penetration of his cock while she writhed against him. He kept his hips moving, the slow pump, deep in, slow drag out, feeling her getting wetter and wetter.

"Lucas. Come with me. I need to know you'll . . . go with me."

He could have exploded without a thought. He nodded.

Cass kept her gaze on his face, the gray eyes, the implacable mouth, the concentration and fire. She couldn't think, her body spasming already, but then she gave a cry of protest as he slid out of her, went down her body and suckled himself on her cunt, lifting her hips and legs so she was yanked half off the bed, clutching the headboard as he plundered her, clever enough not to touch her clit and send her right over. He'd slowed, taking his time now, and she was mewling, any type of self-control or dignity abandoned as she pleaded for what she wanted.

What was he doing? Why wouldn't he just let her go? As he turned his movements into slow licks that took her just to the edge of orgasm, held her there, she whimpered helplessly. He balanced her there with a precision that suggested he knew things about her body that she didn't. The pleading was lost as she accepted it and knew she was all his. Her hands gripping the headboard as if truly bound there said it clearly. Whatever he wanted to do to her, wherever he wanted to take her. Somewhere in the haze of her mind, she knew that was the lesson. Give it all to him, trust him, no control of her own.

He slid down the bed, his hands caressing her legs, and came back up with the belt from his slacks. As if reading her mind, her desires, he bound her wrists, then looped and knotted the belt to the rail. "You'll get very familiar with my belt," he observed in a husky whisper, working his way back down her throat. She turned her face to his temple, pressed frantic kisses there, tried to bite at his flesh. "It will hold you like this. Or I'll use it to slap your pretty butt when you don't trust me. Make you have trouble sitting down in your meetings." He stopped over a nipple, gave it a hard nip as she cried out, another wordless plea. "You'll also bite down on it when I find you for lunch, take you somewhere semiprivate and fuck you up against the wall."

"Lucas, don't do this."

"Don't do what? Back you down, until you know you belong to me, every inch, inside and out? Know that you can trust me with anything, because I consider you mine to protect, look out for? Love? You, and everything that belongs to you."

"Antiquated . . ." She muddled up the word, her tongue not working. "Ideas of male chivalry . . . chauvinism. Don't need you to take care of me."

"Everyone needs someone to take care of them. Now, hush. Believe in me." Lifting his head, he gave her a long look, studied her hungry face, his own taut with desire. "Search your heart, Cass. Is there even one thing in your heart that can help you make that leap? Just one?"

The taste, heavy weight, and steel of him were sending her into bliss as he braced himself over her, his muscles tightening up and down his upper body in delicious display.

With the belt and his words—hell, the past thirty-six hours—he'd pushed her past something in herself, the wall she'd built, right into something that felt more natural and true, a new garden that might just be hers to explore. She sought something there to answer his question. Because he had pushed her that far, she wasn't surprised to find what he demanded just waiting for her recall.

It was a news clipping she'd found during her research. Matt's team had been an active part of the rescue and relief efforts during Katrina. The picture showed Lucas sitting on the tailgate of a supply truck. He'd been filthy dirty, with a group of children sitting with him. Exhausted, he'd been leaning against the side of the trailer, fast asleep. The children, a couple of them, played in the mud near him, but two or three were piled on him, sleeping as well.

She knew children. They might take toys or candy from a kind stranger, come back to him for more of the same, but in the same phenomenon seen around police stations and Marines, children followed and stayed close to those who made them feel safe.

No matter what happened between them, Lucas would take care with her children. And that would give her the sense of surety she needed to be his. To open her heart to falling in love with him, though she was likely most of the way there. He was right. It really didn't have anything to do with time. The deal closed early. Time just allowed all the details to be worked out.

"Lucas, please. I want you."

God, he was everything she wanted. She wasn't looking at his body anymore, but at those serious gray eyes. It made her mouth dry with need in proportionate response to the soaking wetness between her legs. As he waited, she managed the next step. "I need you. I accept you."

The ability to tease him with her opening, the arch of her body for his hard cock, made her tremble. He seated himself in her opening, held her down when she tried to pull him in.

"One more, Cass. You owe me one more before I take you. Look me in the eyes and say it, so we both know there's no going back."

She shut her eyes, wanting to believe so much, wanting not to be afraid, knowing there was no way to do this without being afraid.

"You promised breakfast, right?"

"Chocolate chip pancakes, all the way around. Cassandra, say it."

She opened her eyes, stared up at him. "I'm yours."

Something flickered in his gaze and he slowly, slowly pushed in, going deep into her slickness again.

"I'm yours, too," he said softly. "Come for me, Cass."

"You, too," she breathed, just before her body began to buck, from no more than an artful flex of his hips, a tiny rub against her, inside and out. The feel of him, pushing in where nothing had been for a long time, was like a small, rippling, searing orgasm all its own. It built like a wave as he continued the movements, building higher as she clawed at the belt binding her wrists, knowing her voice was going to be hoarse from screaming, because she was already crying out, and she wasn't even there yet.

Then he started really moving, and fire became conflagration, sweeping through her, taking her up higher, higher as he thrust home, all brutal strength now, taking her in every sense of the word. She exploded, years of catharsis contained in one blinding emotional and physical outpouring that swept her away so she could only hold him with her legs and hope he held on to her. She screamed, pleaded with him, and when he released, she wished she could feel the hot stream of him filling her. But the feel of that cock, rippling with release against the walls of her channel, his harsh grunts, the brutal clutch of his fingers on her hips that would leave treasured bruises, would be enough for this moment. Until the next one.

Plaster had to have been knocked out of the wall behind the headboard, but she'd figure out some way to explain that to Marcie. Maybe to Jessica. Marcie wouldn't be duped.

When she cracked open an eye at long last, the full weight of his body was on hers, his temple against hers as well. Being tied like this . . . Oh God, it still felt arousing, even with her body shuddering in aftermath. Who knew? He reached up, loosened the tie of the belt to the headboard, but left her wrists bound to bring them over his head, her fingers curved against the back of his neck. When he shifted and turned her to hold her in his arms, she smiled. "You're not letting me go?"

"Nope." He had his eyes closed, one hand on her ass in a possessive hold, the other around her back, his hand playing with her hair, making her shiver.

"Why?"

"Because as soon as I get past this postcoital coma I'm in, I'm going to start all over again. I'm going to do this to you over and over, so when the kids come back in the morning, you won't have any doubts about the fact I'm not going anywhere."

"I don't have any doubts now."

He opened his eyes, tilted his face down, filled with surprise. "You convinced me," she admitted. "You did what a great negotiator is supposed to do. I know the world's not a certain place, Lucas, but I'm going to put my faith in you. Whatever happens between us, I'll know it was worth the leap. So, will you untie me now?"

His face was a study of emotions that touched her heart. Then a light smile lifted his mouth. "I promised you a glass of wine." His gaze traveled down her body. "I never said where I was going to pour it, or the type of vessel I was going to drink from. And I find I have quite a thirst."

"You can't possibly."

"No. Men are limited in that way. But women aren't." His eyes flashing with promise, he rose, sliding her hands from around his neck to go retrieve the bottle of wine, as well as a towel from her bathroom.

As he came back, she was still halfheartedly protesting, though the shiver in her limbs and his intent gaze riveting on her bound body told her it would do little good.

"Would you deny me, Cassandra?" He gave her the look that made her pulse leap and told her she was his, body, heart, and soul. No, she wouldn't deny him. Though next time that male propensity for postcoital coma kicked in, she was going to pounce on him, bind *his* hands with his belt, and go to work on every inch of his body with her mouth the way she craved to do.

"Can you do crepes? Talia loves crepes."

He nodded. "I can do things you can't even imagine. Will you deny me, Cass?"

She swallowed, all desire to tease fleeing before that expression. "No."

"Good." He put the towel down, parting her legs with a gentle but inexorable hand upon one. "Because I intend to give you everything."

He did eventually release her hands. And as he held himself on his arms over her, in the small hours of the night, prepared to make love to her the third or fourth time—or maybe it was the fifth—she allowed herself the pleasure of finally fingering the soft hair across his forehead. Was there such a thing as a fantasy that turned into something better in reality? Could she let herself believe what had started over a month ago could be something real that lasted? Could Sleeping Beauty really be roused from her sleep by one kiss, and want to spend her life with the prince? And him with her?

She'd never given herself the luxury of hope in such a thing, with its unacceptable and often disappointing truth. But perhaps Sleeping Beauty had seen in her prince's eyes what she saw in Lucas's now as he slowly entered her once again, keeping his gaze locked on hers as her lips parted, tender body arching to accept him again. Something that wasn't disappointing, something she knew was worth working for, getting up off the princess's dais and following him into a whole new world of possibilities.

When Lucas bent, bringing his mouth to hers in a kiss that melted her, that she suspected always would, she met it. Lifting her head, putting her hands on either side of his neck, she dug into the silky short hair at his nape, finding the rough line of his jaw under her thumbs, feeling his hard body stretched all along her softer one. She gave way before truth again and gloried in it. *His.*

"I'm going to lose that bet," he muttered against her lips.

"What bet?"

He shook his head, taking her head back to the pillow, his forehead resting on it. "Tighten on me, sweetheart. The bet doesn't matter. You're what matters. Tell me again you're mine."

She smiled and kissed him, but didn't answer. Taking Savannah's words to heart, especially in their current position, she decided she wanted him to work for it. All night, and then some.

And then she'd ask for those bracelets back.

Joey W. Hill is a bestselling Ellora's Cave and Heat author. She lives in Southport, North Carolina, near Wilmington and Myrtle Beach. Visit her website at www.storywitch.com.

Don't miss her exciting new novel, *A Witch's Beauty*, coming in January 2009 from Berkley Sensation. Turn to the back of the book for a sneak preview.

Rubies and Black Velvet

DENISE ROSSETTI

One

HOLDERCROFT ON THE CRESSY PLAINS,
PALIMPSEST

When the thunder came again and again, rolling around the tall heads of the mountains, the good folk of Holdercroft village shuddered. "They'm at it again," they said, shaking their heads. But the tavern on the plain was warm and snug, the doors and windows shuttered against the fierce driving rain.

" 'Tis the dragon djinn," grunted old Griddle, wiping his mouth with the back of his hand.

"And the sorceress," whispered his wife. She made the two-handed sign of the Sibling Moons. "Brother and Sister preserve us."

"Seen 'er once." Griddle held out his tankard for a refill. "Ridin' a storm cloud, the night the big tree came down, ye remember?"

"Ye were drunk," scoffed his wife.

"Naked as a bebbe she were. All pale and long." Griddle's rheumy eyes took on a faraway look. "Hair down to 'er waist, flyin' like whips o' black silk. And when she looked at me, 'twas like starin' hell in the eye. So dark, so deep . . ." He buried his long nose in his ale.

"Ye stupid old sot." Griddle's wife poked his shoulder with a bony finger. "Why would a sorceress look at ye?"

Griddle subsided, grumbling into his ale. "She did," he muttered, almost too low to hear. "Like she wanted to chew me up and spit me out. Like she hated me for livin'." Abruptly, he banged his empty jug down on the bar. "Gimme another!"

At evening's end, his wife had to call for the blacksmith's boys to carry him home through the rain on a plank.

Out in the barn behind the Mackie place, John knelt at Meg's feet, grumbling as she toweled his hair. "Give over, Meggie. You're not my bloody mother."

But Meg only laughed, that deep delicious chuckle that never failed to make something inside him flutter. She pulled his head down between her generous breasts and rubbed harder. Giving up, John pushed his nose deep into the warm, fragrant depths of her cleavage and inhaled with tremendous satisfaction.

Meg. His Steady Meggie.

Even at nineteen, he had no doubts. The gods had made Margaret May Mackie just for him. His center, his refuge, when the emotional tempests at home got too much. They wore a man down, his family. Between Ma and Da and his ten brawling siblings, there were times John couldn't think straight unless he held Meggie's hand in his.

He stroked a broad, callused palm over the luscious curve of her rump. The only girl in the Cressy Plains who could match him. Five foot eleven inches in her sturdy bare feet, Meg's cushiony body fitted perfectly against his huge frame, her long legs and smoothly muscled thighs a comfortable cradle for his eager weight.

John fumbled a hand down to rearrange his aching cock. He wasn't embarrassed. With Meg, everything was natural, easy. She knew him, better than he did himself, he thought sometimes. He hadn't got inside her yet, though it was all he'd been able to think about through the long, golden summer, the pink musky flesh between her pale thighs. They'd done just about everything else, though. Grinning, he traced the crescent of freckles on the inner curve of one breast with his tongue. Then he blew on the damp, creamy flesh.

Meg yelped and tweaked his ear.

One day . . . He leaned forward to rub his cheek against the softness of her belly through the fabric of her sensible nightgown. One day, Steady Meggie would swell with his child. They'd make their own family, one without fists and fury and slamming doors. If they were fortunate, her frail widowed father would live long enough to spoil his grandchildren. And before he passed to the gods, he'd see the land he'd loved well tended.

And John would be Meggie's too. For the rest of their lives.

It gave him such pleasure to think of it. His life in her steady, capable hands.

He glanced up, watching her sweet round face as she smoothed the rebellious spikes of his damp hair. He'd slipped out the window of the room he shared with Nathan, Topher, Danerel, and Zem and ridden through the storm to see her. His brothers wouldn't tell. Not that he cared, not when he could have this.

As Meg's hair streamed over her shoulders in a cloud of reddish gold, he had the fancy she glowed in the lamplight, as if her flesh was illuminated from within. John knew he wasn't much of a one for stories or clever words, but it crossed his mind that the freckles scattered across her nose looked like flecks of gold floating in a cream jug. His cheeks heated. He was a farmer, not a fucking poet.

"What's wrong?" asked Meg. "You're frowning."

"Nothing." John smoothed his palms up the back of her thighs, under the nightgown. "Ah, Meggie, you're beautiful." He filled his hands with the soft, resilient flesh of her bare bottom.

She smiled, showing an endearingly crooked tooth at the front. "No, I'm not, but I like that you think so." Her blue-gray eyes very bright, she leaned over him, fingertips caressing the back of his neck. "John, I don't want to wait. I brought a blanket."

John's cock reared like an unruly colt, even as his heart tried to climb out his throat. "Sweetheart, are you sure?" He couldn't continue.

"Oh yes," said Meg placidly, though her cheeks flushed with shy color. "I've never been more sure of anything in my life."

Like the healthy young animals they were, they'd spent the summer in heady, sensual exploration, all with increasing daring and delight. John had never imagined a woman would whimper when he kissed the inside of her elbow, or nibbled the soft flesh behind her ear, but Meggie did. On the other hand, he hadn't been surprised that she gasped when he slid a finger into her wet heat or that her mouth opened on a strangled scream when he bent his head, parted her pink folds, and licked cautiously up and down her slit. The smell of her, the strange earthy-salty taste, had sped straight to the most primitive part of his brain. Then it sizzled down his spine in a blinding rush to that other most primitive part—and he'd spurted ferociously, unable even to find the breath to swear, the feeling was so intense.

That had made him flush and look away, but it hadn't turned out too badly in the end, because after a bit of coaxing, Meggie had let him watch as she brought herself off, his fascinated gaze on her busy fingers, memorizing every motion. And he adored the high, helpless noises she made as she reached her peak. When her back had bowed up in a splendid, fierce arch, she'd gasped his name over and over, as if it was an invocation. The rush of emotion had nearly choked him.

Meg stepped away to spread the blanket over the heap of clean straw in an empty stall, and it occurred to John he'd never seen her waste a motion or appear less than graceful. Brother's balls, she was a miracle. *His* miracle.

Godsdammit, what if he hurt her? Rising, he glanced down his rangy body. Flat belly, long, brawny thighs, huge feet in heavy boots. As for his cock . . . Gods!

Tall as she was for a woman, he was so much bigger. Big-boned, his chest and shoulders dense with the muscle of hard labor, day after day. His mother complained he was still growing, but she'd find a smile for him as she heaped a second serving of dumplings on his plate.

John unlaced his trews and sighed with relief as his organ slapped straight up against his belly. He didn't think it was possible for his balls to get tighter, but the motion pulled his scrotum up hard into his body and his cock rippled as if Meg had brushed her lips against the head.

"What if—?" he said. "If I . . . if you . . . you know. Not that I'd mind, but it's too soon."

She sank gracefully to her knees on the blanket. "Stop worrying.

I've been drinking mothermeknot tea every morning since I turned thirteen. Everyone does. It's good for the female parts and no babies." Her smile turned luminous. "Not until we're ready."

John gripped his cock and squeezed, brutally hard. He'd never felt so thick, so turgid. He'd been brought up on a farm, so he knew he'd fit eventually, but oh gods, she was untried. *Tight.* His head spun and the next words came out in a croak. "I'll hurt you."

Meg's gaze dropped, the sensation so tangible it was as if she'd reached out and stroked him from root to crown. When she wet her lips with the point of a pink tongue, he choked back a groan. "Come here," she said, rising. Then she grasped the nightgown at the hem and ripped it off over her head.

He would never see anything more lovely. Not in all the days of his life.

Outside, the wind doubled in force, howling, and the barn rocked under the lash of the rain. But inside it was warm, scented with the thick, musty smell of animals, the milkbeasts shifting in the stalls, John's horse blowing its content, hooves like dinner plates scuffling in the straw.

Some strange presentiment lifted the hair on the back of his neck, so that instead of lunging forward and throwing her down to ram himself deep, John could only stand like a block, gripping a sturdy wooden post as if he would crush it to kindling. He stared, fixing her image in his mind, all plump, smooth curves, painted in cream and gold. Her lips were parted, shining a soft berry pink, the tips of her full, heavy breasts already furled and dusky. Waiting for him, for his big rough hands and impatient mouth.

"We both know what to expect." Meg's whisper hung in the dusty, lamp-lit air of the barn. Her smile went a little awry. "I'm a virgin. So are you. But it will only hurt this one time. After that . . ." She hauled in a breath, her breasts lifting. The soft curves of her belly went taut.

John lurched forward a step, fumbling with the laces of his shirt. "Ah, love."

Meg brushed his shaking hands aside and did it herself, pushing the garment off his shoulders. "I trust you," she said, while he drowned in her eyes, clear and soft as a summer's dusk. "With my life, now and forever."

Suddenly, she grinned, impish with happiness. "But I'm not doing it with a man who's still got his boots on."

The tension broke. John chuckled and everything was easy again. Hopping from foot to foot, he pulled his boots off, while Meg nipped at his chest, humming deep in her throat. When he kicked his trews away, she lay back on the blanket, drawing him down with her, her thighs falling open beneath him like the promise of paradise. One knee rose high over his hip and the sensitive head of his cock slid thrillingly across a slick warm surface.

Meg's lids fluttered down, her neck arching in a beautiful curve, and a surge of greed took John by the balls and shoved him forward, notching his throbbing tip at the small sucking entrance to her body. Bending his head, he ravaged her throat with open-mouthed kisses while her luscious heat tugged at him and their blood beat together. "Love you, Meggie," he muttered, incoherent with need. "So much, so much."

Meg caught his face between her palms and held him steady so she could gaze deep into his eyes. Her fingers felt rough, raspy against his stubble. There wasn't anything around the farm she couldn't do as well as her father's men, had been doing for years. "I'm yours," she said. "Always." She kissed him tenderly.

John clenched his teeth, caught somewhere between tears and driving lust, and grossly uncomfortable. His balls were going to explode. He wasn't going to last. He'd disappoint her, hurt her.

It was the hardest thing he'd done in his life, but he backed off enough to fumble a hand between them, furrowing the tips of his fingers through her curls, feathering over her folds. The lighter his touch, the more likely she was to climax. John prided himself on being a quick learner. Shaking with the effort of restraint, he used two fingers to bracket the tiny prow of flesh at the apex of her sex. Then he bent his head to devour a nipple like a crinkled velvety bud, pulling it up against his hard palate, knowing from their summer's experience that the combination would send her tumbling over the edge in a few minutes. She came for him so easily, his darling Meggie.

But not this time. *"John."* Strong feminine fingers gripped his hair and pulled his head up. Meg glared into his face, panting, her face suffused with color. "I want you. Make me yours. *Fuck me."* She tilted her hips and clasped her long legs over his buttocks, her heels pressing into the small of his back.

John made a garbled sound that might have passed for assent. The dimly lit barn swung around him, then steadied. He set his jaw. He could do this right, he *would* do it. For his Meggie.

He pulled back, grasping Meg's thighs and splaying her wide, all pink and puffy and ruffled. "Watch us, Meggie," he said hoarsely. "Watch me go in."

Her breasts bobbling with her rapid breath, Meg came up on her elbows.

Gritting his teeth, John guided his cock to the space where he fit, a key for a lock, the gods' gift to humanity. Gently, he pushed, butting against her virgin barrier, his heart thundering as he strove for control.

"Oh," he said. "Oh, Meggie. You feel so damn good."

"Don't stop."

He shifted, rubbing a little up and down again, the smooth slipperiness making his head reel. Utterly delicious.

"Do it." Meg slid a hand down, wrapped her fingers firmly around his girth and lodged him where he longed to go. "There."

Shaking like a tree in a gale, John fought for breath.

"Meggie . . ."

The luster of her smile blinded him. Before he could recover, she'd planted her feet on the floor and shoved upward with her strong hips. Her thin shriek traveled past his ear, but he barely heard it, preoccupied with the intensely luscious sensations assaulting the sensitive skin of his cock from base to tip. He'd had no idea she would be so *hot* inside, or so strong. His balls cramped, pressed right up against her in a glorious ache.

"Won't last," he groaned. "Got to, to . . ." Helplessly, he began to thrust. "You . . . all right?"

Meg blinked, her eyes wide with wonder. "Stings . . . a bit." When he changed the angle to slide deeper, her fingers clawed at his shoulders and she choked. "Sweet Sister, do that again."

So he did. Again and again. Until Meg was making those formless noises of pleasure, her cheeks flying scarlet flags of color.

The seed boiled at the broad root of his cock, a flood he could no longer gainsay. "Going to . . . sorry, love, sorry . . ."

Meg wrapped her arms and legs around him and clung, her face buried against his chest, her breath hot and moist against his nipple. John hunched over her and his buttocks flexed hard. Gone, he was gone, lost in the long ecstatic rush from balls to cock, pouring endlessly inside her, his world made of heat and light and his Steady Meggie.

When his vision cleared and he could catch his breath, he was appalled to see her eyes swimming with tears, though she smiled bravely enough. As gently as he could, he withdrew and reached for the cloth she'd set aside. So practical.

He dabbed at the blood on her thighs and then wiped himself down, trying to think of what to say. Meg lay and let him do it, absently stroking his arm. It was no use asking if he'd hurt her. He knew he had. In the end, he said the thing that was in his heart and prayed it would be enough. "Thank you."

Tossing the cloth aside, he cupped her cheek in one big palm. "You gave me a beautiful gift, Meggie. I love you. I'm sorry I made you cry."

"Fool." Meg struck his biceps with her clenched fist, but lightly. "I'm happy." Her lips trembled as she smiled and she scrubbed at the tears like a child. "It was wonderful, feeling you inside me, so close . . . I've never been so happy, truly."

"Really? But . . ." John frowned. "It hurt, didn't it?"

"Only a little."

"But you didn't—? Did you?"

"Not quite," she said tranquilly. Then she grinned. "Make it up to me next time." Tugging him down beside her, she burrowed into his shoulder. "Hold me," she whispered.

Gratefully, John relaxed onto the blanket, feeling a little dizzy. He'd never felt so *much*, as if his soul wasn't big enough to take it all—a soaring joy, a sense of completion, and underlying all that, a sense of his own mortality, of the fragility of life. He wanted to laugh aloud and he needed to cry. Turning his head, he buried his nose in Meg's hair, holding on to her so tightly that she wriggled in protest.

She reached up to stroke his jaw. "You can stay 'til dawn, can't you?"

When he nodded, she said, "Go to sleep, love."

"Meggie," he whispered. "If you're mine, I'm yours. You won't forget it, will you?"

But Meg said nothing, lying limp and warm and heavy all along his side. She was fast asleep.

Two

"What do you think they're doing down there?" The sorceress stared broodingly across the gulf of night-dark space at the tiny twinkling lights far below. Her dwelling was older than time, built into the shoulder of the peak, carved of living stone. The chilly wind lifted the tendrils of black hair that brushed her snow-white hips, but even naked as she was, she didn't feel the cold.

Huge ebony arms snaked around her waist from behind, the hint of scales under the skin abrading her flesh. "Insects," rumbled the dragon djinn. "Who cares?"

The sorceress smiled without humor, the merest curve of thin red lips. She pressed back against her dragon lover, enjoying the monstrous size of him, towering over her by more than a foot. His massive pointed phallus burned so hot against her cool buttocks, the sensation was just this side of pain. She didn't need to turn to know his reptilian eyes would be flaming with passion, ruby-red.

But in the end, she did turn, because she couldn't help herself. By Shaitan, she hated this strange compulsion, her inability to be done with him, to discard him as she'd done with centuries of lovers. Fifty seasons they'd played together and fifty times she'd tried to extricate herself and failed.

In their hellish dance of lust and blood and pain, she could never be sure who'd triumph in the struggle for dominance. She knew only that she was addicted to the savage beauty of the djinn's body, swaying under the lash, fascinated by his stubborn draconic endurance. Sometimes he was so fierce, she feared for her very life, and her slow ancient blood would run hot and heavy. Then it would be her turn to plead for mercy, cracked and broken and exalted. The razor's edge of peril intoxicated her.

And oh, she loved his magnificent body in either form, man or dragon, black as midnight in the pits of hell. But in general, she preferred something in between, as he was now. The best of both worlds.

Stepping back, the sorceress wrapped long slim fingers around his jutting phallus, though she had no hope of closing her fist. The dragon djinn rumbled his pleasure, his forked tongue flickering over a brutal mouth. His organ writhed in her palm, undulating like a cat, the slitted tip curling back to dab a wet kiss on the back of her hand. A mortal would discover his bodily fluids burned like acid; the sorceress felt only a tingle pleasantly reminiscent of pain.

Her lips drew back from her teeth and she squeezed hard. "Even after all this time," she murmured in her voice of frozen silver, "I am amazed by this cock." When she dug into his flesh with the tip of a pointed nail, the djinn hissed, leathery wings arching behind him. With dainty precision, the sorceress lifted her finger, black with dragon's blood, to her lips. She sucked, purring with pleasure, not taking her gaze from his for an instant.

"You, my love," growled the djinn, "are an evil bitch."

The sorceress dropped a mocking curtsey. "Thank you."

"I have something for you."

Her smile broadened. "I already have it." She used both hands in a vicious twist and the djinn's phallus bucked.

He froze, his vertical pupils narrow with pleasure-pain. "Release me," he commanded, and to her own annoyance, the sorceress did.

"Come." Taking her slender hand in his huge paw, he led her from the dizzying height of the mountain ledge to the bedchamber behind the tall carved doors.

For the hundred thousandth time, she thought how difficult he was to read, how dangerous, how delightfully unpredictable. Her heart began to knock against her ribs, though she breathed hard through her nose in a fruitless effort to control it. Not for Shaitan Himself would she allow the djinn to see her vulnerability. He'd kill her if she did.

My love, he'd said. The first and only time in fifty seasons.

My love.

The shriveled heart concealed behind the veil of her Dark Arts soaked up the words like a thirsty desert, even as every instinct screamed in warning.

The dragon djinn retrieved an unremarkable leather case from the corner where he'd tossed it the moment he'd arrived. Lost in the backwash of turbulent air and flame, alive with anticipation, she'd barely noticed at the time.

"Something different tonight." Like a great cat, the djinn extended a gleaming ruby claw and beckoned her closer, the hulking width of his shoulders dominating the room despite the massive baroque bed of dark wood, the sumptuous hangings of figured crimson brocade and gold. Opening the case, he drew forth a small bundle of ivory velvet.

"What's that?" asked the sorceress, losing the battle with her curiosity. "A gift?" He'd never given her anything before—only ecstasy inextricably linked with pain.

"Yes." Those strange eyes drilled into her. "You will not speak again until I bid you."

The sorceress opened her mouth. Then she closed it again, too intrigued for defiance. The djinn was perfectly capable of backhanding her and stalking out to launch himself into the night, falling like a stone until he shape-shifted scant feet above the hungry rocks, his wings snapping out in a great leathery swathe of black. And when he left, he went Shaitan knew where. She had no idea.

The djinn shook the garment out, revealing an exquisite scrap of a corset.

The sorceress curled a lip. *Pretty.*

With great care, he fitted the bodice to the pert curve of her breasts. One great hand spread over her stomach, the velvet soft and tight against her belly, and he rumbled, "Bend."

When she did, her breasts fell snugly into the low-cut cups, and the djinn smoothed the dark fall of her hair aside with a touch gentle enough to be alarming. One-handed, he seized the laces at the back and yanked, brutally hard. All the breath left the sorceress in an un-dignified whoosh.

Shaitan, she hated to look a fool! The sorceress glared over her shoulder.

The djinn smiled his beautiful, terrible smile. "Stand and face the mirror."

When she did, she was hard put to conceal her shock. The corset was dainty, virginal—and utterly sinful. Wonderingly, the sorceress ran her fingertips over the smooth, plushy velvet, purest ivory, but not cold or stark. Instead, it was suffused with the faintest tint of warm cream. Across the front ran a row of tiny satin roses in the tender-est of shell pinks. The cups were cunningly constructed to cradle and offer the breast flesh, ripe for a man's mouth. The upper cres-cents of her areolas peeped out seductively, a dusky, lip-smacking temptation. The garment framed her mons, its very delicacy mak-ing the ravenous pink of her sex, the dusting of black curls, deli-ciously obscene.

When the dragon djinn bent his dark head to bite her white shoulder, she gasped. His gaze met hers in the mirror. "It's a bridal corset," he said. "Breathe in and then out."

Her heart gave such a bound that she wasn't ready when he set his knee in the small of her back and hauled the laces even tighter. Her head spun as her ribs were unbearably compressed. Godsdam-mit, *bridal*—? Surely he didn't mean—? *Did he?*

"The villagers of the southern plains are deeply superstitious." The djinn concentrated on threading the laces, tweaking each criss-cross with a claw, working down methodically from the top. Watch-ing in the mirror, the sorceress could see they weren't ribbons after all, but finely plaited satin ropes. Pink. "They send me girls dressed as if for a wedding. Fools."

The sorceress hissed as the boning bit brutally into her soft flesh. What did he do with them, those terrified village maidens?

As if he'd read her mind, the dragon djinn licked her throat with his forked tongue. A frisson of hot erotic pleasure ran straight to her sex and she gushed and softened in the most delightfully humiliating fashion.

"This one," he purred. "This one had the guts to look me in the eye as I ripped the gown off her body. She told me to go to hell."

When he threw his head back in a gravelly laugh, his long teeth flashed white and sharp. "I told her I was already there. But in return, I gave her the swiftest death I had in me. And I kept the corset. For your pleasure, love. And mine."

Shaitan, he was magnificent! *Love*, he'd said it again. *Her dark, terrible love*. The only one who'd ever matched her—in power, in wickedness, and in dark desire.

Holding his eye, she made a production out of smoothing the translucent silk stockings over her legs, but when the djinn had her brace her foot against his thigh so he could adjust the rose-trimmed garters himself, her dissolution was complete.

"Tonight, you are mine." Those slit-pupiled eyes bored into hers. "To torture, to control, to fuck." His third eyelid flickered across, a sign of some deep feeling she couldn't interpret. "To eat." A glimpse of fang.

Outside, thunder boomed, shaking the mountains to their stony roots. The wind howled and the rain slashed. And in the red chamber, the dragon djinn played his games of erotic torment. The sorceress had expected a whipping. In truth, she'd been looking forward to it. The djinn was a master with the lash, the only lover she'd ever had brutal enough, ruthless enough, to lift her out of herself to that silent inner place of blood-soaked peace.

Instead, to her furious chagrin, he treated her like a naughty little girl. Seated before the mirror, he turned the sorceress over his knee and spanked her bottom with his scaly palm until the blood rose scarlet beneath the skin and she couldn't prevent the instinctive squirm, though she refused to permit any sound to escape. Her face flushed and sweaty with mortification, barely able to breathe, she dug her nails into his leg and bit her lip until it bled. Her head swam.

The sorceress loved it.

By way of retaliation, she rubbed her velvet-clad belly against the rock-hard erection beneath her and had the satisfaction of hearing the djinn's breath hitch. But her triumph didn't last long.

"Watch," he rumbled, pulling her head up with a fist in her hair. "See how dirty you are." He laughed and slid a long finger into her dripping core, teasing her with the implicit threat of a claw. "How dirty *we* are." When he followed the first digit with a second, a thin whimper fell out of her mouth, despite all she could do to strangle it at birth.

"Keep looking." Releasing his grip on her hair, he returned to hard, leisurely slaps, the fingers of his other hand lodged deep inside her. The sorceress was forced to arch her back in the unyielding corset, fighting to keep her balance, anchored by the clutch of her internal muscles on those diabolical fingers. Desperately, she tried not to grab at his calves, but it was impossible.

After an eon, he lifted her to her feet between his knees and ravaged her mouth, stabbing deep with his hard, forked tongue. The sorceress gave as good as she got, though it must be the constricting corset that caused tears to burn her eyes and tiny lightnings to swim in her vision. When the kiss ended—though it was more a duel of mouths—she sank down gracefully to nuzzle his huge cock, running her tongue over the incised ridges, caressing the scales beneath heated ebony skin. With one hand, she grasped it by the broad root, with the other, she gripped his heavy testicles, hard enough to hover just this side of hurt.

Normally, the djinn relished watching her struggle to service him. Sometimes, his cock writhed so violently, she had to nip at it to keep it still. But not tonight.

Tonight, he used her hair again, wrenching her away, leaving a trail of burning moisture across her cheek. Without a word, he pushed her down to hands and knees on the rug before the mirror and knocked her thighs apart.

"Watch," he repeated as his cock snaked its way between her dripping folds. "And remember!" With a grunt, he shoved himself forward, brutally hard.

The sorceress screamed, high and shrill. Between the giant phallus

wedged deep inside her and the cruel grip of the corset, it seemed
there was no room left for *her*, for her soul, her heart's breath. He'd
never been so deep before, because she'd never been able to take him,
not all the way to the root. But now she was all receptacle, all narrow
vessel stuffed full to bursting with *him*, her perfect dragon lover.
Something in her dark heart sheered off and tumbled willingly into
the cup of his ruthless hand.

Glancing over her shoulder at the mirror, she watched, panting,
as the djinn withdrew, inch by torturous inch. The small pink
mouth of her sex flexed around his gleaming black girth, panic and
arousal sucking at him, pulling him back in. Where he belonged.

The djinn's lip lifted and a snarl of lust rumbled in his chest.
"Good?"

"Shaitan, *yes!*" The sorceress pushed back with her hips, relishing
the edgy bite of the abrading scales on her delicate flesh. The delightful ache would live with her for days. "Harder, harder!"

The djinn's laugh boomed around the chamber, louder than the
thunder of the peaks, and the sorceress thought he'd never looked so
brutally handsome, so compelling, so unholy.

Leaning over her body, he tugged the velvet cups away to bare
her breasts. Then he reared back on his heels, wings spread for balance, and pulled the sorceress, still thickly impaled, into his chest.
His fingers meeting around her tightly corseted waist, he lifted her
and forced her down, again and again, staring over her shoulder at the
demonic image in the mirror.

Tears trickled down her cheeks and the sorceress didn't care,
though no one had seen her cry in long dusty centuries.

The pace grew savage, the djinn's wings thrashing behind him, the
sorceress shrieking her pleasure and pain. With a final vicious thrust,
he froze, his cock swelling, rippling. His hot breath lifted her hair as
he roared, a primal bellow of male satisfaction. The mountain shuddered with the power of it.

But the sorceress heard the sound as if from far, far away, in a
world beyond a veil. Reaching around her with one long arm, the
djinn flicked an expert claw against her clitoris. There was no time

for more than a keening whimper as all the breath left her body in a whoosh. The grip of the climax, the most ferocious she'd ever experienced, was more than doubled by the constraint of the boned corset. Her vision hazed, then clouded over. The djinn's hot seed washed into every crevice, every fold, burning as it went. All the muscles in her body contracted and released in an endless clenching rush.

She sagged, boneless, and her dragon lover caught her effortlessly in his massive arms, lowering her gently to the rug. The sorceress lay, still rigidly encased in the corset, her cheek pressed to the soft pile beneath her, and thought longingly of the cock ring she'd had made specially for him—the one with the cruel silver studs on the inside and the attachment for a leash. Next time.

The djinn disengaged. When she winced, he chuckled, giving her an absentminded pat on the rump. She gazed into the mirror as he used one of her nightgowns to wipe himself down. Very, very slowly, she rolled over and sat up, staring at her reflection in disbelief. She'd never looked more beautiful. Rumpled, yes. Ruined even, with the djinn's smoky seed smeared over her slim white thighs. But *alive*, as if she were mortal still, the skin above the ivory velvet flushed pink with lust and love.

"Ah, that was good." The djinn stretched luxuriously, his dark, handsome head nearly reaching the ceiling. The unreadable, alien gaze dropped to her face and he reached down to haul her to her feet. He stared at her a moment longer, then his mouth curved in a sardonic half-smile. "Good-bye, my dear. Keep the corset. It suits you." The lamplight burnished the pattern of scales on his deep chest with bronze-green sparks.

Despite herself, the sorceress blinked. "Good-bye?"

Three

The djinn pushed her chin up with his big fist. "Consider it a parting gift."

"P-parting?" Distantly, the sorceress heard a crystalline sound, as if something small and precious had shattered. Or perhaps she felt it in her bones, that breaking sensation.

"I make it a rule," rumbled the dragon djinn, "to be the first to walk away." He shrugged. "Or fly, in this case. Less potential for boredom."

"B-but—" stammered the sorceress, fumbling. "It's been—"

"Fifty seasons. Yes, I know. You think the tedium is worth continuing?"

The sorceress choked on the bile in her throat. *"Tedium?"*

"Tonight was amusing, I grant you. But that was the corset." He ran a talon down the flowing curve from armpit to hip, scoring the velvet pile in a single continuous line. "You should wear it often, with other lovers." The djinn shook his head, apparently in sorrow, though the gleam in his eye told the sorceress he was mocking her. "Remember me, love." He swept into an ironic bow, magnificent in nothing but his ebony skin.

The sorceress hauled in a breath and came up against the constriction of the boned corset. The action, small as it was, ignited the dreadful hurt within her, her rage rising until it was white-hot in a matter of moments. For an instant, she was numb save for her terrible pain. And her overpowering fury. *Shaitan, Dark One, help me!*

"No one," she hissed, *"no one* scorns me. I am the sorceress of storms."

"In a teacup, perhaps?" Arrogant as ever, the djinn tapped her on the cheek with a ruby claw. "Once again, farewell. I wish you the best—and the worst." Grinning, he turned to go.

The sorceress snarled a spell and a long dagger with a smoking blade appeared in her hand. Murky smears of evil Magick oiled the shining metal.

Unperturbed, the dragon djinn paused. "Oho," he smiled. "What now? You want to play a different game, love?"

The sorceress stepped forward, right into his arms. "I do not play," she spat. "And I am *not* . . ." In a single smooth movement, she thrust the dagger under his jaw, deep into his carotid artery. "Your love!" With a vicious twist, she jerked the blade free and shoved it back again.

The djinn choked and staggered back, his huge hands clamped against the wound. The sorceress followed, pressing close, avid. With every beat of his great heart, draconic blood spilled over his fingers in spurts. Against the ebony of his skin, it was almost too black to see—until it soaked into the pale velvet of the corset.

The sorceress looked down at the dark stain spreading over her heart and laughed aloud, her silver voice cracked and ugly. "How fitting."

When the djinn fell to his knees, his reptilian eyes growing flat and dull, she reached out with another spell and grasped his fading soul. "Don't go just yet, my *dear*. Leave me something to *remember* you by." Mercilessly, she held him back from death's threshold, feeling his life trying to flee, frantic wings fluttering in her fist. The blood flowed down the blade and over her arm like a coal-black kiss, the velvet of the corset absorbing every drop until the plushy fabric was a matte ebony and the pink satin roses shriveled and fell away, dyed dark with the dragon's death.

"Bah!" The sorceress opened her fingers and the blade dropped to the rug with a dull thud. "Shaitan take you, reptile." Turning away, she released the Magick and the djinn slumped, his soul draining away with the last of his life's blood.

The sorceress glared at her reflection, the black corset a magnificent contrast with her snow-white limbs, the pale swell of her heaving breasts. Her teeth bared in a snarl, she reached for the laces.

There was no warning.

From behind her, a nightmare vision rose, quicker than thought, roaring with hate and rage. The djinn reached a huge taloned hand over her shoulder, his eyes flaming. With the last of his strength, he rammed every claw into her breast, a perfect arc of cold daggers piercing flesh and bone.

"Bitch!" he thundered. Then he jerked free, slid boneless to the floor, and died.

The sorceress stared in utter astonishment at the five welling gouts of scarlet. As she swayed, her vision clouding, she reached out, calling desperately, *"Shaitan! Lord! Avenge Your servant!"*

And He answered.

The last thing the sorceress saw were the five heartsblood rubies glittering on the breast of the corset. *Yes!* Fiercely, she gathered up the only things still living within her—her will and her hatred—and poured them into the black velvet.

By the time she hit the floor, the sorceress of storms had ceased to be.

Only the corset remained.

On the next peal of thunder, her body trembled, shimmering into a pile of gray ash that whirled out the tall doors and away over the high ledge.

Long before the small scavengers had nibbled the djinn's body down to the strong bones, the corset had followed the remains of its mistress, fluttering miles on the wind over the Cressy Plains like some bizarre bird of prey.

⚬⚬⚬⚬⚬

Meg had just helped Da to bed when she heard horses outside in the yard. She dropped a kiss on her father's stubbled cheek and rushed to the window, her heart singing. *John.*

Seven weeks had passed since that night in the barn, and he'd been as good as his word. He'd made it up to her in every possible way and from every possible angle. A hot wave licked down her spine at the thought of his hands, his mouth, his cock. She knew she had no experience, but surely John Lammas must be the best lover in the world. He'd made her come so hard, she'd simply opened her mouth and screamed. Sister save her, she'd damn near fainted!

Her hand on the latch, she watched his dark figure swing down from the horse and walk toward the house. She'd know that purposeful, long-legged stride anywhere. John never seemed to hurry, but he always arrived where he was supposed to be, unflurried and on time. It made him a fine dancer and an excellent horseman. He was the most coordinated person he knew, for all that he was so big.

Meg shivered. Big all over.

His cock was long and thick and straight, with a heart-shaped head that was smooth as silk under her tongue and tasted of musk and salt and man. What must it be like to have a part of your body with a mind of its own? She couldn't imagine, but gods, she could enjoy! She loved that she could drive him wild with her mouth and her hands, until he shuddered all over, his fists clenching and unclenching.

With one hand, Meg rubbed a tingling nipple, assaulted by a delightful vision of John roped to the post in the barn, his huge muscular body entirely at her mercy, his cock jutting up all flushed and stiff while his dark eyes burned with frustration and he ground out exactly what he was going to do to her, the moment he was free. Mmm, sweet . . . Perhaps tonight . . .

Her eyes narrowed. There was a second horseman, still mounted, waiting by the gate. The man turned his head, his profile limned twice over by the light of the Sibling Moons, the Sister and the Brother. Meg frowned, apprehension unfurling in the pit of her belly. Nathan, the next brother along, as mercurial as John was calm. What was he doing here? They were such a volatile clan, John's family. No wonder he liked to lie peacefully after they made love, one big hand stroking her hair. No speech necessary.

She had the door open before John reached the bottom step. "What is it?" She slipped out onto the porch. "What's wrong?"

"Meggie." He caught her hands in his and she went up on tiptoe to kiss him. Their lips met and clung, and for a few blessed moments, she forgot all about Nathan. But then John drew back, his thumb caressing her jaw, and she knew.

This was going to be bad.

"Nathan and Da had a fight." John gave a sour laugh. "The whole family's in an uproar. Ma, the girls . . . Brother's balls, my ears are still ringing."

"But they're always like that. Why . . . ?" Meg glanced at Nathan's motionless figure and he lifted a hand in a brief salute. She'd always quite liked him. He was as quick to laughter as he was to rage, and charming with it.

"Nathan hit him. Da, I mean."

"He *what*?" Appalled, Meg stared at the other man across the shadowed length of the yard.

"Split his lip." John ran a hand through his hair. "Shit, Meggie, it was awful. Now Da says he has no second son, and anyhow, Nathan stormed out. Either way, he says he's going to Caracole. Torza's Band are recruiting."

"Sister!"

"Sweetheart, he's such a hothead. I have to go with him. Get him there in one piece, see they don't cheat him on the contract. Ma made me promise."

"But, John . . ." Meg ran down. Even buried in Holdercroft, she'd heard of Torza's Band. Who hadn't? A mercenary company, the most famous on Palimpsest. She shivered. Killing to order. "How long . . . ?" She cleared her throat. "How long will you be gone?"

"Ten days to Caracole. Ten days back." John shrugged. "It'll take them at least a few days to process him. A month, give or take."

"You can't . . . talk him out of it?"

"Turns out it's what he's always wanted." John shook his head. "Idiot, when he could have all this." He lifted his head to gaze across the fields and fences, to the twinkling lights of the village and the dark bulk of the mountains beyond.

"It's an adventure, I suppose," said Meg slowly. Caracole was a city of blue canals, elegant pavilions, and smiling vice. Country folk said darkly you could buy anything in Caracole if you had the coin. *Anything.*

"Fuck that," said John, not generally so crude. "Everything I want is here."

"John." Tack jingled as Nathan rode forward. "We should go."

"In a minute." John glared at his brother. "You start. I'll catch you up."

"All right." Nathan grinned, a flash of white teeth. He lifted a hand. " 'Bye, Meg. Wish me luck."

"Good luck, Nathan," she said automatically. "Be careful."

Nathan snorted. "Sure." He trotted away into the darkness.

Meg tugged John into the light spilling from the open door. She wanted to see his face. "The Sister hold you in Her hand, love. Come back to me."

She saw his throat move as he swallowed. He pushed a lock of dark hair out of his eyes. "Meggie, wherever you are is home to me. I love you. Now give me a proper kiss and let me go."

And so she did, pressing herself up against him, memorizing the feel of his hard chest crushing her breasts, the bruising grip of his fingers on her hip, the hot depths of his mouth.

Finally, she hugged him with all her considerable strength, making him huff out a laugh. "Don't forget me," she whispered, seized by a sudden terror.

"Not my Steady Meggie. Never, I swear it."

He dropped a last kiss on her nose and wrenched himself away. Almost running, he swung into the saddle and cantered away after his brother. At the gate, he turned for a final wave, his face a pale blur. And then he was gone.

❦

The first month tiptoed by on leaden feet. Meg greeted each dusk with gratitude, because John was one day closer. Then Da caught the shaky ague and she had her hands full for four or five days until he was over the worst of it. Mistress Griddle, who was better than most big-city healers, shook her head over his tall wasted frame and murmured that Meg should be ready.

Although running the farm and coping with Da took all her time and attention, Meg found she was stopping whatever she was doing several times a day to shade her eyes and stare down the rutted path. She missed John with a physical ache so acute her stomach felt like a ball of lead. Often she'd forget and think of something she wanted to ask him. How to speak to the farmhands, for instance. What he thought she should do about the broken pump or the fence in the north pasture. Sister, how she longed for his strong arms around her, his deep voice telling her everything would be all right! Every day she walked over to the Lammas farmhouse, and every day John's mother shook her head, her eyes clouded with worry. The weight fell off Meg and the bloom in her cheeks faded.

Toward the end of the second month, she found her father's crumpled body on the floor of his bedchamber. He didn't regain consciousness until two days later when he peered muzzily at Meg's face and called her by her mother's name. "Sorry, love," he rasped, barely audible. "So sorry."

An hour later, his fingers slipped from her grasp and the life passed from him in a long sigh.

It wasn't until after the simple funeral that Meg discovered the full meaning of that strange apology, what her father had been hiding from her. The following day, Master Montse, the local financier and moneylender, arrived to explain gently, but firmly, that the Mackie farm was so deeply encumbered as to belong to him, lock, stock, and barrel. Would a week be convenient for Mistress Meg's departure? There was much work to be done before he could cry the sale in Holdercroft market square.

Numbly, Meg nodded. How could her life have fallen apart around her in the space of two short months? Dragging herself upstairs, she sat on the narrow bed she'd slept in all her life, staring blankly at the hooked rug she'd made with her own hands. Several hours later, she rose as if in a dream and packed a small bag. Her needs had never been complex. As an afterthought, she found the cheap blade and scabbard Da wore when he went to market. Grimly, she buckled them around her waist. The road to Caracole was a hazardous one, especially for a woman alone.

But John needed her, she'd never been more certain of anything in her life. Her mouth twisted. The Sister knew, no one else did, not any longer. John Lammas was her future, and once she found him, all would be well.

The following day, Margaret May Mackie turned at the gate for a last look, one hand on the worn wooden post. It felt sun-warmed and splintery, remarkably solid for something that would be gone from her life the moment she walked around the bend beyond the copse of stately cedderwood trees.

Squeezing her eyes shut, she disciplined her breathing. Carefully, she closed the gate, heaving the bar into place with the ease of long practice. Then she squared her shoulders, spun on her heel, and started down the rutted path that led to the Caracole road.

Four

When Tansy screamed, Meg froze, her fingers crushing the starched napkin she'd been attempting to fold into a crown. Godsdammit, she'd ruined another one.

The screams went on and on. Seizing Cook's heaviest skillet, Meg darted to the kitchen door. Full of intriguing twilight shadows, The Garden of Nocturnal Delights spread in a broad, gracious crescent before her. The Main Pavilion was situated front and center, convenient for both canal and street. Scattered discreetly among the lawns and shrubberies and water features, the small pavilions revealed themselves in teasing glimpses of warm terracotta walls topped by pagoda-style roofs.

Her heart pounding, she tilted her head, listening. Doors slammed and voices rose, shouts and exclamations colliding in the soft night air. Peering down the winding path, Meg was treated to the sight of two sets of flexing buttocks as a pair of bare-assed Queen's Guards charged past, swords in hand. They'd be off-duty, none too pleased to have their pleasure interrupted, but thank the Sister for their presence. Her breath came a little more easily.

By the time she reached the Pavilion of Clouds and Rain, Tansy was huddled on the fine bricked path outside the small elegant building, her face in her hands, whining like a whipped dog. The tray she'd been carrying lay upside down beside her, the sweetmeats Cook had created so lovingly spilled and broken, the delicate tisane pot a pathetic pile of shards.

Meg laid the skillet aside and crouched, drawing the little apprentice courtesan into her arms. "Tansy, what is it?" But the girl only continued to shake and cry, burrowing her head into Meg's shoulder.

"Mistress Meg?" One of the soldiers stood naked in the open door, his face grim. "They're dead, both of them."

"What?" Meg stared. Blood stained the man's fingers. Automatically, she untied her apron and passed it to him.

The second warrior, a grizzled veteran, appeared at his elbow. "Looks like she killed him and then herself."

"But that can't be. Not Shalla-Mae and her Duke."

The man shrugged. "See for yourself," he said. His gaze shifted to a point over Meg's shoulder. "Mistress," he said, a warning in his tone.

She turned. A small crowd was beginning to gather—clients and courtesans, male and female, a couple of Rose's apprentices. In fact, Rose herself was hurrying down the path, her robe of midnight blue brocade belling behind her. The Dark Rose.

Their eyes met and an unspoken message passed between them.

"Friends." Rose smiled and Meg was struck again, as she always was, by the particular sweetness of her employer's expression, the charm she exuded as naturally as breathing. "Please." She spread her hands, long-fingered and graceful in the deep sleeves. "An argument of the heart. You know how it is."

Still smiling, she gestured at the Main Pavilion. "I have cool sherbet and spiced wine awaiting your pleasure and Cook has prepared a special supper. You wouldn't be so cruel as to disappoint him. All is well here."

A disarming twinkle. "Our Mistress Meg has everything under control. As usual."

Succumbing without a struggle, the little group straggled back toward the larger building. At Rose's discreet gesture, the apprentices shepherded them along, practicing their sidelong glances and small talk.

Rose drew the sniffling Tansy to her side. "Come and find me the moment you know," she murmured to Meg.

"Yes." Meg smoothed her skirts, her heart pounding. Folding her hands before her, she willed herself to be calm. In the five years she'd been Housekeeper at The Garden, there was little she hadn't seen, nothing she hadn't been able to cope with. "I'll do that."

A crisp nod and Rose glided down the path in the wake of her customers.

Meg turned to the older man. "Captain, if you would be so kind?"

"Sergeant," he said absently, completely comfortable in his skin. "Mistress, it's— There's a lot of blood."

"Thank you for the warning." But when he stood aside and Meg stepped over the threshold, the smell took her by the throat. "Sweet Sister," she whispered, reeling.

It didn't seem possible that two bodies could contain so much blood. The silver-shot, misty gray hangings that gave the pavilion its name were splashed with great gouts of it, Shalla-Mae's white-blond hair clotted scarlet. Mercifully, Meg couldn't see her face. The courtesan lay slumped in a graceless sprawl of arms and legs beside the wide bed. Gods, she would have hated to be found so, pretty Shalla-Mae, so careful of her dignity. Her patron, a handsome man in his mid-thirties, hung half off the mattress, his face contorted, a long wound lacerating his throat, just below the ear. They were both naked. On the floor, just beyond Shalla-Mae's clawed fingers, lay a silver blade with an ornate hilt.

Meg dropped to her knees, reaching for the girl's shoulder, but the Sergeant stayed her hand. "She cut her own throat," he said. "You don't want to see it."

Meg drew back, swallowing. "No," she agreed. She lifted troubled eyes to his swarthy face. "But I don't understand. They were going to sign the bedding contracts this evening. Cook and I made them a special celebration supper. The Duke was besotted. I think he truly loved her."

"What about the girl?"

"Shalla-Mae? She was thrilled, swept off her feet. She even bought him a gift." Meg rose. "Aargh, gods!" The fabric of her gown clung to her legs, cold and heavy where she'd kneeled in the pool of blood.

"Steady there, Mistress." The Sergeant's big warm hand closed over her arm, and for a moment, another voice echoed in her head. *My Steady Meggie.*

"I'm all right." She hadn't thought of John for some time now. Not since last night, on the edge of sleep.

"A gift?" said the younger soldier. "What sort of gift?"

Meg glanced at his hard face, the long white scar on his chest. If he'd lived, Nathan Lammas would look like this now, be this sort of man. Sternly, she disciplined her thoughts before they could stray to John for the hundred-thousandth time. Rose was depending on her. "A corset, Shalla-Mae told me, a beautiful corset." She gave a wry smile. "The sort men like."

"Is this it?" The Sergeant held out a bundle of black velvet. Correctly interpreting Meg's hesitation, he said, "It was on the floor over there. But no blood."

Meg took it from him. "Must be." The plushy velvet was luxurious under her fingertips, like the pelt of some beautiful animal. "She would have been stunning in it, so fair against the black."

A glint of red caught her eye and she held the garment at arms' length to see. "Merciful Sister, look at the rubies!" Five of them glittered from the bodice, in a perfect arc of baleful fire, each shaped like a tear—or a drop of blood.

"That's the grade they call heartsblood," said the Sergeant. "Brother's balls, how did she afford it?"

"It was a bargain, in one of those strange dusty shops in the Melting Pot, the kind that come and go. Even then, it took every gold cred she had, all her savings, but she thought it was worth it for her Duke. Poor Shalla-Mae." Meg glanced quickly at that hideous hair. They'd have to wash it before they could lay her out. "It called to her, she said. And she had to have it."

"Give us a few minutes to dress," said the Sergeant, "and we'll find a door or something to carry them on." He paused. "You'll need to make him decent before his family comes." He indicated the twisted body of the Duke with a jerk of his chin.

Meg winced. But she knew what the soldier was thinking—the gossip would be vicious, hurtful. Poor Rose, scandal wouldn't bother her—she was accustomed to notoriety—but the loss of one of her treasures would. The experienced courtesans and the eager apprentices, the boys and girls both—she loved them all with a fierce protective love. There was more than an element of bossy big sister in Meg's employer.

An hour later, alone in her small suite on the second floor of the Main Pavilion, Meg discovered she still had a ball of black velvet clutched in her fist—Shalla-Mae's corset. She had to set it aside so she could brew a calming tisane, but doing so took a surprising degree of effort. How lovely it was! Yet again, her fingers strayed to stroke and pet.

When she heard Rose's light tread in the passage and then her knock, Meg thrust the garment hurriedly into the back of a drawer. As she straightened, she couldn't help feeling like a felon. Not that it mattered. Unaccountably exhilarated, she turned to greet her employer with a smile on her lips that felt almost . . . wicked.

"Thank the Sister for you, my dear," said Rose, accepting a cup. "That was awful." Her beautiful caramel-colored skin, usually glowing with health, still had a slight undertone of gray.

"Yes, it was." Meg poured for herself with steady hands. "But everything's arranged. The Sergeant even went to the Wizard's Enclave with a message for the healer. Shalla-Mae looks as decent as the woman could make her. The Duke wasn't such a problem."

"Poor child." Rose put the delicate cup down with her usual grace. The set had been her gift. "There's no doubt, is there? About what she did?"

Meg shook her head. "No. The Sergeant fetched his duty Captain. They checked everything."

"Valuable man, the Sergeant. Did you give him a chit? It's the least we can do."

"Two, actually. He said . . ." She broke off, conscious of the warmth in her cheeks.

Rose cocked a brow. "Why, Meg, you're blushing." She grinned like a boy. "He asked for you, didn't he?"

The Sergeant had taken the chits with a courteous nod and tucked them into his belt pouch. He'd shot Meg an appreciative glance, one that raked her from head to toe, with lingering stops at the fullness of her breasts and the generous curve of her hips. "You're a fine-lookin' woman, Mistress Meg. I don't suppose . . . ?" A brow quirked and he gestured at the corset in her hand. "You'd look tasty in that, I'm thinkin'." His voice had thickened.

Then he'd caught her expression. "Not now," he added hastily. "I know it's not a good time. Next week, mebbe. Or the week after? I'm a patient man. Rhiomard, at your service." He'd given an oddly anti- quated bow.

Rose sighed. "You said no, didn't you?"

"Rose, you know I don't . . . do that."

The other woman snorted. "You're female, aren't you? You have needs, same as everyone else. Give it to him for free, if the money bothers you."

Meg rubbed her brow. "We've been over and over this. I'll get there, but in my own time, all right?"

Rose looked her in the eye and Meg braced herself. Here it came. Again. "He's dead, Meg love. You found that out years ago. By the Sister, it's past time to let him go. You said he loved you. Wouldn't he want you to be happy?"

"Perhaps."

Because she wasn't sure. How could she be?

It had taken her almost four months to earn enough for the bribe because the pale clerk at Torza's headquarters refused even to speak with her until he saw the color of the creds in her purse. Her first job had been with the merchant who picked her up on the road to Cara- cole. When he'd suggested Meg earn her passage in his caravan on her back, she'd showed him Da's knife and offered to cook the eve- ning meal. After the miracle she wrought with stale biscuits, stringy meat, and dried vegetables, there'd been no more talk of whoring. A woman Meg's size knew how to cook, because she liked to eat. And after the curdle pie, the merchant had asked her to marry him.

Smiling calmly, Meg had refused, and when the caravan reached Caracole, she secured a place at The Garden as a kitchen maid. And now, here she was as Housekeeper, unflappable as ever, and completely indispensable, according to Rose. Meg sighed. If only she could still the turmoil inside her.

Nathan and John had enlisted together. She wouldn't believe it until Torza's clerk pushed the documents across the desk to show her the thumbprints, a thick sprawling signature that looked like John's. Fifth Company had shipped out the next day, en route to a job down the coast. The man riffled through pages, while Meg stood, dumb as a beast, her world unraveling around her.

Deep inside, a small voice whimpered, "But you promised, you *promised* . . . " The urge to drop to the cobbles and curl up in a fetal ball was almost overwhelming. He didn't love her—or at least, not enough. It had been a lie, all of it.

A year later, she learned they'd succeeded in quelling the island rebellion in question, but now the company's contract had been extended for garrison duty. The following spring, with dry disapproval, the clerk revealed that one John Lammas had been disciplined four times, once severely. Severely? She wanted to vomit. The Sister knew John had never suffered fools. Ah gods, why couldn't she hate him?

But worse was to come.

On her next visit, Meg stood shivering in her winter cloak, one of Rose's castoffs. Although it was warm enough, it was too short for her and the wind whistled around her calves. Fifth Company had finished the tour of duty and its ships were returning to Caracole in convoy. Hardly daring to breathe, she watched the clerk's ink-stained finger travel down a column and trail to a halt. "Trinitarian galleys," said the clerk. "His ship went down, Mistress. All hands drowned. Fucking pirates." And then he'd looked up and seen her face. "Uh, sorry." Afterward, Meg could never be sure whether the apology was for the language or the news.

She recalled laying the coins down on the table very precisely, one after the other. Clink, clink, clink. Unable to speak, she'd reeled out into the sunny street and stared for a long time at the bright blue water in the canal. How deep was it? Deep enough? What had the sea and the passage of time done to John's big body, the body she'd loved so much?

"You want children, don't you?" Rose was saying. "I know you do. Can't do that without a man."

Deliberately, Meg inhaled, held the breath, and let it out. "Life goes on, I know that. And he left me, though he promised he wouldn't." She met Rose's gaze and shrugged. "He met someone else, I suppose, someone more to his taste. When I see him in my dreams, his face is always so clear. It's as though the Sister sends him. But when I wake . . ." She bit her lip. "I forget the precise shape of his jaw, his ears, his hands."

"You see?" Rose's lovely face was sympathetic, but determined. "What about that man from the moneylender's? What's his name?"

"You mean Yaso?"

"That's him." Rose waved an elegant hand. "He's definitely a long-term prospect."

Meg chuckled. "Oh yes, long-term, not to mention long-winded. Godsdammit, Rose, he's likely to bore me to death."

Her employer rose in a graceful flurry of blue brocade. "But you're not going to give him the chance, are you?" she said shrewdly. "Ah, Meg."

It wasn't as though Meg had been completely celibate. Two years from that hideous day at Torza's headquarters it had taken for her to select her first lover, but only a month to part from him. No one was quite . . . satisfactory. Even now, she only needed the fingers of one hand to count them. Less, in fact.

How could any man measure up to the memory of John Lammas?

⊰⊱⊰⊱⊰

Meg had the smallest of The Garden's four bathhouses to herself. Gratefully, she dropped the sturdy bar across the door and unlaced her gown. Even though she'd changed her dress the moment she'd returned from the Pavilion of Clouds and Rain, she still felt soiled. Violent death, she supposed. She hadn't seen it before.

Standing naked in the shallowest tub, she sluiced herself with buckets of scalding hot water and scrubbed every inch of her skin with a rough cloth and lashings of rose-scented bath cream. Gods, that was better.

Glowing pink and dripping, Meg padded over to the deep porcelain tub and flipped open the spigots. Sighing with the anticipation of a good soak, she watched the steaming water gush into the bath. Plumbing like this cost a fortune, even in a city as sophisticated as Caracole, but Rose had invested wisely. The bathhouses, with their luxurious appointments and under-the-floor heating, were one of The Garden's most popular attractions. Shalla-Mae had been a specialist in the slow art of the erotic bath.

Involuntarily, Meg's eye fell on her clean clothes, folded and waiting on the padded bench, and her belly fluttered with strange excitement. Seizing a towel, she dried herself off while water splashed behind her. As she watched, the neat pile wobbled and everything slid off the bench to the floor, save for the corset, a small sprawling patch of midnight black, spiced with the wicked flare of rubies. Meg blinked. Strange. How had the corset come to be there? She must have brought it with her, but she didn't recall . . .

Sister, it was a gorgeous thing. Tomorrow, she'd put it in the box she was packing to send to Shalla-Mae's family, but for now . . .

Slowly, Meg reached out and the corset came to her hand like a wild animal condescending to be stroked. As if in a dream, she swiveled to face the mirrored wall, holding the garment up before her nude body.

Oh, oh, oh. It made her look . . .

Meg swallowed.

Hands trembling, she loosened the laces and slid the corset over her head. It settled against her skin in a velvet caress that sent a thick wave of sexual heat spiraling up her spine. Panting a little, she reached behind her and tugged the laces, but she must have pulled too hard because the corset tightened around her rib cage in a sudden, smooth rush that forced all the breath out of her in an undignified grunt.

Her vision grayed out for a moment, and when she came to, the first thing she saw was her reflection, posed like a dark queen in some wicked, erotic dream.

The boning forced her up straight, her back arched and her swelling breasts offered as if on a plate, the areolas candy-pink, tight with arousal. Sweet Sister, had her waist ever been so tiny? She'd always been well fleshed, the charitable might have called her voluptuous, but surely she'd never looked so infinitely fuckable in her life?

Not only fuckable. Edible.

The black velvet made an exquisite contrast with the delicious golden creaminess of her skin. She twisted to peer over her shoulder. The globes of her buttocks were magnificently framed and presented, quivering with every panting breath. And between her thighs . . .

Meg faced the mirror, widening her stance. The pale skin of her inner thighs shone slick with arousal, and from the lips of her plump slit, dark pink folds peeped, so puffy and engorged they looked angry. She could swear her heart beat there, her clitoris sitting up high and hard, like a tight ripe berry. The blood thundered in her ears, a regular, vicious surf, and the rubies on the bodice seemed to twinkle in time.

Her blue eyes had gone so dark they were almost black with lust. Gods, she needed a man! Preferably on his knees before her, worshipping her with his mouth. Meg narrowed her eyes and an image slithered out of her subconscious, complete in every lascivious detail.

Five

The man's back was to the mirror, his face buried between her thighs, the line of a muscular back and buttocks pleasing to her eye. She'd never fantasized in such detail before. Sister, she could see the light gleaming off the cruel silver cuffs that bound his hands behind his back. He'd been whipped, precisely and without mercy, the bloody marks crisscrossing his spine in an aesthetically pleasing pattern.

The blood's so pretty, like rubies.

Meg moaned, her clit quivering under the expert lash of his dancing tongue. In a faraway corner of her mind, she knew it was the familiar touch of her own fingers, but she was lost . . . lost in the cruel beauty of forced submission. Her body sang with power.

He's only a man, a toy.

Yes, only a man, made to serve, to serve her pleasure. Meg slid to her knees, her thighs splayed, and the man went with her, crouching awkwardly without the use of his arms, his ass canted high in the air. But his busy tongue didn't miss a beat.

Now she could see his balls, drawn up tight and hard, the shadow of a long thick cock jutting below. A band of metal cinched him hard, a cock ring. As she watched, it tightened viciously all by itself and the man's low moan of anguish puffed hot against her slick flesh. Meg's empty sheath contracted, her clit convulsing with pure, white-hot pleasure.

Panting, she braced herself on one hand, the other still busy between her thighs. Gods, what was wrong with her? The images were so powerful, they seemed real. She shook her head, trying to regroup, reground. Pain, whether hers or another's, had never held any attraction. This . . . dream . . . these thoughts . . . were horrible, not like her at all.

Squeezing her eyes shut, Meg fumbled for the laces in the small of her back, but for some reason, she couldn't seem to get a grip. She writhed, feeling the silky brush of the man's hair as he pillowed his head on her thigh.

It's him.

What?

Meg's eyes flew open. John's dark eyes gazed up her, with an expression she'd never seen in life. Almost . . . sly.

He left you.

"You promised," whispered Meg, burying one hand in his thick black hair and gripping it. "John, you promised."

Faithless, faithless. Betrayer.

"Bastard, you bastard!" She dug her fingers into the lash marks and watched the blood well under her nails, relishing the flinch he couldn't hide. "Wasn't I good enough?"

Punish him. Go on.

There was a leather quirt in her hand, metal-tipped, barbarous. Growling, Meg raised it above her head, John staring up at her in terror.

Then his expression relaxed and he smiled, a wholehearted smile of love and trust. "Meggie," he murmured. "My Steady Meggie."

And a tide of warm water washed up over her calves and her bare bottom.

Sister! The bath!

Meg leaped to her feet and lunged at the spigots, the boning of the corset stabbing the underside of her breast. Outside, a night bird called shrilly, its voice like the fading echoes of a woman's angry, wordless cry. Staggering a little, she wove her way over to the padded bench and collapsed, her mind confused and foggy.

She must have fallen asleep, surely? Or had it been some kind of waking dream, a hallucination brought on by shortness of breath? Sister, the corset was cutting her in half! Slowly, she reached behind her, grasped the laces firmly, and loosed them. A wriggle and a curse, and she had the thing off, clutched in her hand. Numbly, she watched the water trickle away through the cunningly placed drain holes in the floor. Thank the Sister it hadn't reached the priceless rugs. Getting the marks out would have been a bitch.

Peering at the corset, she gave an irritated huff. Look at that—it had frayed, an inch or so along one seam. What a pity. Such a beautiful thing . . .

She didn't realize she was rubbing the velvet of it back and forth across her cheek until a ruby caught her perilously close to one eye. "Shit!" Meg flung it away and clapped a hand to her cheek. Her fingers came away red.

But the pain seemed to clear her mind. Godsdammit, she had work to do. Reluctantly, she turned away from the brimming bath and reached for her gown.

⁂

The Sailor's Lay hadn't changed. John took a long step sideways the moment he was past the swinging doors. Putting the wall at his back, he waited for his eyes to grow accustomed to the gloom.

And for his guts to stop churning.

He still didn't deal with crowded areas well, but he had nowhere else to begin, no other ideas. This was one of the few places in Caracole he remembered, the rest was gone in a blur. All he knew was that Meg was in the city—or she had been, six years ago.

After his mother had come around from her faint and his sisters had stopped screaming, it had been his first question. "Is Meg still here?" He hadn't needed to ask after Da. His father's aching absence was all too clear, his broad-brimmed hat hanging dusty from its peg. John hadn't been there to say good-bye or to help his brothers run the farm.

The long cruel years had taught him to hide his feelings, but it was hard, so very hard, to tell them about Nathan, how he'd held his brother in his arms as his life ebbed away. He let them assume it had happened in battle, been quick and clean, but it hadn't. It had been prolonged, ugly, an infection developing where the shackles had rubbed Nathan's ankles raw.

But the boy had been lucky. Captain-Pasha Imaran Indivar Imalani had been too busy to notice he was too weak to row. If he had, Nathan would have been tossed summarily over the side. Now that John came to think of it, such a fate might have been more merciful.

No man survived longer than a year on the rowing bench of a Trinitarian galley unless he was made of iron and whipcord. John had lasted three. It would have been better to have drowned, like so many others that terrible day, but the gods hadn't permitted it, curse them. He and Nathan had been plucked from the sea, saved from a quick death only to be granted a slow one.

Ma had wept over his limp, though he'd managed to prevent her from seeing his back. She'd run gentle, work-roughened fingers across the blue tattoo on his cheekbone, just beneath his eye. Three Trinitarian characters in the old script, each flowing and ornate. Beautiful in their own horrible way.

"What does it mean?"

"Property of Pasha Imaran Indivar Imalani," said John shortly. Which stopped the conversation cold.

So now he'd trailed all the way back to Caracole, and to The Sailor's Lay, the nearest tavern to the headquarters of Torza's Band, where the nightmare had started. There was the bar where he and Nathan had bellied up, laughing, for the round of drinks the recruiting sergeant bought them. It could have been yesterday, save for the new scars gouged into the thick wood.

And the scars on his soul, deeper even than the ones he bore on his body.

I should have known, thought John, snarling at a serving wench who stared a fraction too long at his face. *When he looked at me like I was a side of prime beef . . .*

"Lammas?" said a voice at his elbow. "Is that you?"

John whirled, his hand dropping to the long curved blade sheathed at his waist. It, too, was the property of Pasha Imaran Indivar Imalani. Or it had been.

He glared into the stranger's stubbled face, not speaking. Waiting.

The man's hand dropped and he took a step backward. "Brother's balls, it is! We thought you were dead." His face creased into a tentative smile. "Sergeant Rhiomard. I was in Torza's Band before I joined the Queen's Guard. I was in Third Company. I taught you quarterstaff, remember?"

"Yes." John licked his lips. His voice was creaky from disuse. "You whipped my ass." The Sergeant didn't need to know the scars across his back still pulled. They slowed him down.

"Not for long. You were too good, too focused." Rhiomard's gaze flickered across the tattoo and away, but he was wise enough to say nothing. "Buy you a drink?"

"One. Thank you."

They leaned against the bar, almost exactly where he and Nathan had stood that night. The irony of it felt like a boulder in his throat, choking him. Carefully, John swallowed his ale, trying to concentrate on the nutty brown taste, savor it.

The other man was talking, his voice a background rumble. Gossip about the old days in Torza's Band, something about better conditions in the Queen's Guard.

Abruptly, John couldn't take it anymore. The fusty tap room closed in on him, stifling. "Do you know a woman called Margaret Mackie?"

Rhiomard stopped in mid-sentence and his face shuttered. "No," he said, straightening up. "And I'd best be off."

Shit! He hadn't meant to insult the man. Ah, what the fuck did it matter anyway? "They call her Meg," he said.

Rhiomard turned and his gaze narrowed. "What does she look like?"

John's heart began a slow slamming beat, the rhythm of the oars to the sound of the drum. Spots swam before his eyes. "Tall for a woman. Fair." He pulled in a breath. "She'd have a Cressy accent. Like me."

Rhiomard stepped closer, balanced on the balls of his feet, his hands loose and open. "What do ye want with Mistress Meg?"

Shit, he could barely remain upright, his knees had gone. His hands shook so badly, he dug one into his belt, wrapped the other around the hilt of his sword. Words felt like marbles in his mouth. "Is she—? Married?"

The Sergeant thought about that for an eternity. "No," he said at last and the room swooped and spun.

From somewhere out of a deep well, John articulated the question. "Where . . . is . . . she?"

A hard hand grabbed his biceps and he was so rattled, he permitted it. "She works at The Garden. And I ask again, what do ye want with her?"

She was my whole world. She still is.

Aloud, he said, "We're from the same village. What garden?"

❈

Not long after dusk, Tansy scratched on Meg's door. "Mistress Meg?"

Meg had just kicked off her shoes and made herself a soothing tisane of mothermeknot. She wasn't best pleased. "Is it the laundry again? I thought I—"

But the little apprentice shook her head. "No," she said. "There's a man asking for you. He gave me this." And she held out a chit, one with Meg's mark on it.

She sighed. "I've already told him no," she said. "Go back and say I said he'd be much better off with Bertha or Chuoko."

Tansy hesitated, her pretty little face oddly intent. "It's not him," she said. "The Sergeant, I mean."

The Garden was like a family. Or a village. Everyone knew everyone else's business. Of course Tansy was aware of Rhiomard's interest.

"He's one of the biggest men I've ever seen. There's a mark on his face." The girl brushed her fingertips over one perfectly sculpted cheekbone. "A tattoo, I think. Mistress Rose says it's rude to stare, so I didn't."

"Where did you put him?"

"In the Spring Green Parlor. With a tisane and a plate of those nut scones you make. But I can move him to the Pavilion of Fallen Blossoms if you want?" She cocked her head to one side like an inquisitive bird.

Meg's brows rose. Tansy was insightful for one so young. All Rose's courtesans were trained as independent businesswomen and this girl was going to be a fine one, an agile mind working behind a face as lovely as a flower.

Meg had to smile. "Tell me what you would do," she said. "Make it an exercise. What do you think of him?" This was a game Rose played often with her apprentices. A courtesan's livelihood depended on being able to sum up a client's character at first meeting.

Tansy settled into one of Meg's comfortable armchairs. "Dangerous," she said decisively.

"Oh." Meg hadn't expected that. "In what way?"

"His eyes are full of terrible secrets. He limps and when he moves, it's"—Tansy moved her shoulders—"stiff somehow. As if he's being careful. He's wearing a Trinitarian sword and I bet he's got other blades as well, where you can't see them."

"What do you know of Trinitarian swords, little one?"

Tansy shot her shrewd glance. "My uncle had one. From the wars."

"Perhaps we'd better send him on his way then? The doormen will see him off." Meg watched the girl's face.

"Oh no!"

"Why not?"

"He's so sad, Mistress Meg. And the way he said your name . . ." Tansy trailed off, then recovered. "He won't hurt you, I'm sure of it."

Now completely intrigued, Meg rose and reached for her shoes. "All right, I'll go. I can always ring for help if he's a problem."

"Mistress Meg?"

She paused at the door. "Yes?"

"I forgot to say." Tansy grinned. "He's really quite handsome. In a rough sort of way. Smoldering, you know?"

Meg chuckled. She was still smiling when she entered the Spring Green Parlor and the man turned from the window at the sound of her step.

Six

The man's back was to the light, and for a moment, she couldn't make out his features, but Tansy hadn't exaggerated. He was huge, with massive shoulders and a deep chest.

"Meggie," he said. He moved abruptly, then was still.

The world stopped. Just stopped. As though the Sister had raised Her hand and snatched it out of the air like a child's ball in a game of catch.

Meg's stomach surged up into her throat, then dropped just as sharply back into place. She opened her mouth, but nothing came out.

"Meg," said the man, taking a step forward. "Don't you know me?"

"You're . . ." Meg held up a hand as if to ward him off and he halted, staring down at her. "D-dead."

"No, not quite." The man smiled, but it was a travesty of John's smile, the one that used to light up his dark eyes.

Meg fumbled behind her for the door frame and hung on. "The clerk at Torza's told me . . ." She had to stop to breathe. Her fingertips were tingling, in a way that presaged a faint. "The ship went down."

"It did. But I was saved."

"Wait, wait." Meg rubbed her brow. "I have to . . . I need to . . . Are you real?" She stretched out a trembling hand, needing the evidence of her senses.

It was taken in a strong, comforting clasp and John drew her over to the sofa. "Are you all right?"

They sank down together, hands linked. "N-no," said Meg. His hand felt so big, so hard, even the palm covered with calluses. Where they touched, her skin stung with sensation, as if the contact burned. Tremors ran up her arm, entering her chest, making her heart flutter so hard it hurt.

"I'm sorry," said John. "I've had a few hours to get used to it. You haven't."

Completely bereft of words, she stared into his face, drinking him in, the proud, slightly beaky nose, now with a bump on it, the straight, slashing dark brows. So much the same—and yet so very different. There were lines graven into his brow, beside his nose, his mouth. His lips, once so soft and satiny-looking, were tightly compressed. And on his cheek—

Meg reached out with her other hand and cradled his jaw, noting absently that he must have shaved before he came. "Show me," she whispered. And slowly, reluctantly, John let her turn his head to the light.

"What is it?" she whispered.

"A Trinitarian slave brand." The words came out clipped and low, as though he hated the feel of them in his mouth.

"You were a slave?"

All expression smoothed out of John's face. He could have been a statue of himself, hewn in some dark, tortured wood. "Three years on the galleys."

Meg gaped, dizzy with shock. "I can't"—she shook her head— "can't imagine it. What it must have been like."

"No, I don't suppose you can." Though his mouth twisted, John lifted a hand as if to touch her cheek, then dropped it again. It trembled, very slightly. "Meg, you look wonderful. Are you working . . . Do you like it here?"

Regaining her senses a little, Meg stiffened her spine. "Yes, I do. Very much."

The silence lasted a long time while they stared. Eventually, she said, "Did you try a nut scone?"

"I ate them all," said John vaguely. "Meggie, I know I have no right to ask, but—"

Meg jerked herself free and rose to pace to the window. She stared out at the pale gleaming shapes of the night-blooming flowers, their heads tossing a little in the evening breeze off the sea. "No, you don't have any right at all." She squeezed her eyes shut, struggling with a world turned inside out. "You should know . . . first, I have to say . . . it's beyond good to see you, to know you're all right."

Behind her, the couch creaked as he shifted, but she didn't turn.

"John, you left me." She couldn't stop the stupid quaver in her voice. "All the promises you made, they were just lies. What, was I too much the country bumpkin?" Her mouth twisted. "Too fat, too stupid? *You left me.*"

"That's not how—"

Whirling around, she overrode him. "I haven't been whoring myself either, if that's what you're thinking. Not that it would matter if I had, but I didn't want anyone, not after . . ." She had to stop to catch her breath.

This time, he waited her out.

"I started here as kitchen maid and worked my way up to Housekeeper. Rose and the boys and girls, the kitchen staff, Mistress Prue, the bookkeeper, the gardener"—she gestured—"they're my family. My friends." Fortifying herself with an even deeper breath, she fell into that dark gaze. "I've done well."

"Yes, you have," he said, his voice a deep, gentle rasp. "Have you finished now?" That was one thing that hadn't changed, the natural dignity of him.

Meg felt the heat rise in her cheeks. She gave a graceless nod.

John rose to his full height. Sister, there seemed no end to him! He must have gone on growing after he enlisted, because surely he hadn't been so big at nineteen?

"I was shanghaied, Meg. A drug in my beer." A ruddy flush stained his cheeks, making the tattoo stand out dark against his olive skin. "You said it, a country bumpkin. How they must have laughed. You don't have to believe me, but that's the truth of it. By the time I came to and started puking my guts out, we were miles out to sea, with a fair wind at our back."

His lips took on a thin, bitter line. "I spent the first three years learning how to fight. I'm still very good at it." He shrugged, the movement strangely cautious. "I tried to desert four times. They almost killed me after the last effort."

Gods, so he hadn't, he hadn't . . . Reeling, Meg wet her lips. Sweet Sister, what next? She didn't know if she could take any more. "The clerk said you'd been disciplined."

"I was angry, Meg. And I used what they taught me."

All that and then three years on the galleys. Godsdammit, it was a wonder he was still sane. She cast him a sidelong glance, wondering. Anger seethed beneath the surface, leashed by his rigid control. Angry? That was a pale description. *Furious*. Hell, so was she.

"How—how did you get away?"

The look she got chilled her blood. "The Captain-Pasha employed a new whipmaster, an arrogant fool. I taunted him 'til he stepped too close. Then I"—he hesitated for a split second, then forged ahead—"strangled him with my chains and used his keys to free the others. After that . . . we killed them all."

"Sister save me!"

"I've changed, Meg," he said, his voice curt. "I can't bring back the boy I was, but I wanted to . . . I had to see you, explain." He swallowed. "I don't expect anything. I just had to see you."

"Gods, let me think." Meg flopped back on the couch, her head in a whirl, John following her down. She discovered she was gripping his hand with the strength of desperation—the only anchor in a world gone mad.

All she could think of was the waste, the godsforsaken fucking *waste*. All those years they could have been together, making a life, a family . . . Praise the Sister, She'd sent him back, but why had She taken him in the first place? Why torture them both like this? Ah gods, it was cruel!

Because this was not the John of Meg's girlhood. This man was deeply wounded, damaged. And yet she'd spent years blaming him, hunched over the hurt in her heart, unable to forgive. No wonder she'd never moved on. If truth be told, it was an emotional habit she was finding difficult to break even now. She hated him as much as she'd loved and longed for him. Gods, she'd actually believed John Lammas didn't want her, the John who'd sworn he'd loved her! Like a fool, she'd measured her worth by his apparent rejection. No wonder she'd never been able to sustain a relationship with another man.

But none of it had been his doing, none of it at all.

Uneasily, Meg recalled the image in the mirror, the quirt in her hand, the bloodlust in her heart. The bloody stripes on his back . . .

Oh gods, the way he moved. Three years on a slave galley. With a *whipmaster.*

Her stomach lurched and she had to bite her lip hard to get through the pain and the horror.

John's fingers tightened on hers. Then he lifted her hand and pressed a soft, moist kiss over the pulse in her wrist. She choked.

Oh. *Oh.*

That hadn't changed. If anything, the years of his absence had intensified his physical effect on her. Meg's entire body tingled, suffused with warmth, head to heels. The flesh between her thighs throbbed with sweet wet tension. But she got through that, too, disciplining her breathing. Because she wasn't a girl any longer.

I'm yours, she'd said to him that night in the barn. *Always.*

Clinging to John's hand, her eyes closed, Meg thought back over the years, over her lackluster attempts with other men, the new life she'd made for herself. She'd been busy surviving. She hadn't thought of her lost love every moment of every day. But inevitably, as she drifted into sleep, alone in her soft bed, some element of him would weave its way into her fading consciousness—his eyes, his deep voice, the touch of his big hands.

She'd told him true so long ago. Despite his apparent betrayal, there'd never been anyone else for her. Never would be.

A Sister-given second chance for happiness. But oh gods, it was going to be difficult. For both of them.

Meg opened her eyes. "What are you going to do now?"

She caught him staring at her breasts, his eyes hot and hungry. When she spoke, he jerked his gaze up to her face, flushing. "That depends on you. I know what I want." His grip tightened, crushing the bones in her hand. "I want my Steady Meggie back. Nothing else matters."

Abruptly, he released her and rose, as if he needed to put some distance between them. He widened his stance, his hands clenched at his sides. Parade ground rest, she thought.

"Meg, I'm damaged goods." His smile was more like a grimace. "Branded like a milkbeast. I don't see how any woman would still want me, let alone you. But you see, I kept hoping, all that time. It was all I had. I couldn't . . . couldn't help it."

He was shaking, she realized, bone-deep shudders that traveled right though his powerful frame. When she opened her mouth, he held up a hand. "No, don't speak. Let me get through this. You should know. Before you speak." He began to pull his shirt out of his waistband. "I've lost count of the number of times I've been wounded."

"No, you don't have to—"

"Yes, I do," said John grimly. "I caught a halberd to the muscle in the left thigh. That's why I limp. I will always limp. But I won't embarrass you by dropping my trews." He ripped the shirt off over his head and stood facing her, the bands of muscle in his chest washed golden by the lamplight.

Meg caught her breath.

That beautiful olive skin was slashed and pitted in half a dozen places with the white of old scars. But the light mat of black hair that arrowed down over his flat belly and the tight brown nipples were as she remembered.

John said nothing, simply waited for her to wipe away the tears. He'd gone very pale, she noted, his lips almost gray. "I'm not finished," he said eventually. His throat moved as he swallowed. "That's not the worst. This is."

Slowly, he pivoted, presenting her with his broad back, and Meg cried out, coming to her feet.

His back was a ruin, a mass of scar tissue, of stripes and slashes and bumps.

She didn't realize she was standing right behind him until her hand brushed his biceps. John flinched, but he didn't turn. "It's all right," he said to the window. "I'll go."

"No." Meg dropped her forehead to his shoulder blade, the tears streaming down her cheeks. Then she jerked away. "Gods, am I hurting you?"

"No." He turned and lifted her chin. "Don't cry for me, Meggie. Put me out of my misery. Tell me straight."

Meg gulped. What she'd give to take him to the bathhouse. They'd sink into a deep warm bath together so she could pamper and soothe and stroke. And her tears would be lost in the perfumed water. "I have a question."

He tensed. "Yes?"

Sister give her strength! Meg gathered her courage. If it meant John might drop his shields, let her in, she'd be bold, shameless even. "Are there scars on your ass?"

His brow creased. "My—? No. Why?"

Meg blinked hard and smiled, striving for her usual calm. "That's good," she said. "I was always particularly fond of your ass. I still am."

It took him a few seconds to catch up.

When he did, he gave an inarticulate cry and wrapped her in an embrace so crushing that she squeaked a protest. Sister, he was strong!

John loosened his grip a trifle, burying his face in her hair, his breath coming in painful rasps. "Give me a minute," he panted. "Hold me."

Meg gripped his upper arms and hung on, her breasts mashed against his chest. She'd never fainted in her life, but she thought she might not be far off it. Her brain felt mazy and thick, seething with an overload of incoherent thoughts and impressions.

His biceps were hard, the muscles as dense as cedderwood, the skin there hardly blemished, hot and damp under her fingers. She pressed her face against a slab of unyielding muscle and inhaled. Oh gods, oh gods, oh gods, *yes!* This was John. Not a dream of grief and pain in the night, not a fantasy or a vain hope. *Real.* The massive erection pressed against the softness of her belly told her that in no uncertain terms. If she closed her eyes and buried her hands in his hair, it was as if she were back that night in the barn. Instinctively, she rocked her hips against him and he groaned, deep in his chest.

"Meggie, don't."

"No one calls me that," she whispered, going up on tiptoe to bury her nose in the soft pit at the base of his throat. "Only you. Gods, it's been so long."

"Fuck, yes." John pulled back so he could look into her face. "Sweetheart, I'm right on the edge. I swore when I came here I wouldn't leap on you like an animal." He set her a little farther away from him and his mouth quirked. "Even if it kills me. But I have to kiss you, Meggie. *I have to.*"

When he bent his head, she met him gladly, stretching up. The first brush of lips was tentative, almost as if he'd forgotten the fit. A little bemused, tingling, Meg held still while he changed the angle a couple of times, his lips hot and smooth against hers. He was shaking again, shuddering under her hands. When she ventured to touch her tongue to the tip of his, he made a noise deep in his throat, as if his soul had torn loose, and the kiss changed completely.

John yanked her forward, plastering every inch of her against his hard, aroused body, one hand spearing into her hair to hold her still. He devoured her, there was no other word for it, sweeping his tongue into her mouth, overwhelming, unstoppable, carnal.

Only John had ever been able to do this, Meg thought muzzily. Shatter her steady control, so she forgot everything except the heat, the need to crawl inside his skin, his soul, and nestle there forever. Gods, she couldn't tell whether the licks of fire writhing in her belly and flashing up and down her spine were terror or exaltation or both. She ran a hand down his side and over his hip, feeling the unyielding solidity of his large body, relishing it. The muscles of his ass hollowed and flexed beneath her fingers.

John grunted, spreading his long fingers over her buttock, sealing her against a long thick ridge that he rocked against her, pressing fair and square against her quivering clit. Meg whimpered into his mouth. He might as well have thrust inside. Her sheath convulsed, clenching on a weeping emptiness.

Abruptly, John's hand clamped over hers. Ripping his mouth free, he panted, "Meggie, *please*—" He broke off, his cheeks ruddy with arousal and embarrassment.

"Is this what you want?" she whispered, sliding their joined clasp across the front of his trews.

His groan was answer enough.

Seven

John's cock was burning hot, even through the coarse fabric, the pulse of it thudding against her palm. Greedily, Meg wrapped her fingers around the girth as best she could, watching the erotic agony on his face. He hadn't been lying when he'd said he was right on the edge. When she squeezed, he choked and his already dark eyes went completely black with lust.

"Fuck. Oh gods. Sorry. I can't . . . can't . . ." His hand closed over hers, jerking it up and down, faster and more roughly than she would have dared on her own.

Gods, he felt huge. Wonderful. Meg's focus narrowed. The Spring Green Parlor, the slave galley, the lost years, her hurt, they all faded away in the face of the desperation before her, the man thrusting into the circle of her fingers, sweat beading his brow.

There was only John and Meggie. Meggie and John.

"Come on," she said, gripping harder, rubbing her thumb over the broad head on every up-stroke.

She leaned forward and sucked one tight brown nipple into her mouth. Then she nipped it.

"Meggie! Aaargh!"

If the sound hadn't been so guttural, she would have called it a scream. As it was, she was grateful she'd shut the door firmly behind her.

John's cock kicked hard under her palm and his hips bucked. It seemed to last for a long time, the spasms dying away slowly, each one separate and distinct, his hand helping hers to milk the last of his pleasure until he was bent half over her, gasping.

"Shit. Oh shit," he muttered into her hair. "Gods, sorry."

Slowly, he straightened. When he glanced down at the spreading stain on the front of his trews, at their sticky hands, bright washes of color bloomed across his cheeks, making the tattoo look very dark. "Meg, I— Here." Grabbing his discarded shirt, he began fumbling with her fingers.

His head down, he said stiffly, "I'm sorry. I just couldn't—" He shook his head, still busy scrubbing with the shirt.

"John," said Meg gently. Her body was still thrumming. "John, look at me."

"I'm shamed." He refused to meet her eyes. "I only meant to kiss you and I ruined it. No better than a randy boy."

"John," she insisted.

His gaze lifted, his face like stone, and her heart turned over. He hadn't changed so much after all, because this was how he'd always dealt with unhappiness or uncertainty—by locking it away in some hidden place the world couldn't see.

Carefully, she smiled, making sure he noticed. "I pushed you," she said. "Remember? We did it together." She let the smile broaden to a wicked grin. "Was it good?"

His shoulders relaxed a trifle. "I damn near passed out," he admitted. Then he tensed up again. "That would have been funny, wouldn't it?"

"No," she said as tranquilly as she could manage. "It wouldn't. Because I didn't get mine. And you're going to make it up to me." She let the silence run on for a space, her heart knocking against her ribs. "Aren't you?"

John dragged in a huge breath. "Meggie, are you sure?"

And she knew he was talking about more than physical pleasure.

"No," she said again. "But I'm sure I want to try."

John swallowed audibly. Then he sank awkwardly to his knees, favoring the bad leg, and wrapped his arms around her waist, resting his cheek against her breastbone. "Thank you." The words came out rather muffled.

Meg leaned over and dropped a kiss on his hair.

She lost track of how long they stayed like that, but eventually, John stirred. "My leg. I need to sit."

"Me, too." He got to his feet, Meg inserted herself under his arm, and together, they lurched back to the sofa.

Rolling his head against the cushions, John shot her a glance. "I'll do better next time," he said. "Just give me a minute."

A sudden, incredible suspicion entered her mind. She traced the strong complex shape of his collarbone with her fingertip. "How long has it been?"

He didn't pretend to misunderstand. "Six years, two months, and four days."

"What?" Meg reared back.

He smiled, though it hurt her to watch it. "I've only ever had one lover, Meg. Apart from my own hand."

"But—but what about—?" She flapped a hand, completely at a loss. *"No one?"*

"I didn't want a whore. I wanted you," he said, pinching the bridge of his nose. "I tried a couple of times, but in the end . . . I couldn't afford much, let alone a place like this." His gaze traveled over the elegant wallpaper, the fine furniture. "They were dirty. And they weren't you."

"But—*six years?*"

"Don't forget the two months and four days."

Meg opened her mouth and closed it again. Finally, she said lamely, "Are you hungry?"

At that, John grinned, and for a second, she saw the boy she'd once known so well. "I'm always hungry," he said. "You know that."

There was certainly no fat on him, only hard muscle, his body a mere fraction away from gaunt. She'd be willing to bet he'd only started gaining condition the moment he'd walked off that godsbe-damned galley.

She tugged at the bell pull and Tansy answered so quickly, it was clear she'd been hovering. Slipping out the door, Meg pulled it closed behind her and smiled into the girl's anxious face. "I'm fine," she said quickly. "Bring a meal, would you? As quick as you can. Cold cuts will do. And a jug of wine."

Tansy nodded and trotted off down the passage.

"Oh, and a bath robe, please. A large one."

The girl looked over her shoulder, the curiosity that crossed her features tangible. Meg was still smiling as she turned back into the parlor.

"What's so funny?"

And it hit her all over again.

There he was, sprawled across the couch, his huge masculine presence filling the elegant room. John. *John.* She'd never seen anything more thrilling in her life. Nor more terrifying.

The tears welled up afresh, spilling over before she could wipe them away. "It's so good to see you," she whispered. What stupid, inadequate words!

But he seemed to understand. Leaning forward, he held out a hand. "Come here."

Stumbling, Meg fell into his arms, but he didn't even grunt. Instead, he tilted up her chin, bent his head, and kissed her.

He did it slowly, and with enormous pleasure, making it an oral seduction, cradling her face in both big palms. Their breath mingled and warmed, while he nibbled at her lips, feathering his thumbs across her cheeks. His tongue danced and cajoled, coaxed and caressed. He showed no sign of impatience, as if they had all the time in the world—the rest of their lives. It wasn't so much an exploration as a homecoming.

Gradually, Meg relaxed, her body softening, melting into John's. One hand crept up over his arm, his shoulder, to clasp the back of his neck, his hair feathering cool across her knuckles.

When he began to pull back, she murmured a protest and clung harder. Gently, John freed his mouth. "At the door, love. There's someone at the door."

Feeling drugged, Meg untangled herself, John holding her steady until she could stand without trembling. "That's supper," she husked.

It wasn't until Tansy was in the room, carefully placing the loaded tray on a low table, that Meg remembered. Sister, the wet patch on his trews! But when she spun around, John was standing casually behind the couch, slipping into his shirt. Catching her expression, his lips twitched, almost imperceptibly, but her heart ached. The old John would have shot her a wink, his face alight with mischief.

Tansy straightened, her head bent deferentially as was proper, but Meg knew the little apprentice too well to be deceived. She glanced at the array of dishes on the table and sighed. A feast, everything suitable for a special occasion, even two slices of curdle pie, piped with delicate roses of brandied cream.

If Cook knew, then everyone in The Garden would be aware Mistress Meg had an Important Visitor. And that she looked flushed and rumpled and thoroughly kissed.

She bent a cold eye on Tansy and the girl grinned, unabashed. Gracefully, the apprentice sank into a curtsey suitable for a client of highest rank. Then she raised delicate brows, her face the picture of innocent inquiry.

Meg bit the inside of her cheek. Oh well.

"John," she said. "This is Tansy, a second-year courtesan-apprentice." He gave a stiff nod and she realized he was surprised. He'd thought the girl was just a maid.

"Tansy, this is John Lammas, an old . . . friend of mine." Out of the corner of her eye, she noticed John go very still. Inhaling deeply, she clasped her hands before her and said calmly, "We will be seeing a good deal of him, here at The Garden."

"Yes, Mistress Meg," murmured Tansy, a dimple flashing. "I'll remember."

I bet you will, little imp, thought Meg, but the door was already closing softly. Tansy had gone.

Aloud, she said, "The robe's for you." She tossed it over the back of the couch. "So is the supper."

Looking a little bemused, John sat down to tug at his boots and she added, "I'll wash those trews. Where are your things?"

"I don't have much." He set one boot aside and went to work on the other. "I left my pack with the barkeep at The Sailor's Lay."

"Then how—?" Meg broke off, puzzled. "Chits for The Garden aren't cheap."

"You're telling me," he said ruefully, straightening. "I bought it from Rhiomard. He's how I found you."

"But where—?" She clamped her lips shut. All too clearly, she recalled the Lammas pride. Stiff-rumped, the lot of them, especially about money.

John put his hands to the laces of his trews and paused. He set his jaw. "I'm not asking for your charity, Meg, if that's what you're thinking."

"I know that," she said fiercely. "But it wouldn't matter even if you were."

"Ah, but it does." His lips took on that bitter twist she was starting to dread and she cursed her own stupidity. "A Trinitarian galley's worth a lot of money, even split among every slave on board. With that and my back pay, I've got enough."

This time, the silence was awkward.

Finally, John exhaled, a long breath. "Am I staying?"

She'd always been able to read his face, every expression as clear to her as if she were privy to the workings of his soul. Now, though . . .

Her gaze dropped to the fist gripping the robe. The knuckles shone white.

When the Sister sent a second chance, you seized it—no questions asked.

"I'd like you to," she said simply. "We can eat here, but I have a small suite upstairs."

John cleared his throat. "Does it have a bed in it?"

The giggle was undoubtedly part hysteria, but she couldn't stop it bubbling out of her throat. "Yes."

And a corset.

Where had that come from? Though, now she came to think of it . . . he'd adore the sight of her creamy curves showcased in tight black velvet.

He'd worship—on his knees.

John stepped back behind the couch, shoved the trews down in one smooth motion, and kicked them away. He reached for the robe.

"John? You said . . ." She had to pause to clear her throat. "You . . . don't have scars all over."

He froze. "No."

"Let me see," she whispered.

Meg held his eye, her heart thundering, watching while he made his decision.

His cheeks flushed a dull red, he walked slowly forward. Wearing only the open shirt, he spread his legs and set his hands on his hips. "Not all over," he said in a husky rumble. "You see?"

Inevitably, Meg's gaze dropped to his genitals. She skittered away to glance at the lumpy scar on one thigh, then back again, as if drawn by a lodestone. Merciful—!

She had to breathe through her open mouth, panting like a runner. This part of him had fascinated her from the very beginning, the only part of a man's body not completely under his control. Gods, how she'd loved to drive him out of his mind! Vividly, she could recall his thickness, pressed throbbing against her hard palate, while she lashed the underside with her tongue and made him groan. The soft, tense furriness of his testicles as she stroked over the seam with her fingertips. And the smell of him, musky and rich and almost overpowering. Aroused male.

When she licked her lips, he murmured something, but she barely heard the words. Because he was rising to meet her gaze, filling and lengthening. The head emerged, rosy and ripe, already gleaming. She knew it would be dense and smooth to touch, salty-hot against her tongue.

Some dark, female power washed through Meg. This primeval display was for her, *because* of her. It didn't matter if John was shamed by his blatant response; she didn't care.

"Gods," she croaked, running her gaze over him from head to heels, six and a half feet of honed muscle and sinew and bone—only to become entangled once more with the meaty arch of his cock. "I don't believe it, but you've grown."

At his rasping chuckle, a blush scorched its way out of the bodice of her gown and over her throat. Sister, she felt incandescent, as if she'd self-combust at any moment. Her face must be scarlet. And she could barely stand still, besieged by the temptation to shove the heel of her hand against her clit for relief. It throbbed at her, the ache increasing exponentially with every beat of her heart. When she pressed her thighs together, they were slick, her sex as soft and slippery as butter in the sun.

"John?"

His fingers twitched against his thigh. "Yes?"

"Did you think of me when you . . ." She fought for control. Wasn't she Steady Meggie? "Used your hand, the way you said?"

"Every single time." His smile was slow, but very male.

"Show me."

His flush intensified, but eventually, he reached down, running a hand over his muscled belly and down into the nest of springy black curls. His dark gaze never leaving Meg's, he cupped his balls, as if testing their weight. Then he cradled his cock, giving it an affectionate squeeze that lengthened it by another impossible half inch.

He wet his lips. "Meggie, I dreamed of your beautiful tits every night for six years. I want to see. *Please.*"

"I had a dream too." Her hands shaking, Meg unlaced the front of her gown and opened it as far as she could, exposing her breasts almost to the areolas. "The night you left," she said, "I dreamed of you. Tied to that big post in the barn. At my mercy."

John threw his head back, the tendons in his neck standing proud. "Meggie!" He spread his legs, his grip tightening.

"John Lammas," she said severely. "Now you're flaunting yourself."

Another chuckle, rusty with disuse. "I believe so. But there's better things we could be doing." He took a step forward. "Meggie? Love?"

Meg's nipples were so stiff, so distended, the soft scrape of the fabric was an exquisite torment.

They'd look better in the corset.

"Upstairs," she whispered. "Come upstairs with me."

Eight

"No." In two strides John was on her. "I'll explode." He buried his nose in her cleavage and inhaled so deeply she grew a little anxious waiting for him to breathe out. When he drew back, his eyes were sheened, as though with tears. "Dear gods, I don't believe it." He blinked hard. "You smell the same."

Together they fumbled with laces and tapes, until Meg stood, clad only in her open shift, gartered stockings, and shoes.

Chest heaving, John reached out and, with his palms, smoothed the shift back over her shoulders, exposing her body, one creamy freckled inch at a time. His gaze locked on her breasts, and immediately, her skin felt too small, her nipples too big, so proud with blood, they stood up a ruddy rose-brown.

"Gods," he breathed. "You're a banquet." As he slid a hand back down over her breast and cupped it gently, the shift slithered to the floor.

Involuntarily, she thrust up into his touch and they both gasped. Gritting her teeth, Meg said, "More."

"Meggie—" He stopped and started again. "Even after . . . I still don't have much control. I might . . ."

Meg lost her patience, gloriously and completely. She dug her fingers into his shoulders and bared her teeth. "Godsdammit, I don't bloody care," she snarled. "I've been waiting for years. Do it, damn you!"

For the first time, she heard him laugh. No more than a harsh bark, but a laugh nonetheless.

A single step forward, and he had her pinned against the wall, his big hands gripping the generous curves of her ass. Automatically she drew one leg up, over his hip, and he grasped it, hitching her higher, until something blunt and smooth and hot was furrowing through her cleft, setting off a wave of tingles behind her clit that made the breath catch in her throat.

"Oh fuck, *yes!*" It was as much a shout of triumph as a groan of joy. John surged forward, seating half his length in one plunge and Meg cried out.

"All . . . right?" panted John. But even as he spoke, he grabbed her other thigh and rammed her so hard against the wall, a picture wobbled and fell off its hook with a tinkling crash.

Meg tilted her hips, wrapping her legs around his waist. Which meant opening herself completely, trusting herself to his strength. No one but John had ever filled her this way, a delicious discomfort that required movement. No, nothing as paltry as *movement*—pounding, hammering, thrusting.

Fucking.

As if he'd read her mind, he pulled out in a long glide and thrust back, all the way to the hilt, the luscious friction making her sheath convulse, clamping down hard against his shaft. The breath hissed between his clenched teeth. "Gods," he muttered. "Gods, that's good. Oh, Meggie—"

Abruptly, he increased the pace, until he was leaning right into her body, pounding into her with his full, fat length. There was no finesse to it, only a desperate, brutal desire, but he was hitting her clit full on with every stroke. The orgasm gathered in her loins, coiling tighter and tighter, quivering, ratcheted up so far she feared she might literally fly to pieces when it released.

The skin under her fingers was very hot, even through the thin fabric of the shirt. Meg strained upward, suddenly missing him desperately, even though he was right there, filling her so deep with his heat and hardness and need. Little animal noises fell out of her mouth, feral and ravenous.

Without missing a beat, John lurched forward a step, sealing them belly to belly. His dark eyes glared down into Meg's, utterly intent, owning her soul. "C'mon," he growled. "I can't . . ." He squeezed his eyes closed, then opened them again.

"Dammit—woman—*come*." Each word was punctuated by a thrust, the new angle hitting her perfectly.

She'd been right to fear the shocking impact of that climax. When it broke, Meg did, too, wailing her pleasure, the tears streaming down her cheeks as she shuddered and jerked with the all-encompassing force of it. Spots danced before her eyes.

John groaned as if the heart were being torn from his body. He jammed himself hard and high inside her, and froze, shuddering. Against hers, his belly rippled with the force of his climax. It seemed to last forever, six years' worth of love and lust and frustration. But eventually, he dropped his head to the curve between her shoulder and her neck. She felt the gentle press of his open mouth, his breath puffing hot and moist against her skin.

All she could do was clutch his shoulders and sag against him. "John," she breathed. "Oh, John. Love."

He staggered a little, the bad leg giving out. "Shit. Forgot." A pained grunt as he helped her lower her feet to the floor.

Sweet Sister. It wasn't as though she was a light weight and with a wound like that . . . She tugged his arm. "Over here." They collapsed onto the couch together.

Meg turned her head on the cushions to find John watching her, breathing hard, his eyes as black as ink. An instant's charged silence while he searched her face and his expression relaxed, his lips curving. "Gods," he said, "that was almost worth the wait. All those years . . ." He drew her into his arms and she settled with her head on his shoulder, a perfect fit. His hand rose to stroke her hair, but even though the touch was light, the feathery strands snagged, the calluses on his palms reminding her that things would never be the same. Not quite.

John's voice rumbled softly out of the shadows. Dusk had drawn down and the single lamp provided only a small oasis of light. "Do you know, I've had more peace in this last little while than I have since the day I rode out of Holdercroft?"

Meg said nothing, only laid her hand over his heart.

"Meggie, I'm so tired." A long pause while he laid his cheek on the top of her head. "Even my bones are tired."

"Sleep then," she whispered against his throat. "I've got you."

His grip tightened. "Have you? Have you truly?"

Meg shifted so she could stare directly into his eyes. "Whatever we once had . . ." She paused, thinking it through, feeling the rightness of his presence settle deep into her soul, filling all the empty places that had ached for him. "It's still there." She pulled away, studying his expression, picking her words with care. "That night in the barn, I told you I was yours. Forever. I didn't say those words lightly." Her smile came out crooked. "Which is just as well, because it looks like they're still true. In spite of everything."

John touched his fingertips to her cheek. They trembled. "My Steady Meggie. My peace, my heart. I never stopped loving you. Never."

Meg laid her hand over his. "Well, I tried not to love you. You'd left me after all. Sshh, don't speak. I know. But it *hurt*, John. Gods, how it hurt. I thought you didn't love me enough, or perhaps you'd never loved me at all." She ducked her head, unable to bear the anguish in his eyes.

"And now you know the truth?"

She forced herself to meet his gaze. "You don't change a habit of thought the way you change your clothes. I've been angry with you a long time, John Lammas."

His jaw set, and suddenly she had no doubt about who'd led the mutiny on board that galley. "Do you love me, Meggie?" he demanded. "Enough to try?"

"Oh, yes." She suspected she was crying again. "More than that."

John closed his eyes. "Praise the Brother. Come back here." He wrapped his arms around her.

After five soft-breathing minutes, Meg murmured, "Come upstairs to bed. There's too much of you for this poor little sofa."

No answer. She glanced up at his profile, silhouetted against the lamp light, the thick, sooty-black eyelashes, the strong jaw, the dark stain of the tattoo. Relaxed in sleep, his lips soft, he looked more like the boy she remembered. But the tear tracks shining on his cheek gave memory the lie. She'd never seen John cry.

He'd always been stoic, even as a lad, the only recourse of a re-served sensitive nature amid the turmoil that was the Lammas clan. Meg snuggled harder, staring unseeing into the gathering shadows, waiting for sleep. She'd been his sanctuary then. But now? She wasn't sure she could do it, or even that she wanted to. So much pain, bur-ied so deep he could only release the tears in his dreams.

She woke before dawn, completely disoriented. A deep voice mut-tered in her ear, "No, fuck you." A pause. "Stop, stop! Ah, shit!"

John! She shot upright.

Immediately, her wrist was seized in an iron grip. "Don't move!" A big hand grabbed her shoulder, crushing bone and muscle with merciless strength.

Meg yelped.

In the cool light, John's eyes met hers. There was no sleep in his face, only fierce concentration. Sister, was this how he'd been accus-tomed to waking? Battle-ready?

He blinked. "Shit, Meg." Immediately, he released her. "Sorry. Did I hurt you?"

"No," she lied, forcing a smile. "It was a shock, that's all."

Surreptitiously, she rubbed her wrist.

He blew out a long breath. "You sure?'

When she nodded, he rolled his shoulders, releasing the tension. "I heard mention of a bed?"

⚜

She'd done well, his Meggie. John's eyes widened as he took in the two rooms, a small sitting room cum office and a larger bedchamber. The furnishings were solid and well made, and there was a good deal of blue and cream. A Meggie sort of room.

His guts were still tangled in a spiky ball, and if he wasn't care-ful, the feeling spread to his extremities so his hands shook like an old man's. He was aware he was watching Meg like a hungry corpse-bird, but he couldn't help it. *Did it,* ran the primitive litany in his head. *Fuck, I did it. Meggie, Meggie, it's Meggie!* She'd seen his scars, every one of them, and she hadn't run screaming. It had been one of his greatest fears. Second only to finding her married, another man's babe in her arms. He wasn't entirely sure he wouldn't wake and discover she was a figment of a particularly cruel dream. Brother's balls, it had happened to him often enough before.

She'd cried at the sight of his back, the sweetheart. Even through the ridges of thickened tissue, he'd felt the hot splash of her tears. After that, he'd managed to keep the shirt on. Once was enough. She didn't need to see it again.

Gods, how he wanted her! Right now, right here, on the wide bed he could glimpse through the door. He wanted to take those creamy thighs in his big hands and pull them wide so he could gorge himself on her salty-sweetness, hear her whimper with the pleasure he gave her. The spray of freckles on her breast drove him insane with the urge to nuzzle and lick. But most of all—he drew a fortifying breath—he needed to fuck, to feel her slick, honeyed flesh grip his length like a hot muscular fist until he spilled his seed deep inside her in a long ecstatic rush from balls to cock. Gods, he *craved* it.

Every time he inhaled, he smelled her, his Meggie. Fresh and warm and feminine all at once. So familiar, so dear, he was tempted to sit on the edge of her bed, put his head in his hands, and cry like a little boy.

She was unloading the tray in her usual unhurried fashion, and despite himself, John's mouth watered. It had taken him a few weeks to become accustomed to real food in decent quantities again. He'd done it by eating little and often.

"Here you are." A smile lighting her blue-gray eyes, she brought him a full plate.

He didn't trust himself to speak, so he grunted his thanks. Meg patted his shoulder and gestured to one of two comfortable chairs, drawn close enough for an intimate conversation. Gingerly, John sat, trying to recall his long-forgotten manners and keep the robe closed over his unruly cock.

Deep breaths, one after the other. He could do this. Hell, he had his Steady Meggie back, he could do anything! Automatically, John chewed and swallowed while he absorbed her presence through every pore of his skin.

As the light grew and the sun poured in the window, his heart gradually stopped pounding and that horrible spiky feeling smoothed out. The staff of The Garden woke to face their day. Doors opened and closed, feet pattered down the stairs, a cheerful voice was raised in a snatch of song.

"Do you have to go?" he asked reluctantly. Slow and sweet, that's how he wanted it. Until she was moaning his name with every deep thrust, overwhelmed with pleasure. Then he wanted to lie and hold her, just hold her.

Meg smiled over the rim of her cup. Her eyes were the prettiest shade of blue, not bold like a summer's midday, but soft and luminous, like the hour before dusk. "As the Housekeeper, I'm in charge. But I think they can do without me for a day, under the circumstances."

"What does a Housekeeper do?"

So she told him of her duties, all the everyday, ordinary things she did to keep such a complex establishment running. John heard the words, his brain made sense of the sentences, but it was the timbre of her low voice that enthralled him, a balm for his soul.

When she rose, lifting the tray, he very nearly grabbed her skirt and hauled her back. Her sweet lips curved as if she'd divined the thought. "I have something special for us," she said with a twinkle. "I checked the appointment diary and the Bruised Orchid's free. Give me an hour to rearrange my day. Any of the staff will show you where it is."

"The Bruised Orchid? What's that?"

Meg's cheeks went pink. "One of the Pavilions. Top-of-the-range luxury, with its own bathhouse and other, um, equipment."

John quirked a brow. "Equipment?"

The flush deepened. "We don't have to use it. But the Orchid's the very best. It's beautiful and we deserve it."

At that, he had to kiss her. She would have been flat on her back on the bed ten seconds later if it wasn't for the tray.

⨯⨯⨯

Godsdammit, she felt wonderful, as if she could take on the world. Meg strode down the winding path toward the Bruised Orchid, her heart beating hard beneath tight black velvet. She smiled at her favorite touchme bush, as tall as her head. But when she brushed her fingertips across the fringed silver blossoms, instead of the usual happy chime of greeting, the flowers hissed and drew away.

Stupid thing.

Shrugging, she threw open the door of the Bruised Orchid and stopped dead on the threshold.

Merciful Sister! Tansy had outdone her instructions.

On the wide bed, John lounged against a heap of jewel-toned pillows, the sort of hard-edged fantasy only wicked women were strong enough to have. He was wearing a fanciful version of a battle kilt, the linen skirt and studded leather strips stopping at mid-thigh, so she could see the lower edge of the scar. He'd always had wonderful legs, lean and powerful, roped with muscle and dusted with dark hair. Under the kilt, his cock stirred, lengthening as she watched. A vest of bleached linen hung open over his chest, framing it. It left his arms bare, the smooth swelling line of his biceps making her yearn to sink her teeth in and worry at firm flesh.

A growl rose in her throat.

"I feel like a fool, but Tansy said you'd like it." John spread his arms, and her gaze zeroed in on the ugly scars circling his thick wrists.

Meg didn't waste words. With a jerk, she tore open her gown and let it fall.

John was on his feet and in front of her before she saw him move. *"Meggie!"* His Adam's apple bobbed. "You look—" He shook his head, apparently speechless.

"Beautiful, isn't it?" Honesty compelled her to add, "It's not mine, though. I have to give it back."

No you don't, something murmured in her head. *No one will ever know.*

"Oh, I couldn't," she said.

A stitch popped in the corset and John arched a brow. "What?"

"Nothing."

She couldn't take her eyes from his mouth, the firm masculine curves of it, the blood beating beneath the smooth skin. Meg rose to her tiptoes and tugged his head down, gripping the back of his neck. He bent to her gladly, rumbling something deep in his chest, his kiss intent and forceful, dominating.

Meg met strength with strength, her excitement mounting. She pushed harder into his unyielding body, greed swamping her, fraying at her control. Taking his lower lip between her teeth, she worried at it.

Six years. He's only a man, he lied. How many? How many whores? Filthy . . .

Meg nipped hard and John's lip split. She licked at the sweet taste of blood.

"Shit." Despite the grip of her clawed fingers, John drew back, wiping a smear of red from his lip. "Slow down, sweetheart. Let's make it last this time." When he smoothed a curl behind her ear, Meg batted his hand away and he frowned.

"Sorry. I didn't mean to hurt you." Meg rubbed her eyes, her head buzzing. "I don't really know why I did that."

John smiled his slow serious smile and slung a heavy arm across her shoulders. "It's nothing," he said. "Come and show me this Bruised Orchid of yours. I haven't had time to explore." When he skated his palm down over her spine to pat her bottom, Meg laughed, her tension easing.

"It's, um, very dramatic, isn't it?" she said, gazing at the huge four-poster bed, the tall burnished doors that concealed an extraordinary range of whips, paddles, and cuffs. The richness was reflected in the mirrors lining the wall, as if there were a second pavilion, a secret space where fantasies were made manifest. The patina of rich dark wood was everywhere, polished to a high shine. Not a speck of dust. All was as it should be.

Fastened securely against the wall, a heavy wooden whipping cross gleamed magnificently, the light sparkling off dangling chains. Pressed so closely against John's side, she felt the instinctive recoil ripple through him.

"It's all right," she said immediately.

John squeezed her waist. "I prefer the bed."

Meg frowned. There were other Pavilions with magnificent beds, decadent bathrooms. The Bruised Orchid had never really appealed to her, so why had she chosen it?

"The bath's through here." She led him into the adjoining chamber.

"Impressive." John gazed at the deep square tub, at its cunningly curved shelves and steps, his dark eyes bright with wicked speculation. "You could fit six in there."

"I can arrange it, if that's what you want."

Had that been her voice, so mean and shrill?

"No." John's face hardened. "It is not what I want. Why would you think that, Meg?"

Meg's belly turned a slow, uneasy somersault. What was *wrong* with her? "It was a stupid thing to say." When she pulled in a deep breath, she thought she heard the corset creak, another stitch snap. "I apologize." She ran her thumb over a seam. Yes, another half-inch. Perhaps she should loosen it a trifle. "I'm sorry." She gave an uneasy laugh. "Again."

Odd, she could have sworn the laces tightened, just a fraction.

Nine

"All I want is you." John nuzzled her hair. "In that bed. I'm going to make you scream, Meggie."

Scream? We'll see who screams. Left, you left . . .

Meg felt shivery, her brain soupy, almost as if she were coming down with the ague, yet every now and then, a thought appeared out of the fog, honed sharp with purpose.

Now was not the time to succumb to weakness. Meg shook off the muzzy feeling and squared her shoulders, the boning of the corset enforcing perfect posture. Taking John's hand, she led him back to the bedchamber without a word.

"Is it popular, this sort of thing?" He stopped beside the cross and looked it up and down, his mouth thin with distaste.

"Oh yes." Meg's lips drew back from her teeth. "We have clients who crave pain. And courtesans who specialize in the loving administration of it."

John's brows drew together.

"Feel the weight of the thing," said Meg, and the background noise in her head began to boom and recede like a dark surf, timed to the beats of her heart. "It's so solid I doubt even you could shift it."

John raised a brow. "You think?" He slid his palm along one diagonal of the cross, right to the top.

Vain, so vain. Stupid man.

The surf was crashing in Meg's head, so loud, she couldn't think over the roar of it, could only feel, only do as impulse dictated. Swiftly, she stretched up and locked the waiting manacle around his wrist. The snick of the mechanism engaging sounded very loud.

"Meg?" said John, his brow creasing. "Meggie, what are you doing?" He fumbled at the shackle with his free hand. "Where's the key?"

Her lips were numb. "Cupboard," she whispered hoarsely. Sister, the words were difficult to say! "Get . . . I'll get it." She took three wobbly paces and flung open the doors.

Leather, black and red. Silver and steel, row upon serried row, gleaming in the light.

When she turned back, she had the metal-tipped quirt in her hand, the one from her vision in the mirror.

John glanced from her face to the whip and back again. When he lost color, something inside her howled with glee. *Now you see, betrayer. Pay, ah Shaitan, you will pay!*

"Meggie," he said, very low, holding her eye. "What's wrong?"

Abandoned, left. Not good enough. Too fat, too dull, too stupid.

Ruthless fingers poked at the wound in her soul, ripping at the scabs, making it bleed afresh. Oh, it hurt, hurt so much.

He didn't care then. He doesn't now.

"Are you listening to me? Meg, what's the matter?"

"Everything. John, I—" The corset tightened, compressing her ribs unbearably. Meg gasped for air and the rush of blood behind her temples stabbed like knives.

"You haven't forgiven me for leaving, is that it?" His face was grim. "I thought I'd made it clear. I had no say in the matter."

"Yes, I have. Nngh!" Now her vision was hazing, a bestial roar filling her skull like a storm.

"No." She raised the quirt. "No, I haven't. I'll never forgive you, *never!*" On the last word, the whip flashed down, riding on the scream of hate that ripped out of her throat. All her strength was behind the blow, but John twisted aside at the last moment and it caught him across the back of the thigh.

"Aaargh! Shit!" He clapped a hand over the welt and blood trickled from beneath his fingers. "What the *fuck* do you think you're doing?" Fury darkened his face.

Oh, he's easy. It's so good, so very good. Trapped like a fish on a line. More, do more.

Dropping to her knees, Meg clutched at her head, tugging viciously at her own hair. "No," she rasped. "Sister, I must be mad."

She raised her eyes to John's and saw absolute horror replace the rage. "Help . . . me." The words emerged in a tortured whisper.

"Gods, your eyes are as black as the corset. Meg, what——?"

But she sprang to her feet, glorious in her wrath and her vengeance. A quick step sideways, and she was behind him. Insane strength poured through her in a dark stream. Still gripping the quirt in one fist, Meg grasped his vest in both hands and tore it from top to bottom.

John gave a startled grunt that turned to a shouted curse when she caught him fair across the shoulders with a cracking blow. The cross rattled against the wall, but it didn't budge. More quickly than she could credit, he spun around, putting his back to the wood, his chest heaving. "Meg," he said. And then more loudly, "*Meggie!* Stop this, it's crazy." He jerked at the manacle, his triceps rippling with power. "Shit! What the *fuck* is wrong with you?"

Meg stood panting. In some far-off corner of her mind, she could hear herself, screaming, struggling, but waves of bloodlust swamped her mind, overriding her control. She caught a glimpse of herself in the mirror, her hair streaming behind her, her lush, creamy curves magnificently showcased in black velvet, the gems glittering like opened arteries on her breast. Her face was set in a rictus of a grin, and yes, John was right, her eyes had gone utterly black, but they were tinged with ruby flames.

She looked like the goddess of death incarnate.

You are. We *are.*

Look at him, taste his pain. Ah, he's beautiful. Roll the agony around in your mouth, feel it deep inside, better than a hard cock.

Horribly, she was aroused, her sex swollen like a ripe fruit. Moisture trickled down the inside of her thigh. She could smell it, earthy and somehow feral.

Merciful Sister, no. *No!* Meg choked, a sour burn in her throat. But before she could think, could set herself to resist, power rose from the small of her back, where the corset laces pressed against her skin. It spiraled up her spine, a great roaring gout of it, driven by a cruel wind.

There was no room there for Margaret May Mackie, for John's Meggie, only for blood and vengeance. Appalled, Meg watched her arm rise and the quirt whistle down, laying a stripe across John's chest that went white, then filled with an angry pink. On the heels of the blow, he reached out with a warrior's trained reflexes and grabbed her waist, pulling her almost off her feet, strong fingers digging into black velvet.

Almost immediately, he released her. "Fuck!" He shook his hand vigorously. "It burned me! *Burned* me." He'd lost so much color, his lips were gray. His intent gaze fastened on her face. "Meg, take the fucking thing off. Now!" The last word was a barked command any soldier would have jumped to obey.

"Yes, yes!" At least, that's what she meant to say. Instead, Meg felt her lip curl in a sneer. "Am I beautiful?" she demanded. She spread her legs, showing him the puffy folds between her thighs.

One arm still fastened over his head, John straightened, staring, his dark eyes very direct, every muscle tense. Gods, what a formidable man he'd become!

Betrayers come in all sizes. No man is faithful.

With a tremendous effort, Meg whispered, "My father . . ." Cool air kissed her flesh where the side seam opened another inch.

The corset was crushing her breasts against her ribs. It hurt. *Not in his mind. A sewer, like all men. Want to see?*

Holding her eye, John said, "You are *not* beautiful in that thing. It's ugly. Take it off."

The bloodstorm in Meg's head went insane.

As if she'd been whipping strong men all her life, she waded in, the quirt rising and falling, the welts blooming across John's chest, his ribs, his stomach. Tears streamed down her cheeks, yet her mouth snarled, her panting breath scented with hatred.

With a grunt, John swung around, exposing his ruined back to the lash. He set one knee against the center of the cross and gripped the manacle with both fists. The muscles in his massive shoulders swelled and bunched with power. Wood creaked and the quirt lashed down, drawing blood from scar tissue.

Sister, it was the bravest thing she'd ever seen! As if the vision had been conjured from the depths of the cold hells, she saw him shackled to an oar, his hair long and matted, his body bare save for a rough loincloth. A long lash snaked out, curling over his hunched shoulders in a vicious kiss, wielded by a slim, pouty-lipped youth in an embroidered satin jacket. John made no sound, though his jaw bunched with strain. He could have broken the boy over his knee.

Gods, it was the whipmaster!

A cold sweat popped on Meg's brow, her stomach heaved and pitched. In the ensuing paroxysm, she managed to uncramp her fingers. The quirt fell with a small clatter and rolled closer to the bed.

Get it.

Meg shoved her hands into her armpits and hung on. "N-n—" she said through clenched teeth and another half a dozen stitches unraveled.

The silence inside her head lasted for no more than a heartbeat, though it seemed forever. On the periphery of her consciousness, she could hear John swearing, the chains rattling. Against her spine, the laces slithered, slick as sewersnakes. Then they tightened, a half-inch at a time, the beautiful black velvet ponderous as a giant crusher worm.

Get it. A vicious hiss.

Meg fell to her knees, writhing, her ribs cracking. Speech was beyond her. Rolling, she attempted to reach for the laces, but she couldn't suck in enough air to move her arm, though her lungs labored. Sister, she was going to die!

With the last of her strength, she focused her failing vision on John. Blood ran down his arm from under the manacle, but he was ignoring it, his dark eyes burning into hers, full of horror and fury. "J-John," she mouthed.

Pulling in a huge breath, he took a fresh grip on the cold metal. "I'm coming. Hold on." The muscled shoulders that had pulled a heavy oar day after day for three long years took the strain. With a bellow that shook the walls, he gave a final desperate heave, the power of it coming as much from muscular buttocks and strong back as from his upper body. Wood and metal groaned and the manacle ripped free.

But he didn't dive on her as she expected. Instead, he whirled away, out of her sight. Meg must have blacked out, because she roused to the feel of cold metal against her spine, the blessed sensation of the corset falling away.

Air returned to her lungs in a painful whoop, making her choke and splutter. Strong arms gathered her up as if she weighed less than nothing and she was pressed against a hard, warm, breathing surface. "Meggie? Look at me. *Meggie!*"

It took an extraordinary effort to force her eyes open. The moment she did, John blew out a long breath. "Thank the Brother." He rose smoothly, Meg still cradled in his arms, and strode over to the bed. When he laid her down, she clutched at him with desperate fingers, but he drew away. "Wait a moment, love," he said, in a voice as hard as winter iron. "There's something I have to do."

Her head swimming, she watched him scoop up a long dagger from the floor. Sliding the tip under the small patch of midnight velvet, he lifted it with a grimace of distaste and tossed it into the fireplace. The pale, bumpy ridges on his back were crisscrossed with fresh welts and smeared with blood. One forearm was dappled with it. Meg squeezed her eyes shut in an agony of remorse. Oh gods, what had she done?

By the time she'd found the courage to open them again, he'd got a fire going. As she watched, the first hungry flame nibbled the edge of the corset and a flare of green phosphorescence shot up with an angry hiss. Then another and another.

John gave a grunt of satisfaction and padded back to the bed. He stood looking down at her, his face unreadable. A warrior's face. "Where did you get it?"

Meg struggled to her elbows. "Sorry, John, I'm so sorry. I don't know why . . . how I . . ." Tears overtook her.

"I do. Where did you get it, Meg?"

She raised a hand, only to let it fall. No wonder he didn't want to touch her. "It was Shalla-Mae's. I . . ." A guilty flush bloomed on her cheeks. "Took it."

John ignored the last part. His eyes narrowed. "What do you mean *was?*"

Meg abandoned her pride. "John. Please." She held out her arms.

His face contorted. Taking her hand, he dropped to his knees beside the bed and pressed her palm to his cheek. "Sweetheart, I'm all over blood. Look what I've done already." He nodded at her nude body.

Startled, Meg glanced down. A long red smear marred the curve of one breast, another lay across the pale swell of her belly, just above the dark gold of her pubic curls.

"Godsdammit, what does it matter?" Tears choked her voice. "You saved my life. Even after I—" She couldn't go on. Instead, she reared up and brushed her lips across his tanned chest, in the space between two slashes.

His fingers moved in her hair. "I don't think it was you, Meggie. Tell me about this Shalla person."

"Yes." She dashed the tears away. "But in the bath." Cautiously, she straightened. "We should clean those welts, get some healall on them."

John glanced at the fire, still burning a high, vicious green. "Should be safe enough. Can you stand?"

"Of course." Meg swung her feet to the floor and rose. Automatically, she moved close, slipping her arm around his waist before she remembered. Flushing, she pulled away.

John didn't flinch. He leaned down to plant a gentle kiss on her cheek. "I'll be fine, Meggie. The Brother knows, I've had far worse."

"But not at my hand." She glanced up at his face, but all she could think of was his poor back, the old scars and the new. Her guts turned over. Gods, the new scars she alone was responsible for! "Let me get the key for those cuffs and then I'll make it better, I promise."

"Look at me, sweetheart." When she managed it at last, he touched her hair. "Then you can make it better." One corner of his mouth quirked. "Will you kiss it for me?"

Sweet Sister, how she'd missed that expression! Her heart ached.

"Oh, yes." Tugging on his hand, Meg started for the bath chamber, averting her eyes from the fireplace. "Wherever. Whenever."

The bath water steamed, a pale yellowish green. No wonder. Meg had poured three full vials of healall into it, turning a deaf ear to his protests. The welts stung like a bitch in the warm water, but they were nothing really, not even the ones across his back.

It wasn't the injuries that worried him, but how they'd come about. Suppressing a shiver, John leaned back cautiously into the concave shape at the end of the tub, drawing Meggie between his open legs. Deeply troubled, he nuzzled her hair, trickling water over those luscious tits with his cupped palm, watching the soft pink nipples bead up and turn dusky.

He blew out a long breath. "Tell me about Shalla-Mae," he said.

He'd always loved the sound of Meggie's voice, low and pleasing, with the slight burr of the familiar Cressy accent. It had deepened as she'd matured. But as she spoke, his guts contracted with horror, bit by bit, until a cold lump lay hard and heavy in the pit of his belly. Gods, enough hate and despair for a murder and a suicide. From out of nowhere.

Magick. *Shit*. Black Magick.

He must have let the words slip out, because Meg twisted in his arms to stare into his face. "What do you know of Magick, John? Black or otherwise?"

"The Trinitarians have wizards they call diablomen—demon masters. They trap demons and constrain them to their will." He shrugged. "Supposedly."

"And?" Her soft blue-gray gaze was shrewd.

"I've seen them fight, Meggie." He swallowed, remembering thunder rolling across a deck, small lightnings arcing from within bilious green clouds. Throttled screams of horror, cut short by the crack of breaking bones. And chewing.

"Demons?" Her golden brows drew together. "Most people don't believe in demons."

John showed her his reddened palm. "It burned me. And when I saw . . ." He had to force the words out. "Your eyes changed. Like a sheet of blood laid over the blackest pit of hell. That wasn't you. I know it wasn't, not my Steady Meggie."

Meg didn't reply, just shifted until she lay all along his side, hooking one long leg over his. Snugging her cheek into the curve between his neck and shoulder, she spoke into his skin, her voice so soft he had to strain to hear it. "I thought I was just in a strange mood, you know?" she said. "After all, for the last six years, I've hated you almost as much as I loved you. But I've never enjoyed pain, not giving or receiving, and when I hurt you . . ."

The movement of her arm caused gentle ripples as she trailed her fingers carefully over his chest. "Everyone has a dark side, but I didn't think it was possible to feel such . . . such pure venom. Like my soul was a bottomless well of poison."

The whole-body shudders began again and he tightened his grip, trying to give her reassurance with his warmth and strength. "It was eating me alive, John." She met his eyes, hers wide with remembered horror. "Using my selfishness, my doubts." She swallowed hard. "My inability to forgive. And all I could do was weep and howl and try to fight, to stay sane in all that hatred and bile."

"But you did." John tipped her head up with gentle fingers under her chin. "You beat it, Meggie. And so it tried to kill you. But we got it first." Settling a little more firmly into the curve of the bath, he bent his head to kiss an eyebrow, then an eyelid and the tip of her nose. From there, it was no hardship at all to linger over her lips, while he cradled the satin weight of one breast in his hand.

To his relief, she met him eagerly, but he held himself back with rigid control, monitoring her reaction. The kiss became a slow melding of mouths, sweet and hot. A homecoming and reaffirmation, all in one.

Ten

After an eon of leisurely, rising pleasure, John slid a cautious palm over her warm flank, to her hips. Meg murmured something into his mouth, hitched herself a little higher, and parted her thighs. John's fingers slipped over slick folds, hotter than the water. His heart rate doubled, while he stroked and caressed, trying to keep it light, the way he remembered she liked. A gift he could give her.

When he worked a finger inside, she gasped and pressed down, the resilient fleshy walls of her sheath clamping on to him, making his cock kick in sympathy and longing.

"John, please. I need—" Her eyes glimmered with tears.

"Are you sure, sweetheart?"

Shuddering, she produced a watery smile. "I can't stop thinking about it. Make love to me, make me clean again. As deep as you can go."

"Yes." He wasn't capable of more. Setting his hands to her waist, he guided her over him, her opulent curves glimmering pale under the water.

Reaching down, Meg wrapped her fingers around him in a no-nonsense grip that made his eyes roll. Throwing her head back, she held him as she sank down, taking him in slow stages, until he was enveloped in hot gripping bliss, all the way to the root.

On the up-stroke, her soft blue gaze lowered to his. "Ah, that's good." She slid down again until he hilted.

John spread his big hands over her glorious ass and squeezed, relishing her shudder, the way her nipples peaked for him. "Slow," he rasped. "Make it last. My Meggie."

Meg rose and fell, rocking them both toward completion, a slow flush climbing from her generous breasts to her throat and cheeks.

The water surged, slopping over the rim of the bath. For a wonder, she broke before he did, speeding up before collapsing onto his shoulder, tears and laughter mixed. "Oh, oh! *John!*"

Arching up, John let go, losing himself in the luxury of spurting inside her. Gods, it was sweet! He wrapped both arms tight around her, sealing their bodies together, breast to breast, belly to belly, a perfect fit.

They lay like that for a long time, not speaking, until the water cooled. Like a flock of corpsebirds, the worries returned, ominous flutterings at the back of his mind. Shit.

The welts were stinging again. John shifted to ease his shoulders and kissed her hair. "Better?"

"Mmm." She yawned.

"Come on." He reached out a long arm to snag a fluffy towel from the waiting pile. "Let's get you to bed."

Five minutes of murmered nonsense and kisses later, they walked hand in hand into the bedchamber. Only one niggle remained . . .

John turned to the fireplace.

And froze.

"Get on the bed," he barked and such was the command in his voice, Meg had vaulted onto the mattress before she opened her mouth.

"What? What is it?"

This time, he used his Trinitarian sword to lift the corset out of the ashes. "It didn't burn. Look." He turned, the garment dangling, a small dark door opening onto hell.

"Merciful Sister!" Her voice cracked.

Gingerly, John reached out and brushed it with his fingertips. Cool and soft. When he took it from the tip of the sword, it draped over his hand, the rubies winking slyly. His gorge rose. "I cut the laces clean through, top to bottom." He slid a finger beneath them. "But you'd never know. They're perfect. In fact . . ." He held the corset out at arm's length. "The only damage is to the side seams."

"That happened before . . . before . . ." Meg rallied. "I hurt you."

"Interesting." On the word, he tossed the corset into the air, catching it with the sword as it fell. As he'd intended, the razor-sharp edge ripped a long gash in the black velvet. He flipped it to the floor.

Meg stretched out a hand. "Ah, don't—" She broke off, biting her lip. After a short pause, she said, her voice shaking, "Sister, it's an evil thing. I can feel it, calling me."

"You're not wrong." Grimly, John squatted, watching. He wasn't going to touch it again, not with his bare hands. "It's repairing itself. The fucking thing's indestructible."

He rose, backing away until he reached the bed, slipping his arm around Meg's soft waist, drawing her close. "Tell me what happened to the seams."

"What? Oh." Meg started, dragging her gaze from the corset with difficulty. "They just popped. I felt them." She shrugged. "When you're my size . . ."

"Nonsense. It fitted you perfectly." John turned her head toward him, a firm hand cradling her jaw. "Keep looking at me, Meggie. I want you to think. What were you doing when the seams split? Were you moving? Stretching?"

She frowned. "N-no. I was thinking, just thinking."

"Thinking what?"

"That I should give it back. It wasn't mine." Her eyes went wide. "And later, I tried to argue, to fight. First about Da, and then about you. John, what are we going to do?"

John glanced across the room and a ruby twinkled at him. *You bitch of a thing,* he thought, *you're not stealing my happiness. Not when I've only just found it again.* Aloud, he said, "I have a theory, but we need help, expert help."

"The Wizard's Enclave!" Meg clutched his arm. "I'll take it there."

"No, you won't. I will. Sshh." He forestalled her with a finger against her lips. "Can you find me a stout box, one with a lock?"

⋙⋘

Meg paced from one side of her sitting room to the other. She sat at her desk and stared listlessly at the accounts. The bill for the last consignment of mothermeknot was exorbitant, but the girls went through bushels of the stuff. She must speak with Prue the book-keeper. She'd know what to do. Rising, Meg resumed pacing.

She'd given up trying to sleep. John had been gone for hours, The Garden's deed box tucked under one arm.

Dusk was drawing in before she heard his step on the stair, the rumble of his deep voice as he spoke with Tansy. She flung open the door. "John!"

Each time she saw him, so big and dark, so *there*, the shock hit her all over again. He gave Tansy a courteous nod of farewell and quickened his step, his long stride eating up the short distance from the head of the stairs. She'd always loved the way he moved, his gait smooth and powerful. Now there was a slight hitch to it, a stiffness about his upper body. Six years gone, stolen from their lives together. Not only stolen, not only wasted, but besmirched—smeared with the ugliness of blame, the pain of heartache.

Because of it, she made herself smile. Then she went up to tiptoe to press her lips to his. Abruptly, she drew back, wrinkling her nose. "What's that smell?"

The corners of John's mouth twitched. "Purist Bartelm was not impressed. I got a little singed." He showed her a scorched sleeve.

"Bartelm? But he's—"

"Important. Yes, I discovered that—right after I'd finished, ah, insisting."

Meg almost smiled. Relief was making her dizzy. "He's famous, the most senior wizard in the Enclave. Thank the Sister, it's over!" She tugged John into the room. "Come in, come in. I'll organize some supper. You must be starved. And I can give Rose back her deed box."

She laid a hand on the polished wood.

And immediately, she knew. "He didn't take it!"

John walked past her to place the box precisely in the center of the desk. He turned. "He said it wouldn't be any use. The corset's your problem—or to be more accurate, *our* problem."

Just like a man.

An angry flush heated Meg's cheeks. "But he's a Purist, a *wizard,* for the Sister's sake. What did he want? Money?"

"No." John wrapped long fingers around her upper arm and drew her into the bed chamber. He shut the door. "Can you feel it in here?"

"Feel—?" Meg stared at him in dawning horror. "Sister save me! It had me again, didn't it?"

He rubbed her shoulder. "Only for a few seconds. No more."

Meg swallowed. "What did you mean, *our* problem?"

"The Purist did a series of Magickal tests. That's why I was so long. He says it's keyed to you now, hooked into your soul like a barb. He was very interested, once I got his attention."

"That's no comfort. Dammit John, it's just a corset. A foundation garment. How can it do this?"

John shrugged. "Only the Brother knows exactly, the Purist didn't. But it's as near a demon as makes no difference. Female."

Her eyes must be as round as the Sibling Moons at full. "A *demon?*"

John's face grew very grim, the tattoo on his cheekbone shining almost blue-black. "Bartelm found the residue of a dozen souls. Possibly more. Murdered, Meg."

He took both of her hands in his and pulled her down to sit on the side of the bed.

"We tried to destroy it and failed. According to the Purist, whatever we do with it, wherever we leave it, it's compelled to find its way back to you. Because you defied it and lived. When it's finished with you—and me—it'll move on to the next victim. That's what it does, what it's always done."

His chest expanded as he hauled in a breath. "How much do you love me, Meggie?"

"How much? What sort of question is that?" Meg tugged her hands free, her stomach churning.

"The essential question." John leaned forward, his dark eyes gleaming with intensity. "I couldn't burn the damn thing, couldn't cut or damage it in any way. But sweetheart, *you did.*"

"Me?"

"You." He cupped her face between his callused palms. "He was most intrigued with the evidence of the seams, the old Purist. Something you did destroyed the stitching, Meggie, remember?"

"I thought of you, or my father."

"Exactly."

Meg laid her head against his shoulder and they sat in silence for a time. She strove for her usual calm, the efficiency Rose prized so highly. No task was impossible if you broke it into its component pieces. One step at a time. Steady Meggie. It wasn't only John's name for her, it was how she lived her life, her feet planted firmly on the earth. Finally, she said, "The corset is made of hate, isn't it?"

"That's pretty much what Bartelm said."

"And every time I had a loving thought, a true thought, I hurt it."

"Yes." John stroked her hair. "Sweetheart, this is something we have to do. We can't allow such evil loose in the world. It's wrong."

"Yes, but I don't see how— Oh, John, I can't help thinking of the young ones, like Tansy. What if it got hold of—?" She couldn't go on.

"So do you love me?"

Meg pulled back to study his face, seeing the boy she'd known and the man he'd become. Six years of John's life, missing from hers. So much mystery. She would never truly know what he'd endured in that time, could only guess at the ways his character had been molded and changed. Her head told her he was a stranger, in so very many ways. She should be wary.

Ah, shit. Now she was doubting her own mind. What thoughts had the demon planted, like evil weeds? And which had she created for herself, seeded by the pain of John's perceived betrayal? Meg's lip curled. She'd been easy prey, pathetically easy.

And yet . . .

That long ago night in the barn, she'd felt steady and shaking all at once, exalted but nonetheless calm at her center, where it counted. And in this moment, her heart still insisted this man was *John*, her John, the core of him the same in its utter decency, its loyalty. As a girl, she'd stood at his side and gazed out over the peaceful fields of her father's farm. The world had had a particular shape, and John had been the architect of its rightness. Now as she gazed into his dark eyes, she recognized that same stubborn set of values, unchanged by all that he'd seen and done and suffered.

Gods, if there was one thing John Lammas did well, it was commitment.

"Yes, I think so," she said at last.

A crease appeared between John's brows and he squeezed his eyes shut for an instant. Then he shook his head. "Not good enough. The slightest doubt and we're done for. Meggie, I'm not sure what sort of future we'll make together, but I know I'll love you 'til I die. Even if it's tonight."

She rose and went to lean by the window. She'd always loved this view, over the gardens and down to the night-dark waters of the canal. Still low in the arch of the sky, the silvery-blue disk of the Sister was rising over the pavilion roofs. If Meg dipped her knees and peered up, she'd see the Brother's martial red would be dominating the zenith. But she didn't do that. Instead, she fixed her gaze on the Sister. When she was a little girl, she'd believed a beautiful woman lived on the moon, combing the stars from Her hair.

But that was a child's understanding, direct and concrete. The Sister was so much more than a delightful fairytale. She was the wellspring from which Love sprang, made manifest in the world.

Meg pressed a hand to her heart, feeling the regular thud of life beneath the curve of her breast. A delicious warmth spread from the base of her spine to caress her torso and fill the cold empty spaces fear had left behind. And suddenly, she knew what to do.

She met John's waiting gaze. "I trust you," she said, drowning a little. "With all that I am, with my life." When he would have spoken, she held up a hand. "Do you trust me?"

After a pause, he said, very low, "My Steady Meggie. Yes, I trust you."

"Do you know the text of 'The Bridal Gift of the Sister'?"

He shook his head, his eyes brightening. "Not the way a woman would, but I've heard it read at weddings. I've got the gist. Ah, sweetheart, you're clever."

Meg gave a wry smile. "Gods, I hope so." She went to stand between his knees, resting her hands lightly on the broad shoulders. "I'm going to bathe and pray. I suggest you do the same." She kissed his forehead. "Alone, John." On impulse, she brushed her lips across the tattoo, feeling him first stiffen, then relax. "I'll find a copy of the scripture for you, and I'll leave letters for Rose and Purist Bartelm, just in case. Then I'll put that filthy garment on my nice clean body and . . . we'll see." She couldn't prevent the shudder of dread.

"That's what Ma used to say when we were little."

"And it always turned out right, didn't it?"

John didn't reply, only wrapped his arms around her waist and laid his cheek against her breast.

<hr />

Ah, she felt ready for anything, even a godsbedamned demon in the ridiculous form of a corset. Meg twisted, staring over her shoulder at her reflection in the bedroom mirror. Sister, it was a beautiful thing. Look how the black velvet enhanced the smooth, creamy globes of her ass. After this was over and she'd beaten it, she'd keep it in a glass case and take it out to wear on special occasions.

Wait a minute. She leaned forward, peering. Was that—? Her eyes shone as dark as John's, but with a red tinge.

She didn't allow herself to complete the thought. Meg pinched herself on the arm, so viciously she had to curse out loud. But her head cleared a little and the red faded from her eyes. Thank the Sister she'd rehearsed the move in the bath. Many, many times.

"Ready?" John's deep voice came from the door.

"No." She wasn't able to smile. "But let's do it anyway."

She'd asked him to come naked though she hadn't understood why when she'd made the request. But now she thought she knew.

Nude meant vulnerable. In John's case, it meant giving her all that he was, including the scars, symbolic of the history between them, his suffering and hers.

He could have sent you a message . . .

True enough. If he'd been really determined, surely . . .

Doggedly, Meg shook her head. Naked meant beautiful, too. She let her gaze travel over his big frame in a leisurely perusal, enjoying the irrepressible twitch of his cock when she eyed it. Stripped, he was still a huge man, but the width of his shoulders and the depth of his chest were balanced by the long, powerful legs and the trim waist. Every inch of him pure muscle. Her eyes narrowed. He needed feeding up, she'd have to—

He makes you look fat.

Don't be obvious. For the first time, Meg met it head-on. *Bitch.*

Utter silence.

The only warning was the slither of laces. With a vicious jerk they tightened, so brutally all the air whooshed out of Meg on a pained grunt.

"Shit!"

Two strides and John loomed over her. He held up the long dagger he carried, so close to Meg's nose that her eyes crossed. "Try that again," he growled, "and I'll cut her loose. As many times as it takes." Glaring, he lowered the blade until the tip rested against the center ruby. "I'm bigger, stronger, faster. Understand?"

The laces loosened, and suddenly, Meg could breathe again. "That wasn't too bad," she wheezed, her hands on her knees.

"All we did was surprise it." John turned to lock the door. "It overreacted. It knows it's fighting for its life."

"*Her,*" said Meg, irritated. "A sorceress."

John scowled. "You see?" he said. "There are three of us in here." He pointed to the corset with the dagger. "And one's a demon."

"Demons are stupid," said Meg. "They come when you call them. Like dogs."

Like men.

Meg flicked a furtive glance around the room.

Nothing to use as a weapon.

She and John had worked together to remove almost every object, including her crystal vase, her comb, and her brush. All that was left was the bed, the dresser, and a man the size of a house.

Oh. And the mirror.

He'd been following her gaze. "Dammit, I forgot." As if she'd spoken her thought aloud, John lifted the mirror down from the wall. Swiftly, he opened the door and carried it into the sitting room. He was back before Meg could move, the door locked behind him.

He even grinned a little, the insufferable . . .

Meg squeezed her eyes shut. *Merciful Sister, give me strength.*

She moistened her lips. "Remember what we agreed. Don't touch me. The Sister only knows what it might do." Putting her hands on her hips, she brushed her thumbs over the opened seams. Was it her imagination or had they split another half-inch?

John picked up the small illuminated hymnal from the end of the bed and turned to the page she'd marked. "This is beautiful," he said, his big fingers gentle on the yellowed pages, the dagger gleaming in the other fist.

Meg drew a steadying breath. "It was my mother's."

She left you, too.

She was still coping with that one when John began. "From 'The Bridal Gift of the Sister,' Verse one: *Courage is the gift of the Brother* . . ."

He looked up. "Come on, Meggie love. Say it. *Courage is the gift of the Brother* . . . "

Eleven

"*But love . . . love is the gift of the Sister,*" said Meg, obediently enough. Her throat was lined with sand. She coughed. "I need a drink of water."

"No," John said cruelly. "Keep going. *On the night They were wed . . .* "

Bastard. What do you care? You ran away.

"*On the night They were wed, the Sister knelt before Him—Brother, Husband, Lord.*" He should be pleased with that. She'd got it out in a single breath.

"Wait," he said suddenly. "I think you should do it. Kneel."

"What?" Meg choked.

"Do you love me, Meggie?" Gods, his dark gaze was dark enough, deep enough to drown in. The rush of anger floundered and spun in her head.

Meg opened her mouth. *Yes. Yes, I do.* Instead, all that emerged was a low-pitched growl. This time, she pinched the tender flesh of her inner thigh, using the bite of the pain to drop to her knees.

Get his knife and all pain ends.

Her tongue flapped around, too big for her mouth. " '*True l-love is My gift to You, B-beloved,' the Sister said.* John, it hurts."

"Hurts? How?"

"The words. Don't make me say the words." Tears streamed down her face. "They're not true." She shuffled a little closer on her knees, her eyes on the gleaming blade, so sharp it had cut her laces like butter.

"How can they not be true?"

"It's all self-interest, comfort, habit." Meg tossed her head. "*Tedium.*" She spat the last word, her mouth twisting in a bitter ugly shape.

"Getting desperate, are we?" said John with a lift of the brows. "Trust me, Meggie love, life with you will never be tedious."

A giggle bubbled out of her, underpinned with a snarl of rage. A stitch released, one on each side. Meg clutched her head. "I'm going mad."

"No, you're not, you've never been more sane. Second verse, sweetheart. Go on, I'll start you off. *She touched Her starry eyes. She said, 'True love sees what is . . .'*"

It was all hollow, a sham, he knew that. Hell, what did it matter? *"She touched Her starry eyes. She said, 'True l-love sees what is—the good, the bad, and all that is between. Because, because—'"*

Shit, swallowing razors would be easier. Longingly, Meg gazed at the knife in John's fist. Only an arm's length now.

Despair swamped her, a tide of freezing dark. Love didn't exist. He'd gone away, left her looking like the fool she was.

"You can do it," he was saying. "I know this bit's hard, but you can do it. *Meggie*."

Whimpering, she struggled. There must be a reason he wanted her to say these stupid verses, but she could no longer recall what it was. Sister, she was hard put to remember her own name!

Oh yes. It swam up out of the murk. She was . . . Meg. Margaret May Mackie. No one could say Meg Mackie didn't finish what she started. She hauled in a breath.

"Because love l-loves. Aaargh!" She fell face forward on the floor, writhing, her throat and mouth burning as if she'd gargled with acid.

He didn't touch her, the cold bastard. "Look what you did, Meggie!" His voice stung like a lash. "Sit up and *look*!"

Groaning, she pushed herself upright. There was a sprinkle of dust on her hip, her thigh, black dust. Next to the seam, now open another inch, a small section of black velvet had unraveled. Disintegrated.

For a split-second, her head cleared. Sweet Sister, it was working! She'd been right!

The eldritch scream of rage rattled her bones. Spots danced and spun before her eyes. They began to coalesce. Meg swayed.

"Don't faint, Meggie. Hang on, love. *Hang on.*" A direct order, she thought muzzily. In his commander's voice. "Verse three: *The Sister offered Her wrists . . .*"

Never free again. A concubine, helpless. Property.

Gods, she'd worked so hard, saved every spare coin. An image flashed behind her eyelids. John, breaking open her strong box, his long fingers sifting through her savings, his face avid.

Greedy bastard. Stealing. All that effort wasted, come to nothing! NOTHING!

Meg set her teeth. "*The Sister offered Her wrists and cruel ropes appeared, chafing Her silky skin. 'True l-love can bear . . . anything, endure . . . anything.'*"

Her spine was on fire, the corset flexing threateningly against her ribs like a living, breathing creature.

John pointed with the blade. "Don't," he growled.

The constriction eased, but as if to compensate, nausea roiled through Meg's stomach, slow, thick, and disabling. Even her bones ached. She had to grind the words out, one by one, with desperate gulps for air in between. "*Love . . . goes on . . . hoping to the edge . . . edge of forever. It . . . never . . .*"

She had to break off to dry retch. Cold sweat broke out on her brow, dripped into her eyes. Gods, this was dissolution, nerve by nerve, cell by cell. She'd never survive it. But at least it was purely a physical attack. Between the waves of pain, her mind was her own again. If she hadn't hurt so much, she would have been triumphant. She could feel the demon's terror and confusion, taste the foul stench of its desperation. It was utterly determined on victory, its hatred a palpable force. Defeat wasn't possible. No male could be permitted to defy the demon and survive—even if the cost of victory was an eternity pinned like an insect beneath the thumb of the Dark Lord.

Fuck it, Meg felt much the same. If she was going down, the demon was going with her, one syllable at a time. Meg wrapped both arms around her middle. *I've got you now, parasite. Listen and die.*

"It . . . never . . . gives up. Because . . ." Pause for breath. Her vision was tinged with red. *"Love . . . loves."*

The seam on the left ripped two inches, accompanied by shrill screams that made the bones in her skull feel as brittle as glass. Surely John could hear them? Meg cranked one eye open.

Gods, he was overwhelming, so dark and purposeful! So magnificently solid. He stood with his legs spread, the hymnal in one hand, dagger in the other. Intensity rolled off him in waves. He was vibrating with the force of his concentration, his eyes as black as pitch, every muscle tense and ready.

"Don't stop, Meggie. Don't give the bitch a chance, *go on.*"

"Verse four," she gasped. *"The Sister . . . touched . . . Her sweet breast."* Meg pressed a shaking palm to her chest, feeling her heart flutter like a caged bird. *"She said—"* She broke off.

John's voice was rumbling along beneath hers, giving the words a different emphasis from the one she was accustomed to. They sounded sonorous, deeply significant, delivered in that rich bass baritone.

They said the next line together, slightly out of time, their voices overlapping, because Meg was still breathing in great heaving gasps, as if she'd been running. *" 'True love . . . is . . . is patient and kind. It seeks not . . . to alter the . . . beloved.' "*

She met John's eyes. *" 'Because love loves.' "*

In the ensuing silence, all she could hear was her own rasping breath and thundering heart. From somewhere a long way off, a small thin voice wailed with rage and grief. More black dust drifted to the floor.

"Last verse," said John softly. "Finish it, Meggie love. Put the demon out of its misery."

Meg said, *"Reaching out, She took His hand and placed it upon Her head."* John tossed the hymnal onto the bed. Meg grasped his hand and bowed her head beneath it. His fingers trembled on her hair.

She'd expected a last-ditch defense, but when it came, it was shockingly strong. A mailed fist closed over her heart, squeezing and crushing. "J-John," she managed. Gods, it was excruciating! Her lips went numb. "L-love . . . love . . . you."

"'*Faith is mighty,*'" he said. He dropped to his knees before her and cradled her cheek in his rough palm. "Stay with me, Meggie."

"'*Hope is great.*'" Meg mouthed the words against John's lips, his breath puffing warm against her chin as he said them with her. "'*But when . . . all else is . . . gone—sense and . . .*'" The right-hand seam of the corset split, almost the whole way to the top. The crushing pressure eased.

"'. . . *sense and knowledge, and life itself . . .*'" Meg's voice meshed with John's. A woman's voice keened, sustained on a long wavering, howling note, as if her very soul was tearing loose. A hot, ashy wind swirled around the chamber. The bed hangings flapped and the lamp rocked.

"'*True Love alone remains,*'" they said in chorus.

"Me," gasped Meg. "I can— Let me."

John pressed a kiss to her forehead and pulled back to watch her face. He was smiling, the tattoo shining a deep blue. Never had she loved him more.

"*Rising, She clasped the Brother to Her breast and His tears dampened Her hair.*" With each successive word, speech grew easier and Meg's voice rose. By the time she reached the final line, they could probably hear her in the farthest pavilion. "'*Because love . . . LOVES!*'"

The wind dropped. Meg's shout echoed, bouncing off the walls. John froze, listening, the blade poised.

She'd expected a bone-rattling shriek of fury. What she got was a prolonged grating rasp of a noise, horrible and pathetic at once. A death rattle.

A heartbeat later the corset dissolved, falling about Meg's feet in a drifting rain of silky black particles. The rubies tumbled to the floor, five tinkling glassy impacts, each separate and distinct.

Meg gazed at them in dismay. Gods, how were they supposed to destroy *rubies*? She leaned forward to touch, but a brawny arm blocked the way.

"Wait," he said.

The stones were such an arterial red. Sergeant Rhiomard had

been right about them. Heartsblood rubies. Meg wrinkled her nose. They even smelled like blood, that distinctive coppery-sweet odor—

She blinked. Five large drops of blood lay gleaming on the floor in a perfect semicircle.

"Where do you keep your cleaning supplies?' asked John.

"Downstairs, but I have . . ." Naked, Meg stumbled to the old dresser and rummaged in the bottom drawer. "Here." She tossed him an old shift, threadbare with many washings. "This do?"

John's lips pulled back from his teeth in a wild grin. "Oh yes." Effortlessly, he ripped the garment in two and wiped up the blood in a couple of sweeps. Then he walked away, into the other room. "Don't move. Back in a minute."

Meg shook herself out of her daze, reaching the sitting room door in time to see him shrug on a robe and disappear down the passage.

She was standing in the same place when he returned, her mind a pleasant blank, her knees still trembling. John was carrying a dust-pan and brush. "What did you do with it?" she asked.

John's grin grew positively feral. "Tossed it down the privy." He advanced on the drift of black dust, brush and pan at the ready.

＞＞＜＜

Though Meg had fallen almost immediately into an exhausted sleep, it was a restless, uneasy slumber. When she thrashed on the pillow, her brow creased and her lips tight with remembered pain, John had murmured to her, foolish words he hadn't realized he even remembered, loving nonsense. He'd kissed and cuddled and soothed until she dropped off again, smiling, her head on his shoulder where she belonged.

The hours tiptoed past. Finally, well after Sistersrise, a long sigh whispered out of her and she relaxed completely, turning toward him and curving her body into the shelter of his waiting arms, one palm laid squarely over his heart. Whether it was in supplication or ownership, he didn't know and he didn't care. Either or both were fine with him.

Thank the gods for the moonlight that streamed in the open window, the Sister bathing the bed in her silvery-blue. It meant he could lie and watch Meg sleep, his fingertips drifting across warm, silky skin—her shoulder, the tender swell of her breast, the complex line of her collarbone—marveling at the miracle that was his Steady Meggie.

What a warrior she was! He'd seldom seen anything to equal it for cold-blooded courage. Gooseflesh paraded all down John's spine and the arm around her flexed. In this quiet bed, with dawn slowly brightening the room, he could admit to himself how frightened he'd been.

Keeping his distance was the hardest thing he'd ever done, standing with the book in one hand and a naked blade in the other, two feet away. Every cell in his body had screamed at him to scoop her up and get her to safety. Now, now, *now*!

Gods, the alien expressions that had flitted across her face, other features swimming beneath her fair, freckled beauty. At times, he'd even been able to discern a narrower jaw and thinner nose, dark eyes veiled with crimson.

John shivered. He pressed his mouth to Meg's shoulder, inhaling again and again, until the shudders eased.

In the end, he'd had to trust to her judgment and her strength. There'd been no other way. For either of them.

His heart gave a great bound, so violent he had to press his palm over Meggie's hand on his chest. He buried his nose in her hair, breathing in painful open-mouthed gulps.

Shit, it was *over*!

All of it.

The stinking galley, the agony of slavery, of knowing she was lost to him forever. The impotent fury that had burned behind his breastbone like a bonfire, his life wrenched from his control.

All gone.

He'd barely had time to recover from the dizzying joy of finding her again, his Meggie, and the fucking corset—

Shit, shit, *shit*!

He was shaking again, so hard the whole bed vibrated with it. John's vision blurred, and when he rubbed his eyes, hot salty drops splashed down, beading on the inner curve of Meg's sweet breast. Something hard and crusted broke inside him.

He slid down, wrapping his arms around her the way a child hugged a furrybear toy. Desperately, he pressed his face into soft breastflesh, willing the tears away. He'd almost succeeded when her fingers moved in his hair and a sleepy voice murmured, "Sshh, love. It's all right. I've got you."

For a second, he hesitated. Fuck, he was safe, *safe*. He could let go and know he was held. Loved. They had a future together, a lifetime, he and his Steady Meggie.

John surrendered to the storm, all the rage and grief and fear draining out of him in a great flood, while Meg lay in silence and stroked his shoulders, over and over. His soul relaxed into the comfort of that touch, taking shelter in the shining light of her the way he'd done as a boy. How he'd missed her!

It was probably fortunate such a degree of intensity couldn't last long. He raised his head and cleared his throat. "Your breasts are all wet. Sorry."

"Doesn't matter," said Meg tranquilly, rubbing the back of his neck.

There was his favorite spray of freckles, all shiny with tears. John licked the salty moisture away. He was very thorough.

"Mmm." Meg wriggled, her eyes half-closing with pleasure.

"Meggie?"

"Mmm?"

"Put your hands over your head."

"Like this?" She lifted her arms in a sinuous stretch, gazing at him from under dark gold lashes. "Why?" Her lips twitched.

John took a velvety nipple between his lips and tugged, very gently. Releasing it, he blew a stream of warm air and watched it ruche into a crinkled bud, begging for more. "This," he said with a satisfaction that went bone-deep, "is going to take a very long time."

And it did. Until he had her writhing and crying aloud, her legs over his shoulders and a pillow under her bottom, while he licked and nibbled and suckled, caressing and coaxing and demanding, with lips and tongue and fingers. Gods, he'd missed this, the hot musky taste of a woman's pleasure—for him, because of him. Smiling, he sent her over for the third time. Ah, such beautiful noises she made.

When he finally worked his way inside, inch by slow, clasping inch, those long strong legs rose delightfully over his hips, her heels digging into his buttocks.

John wasn't shamed that his eyes were wet, because Meggie was no better.

"Welcome home, love," she said, while he drowned in her blue-gray gaze, soft and strong as a summer dusk. "Now and forever."

⚜

The Bridal Gift of the Sister

Courage is the gift of the Brother, but love is the gift of the Sister. On the night They were wed, the Sister knelt before Him—Brother, Husband, Lord. "True love is My gift to You, Beloved," the Sister said.

She touched Her starry eyes. She said, "True love sees what is—the good, the bad, and all that is between. Because love loves."

The Sister offered Her wrists and cruel ropes appeared, chafing Her silky skin. "True love can bear anything, endure anything. Love goes on hoping to the edge of forever. It never gives up. Because love loves."

The Sister touched Her sweet breast. She said, "True love is patient and kind. It seeks not to alter the beloved. Because love loves."

Reaching out, She took His hand and placed it upon Her head. "Faith is mighty, Hope is great. But when all else is gone—sense and knowledge, and life itself, True Love alone remains."

Rising, She clasped the Brother to Her breast and His tears dampened Her hair. "Because love loves."

Denise Rossetti lives in Australia.
Visit her website at www.deniserossetti.com

Don't miss her exciting new novel, *The Flame and the Shadow,*
now available from Ace Books. Turn to the back of the book for
a preview.

Riding on Instinct

BY JACI BURTON

Available April 2009
from Berkley Heat

Department of Justice agent Shadoe Grayson is out to prove she's no rookie, and eagerly accepts her first undercover assignment at a strip club in New Orleans. Working with the Wild Riders, a government agency of bad boy bikers, her goal is to expose a corrupt DEA agent. All she has to do is learn to strip like a pro . . .

Standing in Shadoe's way is arrogant and smoking-hot Spencer King, her new partner and one of the Wild Riders. Spence thinks Shadoe looks more like a schoolteacher than a stripper, and doubts her ability to do the job. But when he mockingly challenges her to strip just for him, he finds out there's more to the surprisingly sexy agent than by-the-book rules and Government Issue pantsuits.

Now Spencer has to resist his baser instincts while Shadoe learns that taking off your clothes doesn't always equal losing control . . .

Fair Game

BY JASMINE HAYNES

Available June 2009
from Berkley Heat

Josie Tybrook is holding her own—on her own—with a successful career and a bright future. She doesn't need a man to make it brighter—unless it's only for a night of no-strings-attached sex. After a brief erotic encounter, Kyle Perry is a perfect candidate. Except that Josie soon finds they have a professional tie that will bring them together again. And again.

Now, in business *and* in pleasure, Josie and Kyle engage in a battle of wills. What begins as a hot diversion of power and domination turns into an intimate game behind closed doors, where the role of slave and master shifts with each erotic move. But as the games escalate, they find themselves becoming bound by something stronger than they ever imagined—and discovering the ecstasy of what it means to really lose control.

A Witch's Beauty

BY JOEY W. HILL

Available January 2009
from Berkley Sensation

Mina is the daughter of an unholy union—a mermaid taken by one of the malevolent Dark Ones. While helping to rescue Prime Legion Commander Jonah, she exposed herself as a potentially dangerous weapon, susceptible to the darkness in her own blood. Now, for the general good, Jonah has angels watching over her . . .

While other angels see Mina as a liability, David, the human-born angel, feels a connection to her that is undeniable. Perhaps there has never been a Dark One capable of good, but in Mina, David believes he's found an exception.

Though Mina is resistant to being protected, her attitude begins to change when David is awarded the duty. Looking into his eyes, she can sense that he too knows what it means to fight the darkness within. But—as their passion threatens to take over—will it lead them to Heaven or Hell?

The Flame and the Shadow

BY DENISE ROSSETTI

Now available
from Ace Books

Grayson of Concordia, known on countless worlds as the Duke of Ombra, is a mercenary, a sorcerer of shadows—a man whose soul is consumed by darkness. For Gray, the bleak savagery in his heart is manifest in an entity he calls Shad. He has long resisted Shad's enticements, but when he is hired to kidnap a fire witch, he seizes the chance to restore his soul—no matter the cost.

Cenda's heart is ash. Since the death of her precious baby daughter, life has lost all meaning for the fire witch. Slowly, she has worked to master her powers and go on living. But when she encounters Gray, her will is no match for her desire. But her love may not survive the terrible discovery of Gray's betrayal . . .